"Ellen Gable has used a com~~pelling, well-told story~~ to draw a real life picture of the central importance of the sacramental aspect of marriage. Her story of two women — separated by generations, eras and the choices they make, particularly in the way they choose to love — draws a stark contrast. Yet, Gable manages to pull the reader into both worlds and then beyond time and space to a place where faith, hope and love crosses the divide and unites these two women in the bonds of Christ's suffering."

Nancy Jahn, mother of seven,
freelance writer and
senior Parliament Hill staffer

"A thought-provoking story about the innocence of youth and the wisdom of adulthood through which is cleverly weaved the teachings of the Catholic Church. A 'must read' for anyone who has ever had questions/doubts about the sanctity of human life. A truly enjoyable and heartwarming story."

Shirley Riopelle Ouellet
mother of two, public servant

"I thought this was a fantastic book explaining NFP in the face of rampant birth control use in our society."

Rosemarie Colon,
mother and NFP teacher

"An engaging love story, but also the story of a young woman's quest for truth, a quest that takes her on a journey to the past, prompts her to re-examine the present and urges her to strive towards the future with hope and longing."

Patricia Dupuis, mother of nine,
freelance editor

"An inspiring story written with great insight. A 'must read' for both young and old."

Joan Kelly, President
Sandpoint/Braeside
Catholic Women's League

EMILY'S HOPE

a Novel

ELLEN GABLE

Kyle & Laura,

God bless you!

Ellen Gable Hrkach

Full Quiver Publishing, Pakenham, Ontario

Disclaimer: This book is a work of fiction. Though some of the events are based on real life experiences, names have been changed and the characters and events have been fictionalized.

EMILY'S HOPE
copyright by Ellen Gable
published by Full Quiver Publishing
PO Box 244
Pakenham, Ontario
K0A 2X0
www.fullquiverpublishing.com

ISBN Number: 0-9736736-0-5
Printed and bound in Canada

Cover design and photography by
James Hrkach

NATIONAL LIBRARY OF CANADA CATALOGUING IN PUBLICATION

Gable, Ellen 1959 -
Emily's Hope/ Ellen Gable
ALL RIGHTS RESERVED

Copyright 2005 by Ellen Gable
Full Quiver Publishing
a division of Innate Productions

DEDICATION

To God, the Author of life, and to my parents, Elizabeth Power and the late Francis Gable, for giving me the gift of my life.

To our children who, by their very presence, proclaim the Gospel of Life: Joshua, Benjamin, Timothy, Adam and Paul, those we are raising, and to those six precious children waiting in heaven, it is a great privilege to be your mother.

To my best friend, husband, and sacramental partner, James Hrkach: without your loving influence, I would not have become the person I am today.

ACKNOWLEDGMENTS

There are many people who generously gave of their time to support me in the creation of this book.

First and foremost, I would like to thank my spiritual director and dear friend, Father Arthur Joseph, for his wisdom and guidance. As well, my sincere gratitude for offering to read the first draft of this novel and for your ongoing spiritual direction and loving encouragement.

Special thanks to my youngest sister, Laurie Power. I thank God every day for the wonderful gift that she has been to our family. Thank you for reading many different edits of my novel and for offering candid feedback.

Special thanks also to Regina Rolph and Kathy Cassanto for reading several edits of my novel. I sincerely appreciate your enthusiasm for my project from the very beginning.

To my sister, Diane Gable, and to my step-sister, Linda Gill, for helpful feedback, and to all who read a pre-publication draft of my novel: Michelle Sinasac, Sarah Smith, Jessica Smith, Sarah Loten, Marcy Millette, Anne Glenn, Kathleen Whalen, Mary Whalen, Joan Kelly, Shirley Riopelle Ouellet, Marilynn Light, Meredith Light, Marilyn Ensor, Mary Ellen Drapeau, Laura Johnson, Abby Johnson, Renee Timinski, Ingrid Waclawik, Josie Scott, Alison Colotelo, PG, Nancy Jahn, Martha Jahn, Mary Lou DuBois, Mara Indri, Rosemarie Colon, Jerrie Legree, Donna Terry, Ben Hrkach. Your honesty and candor is greatly and humbly appreciated.

To Dr. Maria Kukovica and Maureen Bentz, thank you for helping me with medical terms, and to PG for writing part of the summary on the back cover.

My sincere thanks to Mary Ellen Drapeau for sharing with me the experience of the birth and death of her son, Jacques (which served as the basis for Chapter 28) and to Shirley Riopelle Ouellet for sharing with me the birth and death of her daughter, Natalie.

A great big hug and thank you to Mark Cassanto for creating the Full Quiver website, and to the Sandpoint/Braeside Catholic Women's League for their donation to the website.

Special thanks to Sarah Smith, who patiently spent several hours posing for the cover photography.

To P.M. Dupuis, who professionally edited my novel and to Susan McEwen, who copy-edited the final draft.

A very intimate thank you to my husband, James. I am grateful for your suggestion that I write a novel, your cover design, your thorough editing job, and your continued support and encouragement.

Most importantly, thank you to God for the inspiration to share the Church's beautiful teachings through the stories of Emily and Katharine.

Ellen Gable Hrkach
Pakenham, Ontario
June, 2005

". . .there is no love without hope, no hope without love and neither love nor hope without faith."

St. Augustine

June 1993

The pain in her abdomen became more excruciating with every passing moment. She sat on the sofa and dialed the number of the high school. It seemed like an eternity for the line to connect. One, two rings. *Please, someone pick up,* she silently begged. Hearing the secretary's voice, Emily could barely speak, but she uttered enough to make it clear that she needed her husband. She dropped the phone and tried to take a deep breath. Feeling an overwhelming need to vomit, she rushed to the bathroom just in time to spill the contents of her stomach. She gripped the cold, hard toilet, as if in some way, it would make her pain bearable. Disoriented, she thought of her baby and quickly glanced over at his smiling, inquisitive face, oblivious to his mother's pain.

I've got to stay conscious for my baby, she repeated over and over again in her mind. She moved back to the floor next to the sofa, trying to sit upright with her young child next to her, while drifting in and out of consciousness. Keeping a death grip on him, she woke up as the paramedics were prying her hands off her son and placing her on a stretcher. It all seemed like a dream. She overheard the paramedics talking about what a "little thing" she was.

Too weak to make a sound, she wondered where her young son was. She caught a glimpse of her husband holding him at the back doors of the ambulance.

His right arm cradled their son's little body, while his left hand clasped his small head to his chest as if to shield and protect him from the turmoil that surrounded them both. But her husband's face. . .his face was so broken and distraught that Emily felt the anguish of a wife and mother abandoning her family. Tears welled up in her eyes and for a moment, Emily forgot her pain.

Then his eyes caught hers and he realized that she was watching him. Everything changed. His chin lifted as if for courage and penetrated her being with a look of tenderness, of confidence and reassurance. *Whatever happens, I will be strong for you and for the sons we both love and for God, who has asked so much of you.* He seemed to say all of this with his eyes, all of this and more. As his love reached out to her through the shouts of the paramedics and their frantic procedures, the beeping of machines and the overwhelming wail of the siren, its light already flashing, her terror began to fade and her heart surged within her. Now reassured, she allowed herself to fall back to sleep.

Emily's eyes opened again this time as the paramedics were inserting an intravenous needle in her arm. Although it felt like they were stabbing her with an ice pick, all she could manage was a wince and a quiet moan. It seemed as if every ounce of energy had been sucked from her being. *This is what it feels like to die.*

Then she imagined her little boys' faces, and suddenly the possibility of dying weighed heavy on her heart. *Please, God, I can't die*, she silently prayed. *I don't want my little boys growing up without a mother.* All at once, a feeling of warmth surrounded her, then she felt at peace. There was no bitterness, only acceptance, a calm that was huge enough to quiet an ocean. She silently recited a Hail Mary. *. . .now and at the hour of our death. Amen.* Those last words took on powerful meaning with the possibility that this could be her hour. She knew that whatever happened would be God's will, and she would submit to that, whatever it was.

Drifting into unconsciousness, the last thing she heard was "We're losing her. . . ."

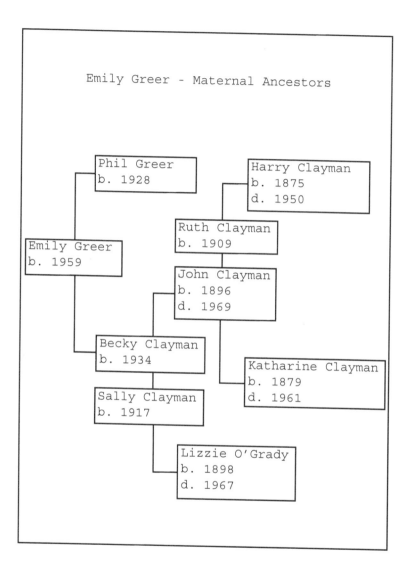

Emily Greer - Maternal Ancestors

Phil Greer
b. 1928

Harry Clayman
b. 1875
d. 1950

Ruth Clayman
b. 1909

Emily Greer
b. 1959

John Clayman
b. 1896
d. 1969

Becky Clayman
b. 1934

Katharine Clayman
b. 1879
d. 1961

Sally Clayman
b. 1917

Lizzie O'Grady
b. 1898
d. 1967

1

Psalm 31:12

October, 1976

Emily gathered up the books from her locker as her mind wandered to the mental list of things that she needed to accomplish before the end of the day. First, she planned to do some research for her English project. Though it wasn't due for another month, she frequently finished within a few days of assignment. Emily had little tolerance for students who left it to the last minute to complete or, worse yet, to start their projects.

Cheerleading practice had ended early, giving her a window of opportunity. She glanced at her watch and figured that she had about 20 minutes before the library closed. Pressing down the halls and out the door, she nearly collided with her English teacher.

"Sorry, Mr. Bishop," she apologized.

"That's all right," he said, with a slight lisp. "Where are you heading in such a rush?" Mr. Bishop was well-liked at her high school. A big bear of a guy, a Fred Flintstone lookalike, he was a gentle man with a big booming voice, who always wore a wrinkled suit with a brightly colored bow tie.

"I've only got 20 minutes until the library closes, and I need to do the research for the project that you assigned."

"Nice to see that someone is actually doing homework, Miss Greer. Good luck with your research," he said with a broad smile on his face. He always seemed so happy and friendly that Emily wondered if he ever lost his temper.

Emily ran out the door, then stopped when she noticed the breathtaking colors of the trees just starting to make their transition from summer to fall. Her favorite season was autumn with its cool mornings, fresh crisp air with a hint of winter to come and, most of all, the colorful trees.

Arriving at the library, she sprinted to the card files.

"D, E, F. . .ah, here's the G's, Genealogy." She jotted down several book numbers, then walked quickly to where the books would be found. "Here they are, Genealogy for Beginners and Genealogy and Ancestor Trees. This should be a good start."

After checking out her books, Emily slipped them into her school bag and, breathing a sigh of relief, walked out the door toward home.

She passed a few other students along the way, glanced up to see if she recognized them and when she didn't, looked down again. Emily was friendly but not overly so. Perhaps because she was small and young-looking, hers was a kind, inviting face even when she wasn't smiling.

She continued walking along the street and passed by the bus stop as the bus was letting off students.

"Hey, Em!"

Her best friend, Carrie, was waving wildly. Carrie's effervescent personality and natural beauty made her popular with the boys. "Hi, Carrie." Emily stopped at the street, by the bus stop.

"I hate going to school so far away. I wish my mom would let me go to the public high school here, but well, you know my mom. She believes that if she's paying for something, it's got to be better."

Emily nodded. "Hey, do you want to come over to my house and listen to records or make prank phone calls?"

"I can't. I've got to stop by Pizza Palace and grab some dinner. My mom's working tonight. Besides, I've got a science project due tomorrow."

"I'll come over to Pizza Palace with you and we can chat while you're eating. Hey, how come you waited till the last minute to do your project?"

"You know me, I work better when I'm under pressure."

Emily rolled her eyes. "Right."

They walked across the street toward the restaurant. While Carrie was ordering pizza, Emily slipped into a booth by the window. She nonchalantly glanced out and watched a young couple pass by. The young man had his arm around the girl's waist and his hand in her back pants pocket. They walked in step as if they were attached to each other. Emily sighed.

Carrie joined Emily in the booth and took a huge bite of her pizza. Still chewing, she asked, "Hey, Em, have you ever thought of getting contact lenses? I mean, those little wire frame glasses you wear make you look like Ben Franklin or, worse yet, like you're studious or something."

"Yeah, well, I don't think so. I mean, I just don't like the idea of putting something on my eyes. Besides, I like my glasses."

"But Em, you have such beautiful almond-shaped eyes. Gosh, I remember the first time I met you, I thought perhaps you might be Oriental."

"Must be the Indian in me."

"Indian?"

"American Indian. Remember I told you that my great-grandfather was an Indian? Don't know which kind, though."

"Well, you certainly have the long hair of an Indian girl," Carrie retorted, swinging her medium length auburn hair as she spoke. "It looks like you haven't cut it in years, for crying out loud. That style went out of fashion last year. Puh-lease! I bet the boys would notice you more if you got your hair cut and shaped."

Emily rolled her eyes again. Carrie was always trying to convince her to wear makeup or to change her little girl appearance. The truth is, she liked her long, waist-length brown hair which, out of habit, she frequently flipped back away from her face. Most of the time, she enjoyed her young looks.

"Don't roll your eyes at me, Emily Greer! We've been friends for seven years. For the last two or three years, you've been complaining that boys just don't take you seriously."

"So?"

"So. . .you need to start dressing like a 17 year old, not like a ten year old. Last week you wore your hair in pigtails. You even had me convinced that you were ten years old."

"Okay, okay. I get your point. I'll think about getting contacts, a haircut and I promise never to wear my hair in pigtails again. Happy?"

Carrie sighed. "Sure, Em. If you get your hair cut, I'll faint right on the spot."

"Very funny."

"By the way, how's Rick doing?"

"I guess he's okay."

"What did he wear today?"

"His blue pullover sweater and jeans."

"He used to look pretty cute in our school uniform, Em. Dark pants, white shirt and tie, a real dream. Of course, I can understand why you like him." Carrie swallowed the last bit of pizza. "I'll call you tonight after I finish my project. See you later."

They strolled out of the restaurant and Emily waved as she watched her friend cross the street. On her way home, she allowed herself to daydream. Though she hadn't yet dated, she constantly eavesdropped on the other girls' conversations in the locker room about their big Friday night dates. Sometimes, the girls would ask who Emily went out with. Usually, out of embarrassment, she would lie and say that she was dating someone from another school. Only her close friends knew differently.

Her daydreams always involved a certain boy, Rick. He was over six feet tall, with light brown feathered hair. To Emily, Rick had it all: he was smart; he was the cutest boy in the school and, in her opinion, the best player on the basketball team. Rick was in some of her classes, but she was too nervous to talk to him.

She continued daydreaming about marrying Rick and settling down with a bunch of kids. Coming to a busy street, she casually looked both ways, saw that no cars were coming and proceeded across the street. All of a sudden, she felt someone's hands firmly on her shoulders yanking her back just as a van, making a sharp turn, skimmed past her. She continued to feel the unknown person's hands on her shoulders, keeping her from falling forward.

For a few seconds, she stood in the middle of the street, unable to breathe or to move. Her mouth open, her whole body shaking, she turned around but saw no one. Dazed, she said out loud, "That van almost plowed into me! It would have hit me had someone not pulled me back." Pedestrians on both sides of the street continued walking, absorbed in their own thoughts, as though nothing had happened. Emily could hear a loud pounding noise, then realized that it was her own heart beating wildly. She continued on her way, distracted and confused, but mostly relieved.

Emily reached her house, stepped up to the little front porch and pushed the door open. The smell of freshly cooked bacon filled the air. "Hi, Dad," she yelled. Since her father, a mailman, was usually home from work by 3:30, she knew that he would be making dinner, a household task that he had done regularly since her mother had returned to work full-time.

She stood at the front door in the living room, took off her jacket and threw it on the chair nearest the door. To the left of the spacious living room was their small kitchen.

"Bacon, lettuce and tomato sandwiches, again?" she asked. "Yeah," he mumbled through the half-smoked Raleigh cigarette. Kissing him on the cheek, she smelled his familiar Old Spice aftershave through the smoke of his cigarette. She stood next to him and watched as he turned over a piece of bacon in the frying pan.

He put out his cigarette, took a sip of his beer and began humming along with the record player. Phil Greer stood about five feet six inches tall, still had most of his hair, and except for a bit of a pot belly from drinking, he appeared considerably younger than his 48 years. He was humming along with the song "My Cherie Amour" by Stevie Wonder. Emily often told her dad that she thought he was a dead ringer for Frank Sinatra; unfortunately, he didn't have Frank's singing talent.

"Can I help?" Emily asked. Though she was anxious to begin her research, she patiently waited for her dad to answer.

"Sure, Em, you can set the table."

"Okay."

"How was school?" her father asked.

"Fine, I guess. Oh, I got an A on my French composition."

"Tray bee-an," he complimented her, sounding more like Gomer Pyle speaking French.

"Dad, it's tres bien, you've got to roll your R."

"I'll have you know I was stationed in Paris during the years after World War II."

"I know you were, Dad, but where in the world did you learn to speak French?"

"From the girls." He raised his eyebrows and grinned.

"Come on, Dad. Were they French girls?"

"Sure." He laughed. He enjoyed teasing his youngest daughter.

Emily finished setting the table, then walked back through the living room and rushed upstairs. At the top of the steps, she passed by her parents' room, turned left, then passed by her older brother, Matthew's, small room and walked further down the hall to the larger bedroom that she and her sister, Susan, shared. Sometimes Emily felt a bit guilty that she and Susan, as the two daughters, were somewhat favored. Their room had a plush carpet and identical pink and blue-patterned bedspreads. Her brother's room, though impeccably neat and tidy, had bare floors and a plain brown blanket. Both rooms had black and white televisions, though the sisters' TV was larger.

Emily was thankful when Susan started working her new job last year. Now Emily could enjoy the privacy of their bedroom until six o'clock. Once inside her room, she threw her book bag on her unmade bed, then walked over to open the small window in the center of the end wall. Their beds flanked each side of the window, tucked into the two back corners of the room.

She then pulled the television stand closer to her bed. She turned on the television and started watching an old rerun of "I Love Lucy."

With the background of dialogue from the television show playing, Emily sat on her bed, then reached into her book bag, took out her library books and began her research. As part of her English assignment, she was tracing her family tree back three generations. She scanned the genealogy books for ideas on where to find important information relating to a person's family tree.

In one book, the authors encouraged those interested in their family's genealogy to talk to every older member of their family for first-hand information and photos. The first person who popped into her head was Aunt Sally. She knew that her aunt would not only have lots of photos, she would also have plenty of information which would help Emily in her quest to find out about her ancestors.

She turned down the volume on the television, then picked up the pink princess phone on the night table and dialed her aunt's number. Aunt Sally, her mother's oldest sister, had been a widow for several years. Now nearly 60 years old, she didn't appear a day over 45, still old in Emily's opinion, but not too old. Emily liked to tell her aunt that she resembled Ava Gardner, but in actuality, she looked and sounded more like Dinah Shore, except without the southern accent.

She always pictured her sitting by the phone because as usual, her aunt picked up on the first ring. "Hi, Aunt Sal, this is Emily."

"Hi, Tootsie Roll. How are you?" Emily moved the receiver away from her ear, as Aunt Sally's voice could be loud and piercing.

"I'm fine. I'm doing a research project in English on my family tree. I need to find out who my ancestors are, perhaps a photo or two for each. I was hoping that you would help me."

"Aunt Sally would love to help you," she replied. Emily remembered how her brother and sister used to tease their aunt because she almost never referred to herself in the first person, always as "Aunt Sally."

"I can bring my photo albums on Sunday, if you'd like."

"That would be great. Thanks so much." They said their goodbyes, then Emily hung up. She turned up the volume on the television and watched the rest of the "I Love Lucy" program.

The rest of the week flew by for Emily.

On Sunday, Aunt Sally arrived.

"Hey, Em, Aunt Sally is here," her mom called up to her. Emily bounded down the steps, passed her mom and rushed over to hug her aunt.

"Sal, you can take your albums into the dining room. There's still a couple of hours till dinner," Becky said, then took another puff of her cigarette. Becky was younger than Sally by 17 years, but taller by three inches, with her short, dark hair starting to go gray.

"Thanks, Beck."

Aunt Sally spread the three bulky photo albums out on the dining room table.

"Gee, these albums smell. . .well, old," Emily exclaimed. A strong musty odor emanated from the three large books.

"Yes, they do. Some of these photographs are from the late 1800's."

In one album, Emily came to a brown, somewhat unfocused photo of a young woman with a taller man behind her. "Who's this?"

"That's my grandmother, Katharine Clayman. She was your grandfather's mother."

The photo of Katharine Clayman showed a stoic-looking young woman, who, Emily surmised, would have been quite pretty had she smiled. As it was, her face had a harsh look despite its youth.

"How old was your grandmother here?"

"Not sure. From the darkness of the photo, this might be one that my father took with his new box camera. Aunt Sal remembers him saying that he saved for three years to buy one of those. He finally had enough money when he was about 15, in 1911. Most of these smaller, darker pictures were from his collection. Perhaps 1912."

Emily's aunt squinted as she studied the blurred, brown-tinged photograph. The camera had caught the gaze of both her grandmother and a man who appeared to be walking behind her.

"Who's the tall man here?"

"Gee, I'm not sure, Tootsie Roll.   Aunt Sal doesn't recognize him."

"Well, whoever it was looks quite tall, don't you think?"

"Sure, but Grandmom was pretty short, not quite five feet tall."

"That's neat, Aunt Sal, kind of like me, huh?"

"Yes, like you, Tootsie Roll."

Emily felt an immediate connection to her great-grandmother, Katharine.

Aunt Sally pointed to another photograph. "This is her husband, Harry Clayman."

Emily studied the photo of her great-grandfather, and saw what at first looked like a frightening face, taking on the appearance of chiseled-out wood. In a few photos, he had a broad toothless smile, which made his face seem less ominous-looking.

"Mom says he was an Indian, a Native American."

"Yes, he was. But he was kind of ashamed of his heritage. When Aunt Sal was a teenager, she used to ask him which tribe he was from and he would always answer "civilized."

"What more can you tell me about Katharine, my great-grandmother?"

"Well, she died in 1961 when she was almost 82 years old. She had quite a rambunctious personality and had two children."

"Two children? That seems odd. I've been reading about the fact that families were generally large in those days. I wonder why she only had two children."

"Well. . . ." Aunt Sally hesitated, then looked away for a moment.   "I know that she had at least one ectopic pregnancy, which means the pregnancy was in the fallopian tube and not the uterus. From my understanding, she almost died."

"That poor woman."   Emily continued studying the various photos, becoming more intrigued by her ancestors. "Who's this?" she asked.

"This is John Clayman, my father, and over here is Ruth Clayman, John's sister, my aunt. This photograph was taken in 1909 just after Ruth was born."

The photograph was a beautiful picture of Emily's great-grandmother, Katharine, and her son, John, sitting in front of her on the floor. The infant Ruth was on her lap.

Emily had met Great Aunt Ruth several times. She had never thought about where Ruth fit in before.

"Here's another photo of Aunt Ruth," Emily's aunt proclaimed, then pointed to a photo taken in the 1920's when Ruth was a young woman of 16 or 17.

"Aunt Sal, you know, Ruth doesn't look anything like my grandfather, John."

"What do you mean?"

"Well, she looks very different from him. Grandpop looks like he's part Indian, very dark-skinned."

"Oh, well . . ." Aunt Sally hesitated, then shifted in her seat. "I guess she just looks a lot like her mother."

"And who's this pretty young woman?"

"Oh, that's Aunt Sal, Tootsie Roll, as a teenager."

"Wow, that's you? Were you around the same age as me here?"

"Not sure, perhaps 15 or 16 in this photograph."

Emily studied the black and white picture of her aunt as a young woman. She was wearing a beautiful calf-length dress and her face displayed a coy smile. Despite that, she had a definite twinkle in her eye, a look of playfulness.

"You were pretty, Aunt Sal."

"You think so?"

"Sure. These photos are so neat. I find it fascinating to think that at the time these photos were taken, these ancestors of mine were all walking and talking with unique personalities."

"You know, Tootsie Roll, Aunt Sal wishes that you could have known some of these people. You were just a toddler when your great-grandmother died and only a small child when my parents, your grandparents, died. It's difficult to experience their personalities through a simple photograph."

"I don't know, Aunt Sal. I mean, I could tell that you were full of mischief in this one picture here."

"Maybe. But pictures only reveal a small part of the story. There's so much more to a person than what you see in a photograph."

"Well, some day, you'll have to tell me more about that, Aunt Sal. Could I get some copies of these for my project?"

"Sure, Aunt Sal would love to do that for you. It'll probably take a week or so, though. Is that enough time for you to finish your project?"

"Yes, I have nearly a month before it's due. Thanks so much."

Emily gathered her project materials, together with all the information regarding her dad's side of the family, and stored them in a safe place. There was something that intrigued her about her family tree, and it gave her a desire to learn more about her ancestry.

Eight months later, Emily lay in bed reflecting on the school year thus far.

Summer had come to her small New Jersey town early. The nights were warm, the days hot. Dawn was just breaking as she lay in bed enjoying a rare cool breeze through the window. She found it hard to believe that she had just turned 18. This was a big year. Legally she was, of drinking and voting age, an adult.

Emily jumped out of bed, slipped out of her nightgown and pulled on a pair of tight-fitting cotton pants, a tee-shirt and her sandals, then made her way downstairs. She sat down to watch the Today show on TV with a bowl of cereal and a glass of orange juice. Her mother and father had already left for work that day. Her older sister, Susan, dragged herself into the living room.

"Morning, Sue."

"Why do you have to act so cheerful in the morning? It gets on my nerves." Susan was several inches taller and two years older than Emily, and had been coloring her hair since she was 16. It wasn't surprising that Susan was years ahead of Emily in the maturity department. Dating since she was 14, she smoked a couple packs of cigarettes daily and she drank socially.

"Hey, you didn't finish the Lucky Charms, did you? You know I like them," Sue grumbled.

"No. I'm having Oat Flakes."

"I need some coffee."

Her older brother, Matthew, was working the midnight to seven shift at his job at Kravitz Department Store. Though he attended night courses at the local community college, Emily knew that he would be walking in before she left for school.

On the Today Show, Tom Brokaw was giving the up-to-date statistics on the numbers of women exercising their right to choose abortion. Emily remembered the previous Saturday when she had gone to Mass. The priest talked at length about the pro-life march taking place this week. He preached to the people that abortion was wrong; in fact, it was murder. For Emily, abortion seemed like it should be kept between a woman and her doctor. *Who am I to tell anyone that abortion is wrong?*

Though she hadn't started dating yet, she assumed that once she did, she would likely lose her virginity if she fell in love. It was certainly not in her plans to wait until marriage. After all, Emily reasoned, it seemed like no one waited until marriage these days. However, she knew in her heart if an unexpected pregnancy ever happened to her, she wouldn't be able to exercise her 'right to choose' an abortion. When it came to other people, she didn't really care whether they had an abortion or not. Then again, Emily believed that she was too smart to ever get pregnant accidentally. That's why birth control was invented. In her mind, there was no excuse for unplanned pregnancies in this day and age.

The door opened and her brother, Matthew, walked in.

"Hi, Matt," Emily said.

He grunted an answer, something she couldn't understand.

Emily studied her brother as he moved across the room. His normally well-combed dark hair was messy after a night's work, and his brown eyes appeared ready to close. He dragged his feet across the room as if he was carrying a heavy load on his back, and shuffled toward the bathroom to take a shower. He was the tallest in the family at five feet ten inches and looked similar to their father. Emily and Susan both resembled their mother.

The bathroom door closed, Matthew began pounding on it. "Sue, you know I take a shower as soon as I get home. I can't stand being sweaty. Hurry up."

"I'll be out in a few minutes. Hold your horses."

Grabbing her books and purse, Emily stepped out on to the small porch and began the long walk to the high school. The sun felt warm and the air smelled of freshly-mowed grass. She loved her neighborhood, a middle-class suburban area where the homes, built right after World War II, were all Cape Cod types, with shutters decorating the windows, bountiful flowers in practically every garden. Oak trees were so numerous that on a rainy day, you could remain dry if you walked under them.

She relished the warm summer days walking to school this past week. It was difficult for her to believe that in a few short weeks, she would be graduating from high school and going to college. She thought about how much her life would change and how much more responsibility she would have then.

Somewhat distracted by the heavy traffic in front of the high school, Emily bumped into two entangled students near the side door of the school. "Hey, watch where you're going," they shouted, as they promptly attached themselves to one another again as if they were two vacuum cleaners. When they kissed like that, it seemed like they were sucking each other's face. That kind of kissing made Emily's skin crawl.

She quickly reached her locker to drop off some books and to grab her history book for first period. Her friend, Maddie, flagged her down. She was taller, at five feet four, with long blonde hair.

"I can't believe we'll be graduating in a few weeks," exclaimed Maddie.

"Yeah. The last four years have just flown by for me," replied Emily.

"I'm really looking forward to college," said Maddie. "I hope to try out for the field hockey and softball teams."

"You won't have any problem. You're a great athlete," said Emily.

The two girls continued their chatter as they walked down the hallway until they reached their history class.

This was Emily's favorite time of day, not because of the subject matter, but because Rick was in this class. He sat behind her, a few seats over. She was always sure to avoid staring at him, instead focusing on the painted cement blocks which served as walls in the newly-built school. After all, she didn't want him to know how much she liked him. Both Carrie and Maddie used to tease her, "The way you act, it's as if you don't like him. No wonder he doesn't ask you out."

Emily recognized that there was a certain measure of truth to that comment. However, she didn't think that she could handle the rejection if he found out that she liked him, yet didn't want to ask her out.

After History was English with Mr. Bishop, her favorite teacher. In his class, she learned something new every day. Emily was also fascinated with Mr. Bishop's face. His features were all large, with a nose as bulbous as Karl Malden's. More importantly, Emily was intrigued by his unique way of teaching. He would challenge the students to earn their grades in several creative ways. Emily remembered an assignment when she visited a nursing home, talked to the residents, then wrote a two-page essay on what she had learned.

At the beginning of class, Mr. Bishop had casually mentioned that he was Catholic. One of the students made a comment about overpopulation and the fact that Mr. Bishop, the father of seven, was contributing to it. He responded by sharing with the class that he had recently undergone a vasectomy. He had announced that it *was* the responsible thing to do. Emily really admired Mr. Bishop. He was a talented, enthusiastic teacher and he seemed to know exactly what to say and how to act in all circumstances. He talked about how there were virtually no side effects to vasectomy, and he predicted that one day vasectomy would be the number one method of birth control.

Emily hadn't really thought much about that, but Mr. Bishop appeared to be so sure that it was the right thing to do.

Next period was French with Mr. Albright. Mr. Albright was not much older than Emily and the rest of the class. He was thin, wore glasses, sported a moustache and was one of the funniest people that she had ever known. The class was small, with only seven students, and there was always opportunity for informal conversation. Usually, Emily got along well with her young teacher. Today, however, after Emily and Maddie mentioned that they would be attending Mass on the weekend, Mr. Albright, a self-proclaimed atheist, remarked, "You girls are wasting your time going to Mass. There is no God, you know."

"What are you talking about, Mr. Albright?" Emily asked. It seemed like two of her teachers were so intense today.

"You're wasting your time. God doesn't exist and never has."

Without thinking, Emily blurted out, "Just because you don't believe in God doesn't mean there isn't a God. It just means that you don't believe in Him."

"If God existed, there would be proof."

"First of all, faith means believing without proof. But I believe there is proof. How do you think the world was created?"

"Have you ever heard of the Big Bang Theory?"

"I've heard of it, but I don't know much about it."

"Well, scientists believe the world was created when an event called the Big Bang happened. They have concluded that there is no God, that the world was created through an explosion."

"That's the most absurd thing I've ever heard."

He ignored her comment, then remarked, "So you see, Emily, people like me who are strong, intelligent people, don't have any need for God. We have ourselves. Belief in a god shows weakness. People like you, especially Catholics and other Christians, can't stand to think that when you die, it's over. So you allow yourself to believe all this baloney about a higher being and heaven." He hesitated. "It's really a bunch of nonsense."

Emily's heart began beating more quickly as her blood

pressure began to rise. *He is making a mockery of everything that I believe in.* Why wouldn't he listen? It felt like she was talking to a brick wall. What about this Big Bang? How many people believed in that? Could he possibly be right? It was hard to hear him judging her as weak.

She remained silent as tears began to well up in her eyes. Keeping her head down, she avoided eye contact with him.

"Listen," she heard him say, "I'm sorry if I upset you. But obviously, you need to think about the possibility that everything you've been taught is a bunch of made-up stories and it's not the truth." He sounded so sure, so right, so confident.

With that, the bell rang. Avoiding her teacher's glance, she scooped up her books and left the classroom. These were the times Emily wished that she went to the Catholic high school. Trying to put the conversation out of her mind, she walked with Maddie to the cafeteria and, as they ate lunch, discussed the debate that had just taken place. As Rick walked into the cafeteria, the conversation turned to a more hushed tone. Her friend whispered, "Oh, Em, there's Rick." Emily rolled her eyes as if to say, "I know, I know. Don't be so obvious."

The rest of the school day passed by uneventfully, and Carrie invited herself to come over to Emily's house after school. Their favorite thing to do was to make prank phone calls. Today, all Emily could do was talk about Rick and how cute he was. Carrie came up with what she assumed was a brilliant idea.

"Why don't we call Rick?"

"What?" Emily shouted. "Absolutely not. I would never in a million years call him."

"Well, what if I call him while you listen in on the extension downstairs?" her friend replied.

Emily was tempted and Carrie was convincing. "Let's just find out if he even thinks you're cute."

"No, it's. . .uh. . .just not right, Carrie."

"Come on, Em. It's a plain and simple fact that you are cute and adorable. I'm sure he thinks so too."

Part of her knew that it was wrong to make a prank call. However, her impatience to know what he thought of her convinced her. She gave in to the temptation and allowed Carrie to dial the number.

She ran downstairs, taking two steps at a time and picked up the extension in the living room. Emily listened as his mother answered the phone and Carrie asked for Rick.   As she heard his deep drawn out voice say, "Hello," her hands started trembling as she was holding the phone.

Carrie began the charade. "Oh, hi, Rick. You don't know me, but I've certainly heard a lot about you. You are supposed to be one the best looking guys on the basketball team." Carrie was obviously comfortable talking to boys.

"Who is this?" He sounded annoyed.

"My name is. . .uh. . .Nancy."

"Where'd you get my number? It's unlisted." Now, Emily felt guilty.   She had begged a friend of hers to get the number from one of Rick's ex-girlfriends.

"Well, I have my ways," she continued.   Carrie's style seemed like it was part of Flirting 101. "Tell me, Rick, do you have a girlfriend?"

"I might and I might not. Why should I tell you?"

"Because I want to know if you'd be interested in dating me."

"I don't know. I mean, I don't even know you. I'm not even sure you're the kind of girl I would date."

"Well, now, maybe you can tell me what kind of girl you would date. I know you've dated a few cheerleaders. Is that the kind of girl you like, rah, rah, short skirts and all that stuff?"

"Maybe."   He paused.   "I guess it depends on the cheerleader."

"What about Jamie Foster?"

"Yeah, I'd probably date her."

"Cindy Cohen?"

He hesitated, then said, "I might."

"Jennifer Hanson?"

"Yeah."

"Well, you've already dated Karen McMann. Would you consider dating Kathy Simpson?"

"I guess so."

"Oh, and there's that little, tiny cheerleader. Gosh, she's cute. What's her name. . .um. . .Emily Greer? Would you consider dating her?"

Emily listened on the extension for what seemed like several minutes, unable to breathe in anticipation of his answer. He finally responded, "No, I definitely would not be interested in dating *her*. Absolutely not. No way."

Oh my God. Emily, now hardly able to breathe, felt crushed but kept silent on the extension.

"Sounds like I've hit a nerve, Rick. What in the world could be wrong with Emily? I mean, I've seen her at some of your games and she's absolutely adorable. Besides, she's an amazing cheerleader too."

"Yeah, I guess." He hesitated. "And I know that she's really smart, but, first of all, I wouldn't want to date someone that looks and sounds like a little kid. You know, the guys on the team, well, we talk in the locker room and stuff and we joke about Emily and make fun of her. I mean, none of us would ever want to be caught dead holding hands with someone who looks like she could be our little sister. . . . "

The phone still at her ear, Emily was now unable to hear what the voices were saying. It seemed as if in one brief moment, all that mattered in life came crashing down on top of her. When Carrie came downstairs a few minutes later, she stood at the entrance of the living room looking over at Emily's ashen face and tear-filled eyes. She watched as Emily slowly, methodically hung up the phone.

"Hey, I'm sorry, Em. I had to keep talking so it didn't seem like I knew you. I never in a million years thought the conversation would turn out that way."

"I don't really feel well. Perhaps you should go."

Tears now began falling down her small cheeks.

"Em, are you going to be all right?"

Staring forward, she slowly nodded. "I just need to be alone."

Carrie grabbed her things and started to walk out the front door. "See you, Em."

"Bye." Her eyes faced downward, her voice barely audible.

"Hey, Em?"

She kept silent, but made eye contact with Carrie, her eyes swollen with tears.

"That Rick is an idiot and a fool. He's not worth your heartache. Someday you'll meet a great guy and have a bunch of kids. You wait and see."

"Yeah, sure." *Someone who doesn't care that I look like a little kid.*

Emily watched as Carrie pulled the door closed. Running up the steps to her bedroom, she replayed the conversation over and over in her mind. For so many months, she had dreamt about having a date with Rick, about Rick giving her her first kiss. And in all that time, he and the other players were making fun of her and talking about her *like that.* With her heart aching, she collapsed on her bed in tears.

2

Prov. 13:19

July 1905

Katharine pulled the blind down over the front windows of the music shop and watched the ice wagon go by. For a moment, she wished that she could be sitting in the back of that truck with all the huge blocks of ice. It was a hot, sticky day, the kind of day where even if you did nothing, you perspired in places you never imagined you could.

She wanted to be anywhere but cooped up in this oven of a store on Saturday. It seemed that at least a hundred people had visited the store today, making the heat almost unbearable.

She wiped her brow with a cool handkerchief and studied herself in the mirror, trying to fix her hat neatly on her head. She was far too short for her liking, though Katharine enjoyed lying about her height. Although she was not quite five feet, she often told people that she was five-one. Because of her small stature, most people assumed that she was a meek, quiet woman, only to discover that she was actually the opposite. Her face often held an unsmiling, uncompromising scowl that offended most people. She certainly wasn't one to put on airs just to impress others. When she cracked a rare smile, her whole appearance changed. She became quite a lovely young woman to behold.

As she was closing the door to the shop, she realized that she had forgotten about the photographer's appointment. "Damn, it's so hot. I wish that we could postpone it." Then, knowing the reason that she made the appointment, she decided to do her best to keep it. Two weeks earlier her next-door neighbor, Marian, a matron in her late forties, had arrived home one day from the photographer's, flustered and smiling.

"You seem happy," Katharine had commented.

"I just came from that new photographer's studio at 2900 Broad Street, and Katharine, I don't think I've ever met such a handsome and comely-looking man."

"Oh?" Now, Katharine's interest had been piqued. "An older gentleman, is he?"

"No, no, he's very young and quite well-mannered and handsome."

Katharine brought herself back to the present and began walking the five blocks to her home. She tried to pace herself so that she wouldn't work up too much of a sweat. Passing a newsboy on the corner, she heard him yell, "Extra, extra, read all about it! House fire on Broad Street kills family of five." Katharine raised her eyebrows, then mumbled, " A slow day for news."

She continued walking down the street, oblivious to anyone strolling past her. She glanced up just as an older man was tipping his hat at her. Katharine forced a smile. Perky, friendly-type people irritated her to no end. After all, if one had to act that happy, then one ought to be that happy. In Katharine's opinion, no one could ever be that overjoyed with life. She reasoned that life was just something to be endured.

She approached her street, then turned the corner and became even more agitated because some children had opened the fire hydrant. She sighed as she realized that she was going to have to walk across the street, now flooded with a inch or so of water. "Kids are such a nuisance," she muttered. Trying to tiptoe as much as she could to avoid getting water on her shoes, she lifted up her skirt to make sure that it didn't soil as well. A child squealed and Katharine jumped. "Be quiet!" she yelled.

She paused as she reached the bottom of the steps leading to her porch. Katharine walked up the steps and opened the door. "Johnnie, where are you?" Though she was small, her loud voice was piercing, loud enough for the entire neighborhood to hear.

She heard, then watched him skip every second step as he

bounded down the steep staircase to the far right of the living room. He was a beautiful, dark-skinned little boy and so smart for nine years old. *Looks like a handsome version of his Pa.*

Before he could speak, she blurted out, "We've got to prepare for the photographer's. Where's your father?"

"Dunno. I think he's in the cellar."

Katharine sighed. "That's all I need, for him to be drunk for this photograph."

She walked across the living room and through the small kitchen to the top of the cellar steps. "Harry, you down there? We're supposed to sit for a photograph."

Hearing no response, Katharine made the trek down the steep cellar staircase. At the bottom of the steps, her eyes caught sight of her husband collapsed on the floor next to his home brew contraption.

She sighed again. In an instant, she started yelling, "Harry! Harry! Get the hell up." She walked over and kicked him in the arm to try to wake him up. He wouldn't budge. "Damn it, Harry." She turned around and slowly went back up the stairs, contemplating her next move. "The simplest thing is to just sit for the photograph and not have him in it. It's just as well, with the kind of face he's got. He'd probably break the camera," she laughed.

She glanced over again at her husband, laying on the floor. He took on the appearance of a little child when he was sleeping, but when he was awake he was the meanest-looking man she had ever known. Of course, he wasn't ill-tempered at all, just the opposite. A full-blooded American Indian, his long, thin face held clearly defined features.

Katharine despised the way Harry let people take advantage of his good nature. She had taken charge of the store to prevent him from giving things away to customers who promised to pay later but never did. She told him over and over, "Harry, you just can't do that in the business world, not if you want to make a buck."

In the living room, Katharine inspected her son and

decided that his outfit, brown knickers and a shirt, would be suitable for the photograph. She stood in front of the mirror by the door and touched up her light brown hair with a comb, then carefully fixed her hat neatly to her head with some pins. Like so many times before, she was momentarily distracted by the model boat her husband carved for her. *That thing takes up too much space on the bookcase.*

She took hold of Johnnie's hand and walked on to the small porch and into the South Philadelphia neighborhood street on which they had lived for four years.

The row houses, lining both sides of the street, were fairly new, built in 1899. They were complete with all the modern conveniences, like small push buttons to turn on the electric lights, spacious cellars that could double as a garage, for those people rich enough to own the new horseless carriages. The front porches weren't roomy, but they were big enough to allow several people to sit and converse. Below the porches were small windows where the coal was delivered every few weeks during the winter.

As they walked down the street, Katharine noticed many people sitting on their porches, staying out of the sun and fanning themselves. A police officer must have arrived and closed the hydrant as the children were now sitting solemnly on the sidewalk, the flood nearly dried up.

Reaching the photographer's establishment in less than five minutes, Katharine and Johnnie sat in the small waiting room. She carefully lifted her hat off and fanned herself with it until a young, handsome man approached them.

"Do you have an appointment?" His voice was deep, and he spoke in a calm and professional manner.

"Yes, we do. Clayman."

"Ah, here it is. It says three people."

"Yes, well, there are only two of us today."

"Fine. In here, please." They were escorted into a small room with a long couch and some equipment. He invited them to sit on the sofa while they listened to him explain what would be expected of them during their appointment. Johnnie was given instructions for keeping perfectly still while Katharine was told just how much all of it would cost.

"What? I can't believe you want that much money for a photograph!"

"Ma'am, I believe we discussed payment when you first made the appointment. This equipment is expensive and professional photographs don't come cheaply."

"My neighbor's box camera costs less than what you charge for one photograph!" she said, getting more bothered by the minute. Then, before she could say anything else, Katharine waited. She remembered that she had sent Harry up to the studio to make the appointment. That inept husband of hers never mentioned anything about how much it would cost.

Katharine wanted to tell the photographer to forget the sitting. Instead, she made a closer inspection of him. Intrigued, she agreed that her neighbor, Marian, was right, this was indeed a handsome young man, not quite six feet tall, probably a bit younger than Katharine's 26 years. His dark hair, ebony eyes and olive skin gave the impression that he was a foreigner, though he spoke perfect English with a slight Philadelphia accent.

She studied the calling card that he had given to her and, to herself, read *Michael Shoemaker, Photographer*.

"So, ma'am, are you ready or. . . ."

"Yes, fine," she nodded. "We'll sit for some —" Katharine was interrupted by the high-pitched sound of the telephone on the wall in the waiting room. Mr. Shoemaker darted out to answer the telephone before it rang a second time.

"Hello. Yes. You want to cancel today's appointment? All right. Would you like to book another sitting? Goodbye."

Katharine studied the photographer as he came back into the room and began working near the large camera. *He certainly is an attractive young man.* She noticed the top of his shirt, which was unbuttoned a few spaces because of the extreme heat. The sight of Mr. Shoemaker's plentiful chest hair started Katharine's heart pounding.

"So, Mr. Shoemaker, how long have you been doing this, taking photographs?" she inquired, while she sat and waited on the green high-backed couch.

"Well, Ma'am, I actually just began on my own a few months ago. I had been working with a photographer on Market Street for several years and decided to start my own business. Wasn't making much money working for someone else."

"Well, with what you charge, you certainly must be turning a profit."

"That's the problem, ma'am. I had to purchase all this expensive equipment and with what I have to pay for that, I hardly make anything at all."

"Ma, when are we going to be done? I want to go play stick ball."

"Yes, yes, Johnnie, just a minute." Her thoughts turned back to the photographer.

"You know, Mr. Shoemaker, my husband and I own the music store over at 15th and Ritner and we actually turn quite a handsome profit. Well, I should take that back. We've only turned a profit since I've taken over at the store. My husband, Harry, has absolutely no business sense at all. That man doesn't have a brain in his head sometimes."

Michael didn't respond, but instead asked, "Mrs. Clayman, could you move a bit closer to your son and angle your body so that you're facing him more?"

She did as she was told. "Like this?"

"That's good. Now, I'd like you to fold your hands and place them on your lap."

Again, she did as she was instructed. *I wonder where he lives.*

"That's good, ma'am. Now, I need your son to put his body at an angle more facing you and to fold his hands on his lap as well."

Johnnie did as he was told.

"That's fine. Now, both of you must stay perfectly still because it takes a while to get the image."

Katharine sat, no smile, no frown, just staring straight at the camera with her chin in the air. She began daydreaming about Mr. Shoemaker and what a good-looking, well-mannered and interesting young man he was. He seemed to be thoroughly engrossed in executing the perfect photograph.

All of a sudden, Katharine heard a pop, then saw a small cloud of black smoke rising from the side of his camera. "There. That photograph is finished. Mrs. Clayman. . . ."

"Oh, please, do call me Katharine."

He hesitated and shifted somewhat uncomfortably behind the camera. The room smelled of burnt powder.

"All right. Uh. . .Katharine, how many different poses would you like?"

"It doesn't really matter to me. That one will be fine. Is it really necessary to sit for more than one?"

"Well, it's not necessary, but I can't be positive that that particular pose will come out well. I would highly recommend you do one more, at least."

"Fine. What should I do now?"

Michael walked over to a small chair and brought it over to the front of the couch. He motioned for Katharine and John to get up off the couch and while they were standing, pushed it off to the side and placed the small chair in the middle where the couch used to be. Looking down, Katharine noticed that there were a few of Michael's business cards on the floor, cards that had been discarded by previous clients. She saw him pick them up and shove them into his shirt pocket. *Those must have been expensive to print.*

"All right. Mrs. — uh, Katharine, please sit in the chair here and I need your son next to you." He motioned for Johnnie to stand to the left of her. He showed him how to put his right hand on the back of the chair with his left hand on the arm of the chair, and while he was doing so, he brushed the top of Katharine's shoulder.

"Oh, excuse me, ma'am. I didn't mean to. . . ."

"Excuse you for what?"

"Well, I —" too embarrassed, he kept quiet and moved back again behind the camera.

Katharine could see that he was watching her through the camera. She decided that this time, she would smile, a simple gesture that she hoped would show Mr. Shoemaker that she liked him.

He pulled his head up from the camera and stared suspiciously at Katharine. She gazed at him, her mouth upturned in a suggestive, flirtatious smile. Since Johnnie was sitting next to her, Katharine wanted to make sure that he understood what her intentions were, without using any words.

As he was looking at her, she smiled broadly, then winked and his shocked face appeared to understand. He peered through the camera and again warned them both to be perfectly still. She continued smiling for the entire time, heard the pop, smelled the burnt powder and when he said, "There, you may both move now," she kept the same enticing smile on her face.

He stood behind the camera and started to write something on the paper next to the large negative when Katharine walked over and stood beside him.

"It was a pleasure doing business with you, Mr. Shoemaker."

He continued writing, his back toward her.

Her usually abrasive demeanor softened as she said, "Mr. Shoemaker, Michael, if you'd like, I can display some of your business cards in my music shop on Ritner Street. It would be a good way for people to find out about you and increase your business."

He finally glanced up, and began staring intensely at her.

Katharine concocted a plan. "Johnnie," she called to her son as he was playing on the sidewalk in front of the photographer's studio, "you run ahead home now. Your Pa will be waking up soon. Just tell him that I had to run a few errands and I'll be home in an hour or so."

"Yes, Ma." Katharine watched him run off in the direction of their home.

"Well, Michael, it might interest you to know that I have a room to rent in my house. It's clean and I provide meals as well. I'm sure you would find it quite comfortable and affordable."

"I'm not sure. I do need a place that is closer to the business."

"Well then, it's settled. You can move in this week."

Katharine moved to stand in front of him. She whispered, "My husband is drunk most of the time. And I do need someone to warm my bed at night." She was smiling and her eyebrows formed a broken arch on her face.

Michael's eyes widened, but he managed to nod his head. "All right."

She reached up and gave him a passionate kiss. Somewhat surprised, Michael took a few seconds to respond. She broke off, and continued in a softened tone of voice. "I only married Harry because I needed to get away from my father. I got the strap every other day until I was 16, still have the scars on my back. Harry, he's a sweet guy and all, but, well. . .I have my needs too, you know."

Michael nodded as they walked back into the studio.

3

John 3:16

April 1978

The sounds of her weeping penetrated her own grief and Emily was moved to feel pity for her mother. It was rare to hear her give in to emotional outbursts, but Becky had retreated to her bedroom early and began sobbing.

Emily walked quietly into the hallway and paused at the door to her mother's room. Moving over to the side of the bed, she whispered, "Mom, you okay?"

"Yeah, Em. I. . .just miss him." She was silent for a moment. "Listen, would you mind laying with me till I fall asleep? I haven't been able to sleep the last few nights. I mean, I haven't slept alone in 23 years."

"Sure, Mom." Emily slipped in, tucked her arm around her mother, and soon, Becky stopped crying and was snoring. She was amazed how quickly her mom fell asleep with just a few minutes of comfort. Emily quietly rose from the bed and tiptoed across the hall to her bedroom.

Climbing into her own bed, Emily tossed and turned, then finally decided to give in and just stay up. The few moments that she allowed herself to close her eyes, her mind kept replaying the announcement of her father's death over and over in her mind.

"I'm sorry," said the doctor. "We did all that we could." At only 49, her father was dead of a heart attack.

How could this happen? In her nearly 19 years, no one that close to her had ever died.

She slowly crept down the steep, pitch-black stairs

leading from her bedroom to the living room. The house was cold, dark, quiet. Usually there was a night light on in the living room. Tonight there was no light, only a brief hint of moonlight coming in through the partly-open drapes. She switched on one of the living room lamps, then walked into the small kitchen.

Emily hadn't realized it when she had gone to bed, but as she had been tossing and turning, it dawned on her that she hadn't eaten in over 24 hours. She knew that she should try to force something down. Opening up the fridge, all she could find were the eight casseroles that relatives and neighbors had delivered upon hearing the news of her father's heart attack and passing. Her mother had never made a casserole in her entire life and now, Emily just couldn't bear to eat food that reminded her of her father's death.

She grabbed the jug of milk, then shut the fridge door and reached up to the cupboard to get a box of Lucky Charms.

She poured herself a bowl of cereal, then began the slow, methodical process of eating. After a few spoonfuls, she realized how ravenous she was and finished the entire bowl in record time.

All at once, the cereal felt like a lead weight in her stomach. Feeling nauseous and needing distraction, she walked into the den. She sat on the sofa, the darkness of the room enhancing her grief and emptiness. Her insides felt as if someone had ripped out her heart and pounded it with a hammer.

Now she began to cry long, hard sobs. *Why did he have to die so suddenly, God?*

The stillness and blackness of the room, now difficult to bear, convinced her to return again to her bedroom.

As she was going upstairs, she could see through the window at the top of the stairs that dawn was just breaking and the birds were chirping. On a normal spring day, she so enjoyed listening to the birds singing first thing in the morning. Now, she became annoyed, almost angry, that all around her life was going on as scheduled. Part of her felt as if the world should just stop, like in the old Twilight Zone episodes. Instead, a new day had begun, the sun was starting to shine and a cool breeze was lightly blowing the curtains in and out.

She sat on her bed surrounded by the many posters of Shaun Cassidy that she had taped to her walls. Devastated at Rick's rejection last year, Emily developed a crush on the popular teen idol. Watching him on the "Hardy Boys" every week and knowing that he was close to her age, she found amusement in daydreaming about him. After all, he was a safe crush and he would never tell her that he wouldn't go out with her. *Seems kind of ridiculous for someone as old as me to have a crush on a teen idol.* She had to admit that it was certainly a way of coping.

She lay down and listened to her sister, Susan, breathing heavily. She became irritated, and wished that she could be sleeping so soundly herself.

Emily wiped away her tears, and allowed her mind to wander back to the previous week. It seemed like a lifetime ago. She had given her dad a hug and he had commented, "You know, Em, you need to find a guy just about my size because you fit so perfectly with me when we hug." Her heart was consoled when she remembered that special moment with him.

The next day, Aunt Sally organized the clean-up in preparation for the reception after the funeral. Emily and Susan were given the job of cleaning the living room. Susan had commented to Emily, "I wouldn't be surprised if Aunt Sal was a drill sergeant when she was younger."

"I know what you mean."

While dusting the knick-knacks on the shelf, Emily glanced over at the wicker hamper in the hallway leading up to her bedroom. Nostalgically, she remembered her escapades inside the hamper. Traditionally, laundry day was Saturday and her mother would empty it. At least once during that day, Emily, then around seven or eight, would slip inside, unnoticed and hidden, for sometimes hours, at a time. She would eavesdrop on conversations or pretend that she was in a small spaceship traveling into outer space.

How she wished that she could crawl back into that hamper and hide away from the awful reality of having lost her father: his touch, his laughter, his soothing words and most importantly, his presence.

When she and Susan had finished the chore of cleaning the living room, Emily sought the comfort and safety of a few quiet minutes alone in her bedroom.   She had hoped that her sister wouldn't intrude on her privacy to allow her to have some time by herself.   As the seconds, then minutes of quiet continued, the solitude of her bedroom now became another source of annoyance.

As she did every day at the same time, she switched on the television to watch her favorite old television show, "I Love Lucy." More than distraction, she desperately needed to escape from the reality of life. She knew that they didn't have to leave for another two hours, but she was dreading those first few minutes at the funeral home.

Though it had been a few days since his death, Emily still could not comprehend that her father was gone. She had expected that her dad would be around until he was an old man. She used to have visions of him with gray hair and wrinkles.   Emily had, for many years, anticipated her dad giving her away on her wedding day. "But, then again, I haven't even had a date yet, so who knows, maybe I'll never get married," she said out loud, feeling more pessimistic than usual.

After "I Love Lucy," Emily watched the "Partridge Family."   This episode involved the teenaged Laurie getting braces and not wanting to tell her new boyfriend. To Emily, Laurie Partridge or Marcia Brady so epitomized what it meant to be normal: pretty, smart, self-assured and popular with the boys. Now, with the events of the last several days, she could care less whether she ever had a boyfriend. The knot in her stomach felt like a never-ending and permanent addition to her body.

As she began to get dressed, she pulled on the nylon stockings, then slipped her dress over her head. She stared into the mirror. Though her appearance hadn't changed much since high school, it seemed to her that in the last few days, she had aged many years. Her eyes, dark with pain, were on the verge of tearing most of the time.

"Em, time to leave, let's go," her mom yelled from downstairs.

She tried to keep her eyes from watering as she descended the staircase and walked into the usually spacious living room, now immaculate after hours of cleaning. Matthew, Susan, her mother and Aunt Sally were standing around waiting for the car to arrive to take them to the viewing.

The limousine pulled up and they all filed into the huge black car, with Becky and Sally slipping into the second seat while Emily, Matthew and Susan sat in the third row of seats. Emily had never ridden in a such a luxurious vehicle. The seats were covered with some sort of black plush material and, as Emily sat down, she could feel the softness through her black-patterned dress. There was an overwhelming aroma of 'new car smell.' Part of her wished that they had just taken their old car, the one that never started in the winter and overheated in the summer.

As the driver began the short trip to the funeral home, Emily studied her mom's face. What must it feel like to be 44 years old and a widow? She pictured her mother as a young bride, naive, innocent and ready to take on the world. Now, her face was distraught but composed, her eyes downcast. Becky's face usually held a constant smile, but there had been no hint of one in many days. She was usually very talkative, but had said very little. Aunt Sally's face was somber and her eyes were also downcast. Susan broke the silence. "Damn, I forgot my cigarettes. Can't we go back?"

"No, Sue." Becky spoke up. "We'll be late if we go back. You can have some of my cigarettes."

"Why do either of you have to smoke?" Matthew asked. "It's disgusting. I hate the fact that my clothes smell like smoke all the time." He pulled out a spray breath freshener and squirted it in his mouth. Then he took a small vial from his pocket and patted the liquid on his face. Emily sighed and put her hand over her nose.

"Well, you know, Matt, you could get your own place. I mean, you are 20 years old. If you don't like it, you are free to move out." Susan's tone was sharp and it was obvious that she was annoyed.

"Look, both of you, stop it. This is going to be hard enough without you bickering with each other. By the way, Matt, it is my home and I am free to smoke if I so choose. And Sue is right, if you're not happy here, you can get your own place."

Emily watched as her brother shrugged his shoulders and became quiet. Normally, he would argue until the other person gave up. Today was different. His normal, somewhat belligerent personality stifled, he sat, head down, mouth closed.

Arriving at the funeral home, the limousine pulled up directly in front of the main doors to allow Emily and her family to exit the vehicle. As she stepped out of the car, Emily was overwhelmed with the numerous cars and the huge crowd of people who had already arrived. She knew that her dad was well-liked, but she never expected such an outpouring of love and affection.

They were escorted into the room where her dad's body was laid out. No one was allowed in until she and her family had arrived. She was thankful that they would be given a few minutes before the throngs of people entered.

Her mother, aunt and siblings walked ahead of Emily as they entered. She was struck by the familiarity of the large room, despite the fact that she had never seen it before. It was obviously designed to appear like a cozy, comfortable living room with soft lights, a non-working fireplace and a light-colored plush carpet.

She watched as her brother and sister stood over the casket staring down at their father, their faces etched with sorrow. Susan began to cry and Matthew, in a rare show of affection, placed his arm around her. Emily moved back and waited while her mom and Aunt Sally knelt before the casket, made the sign of the cross and prayed silently for a few moments. When she saw that they had gotten up, she slowly moved closer. She stopped several feet away from the open coffin. Surrounding his body were at least 50 flower arrangements. The overwhelming aroma of fresh flowers was probably intoxicating, but Emily's senses were dulled, her body still in shock.

Slowly, tentatively, she moved closer to the open coffin. Her feet felt like lead weights. She finally reached the edge of the coffin and forced herself to look down at her father's body. She relaxed slightly. If you glanced at him quickly, it seemed like he was sleeping peacefully. However, if you inspected him more closely, you could see the makeup, lipstick, blush and knew that he was, in fact, dead.

She touched one of his hands, folded neatly across his stomach. It was cold, hard and rough. Emily had never before seen or touched a dead body. It gave her an eerie, yet comforting feeling to see the peaceful expression on his face.

She knelt down in front of his coffin. Making the sign of the cross, she tried to say a few prayers for him. Emily found it difficult to pray. All she could come up with was "Why, God?" Then she noticed the rosary beads in his lifeless, folded hands. It made her think back to the time eight years ago when her mother and father were having an argument, what Emily liked to call a 'shouting match.'

I listen as my parents are fighting again, fighting over bills they can't pay. Each time my mom yells, my dad yells louder. Dad starts to throw things, not at Mom, just throwing things. I'm scared. It makes me feel anxious to see the two people I love most in the world screaming at each other. Don't they love each other, I ask myself. Why won't they stop yelling?

Dad just said something about moving out. Oh, God, please, I don't want my dad to move out. Mom says good. Oh, please, Mom, don't say that. I look at both of them but they don't seem to see me or the panic in my eyes. They only glare at each other.

Dad goes upstairs. I run after him and watch as he gets a suitcase out and starts putting clothes in it.

God, why won't you stop him? I pass by my bedroom and notice my rosary sitting on the bedside table. I grab it, sit down on my bed, and begin saying the rosary. As I say each Hail Mary, I plead with Our Lady, "holy Mary, Mother of God, pray for us sinners now and at the hour of our death. Amen." Please, Our Lady, don't let my Dad walk out.

As I'm saying another Hail Mary, Dad walks by my room and doesn't notice that I'm even there. He stomps down the steps. I can't hear if he says goodbye, but I listen to the door slam shut.

"Oh, God, please, make him come back." I continue saying the rosary, each Hail Mary becoming more fervent than the last. I pray until my heart is bursting. Please, God, listen to my prayer.

I begin saying the Hail Holy Queen prayer and suddenly, I hear the door open downstairs. Without finishing, I stand at the top of the stairs and I see that my dad is standing at the doorway. Mom walks over to him. At first, they're silent.

Then, my dad starts crying. "I can't leave you. I can't leave my family." He and Mom embrace.

I begin to cry. Thank you, God, and thank you, Our Lady, for bringing my daddy back.

She felt Aunt Sally's hand on her shoulder, then heard her whisper, "Come on, Tootsie Roll, people are starting to come in."

She made the sign of the cross, then stood up. With sadness, Emily reflected on the fact that everyone in her family had stopped going to Mass. Everyone that is, except for her. Though she rarely received communion anymore, she continued going to church. Even though she had her own ideas about what she should believe, she always felt a need to attend Mass. One day many months ago, she asked her mom why she and her dad had stopped attending Mass. Her mom had just shrugged her shoulders. Though her dad had stopped going to Mass, he always recited the rosary.

As visitors started to line up to pay their respects, Emily took up her position next to her sister and began talking, greeting and hugging people, accepting their expressions of sympathy.

The rest of the evening was a blur to Emily. It was difficult to keep track of the number of relatives and friends who had come to offer their condolences. In what seemed like just a few moments, they were putting their coats on, leaving the funeral home and driving home in the limousine. As her mom, aunt and siblings sat quietly, Emily glanced out the window at the dark night sky, at what appeared to be millions of stars twinkling in the moonlight.

Within a short time, the limo pulled up to Emily's house and she and her family stepped out. She watched them hang up their coats and proceed to the living room or to the kitchen. She made her way upstairs to the sanctity of her bedroom. Changing into her pajamas, she switched off the lights, turned on the television and tucked herself into bed. Exhausted, within minutes, she was asleep.

All of a sudden, she was in the living room. The front door opened and her dad walked in. "Oh my God! You're alive!" she yelled.

"Of course, Em. I never really died. It was all a hoax."

"A hoax? But why? The doctors said you had died."

"Well, I didn't and everything's fine. Come on, let's go watch some television."

Emily woke up with a start and sat up in her bed. She sighed. Though it was comforting to be able to see her dad alive and well again, it was frustrating to have to wake up and not be with him.

Her television was still on, and some sort of western movie with John Wayne was blaring. She turned it off and climbed back into her warm bed. She lay there quietly and heard Susan come into the room and slip into bed.

After listening to her sister's snores for ten minutes, she quietly crept downstairs, through the living room, kitchen and into the den where she switched on the television. She found an old rerun of "Gilligan's Island." Emily had to admit, even though it was one of those sitcoms that had little to do with real life, Gilligan's Island was one of her favorite old television shows. She and her siblings could never quite figure out where Mary Ann and Ginger were getting all the flour to make coconut cream pies.

Emily lost interest in the show and it soon became background noise. In the cabinet underneath the television, she began searching through the old photo albums, looking for images of her father. Next to one of the albums, she discovered a beige file folder labeled "Work in Progress," written in her father's handwriting. Her pulse quickened as she realized what it contained. *Dad's writing projects.*

She opened up the folder and the first article was entitled, "Freedom Yesterday." As she read the opening paragraph, she could see that her father had written a non-fiction article on the plight of black people and the injustice of treating someone differently because of the color of their skin. Written in 1969, it was obviously something that had moved him to the point of putting his thoughts down on paper.

The writing was mediocre at best, but to Emily, it was a part of her father she knew little about. The emptiness that she had been experiencing over the past few days lessened as she continued reading the unpublished articles that he had labored on.

As she read each piece, she became enveloped by his presence. He wrote with such passion and feeling that Emily was overcome with emotion.

She was filled with gratitude that he had written these articles. And yet, she asked herself, why hadn't she read these before now? Her eyes began to water again as she recalled him telling her about a story that he had written. Teenaged Emily had been too indifferent and too self-absorbed to care.

She held the folder close to her heart. For Emily, her dad's life had just been extended, in a way, through his writing. It was a one-way communication, to be sure, but it was a way of speaking to her and allowing his words to be received and satisfied.

She could hear the ending theme of Gilligan's Island and kept the television on. A commercial for "Old Spice" cologne came on. Emily so wished that she could hear her dad's voice or smell his familiar aftershave. Her heart full of grief, she realized that her mom, rarely emotional and more often matter of fact, might have thought she was acting odd had she found out that yesterday, she had secretly gone downstairs to the laundry pile in the basement and searched for her father's Post Office shirts so she could smell him again.

At the funeral home the next morning, Emily and her family greeted more visitors for an hour before the funeral Mass. Many of Emily's female relatives, including her sister and mother, got in line to kiss her dad goodbye. Thinking it was expected of her, she also got in line and was the last person waiting.

She tentatively leaned down and kissed his lips. It felt strange, like she was kissing a mannequin. The body laying in the coffin appeared to be her dad, but it certainly didn't 'feel' like him.

A short while later, at the funeral Mass, Emily dutifully followed along with the motions but her body, still in shock, paid little attention. In an instant, they were all standing in a circle, around the grave site, while the priest said some prayers. Emily's mother and siblings all laid a single red rose on the top of the coffin as most of the people began walking away.

Emily stood still and watched as the men began to lower the coffin into the hole, then shovel large amounts of dirt onto her father's coffin. With each shovelful of dirt landing on the top of his casket, Emily winced. She hated to think of her dad, cold and alone in that box, dirt covering him.

Then it finally dawned on her that this was not her dad, really. While it may have been his body, it wasn't his soul, his spirit, his memories, his personality, his being.

She believed that his spirit, his being, his very soul was on its way to heaven. And comforted by this, Emily was hopeful that someday she would see him again.

4

Mark 10:14,16

September 9, 1909

Katharine arrived home and ascended the stairs. Just inside her bedroom, a gush of fluid from between her legs splashed onto the floor below her. "Damn! Couldn't it have waited another week? It's so damned hot!" Katharine began slipping off her dress, undergarments and shoes. She complained to herself about the mess, irritated that she would now have to clean up the floor, then realized that she should probably send her son to get the midwife.

"Johnnie, come up here a minute, would you?" she yelled.

She could hear every other step being pounded by her 13-year-old son. "Yeah, Ma, what is it?" he yelled through the closed door to her bedroom.

"Run up to 16th and Porter and get the midwife."

"Can't you use the telephone, Ma? I mean, that's a good six blocks for me to run."

"I hate that thing. People should be in the same room if they're going to talk to one another. Besides, if you go, I know she'll come immediately."

Katharine could hear him race down the steps and listened as the front door slammed. She now allowed her body to relax slightly. She slipped out of her undergarments, grabbed a fresh nightgown and proceeded to clean up the mess on the floor with her already wet clothes.

Her body tensed as she remembered what she had gone through delivering Johnnie. That was 13 years ago and she vowed that he would be her last. Besides the normal aches and pains of pregnancy, labor had been difficult. Johnnie had been a big baby, nearly eight pounds. Calling the birthing process labor was an understatement. She liked to call it 'to hell and back.'

She sighed as she remembered why she was delivering another child. Rarely intimate with her husband anymore, she had relations with her boarder, Michael.

When she was late for her period, she secretly went to the midwife a few blocks away to 'bring it on.' Frequently during the years when she became pregnant, she visited the midwife who used a hat pin or some other sharp object to do the procedure. Katharine knew that it was important to have it done before the quickening, before the pregnancy was too far advanced, before it was considered a baby. Most of the time, the procedure worked and she got her monthly. Sometimes the flow was so heavy that it frightened her. Still, she was determined never to be pregnant again, or at least, never to give birth again.

This time, however, she had gotten a bit of spotting, but definitely not a 'period.' As time went on, the nausea, breast tenderness and other symptoms had increased until finally she felt movement. She had known that as soon as quickening occurred, there would be no turning back.

The banging on the bedroom door jolted her back to the present. "Johnnie, is that you?"

"Yeah, Ma. The midwife said she'd be here in about half an hour."

Katharine sat on the side of her bed and began contemplating the possible outcomes of the birth, but all that she could focus on was the amount of pain that she would have to endure.

In her own way, she held a certain amount of affection for her son, but to her, children were one big nuisance that held little reward. She remembered the diapers, extra wash and sleepless nights. The truth is, she already had one child and was doubtful that she could ever feel the same toward another.

Suddenly, she felt a familiar pain, the gripping of her uterus preparing to expel the child. She tensed her body and screamed out, "Why couldn't that damned midwife have come sooner?"

Several hours later, the midwife's assistant was patting Katharine's forehead and wiping away the sweat as she struggled through another contraction. "Katharine, you need to stop tensing your body. Try to relax," the midwife said, in a hushed, calming tone.

"Annie, you try to relax pushing a cannon ball out from between your legs. I hate every minute of this."

Although it was September, it felt like the middle of July. The occasional engine sound of the horseless carriages could be heard amidst the sounds of the cloppity-clop noises of the horses and buggies. The loud moaning of a birthing woman echoed throughout the neighborhood.

The midwife examined Katharine and discovered that she was completely dilated and ready for pushing. A cool breeze through the open window offered to make the next few minutes more tolerable. For Katharine, it fell like a gift unnoticed.

"Katharine, you can start pushing with your next contraction."

She obeyed the instruction and with every contraction, she continued screaming and moaning. Within ten minutes, she had pushed the child free of her body. The baby slid into the midwife's hands and immediately started crying.

"You have a daughter, Katharine, a fine beautiful daughter."

The midwife handed the baby to her assistant who began to clean her. A few more contractions and Katharine delivered the placenta and the rest of the umbilical cord, the baby's lifeline for the previous nine months. The midwife studied it for several minutes before declaring, "Looks like it's intact. We'll just watch your flow for a few days and you'll be as good as new."

"Good as new. I hardly think so," she complained.

The midwife ignored Katharine's comment, then studied the baby. She was no longer blue and had 'pinked' up. She seemed very fair compared to Johnnie. The assistant handed Katharine the baby to hold.

There was a gentle knock at the door. "Come on in," replied the midwife. Harry entered, head down, avoiding his wife's eyes. "How's my wife doing, ma'am?"

"Just fine, sir. You've got a fine healthy baby girl, Mr. Clayman."

"Well, look at that. She's just a tiny little thing compared to how big Johnnie was," he noticed. The baby was calm, somewhat squinting around at her surroundings. "Almost the spittin' image of my wife," he commented. The baby opened her tiny mouth in a reflexive attempt to nurse. "She's a beauty, so different from my ugly Indian face," he said.

Katharine interrupted him. "Where's Michael?"

Harry's face showed a rare frown. "How do I know? I don't keep track of his goings on."

Ignoring him, Katharine more firmly said, "Go get Michael, Harry. He's probably at the studio."

Harry's eyes became downcast and he nodded.

"I'm gonna get Johnnie first to see his new little sister. He's out playing stick ball." He hesitated. "Then I'll get Michael." Harry quietly left the room and pulled the heavy door closed behind him.

As he left, Katharine felt free to speak. "I can tell you this for sure. This will be my last child, if I have anything to say about it."

"Ah," the midwife replied, "but she's a fine healthy girl. You haven't had a daughter yet and every woman wants a daughter," she said, as she scurried around the room helping the assistant to clean up the mess after childbirth.

"One child is enough for anyone," Katharine complained.

"Your husband seems quite taken with his new daughter."

"It's surprising that he's sober," Katharine responded, her tone without emotion.

A short while later, a quiet knock was heard at the door and Johnnie came in. His smile was broad as he timidly approached the bed where his mother had just given birth to his sister.

"She's tiny, Ma," he said.

"Here," she said to the assistant, "take her for a minute while I visit with my son. Doesn't she need to be weighed or measured or something like that?"

"Sure, ma'am, I'll take her," the assistant said.

"You were making some awful noises, Ma. I was afraid you were gonna die or something. The whole neighborhood heard you."

"That's normal." Katharine hesitated. She watched as the midwife examined the baby. Keeping her eyes focused on the examination, she continued speaking to her son. "It hurts like hell giving birth and I was never one who took well to pain. I didn't think I would ever have to feel that pain again."

Another gentle knock and her husband let himself into her room.

"He's not at the studio, Katharine. I don't know where he is." Harry tentatively approached the assistant and held out his arms. The assistant smiled, then placed the baby in his gigantic, dark arms. Harry cooed at the newborn girl. Her miniature thumb grasped on to his large callused finger and held on tightly.

"Well, this young lady is certainly a beauty, just like her mama," Harry had beamed, careful to avoid Katharine's eyes.

Several months later, Katharine was tending to the musical instruments at the store. It was mid-morning and she was enjoying a quiet moment while the baby slept in the carriage next to her. Few customers visited the store today and for that, Katharine was grateful.

She heard the bells jingle, hurriedly moved a small sculpture to the side of the cash register and looked up as Michael walked in.

At that moment, the infant Ruth let out a wail. Katharine leaned over and picked up her daughter from the carriage and began rocking her in a feeble attempt to quiet the baby. She hated wasting her time on mundane things such as that, but she knew that she wouldn't hear a word if she didn't try to soothe her daughter.

"Just a minute, Michael."

"No rush, Katharine. Settle your baby, that's more important."

"She's hungry." Katharine sat on the stool behind the counter and unbuttoned the bodice of her dress and offered the breast to her child. Ruth eagerly latched on, her small eyes rolling back as she gulped, now satisfied.

She glanced at Michael, his eyes staring down at the floor.

"I don't know why you're so embarrassed with me feeding my baby. You've seen more of me than just my breast."

Michael kept his eyes on the floor and shifted awkwardly from one foot to the next.

"Look, Michael, this is where I keep the sculpture you gave me." She pointed to the area just behind the cash register.

He leaned over, smiled, then moved back to stand in front of her.

"Katharine, I was hoping that you would bring Ruth in to the studio for a formal photograph."

"Whatever for, Michael? We already have taken a few with a neighbor's box camera."

"I know, but no formal, professionally done photographs. I would do it without charge."

"I would expect that."

The baby at her breast squirmed, then began screaming again.

"I hate when she swallows air. It is so difficult to bring up her gas bubbles."

Katharine buttoned the top of her dress and stood up. She began swaying back and forth in order to placate her child. She started rubbing, almost pounding the baby's back. Michael stood still and silent. In a minute or so, Ruth let out a loud burp and settled on Katharine's shoulder.

She walked around the counter and stood in front of Michael. They stood awkwardly for a moment, then he reached out and gently touched the side of her face. "Katharine, I. . . ."

"Michael, someone will see us," Katharine whispered.

He withdrew his hand and stepped back. "So will you come to the studio?"

Katharine rocked back and forth, then bit down on her bottom lip.

Michael's head tilted forward, his eyebrows raised slightly, waiting for Katharine to speak. "I'll have to bring Johnnie and Harry along."

"Of course, Katharine. Tomorrow afternoon, there are no appointments."

"Johnnie's at school and what of my store?"

"You can all come after school and after the store is closed."

"Very well."

"Good day, Katharine."

"Good day, Michael."

She watched as her lover exited the store. Ruth was asleep on her shoulder and she carefully placed her in the carriage next to the counter.

The following day, Katharine began the closing ritual for the store. She brought the carriage closer to the front, then pulled the blinds over both windows and door. She counted the cash, made a few notations in the ledger, then pushed the carriage outside and waited on the sidewalk for Johnnie and Harry. She was thankful that it was unseasonably warm for November and it was unnecessary to dress the baby so warmly.

Katharine began tapping her foot as she impatiently waited a minute, then two minutes. From the corner of her eye, she could see her son running up the street.

"Sorry I'm late, Ma. Pop's drunk again. I just left him. Hope that's all right."

Katharine sighed. "Yes, Johnnie, that's fine. Push Ruth in the carriage for me, will you?"

John nodded.

Within a few minutes, they arrived at Michael's studio. He was waiting on the sidewalk in front of the store. His eyes widened and his smile was broad.

"Katharine, Johnnie, this way."

She walked through the door as John maneuvered the bulky carriage up the two steps into the studio. He parked it behind the counter, then leaned over and picked up his sister, now awake, but quietly looking around.

"Where's all your hair, little one?" he teased her. "Was I this bald, Ma?"

"Just about. Bring her here, Johnnie."

John walked into the studio where the portrait would be taken. It hadn't changed much in four years.

Michael spoke. "Katharine, please, sit on the couch. John, you sit on the floor in front of your mother and," he stopped, leaned over and gently picked up Ruth from John's arms, then hesitated, transfixed.

Katharine watched as he held her daughter and stared down at her small face. Ruth began cooing. Michael smiled. "Aren't you a pretty girl?" he said, in a gentle, high-pitched voice. Ruth reacted by smiling and babbling.

"Michael, what are you doing?" Katharine asked, in an agitated tone. She had never heard his typically low voice sound so different.

He glanced at her, then paused, and placed the baby on Katharine's lap. He stood back, near the large camera, and tilted his head in an attempt to view the pose from different angles.

"There. That will work quite nicely."

"Hurry up, Michael. I don't have all day."

"Yes, of course."

He peered into his camera, and after a minute or so, Katharine heard a pop, then smelled burnt powder.

"Thank you. I shall have that photograph prepared for you within a few days."

"That's fine, Michael."

As Katharine and her son stood up, Michael approached her and whispered, "About the rent money for this month, Katharine."

"You're late, Michael," she responded, not bothering to whisper.

"I realize that, but it will take a few more days. Besides, this photograph could perhaps be partial payment, could it not?"

"Oh? Now I understand, Michael. Why didn't you tell me you didn't have the money?"

"I don't know." His eyes stared at the floor.

Katharine paused. "I suppose the photograph can be payment for this month. But we can't keep taking photographs to pay for every month now, can we?"

"No, we can't. But it would be helpful just for this month."

"Fine. Good day, Michael."

"Good day."

As Katharine was leaving the studio, she turned around. "Oh, will you be home for supper?"

"No, Katharine. I have some work here at the studio."

"Very well. Good day."

Katharine walked behind John as he pushed Ruth in the baby carriage. *I know why he wanted that photograph and it wasn't to pay for the rent.* For a brief moment, she felt sorry for Michael. He would never be able to be a father to his child, to shower affection on her or to teach her or to dote on her or to give her away in marriage. Katharine brushed the thought aside and focused on what she would prepare for dinner.

5

Isaiah 54:4

December 6, 1978

After checking the time, Emily rushed out the door to another day of classes at college. She sighed a frantic sigh as she realized that she was going to be late for her first class. It was a dreary Monday morning, a cold, wet day that made a person yearn to be inside.

When she had finished high school, Emily initially thought that it would be interesting to study to be a paralegal. After a semester of being taught by lawyers, she opted out of that program and took a few months off to figure out just what she wanted to accomplish with her life.

Her mom, a typist for court reporters for many years, suggested that she look into court reporting. After talking with several people in the profession, Emily thought that it sounded interesting and lucrative.

Watching court shows on television such as Perry Mason, the Defenders and Owen Marshall, she had become fascinated by the person in front of the judge who seemed to be 'typing' on a little machine, taking down the court record verbatim. She spent time researching the local business schools and decided on a college about 10 miles away.

During the ten-minute drive to college, she switched on the oldies station. "My Cherie Amour" by Stevie Wonder was playing. Her eyes began to tear as she remembered how much her dad loved this song. Life certainly had changed in the eight months since he had passed away. Her father's death had left quite a void in Emily's life. It was perhaps out of boredom and needing some distraction that she took up the unusual hobby of writing to pen pals from all over the world. As well, she continued working on her family tree album. Emily became fascinated and intrigued by her ancestors and enjoyed looking at endless photos or hearing stories about them.

Even though many aspects of her life had changed, her love life had certainly remained the same. She had started wearing small amounts of makeup, had gotten her long hair cut to shoulder length and had begun wearing more grown-up clothes, though it was nearly impossible to find adult-looking clothes in the children's department. Despite the changes, most people still regarded her as a little girl.

The day before, a young boy began a conversation with Emily as she was leaving the post office.

"Hey, you come to this post office a lot, don't you?" the boy had asked.

"Uh. . .yes, I do."

"Well, you know, I. . .uh. . ."

Emily had watched as he looked away and then down to the ground.

"Do you. . .uh. . .have a boyfriend?"

"No, I don't." *Why is this kid asking if I have a boyfriend?*

"Do you think maybe we could go out some time?"

Emily's open mouth wasn't sure what to say. "Look, you seem like a nice boy, but I think there are laws against someone my age dating someone your age. And if there aren't, there should be."

The boy seemed confused. "How old are you?"

"19. And you?"

It was now his turn to open his mouth. There was an awkward pause before he spoke. "I'm. . .uh. . .13. You're. . .really 19?"

Emily had nodded. "See you around."

Despite the offer, she still hadn't experienced her first kiss or a date. Every night, she prayed that God would send her a man to marry, someone with whom she could spend the rest of her life. So far: no man. At this point in her life, Emily would have been satisfied with a superficial date, something that would help to make her feel 'normal,' like the girls on television. Sometimes, it seemed like her main goal in life was 'to get some experience with guys.'

Her pulse quickened as her mind wandered to one of the guys in her class at college, Eric. He reminded Emily of a suntanned, California, "Beach Boys" type, with a flawless complexion and not too tall, about five feet seven inches with shoulder-length feathered brown hair.

Emily sat next to Eric in most of her classes and she would often talk to him about the weather or current events. He seemed confident and sure of himself, especially around girls.

Feeling attracted to him, she often daydreamed about what it would be like to go on a date with him. She jokingly told her classmates a few times, "I wouldn't kick Eric out of bed." It was an absurd comment for someone with absolutely no experience with guys.

Emily pulled her car into the college parking lot and found a spot close to the entrance. The school was small, a converted office building next to a nursery school, where Emily would often glance outside to watch the children playing.

She arrived just as the instructor came in and began preparing materials for medical dictation. During class, the teacher would read at certain speeds and the students would practice taking the dictation on their stenograph machines. She noticed that Eric was already there, sitting behind his machine and working on something at his seat. He always dressed so impeccably. Today, he was wearing a casual polo shirt and jeans. He glanced up and smiled warmly. *Gosh, he is so handsome.* She returned the smile and began to set up her machine and organize herself for the class.

"How's it going, Emily?" Eric asked. Just hearing his deep voice made Emily's heart start pounding.

Echoing the words of the Carpenters' song, she replied, "Rainy days and Mondays always get me down."

He let out an unexpected belly laugh. "Emily, you've got a great sense of humor."

Okay, it wasn't that funny.

Within minutes, the teacher spoke up.

"All right, class, we'll begin. This is medical testimony at 120 words per minute." Emily enjoyed how the instructor used distinct voices to indicate two different people speaking. She and her classmates often wondered whether the principal had recruited her teachers from the local school of drama.

First in a low voice, then in a high, the teacher began:

"Where was the fracture, Doctor?"

"In the tibia."

"And what type of fracture was that?"

"It was a hairline fracture."

Emily tried to concentrate and to listen to the words, but she found herself distracted. *Should I let Eric know how much I like him?* He was always so nice to her and, at times, somewhat flirtatious. Trying to brush the thought aside, she settled down to the task of taking medical testimony on her stenograph machine at 120 words per minute.

An hour later, while their class was taking a break, Emily stood alone in the hall. She could see out of the corner of her eye that Eric was walking towards her. She tried to act nonchalant and to pretend that she didn't see him coming. Her breathing became shallow and her heart was racing.

"Hey, Emily, a bunch of us are going to Churchill's after school. Would you like to come too?"

Emily turned her head to look up at him. "Uh. . .sure, I'd love to go. How about you?" *Gee, what a stupid thing to ask him. He just said, " us."* She hoped that he didn't notice that her hands were shaking.

"I wouldn't miss it," he replied, seeming not to notice her blunder. "By the way," he continued, "that was a superb read back you did in class."

"Thanks."

"I don't know how you do it. Medical dictation is so hard."

"Just practice, I guess."

"Hey, Em?"

"Yes, Eric?" *He's using my familiar name.*

"You've got a great voice."

A great voice? I thought I sounded like a kid.

"Really?"

"Sure. You speak so clearly. Ever thought of public speaking?"

"No, I haven't. Some of the kids in high school used to make fun of me whenever I read in class. 'Little Emily sounds like a chipmunk,' they would say."

"That's pretty mean. I think you have a great voice."

She glanced down at the floor. "Thanks," she responded, still surprised at his compliment.

The day passed by quickly and as Emily was packing up her stenograph machine and getting ready to leave, Eric approached her and said, "Looks like it's just us today, Em. The others aren't able to join us after all."

"Just us?" Emily asked, with raised eyebrows.

"That's all right, isn't it? I mean, if you'd rather not. . . ."

"Uh. . . ." she hesitated. "I guess it's okay." *Seems too much of a coincidence that everyone dropped out at the last minute.*

They walked out of school together and toward her car. Feeling awkward, Emily found herself wishing that she could have had more time to prepare herself for this new development. Climbing into her seat, she wondered, *What in the world are we going to talk about?* They never had any trouble before, but then again, they were always accompanied by at least three or four other students. Eric said little in the short two-minute drive to the bar. After she parked the car, they got out and walked together to the entrance of the bar. Eric motioned for Emily to follow him as he led the way into the booth section of the bar.

No sooner had they sat down than a young waitress was asking them, "Can I get you both something to drink?"

"I'll have a Budweiser and the young lady will have. . . ."

Emily hesitated. She didn't care too much for the last drink that she ordered a few days ago when the group had come here after school. She decided to try a different drink, one that Susan usually ordered, one in which the alcohol couldn't be tasted.

"A strawberry daiquiri."

The waitress wrote down the order, then her eyes narrowed. "May I see some ID?"

Emily sighed and reached into her purse for her driver's license. Any other time, this would be fun, but now?   It was embarrassing.

She handed the waitress her license and watched as the young woman scrutinized the document. "How do I know this is yours?"

"Look at the height," she said, exasperated.

Emily listened as she read, "57 inches.   Okay.   That's pretty short."

Handing it back to Emily, the waitress smiled, then said, "You sure don't look 19. I would've sworn you were like, 11 or 12."

Emily returned the comment with an awkward, but polite smile, then glanced over at Eric.   He was snickering under his breath.   "You know, Em, the first day of school, I remember thinking, Gee, somebody must've brought their little sister with them.   Then I heard you talk and I said, that's either a genius or she's a lot older than she looks.   As it turned out, you are a little bit of both."

"A genius? I don't think so. As for looking young, it's a bit embarrassing at times, to be honest. I mean, it was fun when I was younger, but now that I'm 19, it can be frustrating."

The waitress returned to the table and set the drinks down. Emily, nervous about being alone with someone that she was attracted to, started drinking her daiquiri like it was a glass of Coke.   Susan was right about this drink.   It was sweet and, thankfully, she couldn't taste the alcohol.

"You're very smart. I'm willing to bet you did well in high school, Em."

"I did all right."

"I bet you did better than all right. It's pretty obvious with how well you do in our class."

"Well, I don't know about that."

She hesitated, then putting the glass to her lips, realized that she had already finished her drink.

"Hey, how about another drink, Em?"

Without thinking, she nodded. A minute or so later, the waitress brought a second daiquiri to Emily. She again guzzled it down.

Now, it felt like the room was spinning. She glanced over at Eric and down at the top of his beige polo shirt, which was unbuttoned at the top button. Some of his dark, plentiful chest hair was spilling out through the opened part of his shirt.

Emily started thinking, *"Eric, you are so damned sexy. Can you unbutton your shirt just one more button? Your chest hair is so sexy."*

As his eyes widened, she realized, with dread, that she had spoken that last thought out loud.

"So. . . you think I'm sexy, Em?" His eyebrows were raised and the corner of his mouth was upturned in a smile.

Somewhat in shock, Emily was speechless. She took a deep breath and smiled sheepishly. With her left elbow already on the table, she placed her left hand under her chin. She stared at him blankly for a few seconds. For a short time, it seemed like she was seeing two Erics. Then, under the influence of liquid honesty, she replied, "Okay, I admit it. I think you're sexy. Your chest hair is sexy, and I'd love to go out with you. There, I've said it, now it's out in the open." She could hear herself talking but she couldn't believe that her most intimate thoughts were being said out loud.

He smiled. "Well, Em, I certainly had no idea that you felt that way. Would you like another drink?"

"No, I'd better not. It feels like I've had about ten drinks. I guess I can't hold my alcohol very well." Emily was now starting to slur some of her words; nevertheless, she was feeling very comfortable around Eric.

"No, I guess you can't. You are pretty small. How much do you weigh? You'd be affected pretty quickly."

"Did you just ask what I weigh? That's not the most appropriate question to ask a young lady."

"No, I guess it isn't."

"You know, I don't feel so well, Eric.   I'm not sure that I'm going to be able to drive home. Do you think that you could drive me home?"

"I don't have a car. How am I supposed to drive you home?"

"Well, you can drive my car home, then I can get my brother to drive you home."

"I've got a better idea," he offered. "Why don't I drive both of us back to my place for a while and you can sober up a bit. Then, you'll be able to drive home on your own."

Emily hesitated before saying, "All right." *This is great. We can go back to Eric's place and get to know each other better.*

They walked out of the bar and he took hold of Emily's hand.   She could hardly believe this was happening to her. A good-looking guy was holding her hand. She felt like Marcia Brady. More importantly, she felt normal. She glanced at him and he smiled. *Maybe Eric will ask me on a date to a movie or something.*

They reached Emily's car and he took the keys from her, opened up the passenger door, then the driver's side. As Emily sat in the front seat, she wondered if Eric had taken a bath in his cologne. Though she hadn't noticed it before, it now seemed so overwhelming that she was finding it difficult to breathe. Eric drove the two of them to a house about five miles from the bar in a beautiful, high-class neighborhood.

"This is where I live," he said, as he pulled her car into the driveway. *Nice house.* It was a split level set back from the road with a front yard stocked with well-kept shrubs and a red brick driveway and walkway. Eric was obviously from a well-off family.

They got out of the car and proceeded up the walkway to his house. The cold biting wind smacked Emily's face and for a brief moment, she wondered whether she should go inside with him. She watched him reach into his pocket, grab his keys, then quickly unlock the front door. He allowed Emily to enter the house first and, as he was shutting the door, he checked his Gucci watch and whispered, "No one will be home until six o'clock, three hours from now." *Okay, I have three hours to sober up.*

Once inside, he walked ahead of her. She tried to follow right behind him, but she continued to be unsteady on her feet. Walking slowly through the plush carpeted hallway, she studied the inside of the house which seemed like an interior decorator had furnished it: neat, tidy and almost clinical. It all seemed so surreal, like she was part of a dream. Certainly, his house didn't really look lived in, not the kind of messy appearance that she was used to at her house.

He walked ahead of her and through a long hallway. Losing track of him, she hesitated, then heard him call her name.

"Em, just turn left at the kitchen." On the other side of the kitchen was a den decorated in light-colored paneling. It was spacious but cozy looking. Emily watched as he walked over to the stereo.

"Do you like George Benson?"

"Sure, I guess."

He put on a record, then sat down on the floor in front of the cold, empty fireplace.

Still unsteady on her feet, Emily plopped down on one of the chairs near the unused fireplace and began some small talk with Eric. His muscular body and hint of chest hair reeked of masculinity. "Eric, why haven't you unbuttoned your shirt?" she asked.

Eric laughed, this time showing his beautiful teeth, then he raised his eyebrows.

I swear he is slow moving. Should I just go up to him and kiss him or what? Uh-oh. What in the world am I thinking? She couldn't believe her audacity. *Did I just ask him to unbutton his shirt?* Unnoticed before now, she felt as if her bladder would burst.

"Do you mind if I use the bathroom?"

"Sure, it's on the other side of the kitchen. You passed it on the way in."

Again walking slowly and at times holding on to the wall for support, she arrived at the small bathroom, leaned over the sink and splashed some water on her face. Waiting a few minutes, she stared into the mirror and whispered, "Eric is so sexy. I can't believe I'm here at his house. I hope he asks me out on a date." She took a couple of deep breaths, then opened the door.

She moved slowly from the hallway through the kitchen and back into the den. It appeared as if he had started a small fire in the fireplace, despite the adequate temperature in the house. The soft lighting in the room suggested that he had turned down the lights. When she stepped into the den, she stopped cold. Even though the lights were dimmed, she could see that he was laying on the floor, shirtless and propping himself up on his elbow. The sight of his naked chest caused Emily's pulse to quicken and her breath to become shallow.

Her open mouth prompted Eric to speak. "Hey, Em, do you give back massages?" Without thinking and still feeling somewhat uninhibited, she responded, "Uh. . .sure, why not?"

She knelt beside him as he laid on his stomach. She hesitated, then started to massage his smooth, muscular back. Rubbing her hands across his warm skin, she heard Eric moan and say, "That feels great, Em." All of a sudden, she pulled her hands away from his back. Now, Emily felt uncomfortable to be doing such an intimate thing with Eric.

"Hey, why did you stop?"

"Listen, Eric, this. . . probably isn't a good idea."

"Why not?"

"Because I may end up doing something I'd be ashamed of." She stood up and walked over to one of the chairs. She sat down, and her eyes darted around nervously.

Emily could see from the corner of her eye that he was moving closer to her as he sat down on the floor beside her chair.

"Hey, Em?"

"Yes?" She avoided eye contact.

"Have you ever been kissed?"

Her eyebrows raised, she looked straight at him. *What in the world would've made him ask that?* She hesitated.

"Uh. . .why do you ask?"

"I don't know. You seem. . .inexperienced."

"Well, I am, very inexperienced and no, I've never been kissed."

He laughed, then said, "You *are* kidding, right? I mean, you're 19!"

"No, I'm not kidding," Emily admitted, her face down.

"Would you like to be kissed?"

"Uh. . .I guess so, only if you want to."

"Come here," he said as he pulled her off the chair and sat her next to himself on the floor. Emily took a deep breath and closed her eyes. Her heart was pounding so hard, she was convinced that Eric could hear it.

She could feel him place his warm hand on the left side of her face. As he brought his mouth to hers, she felt him kiss her lips. With his lips, he appeared to be opening her mouth. Feeling awkward, she tried to move away slightly, but he followed right along with her. Keeping her eyes closed, she could taste the beer that he had had. *I wish he would stop.* Eric broke the kiss.

"There. What did you think of your first kiss?"

"Strange. Why did you open my mouth?"

"Because that's how a girl and a guy kiss."

"Really?" She looked down, then she recalled how the couples at high school used to kiss in the halls and realized that's how Eric just kissed her. *If that's how a guy and a girl kiss, then I'm not going to like kissing very much.*

In a soft voice, he said, "You know, it takes some getting used to."

"Eric?"

"Yes, Em."

"Let's go on a date, like to a movie or something."

"Well, you know, Em, I don't really date anyone and I don't want to get serious with anyone right now."

"Yes, I know, you don't. But you could date me."

"I'm not really interested in getting serious or dating anyone."

"You don't want to date me?"

"Not just you. I mean anyone. I want to keep my options open. Dating ties me down, if you know what I mean."

"No, I don't. Marriage ties you down. Dating is just a fun thing that you do to get to know someone," she replied.

"Em, this isn't personal. As I said, I just want to keep my options open. However, I wouldn't mind getting to know you otherwise."

"What do you mean otherwise?"

Eric leaned over and kissed her again. She had to admit that the second time was less awkward and somewhat more pleasing. It was obvious that Eric had lots of experience with girls. She broke off the kiss this time and gazed into his eyes. He was staring at her in a strange sort of way.

His voice sounded soft and seductive. "I mean, we can still, you know. . . ."

He kissed her, then maneuvered her so that she was in a half-lying position under him. As he was kissing her again, Emily could feel him starting to unbutton her sweater. Despite her intoxicated state, it suddenly hit her exactly what he meant. She pulled herself up to a sitting position. He continued to kiss her neck and her shoulders.

"Wait." Emily was having a hard time breathing. "Eric, I can't do this." He was kissing the side of her face. What could she say that would make him stop?

"I can't do this. I'm only a child." *Okay, so I'm not a child, but I look like one and that should count for something.*

"No, you're not. You're 19." He kissed her lips again. She pulled away.

"Well, then I can't, because I'm Catholic."

"I know plenty of Catholic girls who do it."

"Well, I don't." Not wanting to hurt his feelings, she continued, "I mean, you know, I really want to, Eric, but I just can't."

"You know, Em, everyone does it nowadays."

"But I don't love you."

"That's okay."

He leaned over and tried to kiss her again. Still feeling somewhat uninhibited, Emily began to respond, then broke off the kiss. Suddenly, the whole situation felt wrong and even dirty. His bare chest, the one that seemed so enticing, now became a claustrophobic wall smothering her.

"I need to go," she finally admitted, then she used his chest to push herself up. The floor seemed to be moving. As she tried to steady herself, she wished that she had more time to sober up. Emily walked out to the hallway.

"Wait, Em."

She stopped near the door, now annoyed that he was using her familiar name, what only close friends and family called her. Standing still, she listened as his footsteps warned of his presence behind her. She shuddered when she felt his hands on her shoulders.

"I really like you. I wouldn't do this with any girl."

She turned around to face him. Her tone was sharp. "You don't want to date me but you want to do *that*?"

"Are you mad at me? I mean, you accepted my invitation to come to my house. What am I supposed to think?"

"I was under the impression that I was coming here to sober up."

Eric remained silent.

Emily sighed and looked down at her feet. She began to put the pieces in place. She had known that she was going to be alone with a guy. She had just told him countless times that she thought he was sexy. What else could he have thought? Emily knew that she had a high IQ, yet sometimes she did things that nominated her for the 'Idiot of the Year' award. This was certainly one of those times.

Uncomfortably, she looked up at him, avoiding eye contact. "Look, I need to go and no, I'm not mad." *At least, not at you.* She turned around again to open the door.

"Wait a minute." He hesitated. "Uh. . .you're. . .not going to tell anyone at school about this, are you?" She had never before heard self-assured Eric sound nervous.

She let out a deep sigh and turned to face him again. "No, Eric, I won't tell anyone," she retorted, in a slightly caustic tone. She turned around and walked through the door. A light drizzle hit her face as she ran to her car. She arrived safely inside before her eyes started to tear.

Emily felt stupid when she realized that she had made a fool of herself with Eric. She couldn't believe the comment that she had made about his chest hair. He said he wanted to get to know her? She wiped away her tears and took a couple of deep breaths as her mind kept replaying the experience, her heart becoming more distraught with each passing moment.

Her first kiss, that momentous first kiss, and all that was behind it, for Eric, was lust. All she wanted to do was get away from him, but the remaining smell of his cologne was overwhelming. The odor was everywhere, on herself and even in her car. It was as if the smell was deep within her pores and he was still sitting right there in the car with her.

Emily finally reached her house and pulled the car into the driveway. She was thankful that, despite her intoxicated condition, she arrived home safely. She knew that her mom would be working and she was grateful that she wouldn't have to explain her emotional state.

Turning off the car, she noticed that it had started raining more heavily, not a trickle, but a downpour, the kind of rain that soaks right through you if you are caught in it for more than a few seconds. She felt the car being pounded by large drops of rain. Emily waited impatiently for a few more minutes before getting out of the car and running to the front door. In a few brief seconds, she was drenched. She struggled with the key, but finally opened the front door. Emily ran across the living room, climbed the stairs to her bedroom and painstakingly peeled off her soaking wet clothes. Her trembling hands made the task all the more difficult. *Seems so appropriate.* Though only her eyes wept, she felt her whole body crying out.

She dried herself off and slipped on a pair of pants and a tee-shirt. Switching her television on, she sat back and started to watch a rerun of the "Brady Bunch." She needed a show that offered distraction and resolution. *He didn't even want to date me.* "All he wanted to do was *that.*"

She always assumed that she would lose her virginity before marriage, but she also was convinced that it would be with a boy she loved and certainly not someone with whom she hadn't even had a date.

For a moment, her attitude softened toward Eric. After all, he had been honest with her. He wasn't interested in going out with her. He could have dated her for a while and. . .Emily shuddered to think what she may have given up had he not been so blunt.

She looked in her TV Guide and discovered that this evening, Rudolph the Red-Nosed Reindeer, the popular Christmas classic, was going to be on. Knowing that she never missed it when she was young, her heart ached when she realized that she felt like she was really, truly no longer a child.

She mistakenly believed that a kiss would make her feel normal when, in fact, it did just the opposite. It left her shattered and disillusioned. Though she had now experienced her first kiss, there was an innocence, a naivete that was gone forever. And she had herself to thank for that.

6

Prov. 4:23-5

December 20, 1978

Emily donned her cowgirl outfit and admired herself in the mirror. She knew that some of her co-workers at the fast food restaurant despised the uniform but, most of the time, Emily rather enjoyed it. She had to admit that she did look kind of cute in the western costume. The gingham skirt, puffed sleeves and straw hat framed her small body well.

"Hey, Em," her mother called from downstairs.

"Yeah, Mom?" Emily walked to the top of the stairs.

"Aunt Sally asked me if you would be interested in having some old ledgers from my grandparents' music store. She's cleaning out her attic and was going to throw them in the trash, then thought you may want them for your family tree album."

"Sounds neat. Tell her yes, for sure. Might be interesting."

"Okay, I'll tell her to bring them at Christmas," her mom replied.

Emily skipped down the steps and leaned up to kiss Becky, who was standing near the television in the living room. "Better go. I'm going to be late. See you, mom."

She drove the two miles to the mall where the Cowboy Kitchen Restaurant was located. The mall was extraordinarily busy with Christmas shoppers. She walked through the spacious restaurant, customers at most of the wooden look tables and western bar stools.

Pushing the door to the staff room open, she was immediately struck by the two separate worlds. The bright, country look of the restaurant was in definite contrast to the puny, less-than-adequately-furnished staff room. The greasy smell of french fries and fried chicken hung thick in the air. Two cowgirls were sitting on the only chairs in the room at the small card table set up for workers to eat. She stopped at the punch-in clock as the hushed voices of the two employees caught her attention.

"She hasn't shown up for work in over two weeks. I heard that she got pregnant by a married guy," one of them said.

The other cowgirl spoke up. "I heard the same thing."

Since Emily relished gossip almost as much as television, she spoke up from her spot at the punch-in clock. "Who are you talking about?"

"Stephanie. When she was at work a few weeks ago, she had to excuse herself several times. When I went to check on her, she was leaning over the toilet, throwing up."

"Well, that doesn't necessarily mean that she's pregnant," Emily responded.

"Yeah, well, when I asked her if she was sick, she said that she wasn't, but that this was normal for someone in her condition."

"Oh," Emily said. "Well, these days, I think it's pretty careless. I mean, birth control is so effective that there's no excuse. I just know that I wouldn't be stupid enough to get pregnant before marriage."

"Yeah, I guess," one of the girls said, "but birth control isn't 100% effective. I mean, a friend of mine got pregnant and she was on the pill."

Emily shrugged her shoulders. "She doesn't have to keep the baby. She could have an abortion or give it up for adoption."

"Are you pro-choice, Emily? I don't know why, but I would have taken you for a pro-lifer."

"Well, I guess I'm personally pro-life, but I believe that it's a woman's right to choose. I mean, after all, it is legal nowadays. Better to terminate the pregnancy than to deal with a disturbed child later. It just makes sense to me."

Their discussion ended abruptly when another worker, this time a cowboy, walked in.

"Hi everyone. You guys all look so serious," he said, as he was punching in.

"Hi, Ray," Emily called out, as the other girls dispersed.

"Hi, Emily. You working the roast beef slicer today?"

"Yes."

"That's great. I'm on rolls. That means we'll be working together."

Emily turned around and smiled. She had been thinking of asking the good-natured manager to assign Ray to the roll machine so that she could get to know him. She was thankful that it had happened on its own.

Ray was an affable kind of guy who always made her feel at ease. Besides, in Emily's opinion, he was the cutest cowboy working that fast food ranch. Though he was short in stature, he had an athletic build, one that would probably have lent itself to something like wrestling or soccer. He had dark wavy hair, dark eyes and a beautiful warm smile.

Walking into the restaurant, then positioning herself at the slicer, Emily switched the machine on and started weighing the portions for roast beef sandwiches. The low hum of numerous customers and employees became constant background noise.

Ray took up his position next to her at the roll machine and grabbed a package of large kaisers to prepare them for toasting. "You must be at least 18 if they assigned you to the roast beef slicer," he commented.

"I'm 19. How about you?"

"I'm 17 and a senior at Harding High. Do you go to college?" he asked.

"I go to court reporting school. This is my first year and I hope to be working in court next year."

"Interesting," he remarked.

"What about you? What do you plan to do after you graduate?" she asked.

"I don't know. I'm thinking of joining the army."

Despite the hurried atmosphere and constant rumble of noise inherent in a fast food restaurant, Ray and Emily became so caught up in their private conversation that they completely lost track of time. The manager, a young, stocky, black man, interrupted them.

"You guys can both take your dinner break, if you'd like. I'll take over on the slicer."

"Thanks," said Emily.

"Let's have our dinner break together," Ray offered. She nodded as he grabbed two roast beef sandwiches and a couple of drinks.

As they stepped out into the mall, they searched for a private spot, away from the crowds of people, and sat down at a bench.

"Would you like to go to a movie sometime?" Ray asked.

"Sure. I love movies. I haven't seen Grease yet."

"Grease it is. I'll check the times and give you a call. What's your number?"

Emily reached into her purse, pulled out a pen and a small pad of paper. Writing as neatly as she could, she jotted down her number.

"You're so organized. Thanks." He smiled and slipped the paper into his pocket.

She couldn't believe that it was this easy. After all these years, she was finally going on her first date.

A few days later, on Christmas morning, Emily approached her mother in the kitchen. Becky was pushing the huge turkey into the oven.

"Merry Christmas, Mom."

"Merry Christmas, Em. I thought you guys were all going to sleep in."

"Not me. I'm always the first one awake, remember?"

"Yes, I do."

"I don't mind waiting till Matt and Sue wake up to open presents."

Emily hesitated.

"Seems empty without Dad around," she whispered.

Becky nodded. "Yeah, Em, it does."

Later that day, Aunt Sally arrived with her usual armload of presents for everyone.

"Oh, Tootsie Roll, Aunt Sally left that box of ledgers in the car. Would you mind getting it for her?

"Sure, no problem, Aunt Sal."

Emily hurried out the door, then shivered. A waft of cold air smacked her in the face. Although there was no snow on the ground, it was a blustery, overcast day. Glancing up at the sky, Emily observed that there definitely appeared to be snow clouds, or at least, that's what she hoped they were. Despite the absence of snow, the smell of winter enveloped her. One of her neighbors was obviously burning some wood in a fireplace and she took a deep breath, enjoying the aroma.

She reached her aunt's car and opened up the passenger door. Sitting on the floor in front of the seat was a large cardboard box, one that had seen better days. The top of it was thick with dust and Emily carefully removed the box from the car before blowing the dust off the top. Standing next to the car, Emily peered through the remaining dust to see large letters in faded ink, "Ledgers, Parlor Music Shoppe, 1905 to 1935, K. Clayman."

"Hi, Em."

She glanced up to see Ray's smiling face. "Hi."

"What's that?"

"Some old ledgers from my great-grandparents. Remember I told you that one of my hobbies is working on my family tree? Well, my aunt thought perhaps this would be helpful."

"That's neat. Hey, Merry Christmas." He leaned over to kiss her. "I had to park down the street because of all cars. Here, let me take this in for you."

"Thanks. It's pretty dusty." As he took the box from her, Emily couldn't help but notice how handsome he looked in his dress jeans and green pullover sweater.

He lifted up the box and followed Emily into the house.

The living room was a flurry of activity with Aunt Sally handing out packages. "Jingle Bell Rock," was playing on the stereo, the Christmas tree's blinking lights seeming to flicker to the music. Ray placed the box in the corner and stood beside Emily. "Hey, everyone, this is my boyfriend, Ray."

They stopped and stared at at the young couple. Becky walked over and shook Ray's hand. "Nice to meet you. I'm Emily's mom, Becky."

Ray leaned over and whispered, "Your mom's not short like you."

Hearing him, Becky responded, "No, I'm not. I like to tell everyone that Emily's the runt of the litter."

Ray laughed.

Standing next to the Christmas tree, Matthew and Susan waved hello.

"Gee, Ray, if Aunt Sally had known you were coming, she would have brought something for you."

"That's okay," he replied.

"Hey, Tootsie Roll, what do you think of the ledgers?"

"I think they're great and I'd like to keep them, Aunt Sal. Thanks for thinking of me."

"Tootsie Roll?" he whispered.

"That's her nickname for me."

"Cute." Ray took Emily's hand and walked over to the couch. "You've got a nice family, Em."

Later that evening, Emily picked up the old box of ledgers and took it upstairs to her bedroom. She lifted up the lid and took out the first book. On the front of it, in beautiful letters, was the word *"Ledger,"* with a elaborate ornate design around the letters, set in a faded burgundy-type color and a beige torn binding.

"Neat," Emily said out loud. Holding the dusty, moldy smelling book, she was struck by the unique design of the cover and pictured her great-grandmother holding it nearly 75 years ago, when it smelled new and unused. For a reason that she couldn't comprehend, at that moment, Emily again felt connected to Katharine, despite the difference in time.

Recalling Aunt Sally's comment that "there is so much more to a person than what you see in the photograph," she wondered what this book might tell her about her great-grandparents.

She opened the ledger to its first page, January, 1905. There were many columns: ingoing, outgoing, purchases, sales and appointments. This page had a line for each day of the month. She scanned through a few more pages until she reached July of 1905. Under appointments and the date July 15th, she saw the beautifully handwritten words, *"Michael moves in."*

"Her husband's name was Harry. I wonder who Michael is."

She flipped through a few more pages and saw only numbers. "Seems like pretty boring stuff."

With that, Susan walked into their bedroom. "Hey, do you want to go clubbing with me? Jill cancelled at the last minute."

"No, I think I'll pass, sorry. Besides, you know I only go clubbing if I'm forced to. I hate that scene."

Distracted, she closed the book and turned the television on.

February 18, 1979 10:00 p.m.

Sorry I haven't written in a while. What can I say? I love having a boyfriend! Ray has already told me he loves me. Ray and I were alone on New Year's Eve and I had a few too many drinks. I don't remember much of that night, but I vaguely remember that I offered to have sex with him. I'm so thankful he refused. The next day, I cringed when I remembered the offer. He has character and integrity, which is more than I can say for myself. His words were, "Neither of us will be drunk our first time, Em." He's right. I've decided to stop drinking.

Tomorrow, Ray and I are planning on skipping school.

Can you imagine? I never did that in high school and college has been pretty manageable. But Ray really wanted to do this so we could have time alone here at my house. Mom, Susan and Matthew will all be at work so this could be our chance. I trust Ray and he's the nicest guy I've ever met.

I feel kind of bad not telling Mom about all this. After all, she is pretty cool and not too strict. I've never lied to her before.

Emily finished reading the last entry and set her journal down. She wondered if she should write anything else for tonight's date. Her conscience was starting to nag at her again when she realized that she would have to lie to her mother. That wasn't something she was accustomed to doing. Emily had earned her mother's trust by being honest.

Turning off the light, she slipped into her bed and flicked on the switch for the electric blanket. As her body relaxed and her eyes became heavy, she drifted off to sleep, thinking of Ray and anticipating the next day's adventure.

The following morning, Emily jumped out of bed. Rushing downstairs, she bumped into her mom in the hallway at the bottom of the steps.

"Watch out, Em."

"Sorry, Mom. I'm a little late and have to leave for. . . school."

"Would you mind taking me up to the bus stop?"

"Oh, not a bit."

"Hey, Mom," Susan called, "I don't feel so well today. I hope I'm not getting sick."

Yeah, I hope not. If Susan is sick, it will ruin my plans with Ray.

A few minutes later, Susan emerged from the bathroom, somewhat pale.

"You okay, Sue?" Emily asked.

"I think I'm coming down with something, but I can't miss work today. I'll manage."

Emily breathed a sigh of relief as they all walked out to the car.

"Hey, Mom, what time did Matthew leave for his job?"

"He left early, Em, around 6:30. He's on the seven to three shift today."

Emily nodded and breathed another sigh of relief. At the bus stop, Susan and Becky got out of the car and stood, waiting on the sidewalk. They waved to Emily as she drove off to her meeting place with Ray.

She reached the McDonald's golden arches and watched Ray run out the door and slip into the passenger seat.

"Wow, Em, I can't believe we're doing this. We're actually skipping school just so that we can be together."

Emily smiled nervously. Looking down at her hands, she noticed that they were trembling.

"I don't know, Ray. This whole thing is making me nervous. What if a neighbor sees us go into my house together?"

"Let me think about this." He paused. "Hey, why don't you let me off at the street behind your house and I'll come in through the back door?"

"That would work."

Emily drove to the drop-off point and Ray got out.

"See you in a minute," he promised.

Emily then pulled the car into her family's driveway. Fishing inside her purse to find the key, her hands were shaking so much that she kept dropping it back inside her handbag. She took a deep breath, carefully picked up the key, unlocked the door and rushed inside the house. Running through the living room, she nearly knocked over an end table. Continuing, she hurried through the kitchen and den to the back door. She opened it up at the same time Ray was walking up the back porch.

"You okay, Em?"

"Yeah, yeah. Just nervous, that's all."

"Hey, no need. Let's just sit and relax here in the den," he said, while taking off his coat, an over-sized Army jacket, and tossing it on the chair.

Emily nodded, then walked over to the record player and put on the album "Rumours," by Fleetwood Mac.

"I can't believe that we pulled this off. It was so easy," he commented. "What should we do now?"

"We can just sit back and listen to records."

"And maybe make out on the sofa?" he offered.

She leaned over and kissed him.

"Em, I have to tell you about an incident that happened yesterday," he said, as she snuggled up close to him.

"What?" she asked.

"I was visiting my cousin, who's about the same age as me, and he wanted to show me a model in his bedroom. So we went up to his room and we walked in on his younger brother. . .well, you know. . . ."

"No, Ray, I don't know. What was he doing?"

"He was, you know. . . ." Ray, his face flushed, couldn't even bring himself to say the word. "He was, you know, doing it to himself."

"Oh." She paused. "Gee, that must've been embarrassing for the poor kid."

"Yeah, I guess. But you know, Em, I think it's wrong to do that. I mean, it just seems like it's a selfish thing to do."

"Oh?" Emily was hesitant to tell him that she didn't think that it was such a big deal. After all, no one gets hurt. "But you do think it's okay to have sex before marriage, right? I mean, we have talked about doing it."

"Yeah, I guess. I mean, I think it's pretty important for the two people to love each other, that's for sure. That's one of the reasons I'm still a virgin."

"Well, you love me and we still haven't had sex yet. In fact, we haven't really done anything except kissed."

"I know. To be quite honest, I'm scared. Disease and pregnancy are pretty serious things to have to deal with. Besides, there's nothing wrong with waiting, right?"

"Right."

He kissed her, his right hand holding her cheek. As she

broke off the kiss, he continued to caress her face, then leaned over and kissed her lightly on the forehead.

Impulsively, Emily said, "Let's go up to my room."

He hesitated, then responded, "Uh. . .okay."

She stood up, then she took hold of his hand and pulled him up. They walked hand in hand through the kitchen, living room, then toward the stairs.

As they climbed the steps, Emily found herself pulling him up to her bedroom.

When they reached her room, she stood next to her bed.

"Here's my bed."

"Yeah, that's your bed, all right. It's a nice bed, Em," he said.

"Well, I like it. "

Emily slipped off her shoes and jumped on her unmade bed, then moved aside to allow Ray to sit next to her. He pulled his shoes off, standing still for a moment, then sat on the edge of her bed. She leaned over and began to kiss him. After a minute or so, Ray stopped and said, "You know what? I just don't feel right about sitting on your bed and kissing. Don't you think we should go back downstairs to the den or something?"

Her eyes became downcast. "You're right. This just doesn't feel. . . ."

Suddenly, Emily heard the front door open, then close. She pulled away from Ray.

"Oh no, someone is home. We can't let them see you."

Panicked looks on their faces, eyes wide with alarm, they both jumped off the bed, with Emily frantically trying to figure out where Ray could hide. Her walk-in closet near the door seemed the best hiding place for now. "Over here, Ray." He quickly rushed into the closet and behind some clothes as the unknown person climbed the stairs.

At the top of the steps, Susan stopped and suspiciously eyed her younger sister.

"Uh. . .gee, Sue, what are you doing home?" Emily asked, in a higher-pitched voice than normal.

"I can ask you the same question. Me, I'm feeling really sick. I got on the bus and thought I was going to spill my cookies. I got off at the next stop and took the bus back home. I gotta lay down."

"Oh, uh. . .that's. . .uh. . .too bad." Emily lingered in front of the closet, toe tapping, and stepped aside to allow Susan to pass.

"Sue, that. . .uh. . .perfume you're wearing today smells like a fresh garden after a rain. What's it called?"

"Forbidden by Givenchy."

"It. . .uh. . .makes me want to lie my head on your. . . shoulder."

Her sister made no response as she dropped onto her bed.

Emily continued. "Well, I'm home because, I. . .well. . .you know, I must be getting whatever you have. That's it. I'm getting what you have and I just don't feel well."

Susan sat up in bed and looked around the room suspiciously. Spying Ray's shoes on the floor near Emily's bed, she blurted, "Okay. Where is he?"

"Where is who?" she asked innocently.

"Where's Ray? The shoes gave him away, Em."

"Okay, Ray, come on out." Emily sighed.

Ray slowly stepped out of the closet. "Hi," he said, as he tried to smile.

"Well, this is certainly a first. Little Miss Goodie Goodie has been caught in a compromising situation with a guy. I think I can get used to this."

"All right. What is it going to cost me?" Emily knew that her sister would keep her secret, but it would mean that she would have to take over one of Sue's chores.

"You know, I don't feel very well, which really bums me out because I can't enjoy this moment as much as I'd like. We'll talk later."

Ray grabbed his shoes and quickly followed Emily down the steps. In the hallway at the bottom of the steps, Emily burst out in contagious laughter and Ray joined along.

"You know what, Em?" he said through his laughter.

She stopped laughing and answered, "What?"

"The moment that we got on the bed, I didn't feel right. I should've never insisted you skip school and I should've never skipped school. This whole plan was wrong."

Emily nodded. "I'll feel really bad if Mom finds out, but Susan's pretty loyal. I don't think she'll tell."

"Well, then we're safe."

The ring of the doorbell interrupted them.

"Who in the world could that be?" Emily asked out loud. "Ray, I don't know who it is, so you'd better stay hidden here in the hallway."

She opened the door and was surprised to find her elderly neighbor, Mrs. Stevenson, dressed like Harriet Nelson and smelling like freshly-baked cookies.

"Oh, Emily dear, I'm glad you're all right. I was so scared. A short while ago, I saw a young man in your back yard, walking toward your back door."

The color drained from Emily's face. Mouth open and trying to compose herself, she replied, "Mrs. Stevenson, it's. . . all right." She hoped that her neighbor didn't notice that her voice was shaking. "As you can. . .uh. . .see, there is no one here but Sue and I. Sue is sick upstairs and I'm. . . ."

"Oh, dear, you're not feeling well too?"

"No, I'm not feeling well right now. Quite honestly, I feel like my stomach is turning."

"You poor dear."

"Thanks, Mrs. Stevenson."

Emily closed the door as Ray walked toward her.

"Listen, maybe I should just go and take the bus home. I'm going to do homework or something."

"You'd better slip out by the back door while I go and talk to Mrs. Stevenson so she doesn't see you."

"Does she sit by her window and watch everything?

"It seems that way."

He nodded. "See you, Em. I'll call you later."

April 26, 1979

    It's hard to believe Ray and I have been going out now for four months.   For the last week or so, several guys have asked me out and I found myself flattered and wanting to go out with them. Is it wrong? I like Ray a lot and I sure do love having a boyfriend, but I'm just not sure that I'm in love with him, that special forever love.   For days, I've been thinking of telling Ray that I think we should start dating other people.

    Emily closed her journal. "Hey, Em," she heard her mom calling her. "Ray is here."

    She took a deep breath and descended the stairs.

    For the last couple of weeks, the two of them had been bickering, not fighting, just 'getting on each other's nerves.' Though she still found him attractive, the excitement seemed to have disappeared from their relationship and she felt that it was time to move on.

    At the bottom of the steps, she could see him putting his jacket over the back of one of the chairs. He turned around and stared adoringly at her. "Hi, Em." As she got closer to him, he leaned down to kiss her. They walked hand in hand through the kitchen and into the den where they normally watched television. Even though there was no one there, the television was blaring with the noise of a police show. Emily walked over and turned it off.

    "Rather listen to music tonight, Em?"

    She nodded. "Yeah, all right."

    He walked over to the record cabinet and, knowing it was her favorite old-time album, chose "Johnny's Greatest Hits," and placed it on the record player.   Emily turned around, rolled her eyes and sighed. *Not Johnny Mathis,* she silently complained, *the 'King of Make Out?' Why does he have to choose that tonight?*

    She heard the first few piano notes of "It's Not for Me to Say" and Ray took hold of her to slow dance.   As the music was playing, he started humming the tune.   Ray was one of the nicest boys that she had ever known but he couldn't sing on key. It was one of the things that endeared him to her.

Her heart ached as she agonized about what she needed to do. She glanced over to the far wall of the den. Her mother's Norman Rockwell prints were hanging in a row. In particular, she was drawn to the print that pictured a young girl and a boy sitting on a bench with their backs to the viewer. In the girl's hand was a daisy and the boy had his arm around her waist with his head touching hers.

Emily sighed. Love at its purest, with no thoughts of sex or lust. The music had put her in somewhat of a trance.

"Em," Ray whispered.

She stopped dancing, took her head off his shoulder and stood still, staring at him. "Yeah, Ray?"

"Are you. . .all right?"

"Uh, yeah, I'm. . .fine."

"You seem tense. Is there something wrong?"

Hesitating, she continued staring at him, desperately searching for the words that would be sensitive to his feelings.

"Well, yes, I suppose there is."

Immediately, there was a look of panic in his eyes. *Oh, please don't look like someone who knows they're about to be told something that will break their heart.*

"What is it? Is everything okay? Are you sick? What is wrong? Please just tell me."

She took a deep breath and began her speech. "Well, you know, Ray, we've been seeing each other exclusively for four months." When she realized that Johnny Mathis was still singing in the background, she walked over to the record player and lifted up the needle to stop the music.

Avoiding eye contact, she continued. "I've been thinking about. . .us."

"That's good," she heard him say.

"And, well, I. . .well, I think. . .I think that we should. . . start dating other people." She now made eye contact. He was staring intensely down at her, and his expression told her the suggestion was devastating to him.

"I'm sorry, Ray. I've felt this way for weeks."

She hestitated. "I didn't know how to tell you."

"But, Em, I love you. I can't bear to think of you with other guys. I just couldn't. I can't live without you. You can't do this to me." His voice was cracking.

Emily took another deep breath. "Look, Ray, I just don't feel the same way that you do. It's not fair to you."

"Fair to me?" Now he was raising his voice. "Not being able to see you every day wouldn't be fair to me." His eyes were starting to tear. "I can't live without you, Em. I love you so much."

"I know you do." She said it softly, trying to console him. She hated to see him hurting.

"You told me you loved me," he said, his voice barely above a whisper.

"I do, but it's not the same way that you love me."

Ray approached her and grasped her shoulders firmly. He stared at her, his eyes dark with pain, and said, "Then I need to be honest with you. If you break up with me, I promise that I will drive my car into the nearest brick wall in hopes that I will kill myself." His words hit her in the face as if he struck her with his hand. She could hardly breathe. After a few seconds, she replied, "You'll what? Ray, you can't do this. Please." What could she say to convince him?

He softened the expression on his face. "Em, please don't break up with me. You'll learn to love me the same way that I love you. You can't do this to me. We've been talking about getting married. Please. . . ."

"Ray. . . ."

"It feels like you've taken my heart out and crushed it."

Emily felt guilty. She paused, then lowered her head. Defeated, she replied, "All right. I'll continue going out with you exclusively." She knew in her heart that she was postponing the inevitable, but she couldn't bear to think of Ray killing himself because of her.

"You won't be sorry, Em. I promise you. You won't be sorry." He hugged her, then walked over to the stereo to turn the Johnny Mathis record on again. He took hold of her to slow dance, but this time, he grabbed her more tightly. She tried to relax against him. *What Ray and I have can't really be love, not that forever love.* Emily never expected him to react the way he did. She knew that he would be hurt and she hated that. Her head on his shoulder again, she glanced at the Norman Rockwell prints. This time, her eye caught sight of another print, one with a girl in a white party dress sitting all alone on a blue, old-fashioned couch. The expression on the girl's face was one of loneliness. She felt an affinity with the young girl. Even though she now had a boyfriend, she was more lonely than ever, trapped in a relationship that she knew needed to end.

Working at the roast beef slicer two weeks later, Emily watched as Ray walked into the restaurant and smiled at her.

Emily sliced a few more pieces of meat and weighed it. *This whole dating thing really is such a drag. Why in the world was I in such a rush?* She had to admit that her impatient personality was hard to reason with, especially when it was mixed with envy. It was difficult for her to watch her friends enjoying themselves with members of the opposite sex during her early teen years. She never stopped to think that with the supposed enjoyment came the responsibility and the down side of dating, like breaking up, jealousy, possessiveness.

Just then, the manager approached Emily and told her that Ray had requested that they have dinner break at the same time.

"Really?" asked Emily.

"Yes. And I said it was okay, if that's what you'd like."

"Sure, that's fine."

"You both can take dinner break at seven."

"Thanks."

Out of the corner of her eye, she could see Ray walk over to stand in front of the fry machine. As Emily studied him, it became obvious that he was not his same old perky self but seemed rather subdued and quiet. "How long can this go on?" she mumbled to herself. She really liked Ray, but she just wasn't satisfied with how things were going and wished that he hadn't threatened to 'kill himself.'

Usually overwhelmingly talkative, Emily hadn't told anyone about Ray's threat. She figured that while she stayed with him, it was safe and he wouldn't do anything drastic. She also knew that this was taking all the responsibility onto herself.

The minutes inched by as only a few patrons came in.

A few hours later, in the staff room, she glanced over at Ray as he shoved an entire sandwich into his mouth in just a couple of bites. With the last bit in his mouth, he crumpled up the foil wrapping. He aimed, then tossed it into the waste basket. He smiled as he saw the foil ball fall easily into the garbage can.

"Two points," Emily joked. "Ray, you seem awfully quiet. Is something wrong?"

Keeping his eyes focused on the table, he said, "Yes, Em, there is."

"What's the matter?"

"Well, do you remember a few weeks ago when you said that you thought it would be a good idea to date other people?"

"Of course, I do. How could I forget? You said that you would kill yourself if I insisted. That really scared me."

"Yeah, well, here's the thing. I think it would be a good idea for us to start dating other people."

Emily's jaw dropped in surprise. "You do?" She hesitated. "Wait a minute. What exactly brought about this change?"

"Well, last night when I was walking one of the girls, Heather, to her car, well, we. . .well, we kind of kissed."

Emily frowned. "You kind of kissed? Either you kissed her or you didn't."

"Well, I kissed her." He looked like a dog who had just urinated on the sofa.

Emily sighed. The last few weeks had been difficult with Ray becoming even more possessive.

"You know, Ray, this is not necessarily a bad thing."

Unresponsive, he sat with his head down.

"This might be a good time to break up," she offered.

"I didn't say I wanted to break up. I mean, can't we still see each other?"

"Ray, I don't think we should keep seeing each other. I like you and you're a really nice guy, but I think it's time to move on."

"But I still love you."

His response was too much for Emily. As she began speaking, her voice was calm, but firm. "Real love, true love, stays faithful, no matter how cute the girl is. If you really love someone, you have to make the decision to love that person."

"I've felt so damned guilty for the past 24 hours, knowing that I kissed that girl. I mean, I have never felt this way about anyone before I met you. You're the first girl I've ever loved."

"Ray, I. . . ."

She was interrupted as another worker came into the staff room. "Hi," the cowboy said.

Ray and Emily waved and smiled awkwardly.

"Ray," Emily whispered, "it's time to call it quits. I'm glad you were my first boyfriend and we've had some really fun times." Her mind wandered to New Year's Eve when, after having a few drinks, she had offered to have sex with Ray and he refused. "Thank you for being honest and for having character." She knew that he would think that she was talking about the unfaithful kiss, but in her heart, she had meant the incident on New Year's Eve when he refused to take advantage of her.

As she walked toward the staff room door, she heard him call her name.

"Hey, Em?" Again, she couldn't stand hearing her familiar name at a difficult time.

She turned around, her eyebrows raised.

"I still love you." He said it loud enough for the other cowboy to hear him. Emily glanced at the co-worker and he was grinning.

She turned around, then walked through the door.

7

Job 10:1

March 18, 1912

Katharine's father stood by the bedroom door. *What is my father doing here?* In his arms were two crying babies. As she sat on the side of the bed, her hands began to tremble. She watched as he cautiously approached her, his left leg dragging as a constant reminder of his Civil War injury. He stood before Katharine, towering over her, then turned and placed the infants on the bed next to her. At first he looked at her calmly, almost serenely. Then, without warning, he raised his hand to strike.

Katharine woke with a start. *Dead for five years, he continues to haunt me.*

She pulled the flannel blankets closer to her chin. The sun was starting to rise, but simply thinking of getting out of her warm bed caused her to shiver under the covers. Her feet were ice cold. She had slipped off her woolen socks sometime during the night and now the socks were lost somewhere inside the blanket. These were the times that she missed having another body in bed with her. She and Harry hadn't slept together in many years. And Michael always returned to his bed after they had relations.

She realized that she would have to stoke the coal furnace or even worse, start up the fire. Katharine despised winter. It was the beginning of March and spring should have arrived by now, yet as she lay in bed, she could see her breath as she exhaled.

The nagging pain in her lower right abdomen was beginning to worry her. She hadn't noticed it much before three days ago, but with each day it became worse. She forced it out of her mind and focused on the troubling task of getting out of bed.

She glanced over at her glass of water on the bedside table and shuddered when she saw that it had a hardened crust of ice on top of it. Taking a deep breath, she threw the covers off, quickly reached for her flannel robe and slipped into her pull-on shoes on the floor beside her. Her bare foot brushed against the cold wooden floor as she let out a gasp and a swear word. "I hate winter," she complained under her breath.

Trudging down the steep staircase, her teeth began chattering as she made her way through the living room, small kitchen and into the cellar. Though daybreak had come, it was still black and eerie in the basement. Katharine reached the bottom of the steps, then walked slowly, allowing her eyes to adjust to the darkness. Arriving at the coal furnace near the front of the house, she opened up the cold stove to find only ashes. "Damn." She despised having to start a coal fire from scratch, but she gathered the paper and some kindling, and after ten minutes or so, managed to start a small fire. Taking the shovel, she reached into the coal bin, grabbed a few shovelsful and tossed them into the furnace. She held her breath as the coal dust blew back in her face. Katharine dropped the shovel and smacked her hands to get rid of the dust.

She remained there, tapping her foot and waiting impatiently for the cellar to warm up, then she let out a gasp. The throbbing in her right abdomen was becoming unbearable. For one brief second, she felt like she was going to faint. A few minutes later, the pain subsided.

Still standing, Katharine almost hugged the furnace, trying to absorb as much heat as she could. Her mind wandered to an incident nearly a month ago, when Michael 'accidentally' forgot to withdraw. After that incident, she swore that she would throw him out on the street, she was so angry. When she got her monthly, she breathed a sigh of relief.

Again, she felt cramping and pain in her lower right abdomen. Could it be something that she'd been eating? Whatever it was, she knew that it would be necessary to seek medical attention before the pain got any worse.

As the cellar heated up, she remained to enjoy the warmth. She heard a quiet scratching noise, then watched as a small mouse scurried out from under the coal bin. The slightest sound made her uneasy. Ever since her son had bought his new box camera, he was constantly pestering Katharine to pose for photographs. Just yesterday, he had asked her to pose in front of their porch, just as Michael was leaving for work at the studio. It bothered her that he had chosen that moment because it distracted her and she forgot to ask Michael for the rent money.

Katharine had begun to notice that in the last year or so, Michael had become somewhat aloof. After they engaged in relations, he would hurriedly get dressed and return to his room, without any of the soft words to which she had become accustomed.

It was several minutes before she walked up the dark stairs through the small kitchen and living room and back upstairs to the bedroom.

The process of getting dressed was slower this morning, since the second floor was still icy cold. However, her ongoing pain became the bigger challenge. Picking up her corset, she hesitated, then tossed it on the bed. She realized that she would have to leave that piece of clothing off today. After getting dressed, she passed Michael in the hallway as he was staggering half-asleep to the bathroom. "Morning, Michael," Katharine managed to say. He ignored her and closed the bathroom door. She descended the steps, then stopped at the front door.

Katharine studied herself in the mirror and wondered whether her pale complexion seemed more so. She straightened her hat and slipped a few pins inside to keep it in place. She reached for her coat and, trying to put it on, spent a few agonizing minutes with the buttons. Blinking a few times, she wondered whether she was going to faint again.

She thought of her young daughter, Ruth, who was two and a half years old. Who would watch her while she went to the doctor's office? Harry was gone for the day. Johnnie had already left for school, and there was no other option than to ask Michael.

Still lightheaded, she walked back up the steps and stood outside the bathroom door. Katharine could hear the faucets running and hoped Michael had not slipped into the bath as yet.

She knocked on the door and heard the water turn off.

"Michael?"

"Yes, what is it?"

"I need to speak with you."

He tentatively opened up the door a few inches, "Yes?"

"I need to see a doctor. Ruth is asleep in her bedroom. Would it be possible for you to take her with you to the studio?"

For a moment he looked uncertain, but he then replied, "Uh. . .yes, Katharine, I can take her."

"Thank you, Michael. You can bring her home after school and Johnnie can keep an eye on her."

"All right."

As he closed the door, she winced. The sharp pains in her abdomen had gotten increasingly worse over the course of the last hour or so. She couldn't imagine what it could be, but it was becoming unbearable. The doctor's office was four blocks away and since Harry had taken the car, she knew that she would have to travel by foot. She hoped that she would be able to walk that far.

She left the house and began the trek to the doctor's office. Though it was March, it felt like the middle of January, piles of snow still plastered to the sidewalks and a sharp wind biting her cheeks.

After only one block, she stopped and took a breather sitting down on someone's front steps. She could feel the ice cold steps through her woolen coat. For a brief second, she felt weak and disoriented. "Are you all right, ma'am?" she heard someone say. Without looking up, she replied, "Yes. I'll be fine, just taking a rest." She was surprised that she was out of breath after only one block.

Only three blocks to go. "If I pass out here. . . well, I refuse to pass out here. I will make it, no matter what."

Struggling through the next three blocks, she sat down on

a vacant step at the end of every street to gather enough energy to continue walking. Breathing a sigh of relief, Katharine reached the doctor's office and collapsed on the floor of the foyer.

She woke up on an examining table inside the doctor's office. "What is going on here?"

"Mrs. Clayman, your blood pressure is dangerously low and your right abdomen is bloated. When was your last monthly flow?" she heard her doctor say.

"About two weeks ago, but come to think of it, it was very spotty, hardly any flow at all."

"When was your previous flow?"

"I don't remember, about eight weeks ago or so."

Katharine studied her doctor's troubled face. "We're transporting you to the Pennsylvania Hospital for more tests."

"Doctor, I don't have time to go to the hospital, nor do I have the money to pay for it. Besides, we'll lose money at the store. I can't afford this."

"Mrs. Clayman, if your blood pressure drops much lower, you could die."

"You can't be serious."

Katharine could see a stretcher being brought into the doctor's office. "What is that thing for? I can certainly walk myself."

"Look, Mrs. Clayman, you need to conserve your energy. I have reason to believe you're bleeding internally. Just lie back and relax."

"Relax? I feel like there's an explosion going on in my stomach."

The doctor sighed and helped Katharine onto the stretcher. Placed into the back of an ambulance, she asked, "Can I have another blanket? It's damned cold in here." All of a sudden, she felt weak and dizzy. As the ambulance began moving, she felt the driver jam on the brakes. "It would be better to walk, if he's going to drive like that." All of a sudden, her throbbing abdomen became unbearable. "Sweet Jesus," she yelled. The young attendant asked, "Are you all right, Mrs. Clayman?"

"Damn it, no, I'm not. I. . . ." Katharine felt like all her energy had been drained from her body. The last thing she heard was "blood pressure dangerously low. . . ."

Just let me sleep, she wanted to say. Someone was patting her hand. She heard a voice like it was at the end of a tunnel. "Mrs. Clayman, wake up."

The gnawing pain in her abdomen was replaced now by a sharper, more acute sensation. Katharine tried to mouth a swear word but couldn't. She opened her mouth again to speak but only managed a grunt. It felt as if someone had taken a knife to open her stomach.

"Mrs. Clayman, I'm giving you a shot for pain."

Katharine felt the needle go into her upper thigh and tried to move away but couldn't. She felt weak, useless and like she wanted to die. Trying to keep as still as she could, she felt an uncontrollable urge to vomit, then spilled a small amount of bile down the front of her.

A few moments later, the pain was very slightly less, but it felt better and she was thankful. When the nurse approached her cot, Katharine tried to grab onto her but only managed to touch her arm. The woman turned around.

Her words were labored and slow. "What. . .happened? What. . .is. . .going. . .on?"

The nurse ignored her and left the room.

The pain lessened, she nodded off to sleep. She woke up and overheard two nurses speaking. When she heard "Clayman," she realized they were talking about her.

"Mrs. Clayman will need another hypodermic in three hours."

"Is she the one with the. . . ."

"Yes, she's had a tubal pregnancy. A very rare occurrence."

Katharine kept her eyes closed, but became more alert.
A tubal what? That's absurd. I wasn't pregnant.
She listened.

"The tube had ruptured," she heard the nurse say. "She's very lucky to be alive. She's lost a tremendous amount of blood."

A few minutes later, she was wheeled along a long corridor to a hospital ward. Everything smelled of bleach and appeared so clean, so white and so clinical. It was impossible to think of anything but her excruciating pain. Several other women lay silent in their beds.

A nurse approached her and pulled the curtain around her cot. She appeared to be checking something on Katharine's arm.

The curtain in place, she drifted off to sleep again and was awakened by the soft but deep voice of a man.

Katharine heard some medical terms that she couldn't understand.

"Mrs. Clayman was admitted to hospital and during exploratory surgery, it was discovered that she had a ruptured right fallopian tube caused by an ectopic pregnancy. There was evidence of scarring on her cervix which may possibly indicate some illegal procedures. . . ."

What are they trying to say?

A younger man's voice said something that Katharine couldn't hear, and a minute or so later, the space beyond her curtained-in area was silent.

A nurse approached Katharine with another needle of some kind. Her hair was pulled back in a severe fashion under her nurse's cap. Katharine believed this woman was in definite need of some face paint to soften her rough, masculine appearance.

"For pain, Mrs. Clayman." Despite her harsh features, her manner was caring and kind.

"Oh, yes, thank you. That really does help."

"You almost died, Mrs. Clayman, directly or indirectly caused by some procedures you've had done in the past."

"What are you trying to say?"

"It says here on your chart that you have scarring on your cervix, the mouth of your womb. That could indicate a difficult delivery, but it's more likely. . .well. . .caused by. . . ."

"Tell me you've never experienced an unplanned pregnancy at a time when it was most inconvenient," Katharine blurted out.

"I'm not married, Mrs. Clayman, so no, I've never experienced an unplanned pregnancy. Even so, I know that kind of procedure is downright wrong."

"It's not wrong until the quickening."

"No, Mrs. Clayman, I believe it is. Besides," she whispered, "I thought that only poor immigrants and prostitutes do that sort of thing."

Katharine took a deep breath as she realized the needle was taking effect. Her stomach was still painfully sore, especially when she made any effort to move.

"Look," Katharine said, "I appreciate your—"

"It's just that Dr. Morrow, he's a very kind doctor and he became a physician to help people. It must be difficult for him to treat a patient, knowing that, in part, her behavior has caused her to be here."

Katharine's pulse quickened and she began to grind her teeth. *How did my behavior cause me to be here? What is she trying to say?*

The nurse continued, "Physicians are obliged to take the Hippocratic Oath and part of that oath is 'I will prescribe regimen for the good of my patients according to my ability and my judgment and never do harm to anyone.' I'm sure he takes that oath very seriously."

"I'm very tired now. Could you excuse me?"

"Yes, of course," the nurse responded. She quickly left the room and Katharine lay back on her pillow and tried to relax. *Poor immigrants and prostitutes? Who is she to lecture me?*

8

Matthew 7:7-8

August 1979

"Don't forget to call when you get there, Em," Becky reminded her daughter.

"No, no, I won't forget," Emily promised.

They hugged and she started down the runway. Emily had never felt so independent as she had at that moment, taking her first airplane trip. As she was walking down the tunnel that connected the airplane to the terminal, she heard footsteps behind her. "Excuse me, sweetie," a middle-aged stewardess with caked-on makeup stopped her before she boarded the plane.

"What is it?" Emily asked.

"Unaccompanied minors were supposed to board first. I'll help you to your seat." She took Emily by the hand.

"Wait a minute." Emily pulled her hand away. "I'm not an unaccompanied minor."

"Then where is your mother or other adult?"

"No, no, you don't understand. I'm not a minor. I'm 20 years old."

The flight attendant's shocked face made Emily smile. "Oh, I'm so sorry."

"That's okay. It happens all the time," Emily replied.

Emily stepped onto the plane and was immediately struck by how closed-in everything was. She could smell an odor that reminded her of bus exhaust. A pretty young stewardess said, "Hello."

She proceeded to her window seat on the left side of the plane, in the non-smoking section. She placed her carry-on bag under the seat in front of her and buckled her seat belt. The plane was only half-full and Emily was relieved that no one sat beside her.

The plane landed an hour and a half later in Montreal. *I'm almost there. Only one flight to go.*

She quickly passed through customs and made the long hike to the gate where her flight to Ottawa would be boarding. It seemed so ironic that she was going to Canada. She was barely conscious that there was even a country called Canada before five months ago when she started writing to Rose, her pen pal from Ontario. Emily and Rose had much in common, not the least of which was a crush on TV's 'the Hardy Boys.' When Rose invited Emily to come up to Canada, it seemed like the natural thing to do. Even though they had only been writing for a short time, Emily felt like she had known this girl her whole life.

"Flight 167 non-stop to Ottawa, boarding at Gate 17." She watched as the flight attendants opened the door and guided people outside to an old-fashioned ramp ascending to the plane.

As she walked out to the plane, she found it surprisingly warm. *Wasn't Canada cold all the time?*

Emily boarded the plane, buckled her seat belt, listened to the flight attendant's instructions in both English and French and only a short while later, heard the announcement, "Welcome to Ottawa International Airport, Ladies and Gentlemen."

When the plane stopped, she gathered her things and stepped into the aisle. Nervously, she followed the mob of people getting off the plane and came to an automatic door. As the door opened, she followed a large group out to the airport waiting room and found herself hidden behind them. She strained her eyes to see if she could recognize her pen pal. It was a nearly impossible task, given Emily's size.

"Emily, over here," she heard someone call.

Standing above the crowd at nearly six feet tall, Rose, a short-haired, clean-cut looking girl, struggled to part the crowd to reach Emily. Though she had seen photos of her, Emily couldn't believe how tall Rose was. She could see her clearly above most of the surrounding people.

Rose grabbed Emily's hand and pulled her through the crowd and over to an area where her family was waiting.

"Mom, Dad, this is Emily, my American pen-pal."

"Nice to meet you," Emily said and extended her hand.

"G'day, Emily, how's it goin', eh?" Rose's father said. He was not quite as tall as Rose, but he was a big-boned man with a brush cut and farmer's overalls.

"Fine." Emily stopped and tried to remember where she had heard that saying before. *Who speaks like that,* she wondered. She realized that he sounded a lot like Bob and Doug McKenzie from the Great White North skits on Second City TV. She couldn't fathom that people actually talked like that.

"This is my brother, Kevin." Kevin was a big fellow, not so much tall, but husky, with long brown hair.

"Kevin, take Emily's suitcase and we'll walk over to the car, eh?" said Rose's mom, also big-boned, wearing a pair of jeans and a tee-shirt, with a smile so wide Emily thought her face would burst. Kevin grinned and took her suitcase. He mumbled, "She is so darned cute," to his sister. Emily loved their accents. At the end of every sentence was the word "eh."

Once inside the car, Emily, feeling awkward and nervous, began chattering.

"Wow, that was a really small airport. Gosh, it's really warm up here. I was under the impression that Canada would be colder."

"It's cold in the winter, but the summers are pretty warm," Rose responded.

"Rose, you're a lot taller than I thought you would be. How tall are you?"

"Remember, I told you I'm five-eleven."

"Oh, right. Well, you seem a lot taller than that in person. Then again, I probably seem a lot shorter in person too, huh?"

"Well. . . ."

"Oh, by the way, my mom said to say hi."

"Emily, did you know you're just about the cutest girl I have ever met?" Kevin said.

"Oh, come on, Kevin," Emily responded.

"I mean it. I can't believe you're the same age as my sister."

Rose and her family were so friendly and welcoming that they all wore what seemed to be a perpetual smile for the entire car trip home.

When they reached Rose's hometown of Arrandale, population 2,000, Emily became fascinated by the unique architecture: rough stone, a clock tower, interesting street lamps, turn-of-the-century brick buildings with weathered advertisements painted on their sides.

Rose's family's home was a trailer on the outskirts of Arrandale. The rooms were small, but the home felt warm and cosy.

What especially intrigued Emily over the next few days was that everyone seemed to know everyone else. Her experience of living in a small city was the exact opposite. Now, she was learning that Arrandale had a very British flavor to it, from the union jack flags to the fish and chip stands.

Emily enjoyed sightseeing in the Ottawa Valley and in Rose's hometown. On her second day in Arrandale, Emily casually mentioned to Rose that she was an experienced gymnast. "Can you show me some of your gymnastics?" Rose asked.

"Sure," Emily responded, then demonstrated some stunts.

"Wow, you're really good," her friend commented.

On the third day of her six-day trip, Kevin walked into Rose's small room as they were sitting on her bed listening to a Shaun Cassidy record.

"You girls want to come and hear some really great rock music?"

Emily glanced over at Rose with a 'what is he talking about' look.

"He means, do we want to go to his band's jam session?"

"Sure, I guess so," Emily said, to be polite. In actuality, she had no interest whatsoever in rock music. Her interests were more easy listening or pop, like the Carpenters or Bee Gees.

"Great," said Kevin. "Be there at 7:30. I'll let the guys know that we'll have an audience tonight."

Later that night, as they were walking to the jam session, Emily asked Rose, "So what kind of music does this band play?"

"They play songs from Rush, Boston, stuff like that," replied Rose.

"What is Rush and are they from Boston?" Emily asked.

"No, no, no. Rush is a band and Boston is a band. You know the song 'More than a Feeling?'"

"I think I've heard it once or twice."

"Stuff like that."

Emily felt a bit relieved. She was thinking that perhaps she might have to endure loud, raunchy rock music that would hurt or, even worse, do permanent damage to her ears. Just then, she heard the faint sound of rock music coming from five or six houses away.

"That's the band playing right now," said Rose.

Uh-oh. By the time they reached the house the music was so loud, Emily couldn't hear herself think. She started to regret her decision to be polite.

Rose knocked loudly on the door several times. The music stopped and a few seconds later, a gaunt-looking, long-haired young man opened the door. With no hint of a smile, he nodded, then stepped aside to allow the two girls to enter. As Emily passed the young man, she could smell the odor of beer or some other sort of alcohol on him and she noticed his long hair was in definite need of some shampoo. After closing the door, he ran down the steps and the girls followed him to what appeared to be a recreation room to the right of the steps.

They walked into a comfortable den decorated in wood paneling. A fireplace and piano lined the west wall, a small bar to the upper east corner of the room and a couch and chair lined the south wall. Though it was a big enough den, most of the room was now taken up by various musical instruments and amplifiers.

Rose and Emily walked over to the plaid sofa and sat

down. Emily began studying the members of the band and said a mental thank you to God that they were taking a break from the ear-splitting music.

The young man sitting behind the drum set had long, dark hair as well. As she was studying him, he looked her way and smiled.

Emily couldn't explain why, but she became uncomfortable with the way he gawked at her. Looking away, she saw the young man who ushered them in talking to Kevin. A young black man with a large Afro was sitting at what appeared to be a miniature piano. The remaining member of the band had his back to Emily and appeared to be playing three or four notes over and over again on his guitar. He was wearing a blue plaid shirt and blue corduroy bell bottom pants. *Didn't bell bottoms go out of fashion a few years ago?* Studying him more closely, she noticed his dark and unruly curly hair.

Kevin spoke up. "Jason, you ready?" She heard him say, "Yes," then watched as he turned around. His dark, curly hair, pronounced jaw and olive complexion left her breathless. He looked almost 'ethnic,' like from some Mediterranean country. As he prepared to play his guitar, it appeared like he was embarking on an important mission. Emily couldn't explain why, but she found it hard to take her eyes off him.

"*Who* is that?" Emily leaned over and whispered to Rose.

"That's Jason. He's the only member of the band who actually practices at these things."

Emily nodded and began studying Jason more closely. As the band was playing, he seemed to be concentrating so hard on his guitar playing, that he almost seemed angry. *No, not angry,* Emily thought, *intense.* The music was loud, but Emily had to admit, it sounded pretty good.

After one song, the band took another break, though Jason continued playing his guitar as Emily watched the others walk over and grab bottles of beer out of the small fridge near the couch.

"Rose," she whispered, "Is anybody here of legal drinking age?"

Rose shook her head. "Nobody, except us."

She turned and casually glanced at Jason again and was shocked to find him looking directly at her. Feeling awkward, she looked away and after a few safe moments, glanced back again. This time, his eyes were fixed on his guitar, as he was attempting to play those same three or four notes again.

Rose whispered something to Emily but she found herself so busy focusing on Jason, she hadn't heard what she said. "What?"

"What do you think of my brother's band?"

"Interesting," was all she could say.

She continued watching Jason, trying hard not to be obvious. In two hours, she observed that the band had played a total of five songs, taking a long break after each song. Although Emily's ears were grateful, she was surprised that she found herself wanting to hear Jason play the guitar. The skill with which he played, as well as his dedication to music, was impressive.

"Time to party," the drummer announced. "You girls want a beer?" Emily shook her head, but Rose walked over and picked up a bottle. Then he directed his comments to the members of the band. The drummer grabbed a bottle of beer and threw one over to the young man who had ushered the girls in. "Kevin, here's one for you."

Emily glanced over at Jason again. He had finally set his guitar down and was talking to the young black man. He walked over to the fridge and pulled out a bottle of Coke.

From time to time, Emily stole a glance in Jason's direction. Now that he wasn't concentrating on his guitar playing, she noticed that he seemed more at ease. The young man with the Afro told him a joke and he laughed. Emily could see a warm, inviting smile.

In the now small rec room, taken up by equipment and at least seven people, Emily began to feel claustrophobic. The drummer leaned down, with his strong beer-smelling breath and whispered to Emily, "So what's *your* name?" His presence again made her uncomfortable, but she managed a polite smile, said "Emily," then turned around and bumped into one of the other band members. "Excuse me," she mumbled with her head still down.

"No problem," she heard him say. Looking up, she found herself staring into Jason's hazel eyes. He was gazing down at her with his left eyebrow cocked and one corner of his mouth upturned in a smile. She turned her head away and in a uniquely rare moment, couldn't think of anything to say.

Rose took Emily's hand and abruptly pulled her toward the stairs. "Everyone's going outside." She glanced back to see Jason, his eyes fixed on her. Annoyed that her friend was pulling her away, Emily sighed and followed her outside. She noticed that the members of the band were standing around on the front lawn, but was thankful when she realized that Jason had followed them outside.

With everyone standing around, Rose made an announcement. "Hey everybody, this is my pen pal, Emily, from New Jersey. She's a great gymnast. Emily, show everyone how well you do a cartwheel."

Emily froze. Normally, she enjoyed showing off her gymnastic talent. In fact, as a competitive gymnast for a short time, exhibitionism was a prerequisite for the sport. However, she became nervous when she realized that Jason would be watching her perform. "Sure, I guess so." As she positioned herself, she heard a few of the band members whistle and cheer her on.

She did a skilled cartwheel effortlessly, pointed toes and straight as a line, hoping that it might come off as impressive rather than embarrassing. Everyone clapped and yelled, "More!" She did a few more stunts, then she announced, "That's all for tonight." Some of the guys feigned disappointment and began laughing loudly again.

Emily casually glanced over at Jason to find him smiling at her. Returning the gesture, she commented to Rose, "Gosh, that guy is so handsome." Despite the seriousness with which he played guitar, he had a beautiful, inviting smile.

"Come on, Emily, we need to get going. My parents are expecting us by 11:00." They waved a general goodbye to the group and starting walking up the street toward Rose's house.

"So what did you think of the band?"

"Tell me more about Jason. How old is he?"

"He's 17, why?"

"Just wondering. He's really cute. What's he like? I noticed that he doesn't drink."

"No, he doesn't. I don't know if it's some sort of religious thing or what. We can ask Kevin about him, if you'd like."

The next morning at the breakfast table, Kevin approached Emily. "Hey, I heard that you like Jason."

"Well, yeah, I do. He seems nice."

"You know, there's a dance tonight at the curling club."

"Curling club? What in the world is that? Do people get together and curl their hair or something? I mean, can't you do that in the privacy of your own home?"

Kevin laughed. "No, no, no. Curling is a sport, where you brush the ice with a broom and slide a heavy puck-like object across the ice. But tonight, they're using the arena for a dance."

"Hey, Rose," Emily asked, "are we planning on going to the dance tonight?"

"We could, if you'd like."

"Sure, that would be great. Do you think Jason will be there?"

Kevin answered, "I can call him to make sure he'll be going."

"I'd like that. Kevin, tell me more about him."

"Sure, what would you like to know?"

"What's he like? Does he date? Is he dating anyone now? What's he like in school?"

"Wow, this *is* serious. Okay. He's a pretty talented guitarist, and he works really hard at it, but you probably already know that. No, he is not dating anyone right now. He's very smart in school and gets high marks in Art and Physics. By the way, he's really shy around girls. There, is that enough?"

"I guess so. I suppose I'll have to find out more if he comes to the dance."

Rose spoke up. "You know, Em, if you want to start an interesting conversation with Jason, you can use some great conversation starters." Rose then went on to list some questions which would provoke conversation.

"I don't usually need conversation starters, but thanks anyway." Besides, Emily had doubts as to whether those questions would really provoke great dialogue.

Later that day, as Emily and Rose were walking in downtown Arrandale, Rose whispered to her friend, "Look, Em, there's Jason."

Emily glanced across the street and watched as he stood next to a smaller, middle-aged woman with short gray hair.

"Is that his mom?"

"Uh-huh," she answered.

Rose continued to window shop while Emily studied him. She noticed that today he was wearing a yellow tee shirt and brown corduroy bell bottoms. She watched as a young, heavyset woman approached Jason and his mother. The young woman appeared to be in her twenties and she was holding the hand of a small child.

Jason leaned down and began speaking with the toddler. She couldn't tell for sure, but Emily thought that the small child was probably a girl. As he stood up, the little girl put her hands in the air in an unspoken request to have Jason pick her up.

He leaned over and scooped the toddler up in his arms. Emily became entranced as she watched him interact with the tiny child. Studying his face, she determined that not only was he good looking, but he was at ease around small children.

"Hey, come on, let's go," yelled Rose.

"Wait a minute."

"Come on, you'll get to see him tonight at the dance."

Emily remained still, her eyes fixed on this young man who, unbeknownst to him, seemed to have stolen her heart.

She watched as he placed the child down. The toddler

grasped her mother's hand and they sauntered off. Emily again studied his face as he spoke to his mother.

Then, without warning, his eyes looked past his mother and caught Emily's eyes.

Surprised and uncomfortable, she wanted to look away, but continued staring. He recognized her with a shy wave, and she returned the gesture.

"Come on, Em, let's go."

"Did you see that?"

"See what?"

"He waved to me."

"Neat."

That night, the girls arrived at the curling club and to Emily's disappointment, none of the guys from the band were there.

"It's still early," Rose offered.

For an hour, Emily continued to glance at the door, watching to see if Jason and the band members had arrived. More people had crammed into the curling club and it was becoming impossible to view the door.

When the band members still hadn't shown up, Emily started to become agitated that she had wasted her night at a smokey, loud, crowded place. "He's not going to come," she complained. "Look, Rose, I need to go outside. My eyes are already starting to tear from the thick smoke. I feel like I'm at a bingo hall."

Emily started to move toward the door, trying to maneuver herself between people who were dancing and those just walking around. She bumped into a guy coming in the door, and without looking said, "Excuse me," and heard, "No problem."

She stopped, looked up and realized that Jason was gazing down at her, his left eyebrow cocked and his lips in a wide grin. She could see Kevin and the other guys right behind him.

Kevin winked and mouthed the words, "He knows you like him."

She glanced at Jason and forced a pleasant but uncomfortable smile, one that sheepishly says, 'Now what do I do?'

Kevin pushed his way through the crowd of people and spoke up, "Permit me to formally introduce you Jason, to Emily." Jason brought his hand forward and Emily reached out and shook it. "Do you want to dance?" Jason asked.

Her eyes became wide. "Dance? Uh, not really. I'd much rather go outside and talk," she offered.

"You know, I'm not much into dancing either," he answered, as Emily led the way through the doorway and outside into the warm August night.

Emily spoke up. "The smoke was getting to me in there. My eyes are starting to water."

"I know what you mean."

Emily walked over to a secluded area away from the crowd of people near the door. She nervously stood by the wall and started kicking the dirt. Though it wasn't dark yet, the sun was just setting. After a few awkward seconds of silence, Emily's mind became blank and she blurted out, "Nice trees around here." Struggling to keep her voice from quavering, she despised the fact that she had resorted to the stupid conversation starters.

"Sure are. I love the way the sunset is reflecting off the leaves of that oak tree over there."

Wow, this guy is something else.

More silence. Then she said, "I heard you liked pastries."

Puzzled expression on his face, he smiled and said, "Yes, I do, but where would you have heard a thing like that?"

"Actually," Emily gave up, "those are just conversation starters. I wasn't really sure of what to say, kind of stupid, huh?"

"No, not at all. That's neat. So you're from New Jersey, eh? I mean, you have a neat accent."

"Yes. You have a neat accent too. You kind of sound like the guys from the Great White North skits on SCTV."

Jason laughed. "I love those skits. They really capture the Ottawa Valley accent well. Now, everybody knows how we talk, eh?"

Emily smiled.

"My father is from Bethlehem, Pennsylvania," he offered.

"Really. So are you half-American?"

"I sure am. My dad moved up here in the fifties and met and married my mom. They just separated."

"I'm sorry to hear about that."

"It's been hard on us kids."

Jason changed subjects. "Hey, Kevin tells me you're 20." Emily nodded.

"You don't look 20.   When I saw you at the party last night, I would have guessed that you were 14 or 15."

"Really? Most people think I'm 11 or 12."

"Well, I knew that you were older than that just by the way you spoke."

No longer feeling awkward and unsure, Emily and Jason comfortably settled into easy conversation covering a wide variety of topics such as school, part-time jobs (you have to wear a cowgirl costume to work?) and family.

As the sun went down, the air suddenly became cool. Emily began to shiver. After spending several days in Canada and knowing that the nights were cool, she still hadn't gotten into the habit of bringing a sweater with her.

Jason, the Canadian, had a sweater wrapped around his waist. Emily, not one to hide her discomforts, started rubbing her arms to keep warm.

"Do you want to borrow my sweater?" he asked. "I'm not cold. You're not used to the cool Canadian summer nights, eh?"

Emily shook her head. "No, I'm not. Thanks."

He slipped it off and draped it around Emily's shoulders. "Is that better?" he asked.

She nodded.   The sweater was warm from Jason's body and smelled of him.

They stood side by side facing out from the wall. The sound of crickets was smothered by the loud rock music coming from inside the curling club. Although it was early August, the cool crisp air smelled of autumn.

Three hours passed before Emily heard Rose say, "Hey Em, it's time to go."

"Already?"

"It's been three hours, for crying out loud."

"Just a few more minutes?"

"Okay. But we've got to get home." Rose ran back toward the entrance of the curling club.

"I have to go soon," she said, with a hint of sadness in her voice. He was so easy to talk to, so gentle.

Jason had his back to the side wall of the building and Emily moved so she was facing him.

He offered his hand. "It's been nice talking to you, Emily. I better go find Kevin and the rest of the band."

"Okay."

As he started to walk away, Jason turned around. "Oh, by the way, there's another jam session tomorrow night. I hope you'll be able to come."

"Me too. See you."

He waved, then hurried off.

Emily stood transfixed for several moments before walking over to the entrance of the curling club to find her pen-pal, Rose, close to the doorway.

Rose walked up next to her. "Nice sweater."

"Oh, no, I forgot to give him his sweater back. I guess I can do that tomorrow. Besides, it smells like him."

Rose's eyebrows raised. "Right."

The next day, Emily found herself feeling nervous and anxious again as she anticipated a night of listening to Jason play guitar, then sharing thoughts and feelings between the two of them. Knowing that this would be their last chance to be together before her departure, she found herself hoping that they would have an opportunity to be alone, one last time.

Arriving at the house for the jam session, Rose and Emily went downstairs. Jason had his back to them, busily practicing a few notes of a song. She resisted the urge to run to him, and walked over and tapped him on the shoulder. He stopped playing, turned around and with a mixture of joy and relief, smiled.

"Hey, good to see you came, Emily."

"You too."

"We're going to practice two songs tonight, then the guys want to have a party."

Emily nodded but kept silent.

"Are you all right?" he asked.

"I guess so. It's just. . . ."

"What's wrong?"

"This is my last night here and I was hoping that we could just talk to each other all night."

"Me too."

"Do you mind if I take some pictures of the band? Would that distract you?"

"No, it wouldn't distract me and no, I don't mind. That would be great."

The young black man walked up to them. "My name's Evan." He held out his hand. "I'm Jason's brother."

Emily's eyes widened, "Brother?"

Evan laughed out loud. "Just kidding. Jason and I have been friends for a long time."

The drummer slapped the side of Jason's head in a playful, yet rough gesture. "Time to work, lover boy."

"Gotta get back to playing," Jason said, while taking a guitar pick out of his pocket. As he turned around, Emily noticed that a second pick accidentally fell to the floor. She stuck it in her pocket. *I'll give this to him during the next break.*

Emily walked over and sat next to Rose on the couch near the door. She watched as the band members took up position at their instruments.

As they began playing, Emily started taking some photos with her small camera. The light was dim in the rec room, but she hoped that her flash would work well enough to allow her to take some decent pictures.

Once the second song was finished, the band members began packing up their instruments. Emily then asked Rose if she would take some pictures of her and Jason.

After posing for a few photos, Emily took Jason's hand and they walked out the door to the backyard.

Jason positioned himself against the back wall of the house with Emily directly in front of him. She looked up into his eyes. Emily so wished that he would kiss her. As if he had read her mind, he leaned down and kissed her lips, a soft, gentle kiss. His lips were soft and smooth and it didn't last long enough for her.

She placed her arms around his waist in a hug and laid her head on his chest. Silent for a few minutes, she stepped back and studied him.

"Hey, how tall are you?" she asked.

"I'm not sure, about five-seven. Why?"

Emily remembered the time that her dad had been hugging her and said, "You need to find a guy about as tall as me because you fit perfectly with me when we hug." She told Jason the story and he smiled. "I wish I could have known your dad."

"Yeah, me too. He would've liked you, I'm sure." She hesitated. "For many years, he had hoped that I would become a nun."

"Are you Catholic?" he asked.

"Yes, I am. What religion are you?"

"I'm Catholic too and I play guitar every Sunday at Mass."

"Really?"

"Yes, really. We go to church, and I went to Catholic school, but I don't really know all that much about my faith."

He paused. "How about you? Does your family go to Mass?"

"Well, my family doesn't, but I do. I'm not sure why I've continued to go to Mass all these years. I mean, there are a lot of things I don't agree with, but I get a peaceful feeling from going to Mass." Emily looked down at the ground. "I'm leaving tomorrow."

"I wish you didn't have to go," he said.

"Me too."

"When do you think we'll be able to see each other again?"

"I'm not sure. I have two weeks of holidays at Christmas. Maybe I can fly up then."

He leaned down and tenderly kissed her forehead. "I've never met anyone like you, Emily. You're so easy to talk to."

"You will write to me, won't you?" she asked in an almost pleading tone of voice.

"Of course, I will, but you write to me first."

"Okay."

They embraced again, this time not kissing, not talking, just holding each other, not wanting to let go. As each minute passed, Emily wished that she could just stop time so they could hold on to each other longer. An hour, then two hours went by.

"I have to go now."

"I know."

They kissed, then hugged, this time with more urgency as they both realized that it would be many months before they saw each other again. She looked up to see Jason gazing down at her. No cocked eyebrows, no smile, only sadness. He gazed at her with such intensity that it almost scared her. The expression in his eyes suggested that he was peering into her soul.

Holding hands, they slowly walked to the front of the house. Emily studied him one last time, trying to remember the expression on his face, the sound of his voice, the touch of his lips. A feeling of loneliness enveloped her as she wondered when, if ever, she would see him again.

Emily, her eyes filling with tears, turned around, and along with Rose, began the long walk to Rose's house. She didn't look back.

Emily was unusually quiet. "You really like this guy, don't you, Em?"

She nodded. "He's one of the nicest, sweetest guys I've ever met."

That night, while Emily was getting ready for bed, she discovered Jason's guitar pick in her pants pocket. *I forgot to give this to him.* It felt so comforting to be able to hold something of Jason's that would remind her of him.

As she lay in bed, Emily reflected on how much her life had changed in a few short days. She never felt this way about anyone before. She thought about the times that she had asked God to send her a man to marry. Could Jason be the one for whom she had been praying? *If he is, God certainly has a sense of humor. I ask him for a man and he sends me a boy. Ah, but what a boy. Even though he is only 17, he seems to possess wisdom and maturity far beyond his years. He's sensitive, intense, talented, kind. Indeed, what a boy. . . .*

9

Song of Songs 5:10

October 1979

Soon after she arrived home from church on Sunday morning, Emily turned on the television in her bedroom. The Pope was giving his homily during the televised Mass from Washington DC. Emily wasn't in the mood for another Mass and was somewhat perturbed that there wasn't anything else on television. No matter which channel she turned on, the Pope's visit was being broadcast. She sat on her bed as she heard the words "human life. . . ."

"Human life is precious because it is the gift of a God whose love is infinite; and when God gives life, it is forever. Life is also precious because it is the expression and the fruit of love. This is why life should spring up within the setting of marriage and why marriage and the parents' love for one another should be marked by generosity in self-giving . . . every human person, no matter how vulnerable or helpless, no matter how young or how old, no matter how healthy, handicapped or sick, no matter how useful or productive for society, is a being of inestimable worth created in the image and likeness of God."

Emily wasn't paying close attention, but as he spoke about the "inestimable worth" of every human being, she listened more closely. It occurred to her that this new Pope was quite the orator. He seemed to give meaning and substance to every word and sentence he spoke. She quite admired him even though he seemed way too conservative for her liking.

She picked up Jason's last two letters from her bedside table. It was unusual for her to receive two letters in one day. Her heart filled with anticipation as she read the first letter again:

September 30, 1979
Dear Emily,

I'm finally starting another letter. I'm really slow at this, aren't I? Anyway, the amount of letters I send is not directly related to the amount of feeling I have for you. I mean, I do some intense thinking about you but every so often it occurs to me that my thoughts aren't much good unless I let you in on them or at least let you know that I am thinking about you. I can assure you that a day hasn't gone by since your summer visit that I haven't thought about you.

Last Friday night, I went to the high school dance and guess who was playing the music? The same group that played at the curling club that night when you and I 'officially' met (I mean, when we shook hands.) Well, you can imagine what kind of a mood I was in that night. While I was watching the band, I kept flashing back to that night. It just made me feel like being outside somewhere talking to you. That's what I feel like doing right now. Though I can't explain why, I really enjoy talking to you.

I can't believe the impression you've made on me in the little time we had. It's beyond me how any of this happened. It's difficult to be sure about this situation when you look at the facts. That's why in my case, I turn to my feelings to confirm things. It's all I have to go on. Except for your mail, of course. Your continuous letters and cards make it very hard for any doubts to enter my mind. Do you have any doubts?

Emily stopped reading. "Doubts? There's no doubt that I have a pain in my heart. There's no doubt that my soul feels lonely for him. There's no doubt that I've never felt this way about anyone before." She took out the second letter that was waiting for a response:

October 1, 1979

 Dear, Most Wonderful, Fantastic, Incredible, Lovable, Beautiful, Thoughtful, Warm, Sweet, Kind, Generous, Emily,

 Did I miss any? Of course I could go on but you get the drift. You know, I always think about you, Emily. I often pick certain moments when we were together and imagine what the expression was on your face, what you were saying and how you said it. It's funny how little things stick with you.

 I wanted to let you know I had a little chat with my friend St. Jude. A one-way conversation, of course. I pleaded with him about our 'hopeless' situation, and he just sat there and listened (I hope.)

 By the way, we never got around to talking about my faults. For one thing, I'm absent-minded which isn't very good when I have to remember dates or appointments or stuff like that. I also worry a lot which goes along with procrastinating and thinking too much. Another might be that I'm basically serious. I'm not very good with joke-making or being in crowds. In fact, crowds especially bother me. That's why I was relieved when you wanted to go outside the curling club and talk. I much preferred it that way. I sometimes have a hard time expressing myself so I don't really open up unless I feel comfortable talking to someone. Take yourself, as an example. I liked talking to you (by the way pastries are dull and the trees have lost their leaves.) Finally, on the last night you were here, I felt comfortable talking with you. That might explain why I didn't appear shy to you that night. As you may know, I was thought of as shy before that night. But on your last night, I guess I couldn't let that part of me stand in the way. Besides, by then I was so 'hooked' on you, I wanted to at least show you I was interested!

 Emily sighed as she re-read the letter. What a sensitive, wonderful guy he was. He sure knew how to melt her heart. *It's hard to believe he's only 17.* Then she glanced at the bottom of this particular letter.   Sometimes he drew small scenes on the outside of the envelopes.   In this case, he drew himself crawling on the sand in a desert, passing a glass of H2O and saying, "Emily, Emily." *Now, if that doesn't make me fall in love with him, I don't know what else could.*

Emily was beginning to hate this long distance business. Why did she have to meet and fall in love with a guy so far away? And, did she really love him? Well, if she didn't, it was the worst case of 'like' she had ever had.   Emily never felt this way about any other guy that she had known.   Her upcoming visit at Christmas would either confirm or deny their love for one another.

Emily felt confident that it would be the former. Jason never told her he loved her but that last night, he had gazed at her with such intensity, words weren't necessary.   If she had any doubts before that, she felt sure that he would, at the very least, write to her.   What surprised her was the frequency and substance of his letters.

She finally picked up her pen and prepared to write another letter.   How could she explain to him that no other person had ever made her feel the way she felt? How could she tell him that she felt incomplete without him? How could she share with him that she connected so closely to him it felt 'spiritual?' The strange thing was, it wasn't a purely sexual thing. She found him attractive, but she didn't only think of him like that. She yearned for his presence, to share feelings with him.

"No," she said out loud. "I can't write all that." After all, she didn't want to scare him.

October 7, 1979
Dear Jason,

Just received two of your letters. I loved your little drawings! Please keep sending them. By the way, you really make me feel wanted. And while we're on the subject of 'you', you know you've made quite an impression on me too.

I also wish we didn't have to spend so much time apart.

I suppose it's good because "absence makes the heart grow fonder." But it's bad because we never get to see each other! It scares me sometimes when I think of the 500 miles that separate us, not knowing what you're doing and thinking this very minute, it really bugs me.

As for doubts, sure, I have doubts, not strong doubts. But once in a while, I wonder whether it's worth the extreme heartache I experience when I think of you 500 miles away and that in the next five years, we probably won't see each other more than two or three times a year.

I've got to go for now. Know that I'm missing you and counting the days until we can be together.

Emily signed and sealed the letter, writing her normal SWAK on the back of the envelope. She knew if she took the letter right to the post office, it would go out first thing in the morning and Jason would get it within the week. It seemed like one of the most frustrating parts of this whole situation was that you write a letter full of feelings and you know the person won't receive it for at least a week. Emily wished there was a way he could get the letters instantaneously.

Emily slipped on her shoes and picked up the letter. Leaving the television on, she walked out of her bedroom, down the steps and into the living room, where her mother was watching the Papal Mass.

"Where are you headed, Em?"

"Going up to the post office, Mom, to mail a letter to Jason."

"You know, Em, I don't think it's such a good idea not to date others. I mean, you only just met this boy."

"I know, Mom, but he's different. I know he won't be dating any other girls."

"How do you know that? Did he tell you?"

"Well. . .no. But I just know."

Emily stared at her mother's raised eyebrows and realized that it would be impossible to convince her right now.

Becky would need to meet Jason to fully appreciate who he was.

"Look, I have to mail this letter immediately. I'll be back in ten minutes."

Emily walked the five blocks to the post office to mail her letter. As she began the hike back home, she heard a horn honk. A car pulled alongside her. He was a guy in his late teens with blond feathered hair and sunglasses. Emily recognized him as a customer who frequented the Country Kitchen restaurant.

"Hi, Emily. You look so different out of your cowgirl outfit, so much more grown-up."

"Really? Is that supposed to be a compliment?" she played along.

"Absolutely. Hey, I was wondering if you're doing anything this Friday night. I'd like to take you to a movie," he offered.

"Well, I'm seeing someone right now," Emily said without hesitation. "But thanks anyway."

"Okay. See you later," he waved and sped off.

Emily sighed. "Boy, when it rains, it pours," she said out loud. She wondered if there was some kind of hormonal signal given off by our bodies when we're already interested in someone. In the past two months since she returned from Canada, no less than four guys had asked her out on dates. Each time she told them that she was already dating someone exclusively.

As Emily continued walking home from the post office, she was confident, regardless of the 500 miles that separated them, that he would not date or even look at another girl. She hoped that when they did get together in late December, it would be a poignant reunion. The romantic in her was convinced that he would, early on, express his love for her. He had definitely given her that impression when he kept signing 'Love, Jason' and underlining the 'Love' part with a dark marker.

A few minutes later, she arrived home. To distract herself from missing Jason, Emily decided go back upstairs to her bedroom, the television still on, the papal Mass still being broadcast. With the Mass as background noise, she began to read her great-grandmother's ledgers laying next to her bed to see if they might contain some interesting information regarding her great-grandparents' store. Sitting on her bed, she opened the first book, this time, focusing on the beautifully handwritten words, *"Michael moves in."*

Keeping the book open, she walked down the steps and called to her mother.

"Hey, Mom, where are you going?"

"To Acme. Need anything?"

"No. Just wanted to ask you if you might know what this means. Down here, next to July 15, 1905, in handwriting, it says, *Michael moves in.*"

Becky paused, then offered, "Could be one of Grandmom's boarders. She used to take in boarders on a regular basis to make extra money."

"Neat," replied Emily. *That mystery is solved.*

The book still open, she sat down on the couch and turned page after page. Only numbers for five months' worth of entries. Then, next to December 15, 1905, the initials, *"BPO midwife, 2:00."*

"B.P.O. I wonder what that means."

More months, more numbers and no other handwriting, until October, 1907, the same message, except this time, *"12:00."*

Intrigued, she read on.

On January 29, 1909, another *"BPO, midwife, 4:00."*

Emily sat back and reflected. "BPO," she said over and over. *Maybe it has something to do with blood pressure.* Would a midwife have been able to check blood pressure at that time?

Reading further, on September 9, 1909, she read, *"Ruth born at home,"* in the same elegant handwriting. "Wow, that would be Great Aunt Ruth. And a home birth. I guess most births took place at home back then."

This notion of family life caused her to look forward to her own future and to Jason. Could he possibly be the one that she would marry, the one with whom she would have children? The whole idea of home birth appealed to Emily and according to the news, it was making a comeback. Now, her heart ached more. She seemed to live each day waiting for another letter from him.

How would she be able to wait three more months until she saw him again? Before this, Emily had to admit that her level of patience, even with the most commonplace situations in life, was almost nonexistent. Now, she had no choice but to be patient and wait. Then what? What if they did love each other, how often could they possibly see one another over the next five years?

10

2 Chronicles 29:6

April 18, 1912

Katharine, still weak, insisted on working at the music store today. To her way of thinking, she had convalesced long enough. Harry couldn't convince her to remain home any longer, though she was still pale and hadn't yet gained back her strength. It had only been four weeks since her operation, but she refused to take more time off. She could imagine how much business had been lost since Harry took charge at the store. He always allowed people to purchase items without payment, then he would forget to write down the names. It was a miracle that they still owned a store.

Taking her time, she walked the five blocks to the music store, stopping on a street corner to buy the Inquirer from the newsboy. "All these stories about the Titanic sinking, I wish the damned paper would print other news," she mumbled. Even a week later, the majority of the stories pertained to the disaster. It seemed like it was the only thing people wanted to hear or talk about.

She unlocked the door to the Parlor Music Shoppe and hurried inside. It was dusty and smelled of mold. Harry obviously hadn't been keeping the windows opened. "I swear that man's not got a brain in his head sometimes," she said under her breath. She gritted her teeth as she realized that she would now have the daunting task of tidying up before the first customer came in. Glancing at the clock, she could see that she had about 15 minutes to accomplish a mediocre job. She tossed the paper on the counter, grabbed some rags and proceeded to dust the store, instruments, counters. Frustrated that she wouldn't have time to mop the floor or wipe the walls down, she reluctantly accepted that a good sweeping would have to suffice for now. She wished that she had a fresh bouquet of flowers to cover up the moldy smell.

As she was sweeping the floor, she caught sight of herself in the full-length mirror by the door. Still holding the broom, she moved slowly toward the mirror and stared at her reflection. Katharine now regretted her decision not to apply rouge and lipstick. Her face appeared emaciated and pale. She felt lightheaded and weak again and decided that she should take a well-deserved rest. She carefully dragged the stool around to the area behind the counter so that she could sit while serving customers. As she pulled on the stool, her abdominal area ached as she could feel the long-range effects from the surgery. She sat on the stool, then remembered what the doctor had said, "Mrs. Clayman, you almost died."

"Maybe it would have been better if I had died," she mumbled under her breath. "Then I wouldn't have anything to worry about."

She laid the newspaper flat, smoothed out the creases and began reading. Of course, the only thing that could be read about was the sinking of the Titanic. "Survivor's Account," was the title of the story that she would scan while waiting for customers to arrive.

She read about how this particular survivor, a second-class passenger named Lillie had escaped on Collapsible D lifeboat with 43 other women and children. "As we were rowing away, I could hear the band play Nearer My God To Thee." Katharine's eyes widened. *That's the most ridiculous thing that I've ever heard. God certainly didn't help those people who died on the ship, or the many people whose deaths were caused by exposure.*

She glanced down again at the newspaper and at an advertisement for men's clothing. The illustration showed a man wearing a suit similar to one that Michael often wore. With her heart aching, she allowed herself to think of him. After the surgery, when Katharine had returned home, Michael had already been gone for days. When she had tried to contact him at his studio, she found that it had been closed, no forwarding address. When she had asked Harry about him, he had shrugged his shoulders and, in a low voice, said "How do I know what happened to him?"

Katharine certainly didn't see any need for her husband to get abrasive with her. Michael never did him any harm. He was polite enough with Harry. Michael was so quiet, that sometimes Katharine forgot that he was there. She recalled how paranoid Michael was that someone, namely Harry, would walk in on them. "That's what locks are for," she would tell him. Now he was gone, and her heart was grieving.

Her eyes caught sight of the miniature paperweight sculpture of Rodin's "The Kiss" that Michael had given her several weeks after he moved in. It always remained hidden to the side of the cash register and behind some books where only Katharine would be able to see it. Otherwise, the police might arrest her for exposing indecent objects.

She picked up the small statue and held it to her breast.

Her mind wandered back to about three weeks after he had moved in. It was an unusual, middle-of-the-afternoon rendezvous. Michael had immediately begun pulling his pants on in order to rush back to his room so as to not make Harry suspicious.

"Michael, it's fine. Harry's drunk most of the time. Don't worry."

She had reached up to kiss him and he had pulled away. "Katharine, I. . . ."

Katharine had turned her body to retrieve her robe. She heard Michael gasp.

"Katharine, your back," he had whispered.

"Yes, my back. I already told you about the scars, didn't I, Michael?"

"Yes. . .but, Katharine, they're. . .bad." The sight of her injuries prompted him to gently caress her shoulder.

"They are, I know. My mother kept telling me how wonderfully they healed over the years and then I would get another new gash to add to the ones which were supposedly better. But, you know, Michael, though they may appear healed, they still feel like open, gaping wounds. I remember each lashing every time I lie on my back. He made sure any whipping was in a place no one could see, no one, except for me or my mother."

"I wish I could have been there to help you, Katharine."

"You wouldn't have been able to help." She had paused. "You know. . .I love you, Michael," she had said casually and with little emotion.

"You do?"

"Of course. Why would you doubt that?"

"Well, for one thing, you're married."

"I know, but I told you I only married him to get away from my father. I was just a kid, 16, and 17 when I had Johnnie. I mean, look at him. How could I be attracted to him? Now, you, on the other hand. . . ." She had leaned over again and had kissed his lips.

"And for another thing, we've only known each other for a few weeks, Katharine." He had broken off the kiss and had reached over to his coat pocket and lifted out a package.

"For you, Katharine."

Katharine's eyes had widened. "For me?" As she had unwrapped it, she nearly gasped when she had seen that it was a miniature sculpture reproduction of Rodin's "The Kiss."

"Why, Michael, it's beautiful. How did you know that Rodin is my favorite artist and this, my favorite sculpture?"

"Your library book. It was laying on the kitchen table a few days ago and it was opened to the section on Rodin and this piece."

Several pedestrians walked by the music shop, distracting Katharine from her nostalgic interlude. Still clutching onto the small reproduction of "The Kiss," Katharine took a deep breath. Refusing to give in to the aching of her heart, she said out loud, "Well, I'm certainly not going to get upset over a man leaving me, that's for sure. With all I did for him, giving him room and board for practically nothing, and this is how he repays me."

The bells on the front door jingled as her first customer came in. He was a regular who frequented the store to buy sheet music for his teenaged daughter. He was a big man, not so much tall, but very rotund, with a handlebar moustache and a balding head under his derby hat.

"Mrs. Clayman, you're back. I'm glad you're feeling better. Me and the wife have been praying for you, that you would make a quick recovery," he said, with a slight Irish accent.

"Thank you, but I don't believe in all that prayer business. I am getting better because I choose to do so," she retorted.

The customer shifted awkwardly as he stood in front of the counter. He forced a smile and asked, "Hey, what do you think of the Titanic sinking? What a shame, all those poor people dying."

Katharine remained silent as she listened to the customer babble on.

"I was reading yesterday of several survivors telling of how the band played "Nearer my God to Thee." Must have been an emotional moment to be on a lifeboat, listening to that song and knowing that many of the people left on board were going to die."

"If you ask me, I think it sounds like a ridiculous story."

The man sighed, then walked over to the rack of sheet music. After scanning it for several minutes, he chose two selections, paid Katharine, tipped his hat and walked out the door.

She glanced down at the newspaper again and re-read the story of the young survivor, Lillie. She was drawn to another survivor's story, this one a man, who was plucked from the icy waters, nearly frozen to death. He talked of watching a priest go from frightened passenger to frightened passenger hearing confession and giving absolution in the last moments before the ship sank.

Katharine shook her head in disgust. She couldn't imagine at the moment of death that she would be concerning herself with superstition like that. "I don't know what I'll be thinking at the moment of my death, but I'll be damned if I'll be trembling with prayer."

Hearing the bells jingle again, Katharine nonchalantly glanced up and was surprised to see Michael standing in the doorway. Her heart began beating rapidly. She watched, stone-faced, as he took off his hat and moved closer to the counter where she was sitting.

"I thought I'd never see you again, Michael," she said, trying not to show any emotion, her hands now trembling.

"I knew that I just couldn't leave you like that, Katharine. I was getting on the train this morning and I felt like I owed you a goodbye and an explanation for my leaving. I went to the house first and Harry told me you were here." Beads of perspiration acted like freckles on his forehead.

"What in the world could there be to explain?" she asked sarcastically. "You waited until I almost died before you left. What a cowardly thing to do, Michael."

"Yes, I know." His voice was quiet, but firm, his eyes downcast. He paused, then made eye contact with her. "Honestly, Katharine, this whole arrangement, especially after Ruth was born, with me sleeping in the same room as your husband, then committing adultery a few rooms away from him. Well, at first, it was enticing enough but after a while. . .well, it was getting to a point that I just couldn't live with myself. I want a wife and children. I want. . . ." He paused.

"You have a daughter, Michael."

"No, Katharine, I don't. Ruth doesn't know me as her father and she never will. That became even more clear to me when you asked me to watch her the morning you became ill. She cried and fussed and there was nothing I could do for her, for she hardly knew me." His voice was now quavering.

"I want a legitimate wife and children. Katharine, I tried to talk to you about me leaving. I've been miserable for years.

The one time I actually got a word in and told you that I was unhappy and thinking of getting another place, you told me not to be stupid. Once you were in the hospital and I found out that you were going to be well, I knew that this was my opportunity to leave." His dark eyes stared intensely at her. "You know that I love you, but I don't love you enough to keep playing this charade. If that hurts you, I'm sorry."

Katharine felt the hair on the back of her neck start to stand up. "To tell you the truth, Michael, it doesn't hurt one bit. You go ahead," she said, her face turning red. It wasn't the first time that Katharine had lied. What was so astonishing was that she did it so well, so convincingly.

He shifted his feet as a stress line formed his brow. "By the way, I wanted to let you know that I started going back to church and. . . ."

"Oh, that's the problem. Churches with their ridiculous rules cause you to feel like you're doing something wrong."

"No, Katharine. All along, I've known what we were doing was wrong. I went along with it because I was attracted to you and well. . .I enjoyed it, for a while. When you became pregnant with Ruth a few years ago, it made me realize that we were going nowhere. You weren't leaving Harry. I mean, you never planned on leaving him. I knew that."

She remained silent, eyes fixed on her feet.

"It took me a long time to gain enough courage to leave, let alone to tell you like this. But I am here, and I just wanted to say goodbye." He placed his hat back on his head.

"Goodbye, then," she said, in an unforgiving tone. *And good riddance*, she wanted to say.

"Goodbye, Katharine. I wish you all the best and I hope you're feeling well." He tipped his hat.

She kept her face down, remaining unresponsive. Katharine listened as the bells jingled when he opened the door, then quietly closed it. The room suddenly felt more empty than before he came in.

Her thoughts began to spin around. Michael going to

church? Why is it that so many people depend on a supposed God that they can't see? What in the world could it possibly do for them? Katharine reflected on the story that she read a few minutes ago about the Titanic. It was purported that the band had played a hymn and that a priest was running from distraught passenger to distraught passenger. Could it be that perhaps there was a God?

If she was convinced that there wasn't a God, why did she and Harry have Johnnie and Ruth baptized at the local Lutheran Church? Katharine shook her head and banished the thought from her mind. Her heart still hardened, she remembered all those times that her father abused her. *When I was just an innocent child, what kind of God would have allowed me to be beaten by my father every night?*

The store's ledger lay open in front of her. *Harry's handwriting is atrocious.* After copying some numbers into the book, she wrote, "*Michael left today.*"

"The only one that I should depend on is myself. I know that I exist and I know where I stand," she said aloud. With that, Katharine started arranging the sheets of music next to the instruments.

11

Song of Songs 2:6

late December, 1979

As she sat in her coach seat by the window, Emily looked out and saw the plentiful clouds which formed a never-ending puffy floor. Her whole body tensed with excitement as she daydreamed about their reunion. She couldn't decide whether she was more afraid or excited to see him again. Part of her couldn't believe that such a wonderful guy had actually liked her and had written back to her. There was also the fact that they had only spent a few days together that first time in Canada. It seemed that getting to know him through his letters was the one thing that convinced her that she was in love, and that this might be the 'real thing.'

In only a half-hour, she would be in Jason's arms. Emily again daydreamed about what it would be like. Would he look the same? Would he act the same? Emily wished that she could run up to him at this very moment.

Within minutes, the stewardess was announcing that the plane would be landing shortly.

Suddenly, Emily began fidgeting in her seat and she became lightheaded, almost breathless. She nervously spent a few minutes combing her hair, then studied her shaking image in her pocket mirror. Once the plane came to a stop, she waited until everyone had gotten off. Taking two deep breaths, she moved down the aisle, off the plane and into the connecting tunnel.

She followed behind a group of people, but she found it impossible to look over them. These were the times that she disliked being so short. It wasn't until she was completely out of the tunnel and inside the airport waiting room that she heard him shout, "Emily!" Her head turned in the direction of his voice and she ran toward him. They met in a long embrace. After all these months, she was finally touching him, holding him.

He pulled her away and gazed at her with a wide smile. "You've made it! You're here and you are so *beautiful!*"

"I can't believe I'm here!" she said as he pulled her close and they embraced again.

They stood still, hugging. If being apart from him was like the greatest torture in the world, then this was certainly the greatest pleasure that she could ever feel. Even though Emily was in a foreign country, she truly felt like she was 'home.'

During the 40-minute trip to Arrandale, Emily positioned herself in the middle seat, next to Jason. She was thrilled to be with him again, but part of her felt awkward. It seemed like they had to become reacquainted, despite the many letters they had exchanged over the last five months.

"Hey, my mom has a huge meal planned. My family's nervous about meeting you."

"Really?"

"Yes," he replied.

"It feels like a dream to be with you again."

"Yeah. I feel the same way."

After a few minutes of silence, Jason spoke up. "I loved your last letter, the one you wrote in a hundred page notebook. That was a great idea and it took me a long time to read."

"I knew that you would like it. I had a fun time doing it too."

Jason cleared his throat.

"So what time do you have to be at Rose's tonight?"

"Not until ten o'clock. We have lots of time."

"Great. I have a surprise for you at home."

"You do?"

He nodded. "I hope you like it."

"I don't think you have anything to worry about there."

After spending several hours meeting Jason's mother and siblings and receiving an original oil painting from Jason, a beautiful landscape mountain scene, he nudged Emily, "Time to take you to Rose's new place."

"But it's only eight-thirty."

"I know," he whispered, "but I was hoping that we could have some time alone before I drop you off." He winked and smiled at her. She gathered her things, said goodbye to Jason's mom and siblings, then walked out the door with Jason.

"This is my mom's car so I can't use too much of the gas." He opened up the passenger side to allow Emily to get in, then walked around to the driver's side. He drove for a minute or two before pulling the car into a remote piece of land near the boat launch at river's edge. It was bitterly cold and the black moving river reflected the moon's brilliance like it was glass.

"I have to turn the car off to save on gas," he apologized again.

"That's okay."

Grateful for the solitude with Jason, Emily pulled out a small gift-wrapped package from her purse. "For you," she said. "I was going to give it to you back at your mom's, but I decided to wait and give it to you privately."

He smiled and slowly unwrapped the package. He opened the box then sighed. "Oh, Em. It's perfect. I love it."

"I knew that you would."

He took it out of the box and slipped it around his neck. "A St. Jude medal. Thank you so much, Emily."

He tried to read the inscription on the medal and, not succeeding, turned on the interior light of the car, "St. Jude Thaddeus, pray for us."

"Read the back," Emily whispered.

"To Jason Love Emily, 12-25-79. What a beautiful gift. Thank you so much. I'll wear it all the time." He hugged her and she snuggled up close to him, laying her head on his coat-covered chest.

"I got a Miraculous medal at the same time, see?" She

held up her medal with the picture of Mary and the inscription around the edges, "Oh Mary, conceived without sin, pray for us who have recourse to thee."

"It's beautiful, Em. It looks perfect around your neck."

She leaned up to kiss him and their lips were reintroduced tentatively. "I've waited so long to do that."

"Me too," he replied.

She placed her head and hand on his chest as he simultaneously slipped his right hand and arm on her shoulder. For the next several minutes, they sat in the quiet solitude of the car. Jason finally broke the silence.

"This is the first time in many months that I haven't felt lost and alone. In fact, I feel complete now that you're here," he said softly.

Emily lifted up her head to find Jason gazing down at her with that same intense piercing expression that she experienced last August.

He continued. "I wasn't sure how I would feel once I saw you again, but now that you're here, there are absolutely no doubts in my mind."

He paused. "I love you, Emily." She could see his breath as he said it.

"I love you, Jason," she replied, her breath becoming more visible as the air in the car became colder. "You know, I had some doubts too, but I knew how I felt about you and I just needed to confirm that." Emily paused. "I think the thing that really made me fall in love with you were your letters, the outpouring of emotion and caring. I've never known anyone like you before."

"Me too." He hesitated. "Do you want to know what I told Evan as you were leaving last summer?"

"Of course."

"I told him that I just said goodbye to the girl I was going to marry."

"Really?"

"Really. I can't quite explain it, Em, but holding you that

night, it felt so right. It seemed like I had known you my entire life."

"I feel the same way."

"I just can't believe it. One minute my life is normal and the next minute I love someone so much I would give my life for her if I had to."

"I know what you mean." Emily's voice started to stutter as she shivered in the frigid air of the unheated car.

He tenderly picked up her cold hand off the front of his coat and, holding the palm of it in front of his face, placed a soft, gentle kiss on it. With his other hand, he unzipped his blue ski jacket, unbuttoned his shirt and placed her frigid palm against his chest. In his initial discomfort, he gasped. Emily tried to move it away, but he held it there. She could feel the very slight vibration of his heart beating.

He kissed her forehead, his warm breath still visible above her, as Emily found her niche, laying her head on his chest while keeping her hand on his warm skin on the inside. The emptiness that she had been experiencing for the past several months was now gone. They held each other, silent.

Jason turned the key and the car started. "Let's get some heat in here. It feels like an igloo."

Emily glanced at her watch. It was almost ten o'clock. Feeling a bit like Cinderella, she said, "I wish we could stay like this all night, with heat, of course."

"I know. I don't think that I'll be able to sleep at all tonight."

The five-minute drive was spent in silence. Arriving at the front of Rose's apartment building, Emily asked, "Will you be going to Mass tomorrow?"

"Yes. I go to the ten o'clock Mass with my family. Do you want to go with us?"

"Sure. Would you be able to take me? I think it would be okay with Rose."

"I would be glad to. We'll pick you up at nine-thirty. Hey, you'll get to see me play my guitar and sing at Mass."

Emily smiled. "I was hoping that I would."

"I sing with my friend, Liam."

"I'm looking forward to it."

They kissed again, then she got out of the car and hurried up the steps. She waved as she watched him drive out of the parking lot.

Emily stirred on the sofa as she heard Rose moving around in the kitchen.

"Good morning, Rose."

"Good morning."

"What time is it?"

"Almost nine."

"I've got to get ready," Emily said, as she pushed the covers off. "Jason and his family are taking me to Mass." She pulled on her slippers and, grabbing some clothes from her suitcase, walked over to the bathroom to shower.

As she was getting dressed, Emily recalled the intimate moment that she and Jason had shared last night when he warmed her hand. What an unselfish gesture that was.

"Don't you want something to eat, Em?" she heard Rose call to her.

She opened the bathroom door and said, "No, thanks, I'll eat after Mass."

A half-hour later, Emily heard an almost quiet horn beep, and glanced out to see that Jason had driven up to the entrance. She hurled her coat over her shoulders and hurried out the door to a blast of cold air. Running over to the car, Emily waited as Jason's mother got out and allowed Emily to sit in front in the middle between her and Jason. They all participated in some small talk as Jason drove to a small country church, just outside of town.

"What a quaint little place," Emily said, as they all walked into the old-fashioned church. Jason's younger brother went to the back of the sacristy to don an altar boy gown while Jason walked to the front of the church to set up the music stand and tune his guitar.

As Mass was about to begin, Emily could see Jason and a taller man, whom she presumed was Liam, prepare to play their guitars and sing. She could see the priest and Jason's younger brother enter as the two-man choir began to sing the entrance song.

It was a different experience watching her beloved sing and play guitar to a church song, quite a contrast from the way he sang those ear-splitting rock songs.

As the time approached when they would be invited up to the front for communion, Emily again thought, like she had so many other times, about the fact that she hadn't been to confession in a long time. She recognized that she had participated in some questionable activities with Eric and Ray. Brushing the thought aside, however, she knew that she was basically a good person, despite those activities.

She recited the "Lord I am not worthy" prayer and walked behind Jason's mother to receive the Eucharist.

Several days later at the airport they stood at the gate, oblivious to everyone around them, holding on to each other, desperately needing to prolong their last moments together.

"When will I see you again?" he asked, pleading.

"I'm not sure."

Jason began to blink as his eyes started to tear.

"Flight 279 to Montreal now boarding at Gate. . . ."

Emily's own eyes filled with tears. She had dreaded this moment for seven days. Just as her heart was full and alive as she began her trip, it was now filled with despair as she attempted to say goodbye.

"I have to go."

"I know." Jason paused. "I wish I was older. Then we could get married right away. As it is, we have to wait four or five years."

With her heart already aching and her eyes already

watering, it was the last thing Emily needed to hear. Her tears fell like droplets onto Jason's blue ski jacket. He leaned down and gently kissed each of her wet eyelids. His lips were still glistening with the moisture of her tears as she looked up one last time.

"Last call for Flight 279. . . ."

Emily reached up and putting her arms around his neck, kissed him in a rough and hurried manner. Then she broke away and ran to the gate. Afraid to turn around, she continued running through the connecting tunnel until she boarded the plane.

Trying desperately to compose herself, she focused on placing her bag under the seat and fastening her seat belt. She sat back and took three long, slow deep breaths to gain control of her tears.

She glanced across the aisle at a woman with a small baby. The infant reminded her of the awkward conversation that she and Jason had a few nights before. Alone in the living room of her friend, Rose's, apartment, they had been kissing on the sofa. Emily had been in a somewhat reclining position, with her back on some pillows and Jason was leaning over her, kissing her.

Jason had stopped and had abruptly sat upright with his head down.

"What's wrong?"

"Em, I'm afraid."

"Afraid of what?"

"Of going too far. I mean, I have never wanted to do anything like this with a girl before. I've never even wanted to kiss a girl before."

"But we love each other."

"I know we do. But Em, I had hoped that we would wait until we're married to do *that*. I mean, you do want to get married?"

"Of course, I do. But you're only 17 and we're not likely to be able to get married for four or five years. I mean, everybody does it. . . ." Emily had stopped herself and cringed as she recalled the incident that happened over a year ago when Eric had said the same thing. She became disgusted that she had spoken that line, one that was probably used frequently by Eric and young men like him.

"I don't know, Em. I mean, I had always supposed that I would wait until marriage to do that. There's something inside me telling me it's wrong."

"Not if we love each other, it's not. Besides, we both know we want to be married to each other."

"And what if you get pregnant?"

"Well. . .uh. . . ." Emily had hesitated. "I won't. I'll go on the pill or something," she had said confidently, as if she had all the answers to the dilemma.

"I wouldn't feel good about you putting chemicals in your body. Besides, the pill is not the answer, and no method is 100% effective in preventing pregnancy."

"Well, most people wouldn't have a big problem with a. . ." Before she could get the word 'abortion' out, she stopped and studied his face.

His eyes had widened. "Emily, please tell me you would never consider that."

"Well, no, probably not, but it needs to be kept legal for those. . .who. . .choose. . .to?" As she said the last few words, she realized that he was staring intensely at her.

"So you would never have an abortion?"

"No, I. . .don't think so."

"Why?"

"Because I don't think I would ever be able to do that."

"But why?"

"I don't know. I wouldn't be able to kill my child, no matter how small."

"Do you understand what you're saying?" The firmness in his tone of voice had made Emily feel uncomfortable. She had never heard him speak with such conviction. "It's like saying that you don't believe in child abuse but you want to keep it free and legal for those who want to do it. That's one of the fallacies of those who call themselves pro-choice."

Emily hadn't known what to say. Quite frankly, she had

never thought of it that way before. Maybe she hadn't really spent enough time thinking about it. What he was saying made a lot of sense.

"As for keeping it legal, that's like saying we need to allow murderers and rapists and thieves to continue breaking the law so they don't get hurt."

"But abortion is legal now."

"I know, Em. That doesn't make it moral. Look at the issue of slavery. How many years was that legal?"

"I don't know."

"Look, I realize that many women who choose to abort feel like they're backed into a corner, sometimes by their husbands or boyfriends, the person who should be protecting and supporting them the most."

"Abortion helps to eliminate unwanted pregnancies, doesn't it?"

"Yeah, by killing the unborn child."

"But isn't that better than seeing the baby abused?"

"No, it isn't. The answer isn't to kill the unborn child, the answer is to place the baby with adoptive parents." He had paused, then spoke softly. "I'm sorry if I was abrupt with you. But I have always felt very strongly about this. In fact, I wrote a pro-life song last year."

"Really?"

"Yes. I need you to understand this. This is not my opinion. It's the simple truth that abortion is evil."

Emily had nodded but kept silent. Did he make sense because she loved him or because what he said actually did make sense? She needed to take some time and think about it.

"I'd like to hear the song that you wrote."

"Sure, maybe tomorrow when you come over to my house."

Emily had recalled the next day, when she had gone to his house, she reminded him to play for her the song that he had written called "If the Morning."

She had studied him as he tuned his guitar. It seemed to her that he did everything to the best of his ability.

He began playing and singing:

If in the morning the Savior didn't rise
Would there be sunshine in your eyes
And in the springtime, if the world wasn't new,
Would love still see its way through
And do we stand only to lose it all
By standing just a little too tall

Save the baby, save the baby
Because I know he's got the right
I know he's got that right
Save the baby, save the baby
Because I know He's got it right
And I know that we have got it wrong

And if the dreamer never woke to tell his tale
Would hope be born still by our hands
And if the baby never sees the light of day
Will nightmares conquer all man
And do we stand only to lose it all
By standing just a little too tall.

Save the baby, save the baby
Because I know he's got the right
I know he's got that right
Save the baby, save the baby
Because I know He's got it right
And I know that we have got it wrong.
And if the baby never saw the light of day. . . .

As she had listened to him, he had the voice of an angel, a pleasant-sounding, melodic voice. But what had affected her most deeply was that he had sung with such conviction.

"Wow," was all she could say. "You wrote that?"

He had nodded. "I was watching a pro-life program on

cable TV and they were singing folk songs, no song that was specifically pro-life. I thought, I should write a pro-life song, so I did."

He had continued, "You know, Em, I don't mean to nag you about this, but abortion is immoral. Every human being has a right to life. No matter how some people try to justify it, it's wrong, despite what the law says."

The baby's squeal brought Emily back to the present as the plane taxied to the runway. How could she have believed that abortion was okay? Did she just think that abortion was wrong now because Jason said it was or was it really wrong? She had to admit that she hadn't thought much about it. Much of what he had said made perfect sense. Abortion was certainly not the way to solve problems.

A few nights ago, nothing else seemed to matter except that they loved each other. Their love was so all-encompassing that if he hadn't stopped, Emily would have gladly given herself to him regardless of the possibility of pregnancy. She remembered past comments that she had made, that women who become pregnant before marriage are stupid. *I guess I could be classified as stupid, then.*

Though she was now feeling challenged on the immorality of abortion, she wasn't yet convinced that sex should be saved only for marriage. In her mind, that was something totally different. She loved him and, for Emily, that was enough.

12

Song of Songs 3:4-5

January 4, 1980
Dearest Emily,

I cried as I watched your plane taxi away but by the time you were in the air, it was too cold to cry. As you already know, I cried while you walked down the hallway to board.

When your plane was taxiing away, I had this wonderful thought that perhaps you didn't really get on the plane, that you didn't really leave.

You don't know how much I wish we were living together (married, of course!) Well, I guess you do know.

> *I love you and*
> *miss you*
> *Jason*

January 4, 1980
Dearest Jason,

It's so hard to believe all this is happening to us. It seems like it's out of a dream or a television show. I just wish we could be together more often. I can't tell you how much I love you. I've never felt this way before and it's such a fantastic feeling. What makes it better and more complete is the fact that you feel the same way toward me.

At least this time, nothing is left 'hanging,' so to speak. Both of us know exactly how we feel: that we want to share the rest of our lives with each other.

I'm grateful that we found each other. What we have is so right and so special that any doubts I had before are completely gone. I know we will be faithful to one another. I have no doubts about that.

In my darkest and depressing moments, I wonder whether everything will work out for us. But when I'm with you, I have no doubts that it will.

Loving you and missing you,

Em

January 12, 1980
Em,

I know what you mean when you say it was all like a dream. But I can assure you that this is real and true. And you can be sure that I feel the same way toward you.

I do feel grateful that we have each other too, but it was hard to be thankful while I was thinking that less than a week ago, I was with you. Boy, what a terrible goodbye that was. I get so choked up when I remember how I felt as we parted.

You are the most important person on earth! This situation really hurts, you know? Yes, I imagine you do know. It's unlike any other pain I've ever known. And even worse and more hopeless is knowing that the medicine to cure it is 500 miles away, and also knowing that I can only take a sip at a time (a very long time). I love you.

Jason

March 30, 1980
Jason,

I can't believe that in just a few days, you will be here with me in my home. It's hard to believe that you will actually get to meet my family. I've loved you for so long and my family hasn't even met you! I'm so thankful that you're able to come down here for Easter. I can't imagine a better way to spend this holiday than with you.

I miss you so much. Every night when I pray, I ask God to allow us to be able to get married sooner than we thought. I dream of the day when we can look into each other's eyes and know that we will never have to be apart. Dreams do come true, you know? *Yours,*

Em

Emily stuffed the letter in the envelope, sealed it and reached for her coat to take it up to the post office. She couldn't believe that in a few days, she would be seeing her beloved again, this time, in her home, meeting her family. She had no doubts that they would love him as much as she did. After all, what wasn't there to love about Jason?

Several days later, on Holy Thursday morning, Emily sat in the seating area of the terminal where Jason's plane would be arriving at any moment. She hoped that his flight would be on time and that impatient part of her wouldn't have to wait.

Though she was grateful to be with him again, she thought about the overwhelming temptation she felt to consummate their relationship every time they were together. On the one hand, being with him brought so much joy. However, with the joy came the temptation. Living 500 miles away from him certainly made it easier to resist the temptation.

She watched as people started to line up at the gate, waiting for passengers to disembark. Lining up behind a family with several children, she stood and waited for Jason to come through the doorway.

Almost immediately, he appeared. Emily moved in front of the group and ran over to him. Still holding onto his small bag, he picked her up and they embraced. Her restless soul was now calmed, and she felt whole again.

After they arrived at Emily's house and Jason was introduced to Becky, Susan and Matthew, the young couple retired to the quiet solitude of the den, savoring each other's presence.

"You're sleeping here tonight." She patted the couch.

"Looks comfortable."

"It opens out into a sofabed."

"Neat."

"I wish we could sleep beside each other all night."

"It's probably best that we don't, Em. I mean, the temptation would be far too much."

"I suppose. But we love each other. What could be wrong with merely sleeping together?"

"Nothing, I guess, but well, I don't know. I sure would love to sleep with you too."

"Let me help you get this thing opened." She pulled off the cushions and reached for the metal bar to lift the bed out. She then placed some flowered sheets on the mattress.

Emily sat on the side of the bed, at first silent. "I hope you'll be comfortable enough."

"I'm sure I'll be fine."

"I better get going to my own bedroom."

"I'll miss you."

"And I will miss you." They kissed and she hurried off.

"Good night, Mom, Sue," she said as she passed her mother and sister in the living room.

"Good night, Em," her mother responded.

"Night," replied Sue.

After she slipped into her pajamas and settled in bed, Emily tossed and turned, attempting to get drowsy.

It bothered her that at this very minute Jason was downstairs in her home. She hated saying goodnight to him. Wouldn't their short time with each other be better spent with their nights together as well?

Her family occupied a home that had only a few creaks in the floors and a mother who slept through earthquakes. So Emily concocted a plan. She would wait until her mother and Susan went to bed (and were obviously snoring) to sneak down to the den and sleep beside Jason, even if it was for only a short time. Trying to rationalize, she promised herself that it would only be to sleep, to simply be close to the one that she would love forever. She understood that Jason wanted to wait until marriage. So she asked, "What would be the harm of simply sleeping together?"

An hour or so later, she listened to her mother's snores across the hall. *Now, I just have to wait for Sue to go to bed.* With that, Susan walked into the room and plopped onto the bed. Pretending she was asleep, Emily waited until Sue was snoring as she prepared to execute her plan.

Within minutes, her sister was breathing heavily. Emily

now sat upright in bed, pulled on her slippers and began what she hoped would be a quiet journey down to the den to surprise Jason.

She tiptoed into the hall and past her mother's room as she listened to the loud snoring. Emily's hands were shaking and her heart was beating so loudly that it felt like she was part of a "Mission:Impossible" episode. Thankful that she had gotten this far, she walked tentatively down the steps and out into the dark living room and through the kitchen.

Emily tried to adjust her eyes as she reached the darkness of the den. Jason was breathing heavily, in calm, even breaths. She knelt down next to the bed and studied his face. In slumber, he was even more handsome. His profile reminded her of a Greek statue. She picked up the covers, slipped in and snuggled up close to him. Emily was surprised to find that he was shirtless and wore only his sweat pants.

Jason moaned and began kissing Emily. He roused enough to say, "Em? What are you doing here?"

They began kissing again. With every passing minute, they became more entranced in each other's embrace. Emily, who was wide awake, was surprised by Jason's uncontrolled affection.

All of a sudden, she felt a tapping on her shoulder, at first slight, then a more urgent poking. She jerked away from him and sat up in bed, looking wildly around in the darkness.

"What's wrong?" he whispered.

"I don't know." She paused. "We should stop."

Jason's head lowered and he remained quiet for a few seconds.

"You know, Em, for a minute, I thought I was dreaming. I was definitely giving in to the moment. If you hadn't stopped us, I probably would have. . .I'm so sorry, Em."

"No, no, Jay. I'm the one who's sorry. I should never have come down here. I should have respected your desire that we wait. I mean, to tell you the truth, I would've been fine if we had gone all the way. I still don't see anything wrong with it."

"I know. Besides, I was awake enough. I should've stopped too."

"I kept telling myself that it would be okay for us to simply sleep together, but I guess I was wrong."

"It sure is tempting to have you lie next to me, Em."

"I know. But I was sure we would be able to. . . look, let's pray. I don't know why, but I feel the need to pray."

Jason nodded. "Me too."

"You lead it, Jay."

"God, please help Emily and I to make the right decision about our love. This is really tough for us and we need your help."

Emily answered, "Amen," and she kissed him on the cheek. "I suppose I should be going up to my own room now. It's so difficult to think of you here in my house while I'm upstairs just rooms away from you."

"I know it is, Em."

"I love you so much," she whispered.

He nodded and sat on the side of the bed as she quietly ran back through the kitchen, living room and up the stairs to her bedroom.

The next morning, Emily rushed downstairs to be with Jason. As she was walking through the kitchen, Becky was holding her hand up in a "stop" motion.

"Hold on," Becky whispered, not wanting to wake Jason in the next room.

"What's the matter, Mom?"

"First of all, Jason's still sleeping."

"So? I was going to wake him."

"Before you do that, I'd like to speak to you about something."

"What is it, Mom?"

"Well," she whispered, "I know you came down here to be with him last night."

"Oh," she said, her head down.

"I'm disappointed in you, Em."

"Yeah, well, we didn't do anything."

"Okay."

"That's it, okay? You're not going to question that we didn't do anything?"

"No, I'm not, because you've never lied to me, Em." Now Emily felt guilty as she remembered the incident last year with Ray, when she lied and told her mother that she would be going to school and instead skipped school, then came back to the house with Ray. She never revealed to her mother the story of that day.

"Yeah. Well, to tell you the truth, something stopped us. I'm not sure what it was, but I felt tapping on my shoulder. It scared the pants off me, to be quite honest. For a split second, I thought someone was standing over us."

"Really? You know, Em, things like that don't happen. Your guilty conscience was probably imagining it. It might be a good idea to refrain from sneaking down to sleep with your boyfriend."

"Jason wants to wait until we're married, Mom."

"Oh, really?"

"Yes, really."

The four days seemed like four minutes and soon, Emily and Jason found themselves again standing at the airport, clinging to each other.

"Why does this have to be so hard?" she asked.

"I don't know, Em."

"Last call for Flight. . . ." the loudspeaker blared.

They embraced one final time and it was Jason who broke away and ran toward the gate.

Once again, Emily's heart and soul felt the all-too-familiar emptiness.

April 28, 1980
Dearest Jason,

I feel so lost, so alone and my heart aches for you. Why do we have to live so far apart?

I hate this situation. It seems hopeless. How can I be positive and cheery when it's at least three or four years till we can be together forever? It seems like such a long time because it is a long time from now. Why does this hurt so much? Why can't I be positive and optimistic about our situation? Why am I crying right now? Because I need you and I can't have you.

Em

May 14, 1980
Em,

Well, I finally got that depressing letter you warned me about. It really hit me. I mean, despite the fact that it was depressing, the overall atmosphere was extreme emotion and it was just . . . beautiful to get that all out of a letter. When I'm with you, it's much easier to share emotions and as we know, in letters, there is usually a lack of 'presence.' But in this one, the words seem to reach out and strangle me.

You know, it seems that each of our visits is only a moment long. They are so short but so good. We have had some beautiful moments. I get such a special feeling whenever we say 'I Love You' to each other. It's like, I'm thinking to myself, there is no phrase which comes from as deep a part of my heart as 'I love you' does. And when I think of my heart being opened like that when I say those words to you, all loneliness leaves me, except that which we always, for the time being, have to face at the end of each visit.

It's really hard to be apart. But every painful minute of waiting brings us closer to that date when we shall meet again! And every painful goodbye brings us closer to that most important date sometime in the future when we will be married. I love you and I'm yours forever.

Jason

Emily placed the letter back into her drawer and reminisced. That letter was written eight months ago. It was now January 2nd, and she and Jason were in the midst of 14 days of togetherness. She finished dressing, then rushed downstairs to the den, where Jason would be waiting.

He was sitting on the floor, knees up, in front of the sofa with his sketchbook. His left hand was propped up on one of his knees and his face was intense with concentration as he busily tried to draw his left hand.

She knelt down besides him. "Hey, that's really good. Looks just like your hand."

"Thanks, Em."

She snuggled up close to him, as he continued sketching.

"I can't do this any longer, Jay. I need to be with you."

He put aside his drawing materials and faced her.

"We have to, Em. What other choice do we have?"

"Isn't there some way for us to get married?"

"I'm not even 19 yet."

"I know, but I'm working now. Couldn't we at least become engaged and set a date?"

Emily was staring intensely at him. They had been together for 12 straight days during the Christmas holidays and in two days they would again be separated. She reached up to touch a piece of his hair, an unruly curl that seemed to have a mind of its own.

"Jay, I know that you're young, but it's not as if I'm asking for us to be married right now. We've already discussed May of '83 as a possible date to be married. Can't we just move it up one year? That would only be a year and a half from now."

Jason gazed down at her. "There would be nothing that would please me more than to be married to you *right now*. But Em, I'm only 18."

"I keep forgetting that because you act so much more mature than most guys much older than you. You're more mature than me."

Jason smiled. "Yeah, but you only look 12."

Emily continued. "I'm serious. I'm now finished college and working full-time. A year and a half would give me time to save money for our new life together in Canada. By the time we're married, you'll have completed your first year of university and I can get a job to support us until you're finished."

Jason sighed. "Well, it certainly sounds like a well-thought-out plan, Em. I know that I want to be married to you. I'm usually an overly cautious person. I never expected that I would even be thinking of marriage at this age."

He pulled her toward him and held her. Emily's eyes pleaded with him, "All I know is that I need to be with you. Right now, we're lucky if we can be together for a few days every four months. We can't go on like this."

"I know. I also realize that if we formally got engaged, it would, in one sense, make this situation more bearable because we would have a date that we could anticipate never being apart again." Jason kissed the top of her head, pulling her close to him.

"I never realized how much love would hurt. All those years I prayed for God to send me someone to love, I never knew how much pain it would cause, not being able to be with you."

Jason began stroking her hair, then pulled her away from him. He whispered, "Let's do it. Let's get engaged."

Emily, eyes widened, replied, "You mean it? Really? We're going to be engaged?"

Jason nodded. "I can't believe it, but yes, we are engaged!"

"Can we tell people?"

"Of course. Isn't that what it means to be engaged? I mean, both you and I have known since last year that we wanted to be married to each other. Now, we can tell people that we are officially engaged."

"I just can't believe it."

"Are you sure this is what you want, Em?"

"How could you even ask such a question?"

"I just want you to be sure that this is what you want. If

we get married, which is what I want as well. . . ." He paused.

"Yes?"

"Then we are getting married for life."

"Of course we are."

"We won't ever be getting a divorce. . . ." He paused again. "Because I won't put my kids through that." His expression was a somber one. "In the midst of the joy, I want you to be sure that this is what you really want."

"This is what I want, Jay. To be married to you forever."

Emily normally dreaded the time after the holidays. It was always such a let down after the excitement of Christmas. But this year, she was determined to remain positive. After all, she now had a date to look forward to, less than a year and a half away, when she would be joined to her beloved for life.

13

1 Corinthians 13:4-8

January 10, 1981
Em,

I agree wholeheartedly with you. This long distance situation is unhealthy. I can't tell you how satisfied I am with how our relationship is progressing and just think, in only 16 months, we will be husband and wife! I need you to be strong, Em. I'm so happy we have each other but it's more a tormented happiness because of our lack of togetherness.

By the way, my mother wasn't too thrilled to hear we're engaged. I mean, I'm not quite 19 and she's concerned because she thinks I'm too young. She seemed somewhat relieved when I told her the date would be a year and a half from now. My dad seemed more open, but I know he's concerned too.

I love you, Em. Try to imagine me sitting with you right now, all alone, and imagine that I say, I love you. It has to be in a sort of low tone of voice, quiet, but very intense and with a lot of feeling. That's what I want you to think of every time I write those words 'I love you.' Somehow, the written words themselves just don't seem good enough.

Jason

Emily sighed. Getting his letters was like a breath of fresh air, though it was a poor substitute for the real thing. It was one of the aspects about a long distance relationship that she despised. Phone bills were expensive and the most economical way to communicate was by letter.

"Hey, Em!" she heard her mother calling to her.

It was an early Monday morning and she was thankful that she didn't have to work today.

She hurried into the hallway and heard, "I'm in here, Em, in the bedroom."

Her mom had remarried, and Emily held mixed feelings about it. She liked her new stepfather. He was funny and easygoing. But it was awkward watching her mother act like a teenager and now sharing her room with her new husband, the bedroom that she had shared with her father, the room where Emily and her siblings had been conceived.

When she reached the bedroom, she stopped cold when she saw her mother, huge grin on her face, sitting on the edge of the bed. Emily couldn't explain it, but there was a glow emanating from her mother's face, unlike any she had seen before.

"I want to show you something, Em."

"What, Mom?"

Becky remained seated, radiant smile still on her face, and pointed to the top of her bureau. A contraption that Emily was not familiar with stood in the middle of her bureau, a small stand with a tube in it, a donut-shaped dark ring visible in the mirror below. It looked strangely out of place even on top of her mom's cluttered bureau.

"What's this?"

"A pregnancy test. You can do these at home now." Becky's face still held joy as she watched her daughter's reaction to her surprising news.

"A what?" Emily shouted, her eyes now widened.

"You heard me, a pregnancy test."

"And you wouldn't be showing this to me if it were negative, so it means you're. . . ."

"Yep."

Emily opened her mouth but couldn't speak. Becky was now 48. Before Emily's father had died, she had pestered her parents, on a daily basis, to have another baby. Emily was now engaged to be married and would be moving to Canada shortly after the baby was born.

Emily kept silent, her eyes fixed on her feet.

"I thought you would be happy. I mean, you're always talking about how much you want to have kids. This is the perfect opportunity for you to get some experience with babies."

"And how am I supposed to do that from Canada?" she answered, somewhat curtly.

"Well, you're not moving to Canada until next year. The baby will be nine months old then. There will be lots of time before that."

Emily sighed. "I bugged you and Dad to have a baby for many years. I'm moving to Canada and now you decide to have a baby?"

"Em, I had no idea that I could have any more children. I thought I was past menopause. I haven't had a period in a couple of years."

Emily looked at her mother and despite her negative reaction, Becky continued to radiate joy.

"Look, Mom, I'm sorry. I really am happy for you. It's just a real shock, that's all. I just keep thinking how this baby won't know me since I'll be getting married and moving away." She leaned over to hug her mother.

"That's bull, Em. We'll make sure that doesn't happen. You know, I was hoping that you would go to the doctor's office with me today since you're not working. I made an appointment for two o'clock."

"I guess so, Mom."

Several hours later, as she and her mom were driving to the doctor's office, she thought of her new sibling growing and developing inside her mother's womb. She now began to focus on what this child would mean for her family. As they were sitting in the waiting room, Becky commented to Emily, "This is the doctor who delivered you 21 years ago."

They were ushered into the examining room as Becky revealed to the doctor why she was there. Emily watched as the his non-emotional face took on a stern, almost angry expression.

"You certainly don't intend to have it, do you?" When he said "it," it sounded like he was talking about a cockroach or something disgusting.

"What do you mean?"

"Come on, dear, don't you realize that you have a one in ten chance of having a baby with Down Syndrome? And that's not the only thing that could be wrong. There are a whole host of deformities associated with elderly mothers like yourself."

Dear? Her 48-year-old mother was being called dear?

Emily watched as her mother's eyebrows formed a frown.

"I'll take my chances."

"Well, then, you'll need to find another doctor because I won't keep you as a patient unless you have an..."

"I'm not having an abortion. Come on, Em, let's go." She stomped out of the examining room, through the waiting room and out the door to the parking lot.

Now, Becky was almost running. Emily was having a difficult time keeping up with her mother's long legs. Becky began to speak loudly: "Telling me to go elsewhere, imagine! Delivering someone's baby is a privilege. I wouldn't go to that SOB again if he were the last doctor on earth!"

Emily began digging her nails into her palms when she thought about the fact that this man was the first person who touched her, since he delivered her 21 years ago. *Goodbye and good riddance,* Emily silently said to the doctor, as her mother drove them out of the parking lot.

September 10, 1981
Dearest Em,

Perhaps by now you have a new little brother or sister. Please call me and let me know when the time comes. This is a unique opportunity for you to get some experience for when you and I start our family.

I crave so much to just be with you, hugging you, kissing you. Also, I crave to sit on the porch steps with you on a fall night and talk about things, any things. And I crave being in church with you and holding your hand when we stand for the gospel. And I crave the feeling we sometimes get after a deep, perhaps frustrating, perhaps delightful discussion about our thoughts and ideas. That's the feeling when I wish we were physically one and experiencing the beauty and unity of intercourse.

This is not going to be an easy life, Em. But no matter how hard it is on us, how good it is depends on our attitude towards it. I might have told you before, but I believe that a person can't have a good life without looking at it in a positive way.

I mean, look at the saints who died for the good of others. Being stoned, burned, thrown to the lions or crucified upside down, must not have been an easy part of one's life. But the saints stayed true to God to the bitter end and looked at it as a good thing.

I love you so much, and as you can tell by how much I've written tonight, I could have really made good use of a good listener, as you already are.

Yours always, Jason

September 15, 1981
Jason,

I have a beautiful new baby sister! She's so tiny and cries a lot and is adorable. Of course, I think she looks like me! I can't wait for you to meet her.

Six months later, March 1982
Jason's university dorm room

Jason fidgeted at the door to his college dormitory room. First, he dropped his key, then inserted it wrong side up. Emily couldn't quite explain it, but during the four-hour drive to the college from Arrandale, he seemed quiet, almost nervous. He finally opened the door, then allowed Emily to enter before he pulled the door closed.

"Nice room."

"I suppose it is. I'm glad that I have a private room. With all the partying going on in this place, it's a miracle other students are able to study at all."

The room was small, perhaps six feet by twelve feet with the twin bed immediately to the right as one entered, his desk at the corner past the bed, and a chair to the left of the desk, below the small window.

"Nice bulletin board," she commented, as she pointed to 20 or so photos of herself above his desk area.

"Glad you like it, Em."

She walked over to the window and parted the small curtain. A soft snow was falling, its huge flakes glistening on the outside window ledge. "I love snow like this, Jay. It's so pretty."

Emily moved to stand in between the bed and the desk. She sat down on the mattress.

"Nice bed."

"It's comfortable." She noticed his eyes darting around the room then focusing on his desk drawer. He reached out and pushed it shut, although it had only been open a crack's width.

"So what do you want to do now?"

As Emily asked the question, Jason's face became pale, his eyes downcast. In nearly three years of dating, for a reason she couldn't explain, it was one of the most awkward moments the two of them had shared.

Within a few seconds, Jason's face lit up. "I've got it, Em. Pose for me. I have a drawing due next week and I need some practice. Besides, I haven't done much sketching of you."

"Sure, okay. Where do you want me?"

Jason dragged the wooden chair from his desk and placed it in the middle of the small room.

"Sit here, Em."

Emily sat down. "Now what?"

"Do something with your hands."

"Like what?"

"Well, perhaps place them on your lap or beside you."

Emily folded her hands on her legs. "Is this all right?"

"Great. Now tilt your body to the right a bit and turn your head to face me."

"Like this?"

"Good." He removed the sketchbook and pencil from the top of his desk, then sat on the floor several feet in front of her.

As she watched him drawing her, it seemed as if the awkwardness had fallen away, and the only thing left was her, the object of his study.

Twenty minutes later, Emily shifted slightly as she realized that her right foot was asleep. She studied Jason, still intensely focused, glancing up every few seconds, then moving his pencil on the paper, in small fine movements as he drew her face.

"So, is your Aunt Suzie going to be able to attend the wedding? And what about your father's sisters? Will both of them be coming?"

"Em, shhh. I'm concentrating. And you need to stop moving. You have to try to keep still."

"But I can't keep still for much longer. I need a break. This is hard work. I bet models make a lot of money sitting still so long."

"Be quiet. I need to focus."

"Can't you finish it later?"

Jason stuck the pencil behind his ear and stared at her, his eyebrows raised and his mouth curved in a smile.

"I guess I'm being too hard on you. Hey, come and see what I've drawn." He took the pencil from behind his ear and continued to draw lines on the paper.

Emily stood up and stretched, then began to shake her foot to rid herself of the pins and needles sensation. She moved closer to Jason, while continuously shaking her foot. He stopped sketching and held out his drawing as she studied his portrait of her.

"Is my forehead that big?"

"Yes, Em. You have a big forehead."

"I didn't think I had anything that was big."

"Well, you have a big forehead."

"How come I didn't know I had a big forehead before now? Why do photos not show my big forehead?"

Jason sighed. "You know, Em, photography is not the same as sketching and painting. Drawing is part observation and part interpretation. It's not my intention to draw something so exactly."

"What about my hair? I mean, it looks like I have about five strands of hair."

"Come on, Em, your hair is pretty thin."

"Are you trying to say there's something wrong with my hair?"

"No, I'm not. It's just an observation, not a criticism." He hesitated. "I guess you don't like it."

"Well, it's not that I don't like it. It just doesn't really look like me."

"As I said, it wasn't my intention to draw you so exactly. I mean, I could have taken a photograph if I wanted an exact representation."

"Whatever."

She watched as Jason pinned the sketch onto the bulletin board next to the plentiful photos of her.

He stood in front of his desk, his eyes again focused on the top drawer. Emily moved to stand behind him, then embraced him and kissed his back through his shirt. "I love you so much, Jay."

He remained silent with his back toward her.

"Isn't this where you normally say I love you, Em?" she whispered.

"I do, Em. I love you."

"Oh, you're not feeling badly that I criticized your sketch, are you?"

"No, no, Em."

As he turned around, she studied his face. He gazed at her, his eyes a mixture of desire and confusion. It was a look that she had never seen before.

"Okay. What's wrong? You've been so quiet and distracted today."

His eyes downcast, he embraced her, then broke off and reached over to his desk. Opening the top drawer, he lifted out a package and tossed it on the bed.

"There. That's what's wrong."

Emily leaned over and studied the box. When she realized what it contained, she blurted out, "Oh my gosh. I can't believe you bought. . . ." Hesitating, she asked, "So when did you buy these?"

"A few days ago. I woke up one morning last week after having this. . .well. . .intense dream about us. For days, it was all I could think about. I couldn't study. I couldn't think. I knew it was wrong to think about and to dwell on. But when I realized that we would be coming here to my dorm room, my thoughts became consumed with the idea that we would have an opportunity to. . . well, you know. I tried to pray but I couldn't. I guess I didn't want to."

"Oh, Jay," she pulled him down to sit beside her on the bed.

"So I went to the drug store. It took me 45 minutes to gain enough courage to buy these, well. . . ."

"Condoms, yes, I see that. Now what?"

"You know, Em, since I bought these, I've been feeling so guilty. I mean, all along, I knew that planning for this whole thing was wrong in and of itself. God, I feel like I'm in confession. I mean, I had every intention of following through with this plan."

"Okay."

"Part of it was because I wanted to please you. I know how much you've wanted to do this all along. Then, of course, there's the whole pleasurable aspect."

Emily remained silent as he continued.

"I began debating with myself: you love her, she loves you, you're almost married. . . ."

"Well, we *are* almost married."

"I know, Em, but almost isn't married. I mean, we've waited for almost three years now."

He continued. "After I bought these, I was lying in bed and I got this horrible feeling that if we did go ahead, that we would be spoiling something, ruining an experience that we will only be able to share once in our lives, the act of giving ourselves physically for the first time."

"But we love each other."

"I know, but we aren't married yet. Even though we love each other, if we went ahead now, it would be more physical than spiritual, more physical than emotional."

"So that means we're not going to do this, right?"

He nodded. "Right. I just can't, Em. I can't do this and I'm sorry if you're disappointed." His eyes were now a mixture of relief and strength.

"Well, I'm more shocked than anything that you even bought these."

"Believe it or not, I've never seen or touched one of these things before. So I took one out of the package. It reminded me of a doctor's rubber gloves, so clinical, so mechanical. I was holding it in my hand, studying it, reading how these things are used. And it just hit me. I mean, it made me realize more deeply how wrong these things are, even in marriage."

"What do you mean?"

"The way I picture it, Em, when we consummate our marriage, it should be you, me and God. That's all. Why should any contraceptive company and their business plan and their advertising strategy have anything to do with our intimacy? When I think of me using this, it means that I'm actually holding back a part of myself. And if you were using a diaphragm or the pill or something, you would be keeping a part of yourself from me. When we give ourselves to each other, it should be a total gift, not a partial one.

"Besides," he continued, "the Church says 'no' until you're married. I've seen no reason why it can't be seen as a good law, one there for our protection and to help us on the road to being good people."

Emily sighed and leaned over to lay her head on his

shoulder. As she waited in the silence of his room, part of her resented the Church with all its rules and laws. She still couldn't see anything wrong with consummating their relationship now. Perhaps she didn't want to. Emily so often tried to justify her desire to 'go all the way,' despite Jason's hesitant suggestion that they wait.

"You know, Em, you matter to me more than any person or thing, except for the One who gave me you and who will allow you to be given to me in marriage."

"I know." She took her head off his shoulder.

"I'm sorry if that causes jealously, but it shouldn't. You are, after all, a reflection of God's love for me just as I am a reflection of God's love for you."

"I'm not jealous. I just never thought of it that way." They sat together in silence for what seemed like hours, just holding on to each other.

"So what do you think we should do about avoiding pregnancy? I mean, you said we should wait to get pregnant, right?"

"Yes, I think we should. Did you ever read that book I gave you called No Pill No Risk Birth Control?"

"Uh. . .yes, I did, a few months ago."

"And?"

"And. . .I. . .well. . .I don't mean to be pessimistic, Jay, and I don't have anything against this natural birth control, but. . . ."

"Liam calls it Natural Family Planning."

"Whatever. This book is against using anything other than this, what do you call it. . .Natural Family Planning? I know I ovulate twice a month, Jay, and my cycles are very short. How long would that give us to be intimate? We might as well not have sex at all if it means we can hardly have sex. Besides, I want something that is foolproof."

Jason sighed and then pulled her close to him. "Try to be optimistic, Em. I know this method works."

"Natural Family Planning just doesn't sound like it's the right thing for us. I want to be able to express my love for you physically and it sounds as if this method won't allow that."

"You said you wanted a foolproof method. Other methods aren't 100 percent effective. I know a girl here on campus who got pregnant on the pill and that's supposed to have a very high effectiveness rate. Besides, this is not about how we can make love every day, several times a day. This is about doing what is right."

"Well, we might as well not be intimate at all if we can only have sex once a month," she complained again.

"You know, Em, I would rather have sex once a month without any kind of contraception than five times a day with birth control. And I know how difficult it is going to be. Remember what I just said about giving ourselves totally?"

For a brief moment, Emily controlled her urge to retort. Sometimes, it frustrated her because he seemed to have all the answers, like his philosophies were without error and not open to discussion.

"I want our wedding night to be special," she whispered. "After all, we will have waited for three years, right?"

"Yes, and I realize that you feel special about our wedding night and that symbolically through sex we can physically, emotionally and spiritually be one, and I also realize that we both have desires, but if these can't be suppressed by our need to be true to each other and to God, to be as good as we can be, then we need greater strength than we have in our relationship."

Emily tried to comprehend all that he was saying.

"Em, I am keeping my mind open that NFP can work for us. If we used something like the condom or diaphragm, I would not be able to ignore the fact that there was a piece of latex involved in our consummation. What would this do to the symbolism? To me, it would be like attending Mass on Sunday with earplugs in your ears. You can just make out what's being said but everything has been dulled and you can't respond properly, but physically you are there and your presence is noted."

"Why are you making such a big deal out of this?"

"Because I believe it is a big deal, Em. So much so, that I'm willing to postpone sex even after marriage until we can find out how to use NFP."

"Why are you being like this? I mean, every couple I know uses birth control. Even the priest at the marriage preparation course told us it was okay in marriage."

"I just can't believe God would want a couple to separate themselves or harm themselves by using devices."

"I don't want to fight."

"Who said we're fighting?"

"Well, your tone suggests it."

"I'm sorry about that, Em. This is so important and maybe you don't realize that right now, but someday you will understand and you will know that this is the right thing."

"What do you want me to do? I have no idea where we can take classes."

"Perhaps you can talk to your doctor and see if he can give you any information."

She nodded and again, leaned her head on his shoulder. Jason turned toward her and kissed the top of her head. "I know this is the right thing, Em."

For Emily, this information was overwhelming. It seemed so foreign to think that birth control was wrong. After all, it had helped people to avoid unplanned pregnancies and isn't that a good thing?

For now, she decided to banish the subject of contraception and NFP from her mind so that they could enjoy the rest of their time together.

14

Jer. 31:15

July, 1918

Katharine couldn't believe her predicament. She and her new lover hadn't used precautions in several months. Now, she was six weeks late for her period. Angry at herself, she had to admit that she had become lazy in that area. At 39, she had figured that she was just too old to get pregnant.

Still attractive and thin, it hadn't been difficult for her to find a boarder who would double as her lover. Her newest paramour had moved in just four months ago. She met Walter, a plumber, when he had been repairing some pipes at Katharine's house. Their conversation quickly turned to the man's lack of living quarters. He had been living at his place of business for a few weeks, since losing his rented room during a house fire. As he had recounted his story, Katharine had studied the man. He was reasonably attractive with a receding hairline and few, if any, teeth missing. At this age, Katharine had told herself, she couldn't be too picky. No one would ever measure up to Michael.

Sitting on the edge of her bed, she tried to reassure herself. She initially believed that she was going through the menopause. "Women don't get pregnant at this age. I'm a grandmother. That's absurd." Then she started feeling the nausea. Her breasts were tender to the touch. There would be only one reason that she could be overdue. She finally said it out loud. "I am not having another baby, that's for sure."

Gathering up her pocketbook and gloves, she slipped on her bonnet and stared at her reflection in the mirror. She had to admit that she was still rather attractive for a middle-aged woman, especially in her cream and magenta-patterned dress.

She stepped outside onto her porch and down the steps to begin the trip to the midwife's house six blocks away. She walked as quickly as she could. Every few feet, she would almost knock into the large numbers of mischievous children playing on the sidewalks, gritting her teeth as she did so.

She arrived at the door to the midwife's small row house, took a deep breath, then decided it was too hot to take a deep breath. The midwife was just coming through the door.

"Oh, Katharine."

"Annie, I need to speak with you."

"I can't. I'm on the way to a birth right now. Fifth child and it's going to be fast so I need to go. Sorry, Katharine."

"I'm late. . . ." She paused. "And I need for you to bring on my period. You've done it many times before."

"Yes, Katharine, I have, but. . . ."

"But what?"

"How many weeks since your last period?" The midwife spoke in hushed tones.

Katharine made eye contact with her. "It's been about 10 weeks."

The midwife took a deep breath as she wiped sweat off her brow. "Why didn't you come to me sooner?"

"I'm older, you know, and I didn't know if I was going through the change. Now, I'm convinced it isn't that."

"I can't really help you now, Katharine. I have to attend a birth. Besides, the police are watching the midwives in town after that woman died last week from hemorrhaging."

"Yes, but she wouldn't reveal to them who was responsible for that. It could have been a doctor for all we know or someone who doesn't know what they're doing. You know what to do."

"Katharine, I'd like to help you, really I would. But I just can't. I need to go." The midwife hurried away, leaving Katharine on the steps of the small row house.

Outraged, she mumbled, "Damn. She could bring on my period and still be in time for that birth. Well, if she isn't going to do it, I will find someone else who will. I will not give birth again, even if I have to do this myself."

She walked a few blocks closer to Broad Street where she could take the trolley to downtown. Within minutes, the streetcar had arrived. Relieved, Katharine lifted her skirt to step onto the car and deposited the tokens into the box at the front. She sat down close to the driver and with her head down, she searched her handbag for a slip of paper with the name and address. One of her customers had once gone to a doctor who brought on a period from a small office in the alleyway of one of the new high rise buildings in the city. The woman had written it hastily and it was almost illegible. "If I can just try to decipher the address. . .625 or is it 627 Market Street?" she mumbled.

Katharine sighed and glanced up, just in time for the trolley to pass by Lit Brothers Department Store. She was always in awe of the breathtaking architecture of this building with its unique style and octagonal towers at the corners. She enjoyed shopping there, but it was far too big a place with its five floors, and Katharine, who normally had little money to spare, usually did more looking than shopping.

She stood up and gripped the pole as she waited to get off at the next stop, 6th and Market. Katharine stepped off the trolley, then stood still, trying to figure out which direction she needed to take.

She began walking, then noticed a building marked 625 Market Street. She cautiously moved around to the back alleyway to see if there was a door. Katharine turned right into a less-than-clean area behind the skyscraper. She tried to hold her breath as she maneuvered between several metal garbage tins.

"Oh," she screamed as a fat rat with a long tail scurried past her feet. For a brief moment, a voice inside told her, "Don't do this." Ignoring the voice, she concentrated on finding the correct address.

She tried the first door, but it was locked. "Damn," she mumbled. Turning to walk away, Katharine looked with disgust at the rat eating a piece of meat in the corner behind one of the trash cans. From behind her, she heard a young woman whispering for her to come ahead in.

"Perhaps I have the wrong address. Is this a place where a woman can come to bring on her period?" Katharine asked.

The woman continued to speak in a hushed tone. "Yes, yes, it is. Come right on in and I'll have the doctor speak with you." She rushed off to the other part of the office, the part Katharine imagined was in the front section of the building.

Katharine stood in a small waiting room, one without any windows or chairs. A feeling of loneliness enveloped her as she stood, silent and alone, for several minutes. She tapped her foot and sighed several times, irritated that she was being kept waiting.

An older man in a doctor's coat came forward and introduced himself. "I'm Dr. Harvey. My nurse tells me that you need to have a procedure to bring on your period?"

Though Dr. Harvey's clothes appeared to be professional, he smelled of chewing tobacco and when he spoke, Katharine could see that his teeth were quite yellowed from the habit.

"Yes, that's correct. I've had this done several times before, by the midwife."

"How many weeks overdue are you?" he asked.

"About three or so. I have all the other signs, like nausea and sore breasts. I've been overdue many times. I would think I'd know if I needed the procedure or not," she said confidently, careful to avoid mentioning the word 'pregnancy.'

"That'll be $35 paid up front. Do you have the cash?"

"Yes, I do," she replied, handing him the money. She knew that it was $10 more than the midwife used to charge, but she felt confident that it was money well spent.

"All right, then. Come ahead in."

He ushered her, in a standoffish manor, through a small hallway and into an even smaller examining room. Again, it was an eerie, lonely place, with no windows and only the door to enter and exit. The walls appeared to have water damage and she noticed that the floor had spots of dried fluid of some kind.

"While I'm gone, put this on and I'll come back to examine you." He tossed the shapeless cotton gown on the table.

After he closed the door, Katharine quickly slipped off her dress, corset and undergarments. She struggled as she opened up the hospital gown. She admitted that she was nervous, but she tried to convince herself there was no reason. *He's a doctor, fully trained. He knows more than that ungrateful midwife.*

As Katharine was lying on the examining table, it felt like her whole body was shaking. She found herself having to concentrate on breathing slow, deep breaths. Within minutes, the doctor walked in. Ignoring her, he began rummaging through some drawers. He methodically and carefully laid out several metal instruments on the small tray next to the examining table, then sat himself at the far edge of the table.

"I need you closer," he ordered her. As she moved her body down slightly, he immediately began prodding around in Katharine's private parts. Without speaking to her, he stuck the instrument way up and caused her to cry out. Reflexively, she arched her body away from him.

"I'm using this to open and scrape out your womb. It'll be over in a few minutes."

Soon, it felt like her insides were being torn apart. *I haven't ever felt like this before*, she thought, terrified. She was gripping the sheets at the side of the table and finally blurted out, "Stop, I can't take this anymore. You're ripping out my insides."

"Of course, I am, my dear. That's what you wanted, isn't it? I mean, you want me to take care of your problem and this is what needs to be done. So be quiet, like a good girl, and let me finish."

After several more agonizing minutes, the doctor pronounced that he was done. "No relations for several days, unless you want to get an infection," he mumbled as he exited the room.

Katharine's stomach felt like it was in knots and the room began to spin around. In spite of that, she was desperate to leave immediately, so she lifted herself up off the table and pulled her clothes on as quickly as she could.

She hurried through the alleyway and, forgetting about the stench, took a deep breath and almost spilled the contents of her stomach.

She walked a few blocks and waited for the streetcar, again feeling nauseated and faint. She held onto the lamp post and instinctively felt wetness on her undergarments. "Ma'am, are you all right?" she heard someone say.

"Yes, yes, I'm fine, thank you," she replied as she heard the bell, then saw the trolley car pull forward.

A man stepped back to allow her to board, then she dropped the tokens into the box and took the first seat available. Feeling weak, she silently hoped her stop would come quickly. As the streetcar raced along, then halted abruptly at the next stop, Katharine felt a tingling at her mouth, like she was going to empty her stomach all over her lap.

A short while later, she looked up as the trolley was passing the storefront where Michael's studio used to be. Now, it was a dress shop, with no hint of ever having been anything else. Feelings of loneliness consumed her. For a brief moment, she was back in his arms, listening to his gentle murmurs.

"Broad and Pollock," the conductor shouted. Relieved, she stood up and in horror saw the red blotch that she had left on the seat. She quickly disembarked, hoping that the stain remained hidden in the folds of her dress.

She struggled to make it home, taking one step at a time. At the end of the block, she leaned and allowed the side of a building to hold her upright, as she tried to catch her breath. When she reached her street, Katharine found renewed strength with her house in sight. Walking through the doorway, she placed her bonnet on the hat rack and laid her handbag down on the chair. As she started upstairs to her bedroom, Harry came in from the kitchen and, noticing her pale complexion, said, "You all right, Katharine? You don't look so good."

"Yes, well, I don't feel so good. I went to have my period

brought on by a doctor." Katharine, still dizzy, gritted her teeth as she recalled how patronizing the doctor had been.

Harry exclaimed, "You what? Oh, Katharine, let me help you upstairs to your room." He gently assisted her up the steps to her room at the far end of the hallway.

As he helped to lie her down, he could see that she had already soiled her under things and the blood was starting to seep through her dress.

"I'll be fine. Don't dote on me, Harry. Just leave me be and let me rest. All's I need is a rest and I'll be fine."

"Katharine, this is serious. We need to call a doctor or get some help," he pleaded with her.

"Well, a doctor is why I'm so sick. This never happened with the midwife. I thought a doctor would know more about what to do. Guess I was wrong. . . ."

"I'm going to get the doctor. . . ." he quietly left the room.

"No. No doctor," she yelled to him. "We can be arrested if he realizes what I had done. Get the midwife. She'll know what to do."

Katharine heard Harry race down the steps. It sounded like he knocked over the spittoon by the wall at the bottom of the steps. She heard him speaking. "Your Ma's not well. Going to get the midwife, Johnnie. Lizzie, go up and see to your mother-in-law."

Katharine thought about her son. John had grown into a handsome young man. His dark skin and rugged good looks made most young girls sigh. The brightness of his smile lit up a room. He had fallen in love with a pretty, Catholic girl named Lizzie and one night, their romance had gone a little too far and she had gotten pregnant. Not knowing what to do, the young couple confided in Katharine who had strongly encouraged them to go to the local midwife to "take care of the problem."

Katharine remembered her daughter-in-law's reaction. Lizzie was horrified. "I'm not going to take care of the problem. This is our baby. We're going to get married." Since John was not Catholic, they had to get married in the back of the rectory under the disapproving eyes of the parish priest.

Upstairs in the bedroom, Lizzie asked Katharine, "Can I get you a glass of water?"

"No, no. How's the baby doing?" she asked.

"Fine, growing, eight pounds already," she responded.

"Get my son, would you? I want to talk to him before the midwife gets here and before I pass out."

Moments later, John quietly walked in and saw that his mother's eyes were closed. Her skin was so pale and her body seemed so still. As he walked closer to the bed, the floor under him creaked and she opened her eyes in an instant.

"Johnnie, don't scare me like that."

"Sorry, Ma. What's wrong? You're white as a ghost."

"I went to have my period brought on," she blurted out. "There's so much blood here, seems he brought on the last ten periods, for goodness sake. Johnnie, if something happens to me, would you promise me something?"

"Sure, Ma, what is it?"

"Would you make sure your father doesn't throw Walter out? He'd have nowhere to stay and someone needs to take care of him. Would you make sure he's taken care of?"

"Ma, please. . . ."

Katharine could hear the stampede of footsteps coming up the long stairway. Immediately, she could see the local midwife and Harry right behind her. Annie approached Katharine.

"I wouldn't be in this condition if you had just done what I had asked."

"Katharine, I had good reason for not. . . ." The midwife was interrupted as Ruth rushed into the room.

"Ma, what's going on?" Ruth was now almost nine years old, with a dark head of hair and a beautiful fair complexion.

"I'm fine. You go downstairs and stay with Lizzie." The small girl, frown on her face, stood still, making no attempt to move.

"Go on, Ruth. Downstairs," Katharine urged.

"Come on, honey," Harry said and he took the child's hand in his own.

15

1 Cor. 6:19

May, 1982

"The Mass is ended, go in the Peace of Christ," the priest proclaimed.

'Thanks be to God," the congregation replied.

Emily made the sign of the cross and remembered that she needed to stop and ask her pastor about NFP teachers. She wished that Father Ben, the priest who would be officiating at their wedding, had been available during the last several weeks. Unfortunately for Emily, he had been away on holidays. He always seemed to be in a good mood.

Now she knew that she would have to speak to the elderly, somewhat grouchy, priest after Mass. She waited in line in the foyer of the church behind four people who had stopped to talk to him. As the minutes ticked by, she tapped her foot nervously and flipped back her long feathered hair.

Finally, she was next in line, and when the person in front of her moved, she looked up at him and asked, "Father, I'm wondering if you could tell me the name of a Natural Family Planning teacher. My fiancé and I want to take classes before we get married."

"Natural Family Planning? Oh, you mean rhythm?"

"I think it's called NFP now. Do you know of any teachers?"

"Not offhand. You know, that issue is really up to your conscience."

"Thanks." Disappointed, Emily prepared to leave. She really had expected that he would refer her to someone. "Now what?" she mumbled. Emily's eyes squinted as the sun began streaming in through the small windows onto a brochure rack. She walked over and casually scanned the information. "Charismatic Renewal," "Engaged Encounter," "Divorced Catholics." There didn't appear to be any brochures on NFP.

Emily turned around just as the sun was shining through the small window. Blinding her, she tried to escape the light and saw that the sun was illuminating an area behind several other pamphlets. She reached back and lifted up what appeared to be a green brochure. It was entitled, " Natural Family Planning, Good News About Birth Control."

She let out a huge sigh of relief. For many weeks, she had been searching for information at the library and doctor's office. Why had it been so difficult to find any information on NFP? She flipped the brochure over and read the names of the teaching couples listed. Slipping it into her pocket, she walked through the church doorway and started her short journey home.

Emily's mind wandered to the conversation that she had had with Jason a few months before. He talked of "postponing sex even after marriage." She had to admit that she was worried. She couldn't believe how strongly he felt about not using contraception. He had said, "I wish we didn't have to physically join for the first time with a piece of latex between us." Really, when she thought about it, she shouldn't have been so surprised. *How many men nowadays would even have insisted on waiting until marriage to have sex?*

However, the more that she thought about it, the more it sounded intensely romantic. Though she wasn't quite sure, she finally made the decision to trust her husband-to-be and do her best to find out how they could use NFP.

Reaching home, she ran upstairs to her bedroom, then she scanned through the NFP brochure. Still unsure whether this method would actually work for them, Emily began studying the information in earnest. With all her unanswered questions, she could only hope that this would indeed be 'good news.'

Under the section, "What is involved in Fertility Awareness," Emily read: "During each cycle a woman normally becomes fertile and then naturally infertile. As this happens, her body provides certain signs or symptoms which indicate her fertility or infertility. Couples can learn to observe, record and interpret these signs with a very high degree of accuracy. They can then use this awareness either to plan or postpone a baby accordingly."

Okay, that seems simple enough.

Several paragraphs later, there was a section entitled, "How Effective is Natural Family Planning?" She began reading: "Various studies have shown that well-instructed couples can achieve effectiveness rates at the 99 percent level." Emily shook her head. She found it difficult to believe that this method could be so effective. If that was the case, why hadn't she heard about NFP before Jason told her about it last year? Last week, when she had asked her doctor about it, he had said, "Well, it's a great method to use if you want to get pregnant, but it's not very effective in avoiding pregnancy." If this method worked so well, why didn't her doctor have accurate information about it?

Under the section "Can NFP Work with Irregular Cycles," Emily read the following: "Modern NFP assumes that every woman is irregular. The rare occurrence of multiple ovulations offers no problems because these ovulations occur within a very short time of each other." That piece of information allowed Emily to feel more at ease.

She dropped the brochure onto her bureau and focused on how exciting and memorable the next few weeks would be.

It was hard to believe that in less than a month, she and Jason would never have to be parted again. They had been carrying on a long-distance romance for three years and it seemed like the longest, drawn out and somewhat painful period of her life.

She imagined what it was going to be like to be married to a perfectionist. She had already seen glimpses of Jason's near perfectionist attitudes about all kinds of things, like music, writing, painting. . .even sex. She recalled a phone conversation a few weeks ago in which he asked her to try to stop talking loudly. He had said, "You know, Em, I like the image I have of

Jesus. I mean, the way I picture it, Jesus wasn't a yeller and I doubt if he screamed the word of God all over the place. He was said to be gentle, you know? And he was forgiving and caring too. That's what I'd like to be like. I'll never be perfect, Em, but I figure if I shoot for perfection and always try my best, I might get a 70 or 80 percent."

She knew that it would be challenging at times. However, it was going to be heaven being with Jason, the person she loved most of all in the world, the person who in less than a month, would be joined to her in the sacrament of marriage.

"Hey, Em?" she heard her mother call from downstairs.

"Yeah, Mom?"

"Get the phone. It's Carrie."

"Okay."

Picking up the phone, she said, "Hello."

"Hi, Em. You must be getting nervous now. Only a month to your wedding," her childhood friend, Carrie, said.

"No, I'm not really nervous, just excited and happy."

"Did you get my RSVP?"

"Sure. I'm glad to hear you'll be coming."

"Wouldn't miss it, Em. We've been friends for a long time. I just wish we kept more in touch. I haven't talked to you in two years."

"Yeah, I know. We've both been busy."

"Hey," Carrie laughed. "When I talked to you a few years ago, you still hadn't had sex yet, Em."

"That's right."

"Well?"

"Well what?"

"Well, what do you think about sex?" Carrie whispered over the phone.

"What are you talking about?"

"Well, you guys have had sex by now, haven't you? I mean, nowadays everybody does it before they're married."

"No, Carrie, we haven't. We're going to wait until we're married."

"Are you kidding? Em, you can't marry a guy unless you know that the two of you are sexually compatible. You still have time."

"To tell you the truth, I would've gladly given my virginity to him years ago, but Jason has been pretty adamant. Besides, I'm beginning to realize, after all this time, that it is the right thing to wait."

"Look, Em, you may be in for a lot of trouble if you find out you're not compatible in bed."

"No, Carrie. Besides, this whole waiting experience helped me to realize what a great gift sex will be for us after we're married."

"I don't know."

"Recently, I made a list of all the disadvantages of having sex before marriage and all the advantages. And I could only come up with one advantage to having sex before marriage and that's how good it would feel. I came up with at least ten disadvantages, like getting pregnant."

"Even if you got pregnant now, Em, no one would know. I mean, you're getting married in a month."

"I would know and Jason would know, and most importantly, God would know."

"All right. Hey, you're going to love the wedding present I got for you and Jason."

"Just having you come to the wedding is great, Carrie."

"Listen, I've got to go, Em. See you at the wedding."

"Bye."

Several weeks later, Jason and Emily sat together at the far edge of the sofa in the den. "In only two days, we will be husband and wife. I can't help but be disappointed that we will not be consummating our marriage on our wedding night. I mean, why do I have to be in the fertile time?"

"Try to remember that our fertility is a great gift from God, Em. But we have already decided that we would avoid pregnancy for the time being and that means abstaining in the fertile time."

"Yes, I know."

"This is the right thing, Em. We have our whole lives to share and lots of time for that kind of intimacy only days after we're married."

"I know."

"Hey, Em?"

She looked up at him, her eyes making no attempt to hide their disappointment.

"Would you still love me if we weren't able to have sex?" he asked in a soft-spoken tone of voice.

"What kind of question is that?"

"Well, if something happened to me and we weren't able to have sex, would you still love me?"

"Of course I would. That's a ridiculous question."

"Em, I look forward to intimacy and making love perhaps more than you do, but our marriage, our spiritual oneness, is far more important than our physical oneness. We would still love each other without the physical, right?"

"But we've waited so long."

"I know we have, but we can't focus only on that aspect of our marriage. I mean, it's only going to constitute a small percentage of our married life, right?"

"So, what's your point?"

"It's good for us to look forward to it and to anticipate having children, but we need to think about the fact that we will be together, forever."

"All right." Emily, somewhat frustrated, stared at him and again wondered how in the world she ended up with this man. She had to admit that she had been moping around, complaining about the fact that they had decided to wait to consummate their marriage, instead of spending all her time thinking of the fact that they would never again have to say goodbye.

"Hey, Em, I almost forgot to tell you about the horrible dream I had last night."

"What was so horrible about it?"

"Well, all I remember is seeing you on a stretcher in a hospital with all kinds of tubes coming out of you, and you were hooked up to a machine. The doctors told me that you were probably not going to live through the night. Well, in the dream, I just collapsed and felt like my world had ended. I don't know what I would do if that happened in real life."

"If it did happen, I would hope that you would be strong. Remember what you told me a month ago in one of your letters, that if one of us died, whoever was left would have to be strong."

"Yeah, I remember that, Em. Being in love with someone is one of the most wonderful experiences in the world, but it sure can make a person vulnerable. I mean, if I could, I would give up my life for you rather than see you die, especially at this age."

"I don't know what my life would have been like these past three years without you, Jason. It's been impossible being apart from you and it's been hard to be grateful for your presence in my life when you have been so far away from me at times. But now, we have the rest of our lives together, whatever that may bring."

She laid her head on the side of his shoulder as he leaned down to kiss the top of her head. Emily loved the way he smelled: no cologne, no aftershave, just him. He began stroking her hair, then started quietly humming a tune, stopping after about fifteen notes.

"That's beautiful,"she said. "Please don't stop."
 The notes became words:

My young love said to me
My mother won't mind
And my father won't slight you
For your lack of kine
And she stepped away from me
And this she did say
It will not be long love
Till our wedding day.

She stepped away from me
And she moved through the fair
And fondly I watched her
Move here and move there
Then she made her way homeward
With one star awake
As the swan in the evening
Moves over the lake.

I dreamt it last night
That my true love came in
So softly she entered
That her feet made no din
Then she came close beside me
And this she did say
It will not be long love
Till our wedding day.

"I can't imagine ever loving you any more than I do now. When you sing to me like that, my heart just absorbs the words and wants to scream out how much I love you." Emily paused. "I've never heard that song before. What's it called?"

"'She Moved Through the Fair.' Liam and I sing it sometimes. It's a traditional Celtic folk song."

"It's beautiful."

"In only a few days, it will be our wedding day, Em. We've waited a long time for this, haven't we?"

Emily nodded.

He leaned over and kissed her.

Does life ever get any better than this?

16

Tobit 8:7

May 22, 1982

Emily awoke at dawn and took her temperature. It was still low. Now it was official. They would be waiting at least a week to consummate their marriage.

Moving toward the window, she also decided that the pouring rain wasn't going to destroy the day on which she and Jason would be married and begin their life together. Despite the drizzle, her heart was bursting with excitement and joy.

She sat on the side of the bed and spent a few minutes studying her room. Though the walls were now bare, the tape marks reminded her of the posters of Shaun Cassidy which she hung as wallpaper a few years ago. Now, her bedroom with its storehouse of memories would remain here as she left to begin her new life with Jason in Canada.

The small window beside her bed was open slightly and the cool, damp breeze was blowing her curtains back and forth. Emily was somewhat disappointed that it was raining, but she savored the fragrance on a rainy day, the smell of earth, the crisp clean aroma of nature's shower.

Her eyes wandered to the photo of her and her dad on the bedside table. Though she had packed most of her belongings for the move to Canada, she had kept this small picture displayed. *I miss you, Dad. I wish you could have given me away today.*

Downstairs in the kitchen, she was surprised to find her mother doing dishes. "The baby's still asleep?" Emily asked.

Her mom nodded.

"She's got quite an exciting day ahead of her," Emily observed.

"You won't be able to get any photos taken outside today," Becky said rather somberly as she glanced outside.

"Yeah, I noticed."

Soon the house became a hubbub of excitement, as people started to rouse.

Flowers were delivered just as Susan, Becky and the other bridesmaids began to dress. Alone in her bedroom, Emily pulled on her gown, with a long-sleeved lace bodice, a white satin skirt and long train. She turned around to look in the full-length mirror. The young bride certainly understood why white was such a perfect color for a wedding dress. Bright and feminine, it was as if she was wearing her joy.

Susan walked in as Emily was admiring herself in the mirror. "You look very pretty, Em. Here, let me button up the back for you."

"Thanks."

As she continued to gaze in the mirror, she also felt empathy for 19th century woman who wore dresses like this all the time. Emily couldn't imagine life without comfortable blue jeans.

Carefully maneuvering down the staircase, Emily found it difficult to walk. Reaching the hallway, she stood still to allow her mother to attach the veil to her head while keeping the thin material for the front of her face fixed back. After a few minutes, they all walked out to the living room for photos. When she exited the hallway, there was a gasp from the visitors staying at her home.

"Emily, you look beautiful," she heard someone say.

Another relative commented, "You look like the bride on the top of a wedding cake!" Everyone laughed.

She turned around again, this time in the living room and studied herself in the mirror above the television. Her appearance wasn't the whole point of this day. But how many times had she dreamt of this moment? It felt so surreal, like something from a television show. However, she knew that it wasn't a dream or a show, as she tried to appreciate every moment of the day.

Arriving at the church, Emily was grateful that the rain had stopped for a brief time and she didn't have to endure the downpour. She stood at the side of the car while her sister helped to carry her train. If one looked around, the day appeared gloomy and dull. What a contrast to the bright way her heart was feeling at that moment. She savored the intoxicating fragrance of the rain and the aroma of her fresh flower bouquet.

Once inside the foyer, as Becky slipped the veil over Emily's face, she reflected on the significance of what that meant. Traditionally, the veil covering a bride's face symbolized virginity. She was a virgin, but how many times had they allowed themselves to be in tempting situations? Emily felt somewhat unworthy. Years ago, she would have gladly given up that one-time gift, and now it seemed so right that she had waited. As Jason had asked her a few months ago, "Em, do you think we will ever regret waiting until marriage to have sex?" Emily had answered, "Probably not." Jason responded, "What about if we go ahead and have sex? Do you think we would ever regret not waiting?" She had hesitated, then said, "Probably." That simple conversation seemed to put things into perspective for Emily. As difficult as it had been, they had waited, and now, in just a few moments, they would be married, in the eyes of God, in front of their many relatives and friends as witnesses.

Emily casually glanced at the wall display dedicated to St. Maria Goretti, the saint for whom the church was named. She reflected on the irony of getting married in a church named for a girl who gave up her life rather than be raped by a young man. The night before, after the rehearsal, while Emily was waiting to go to confession, she spent several minutes reading the story. Though she had been attending this church for many years, she had never bothered to read about the young girl from Italy who had lived a life of purity and service, then died defending her chastity. Emily had read that, as the young man approached Maria with a knife, she told him, "No, Allesandro, it is a sin." Enraged and overcome with lust and passion, he stabbed her 14 times. Even as she lay dying, she forgave him unconditionally.

The young man eventually repented and converted. Then, after spending many years in jail, he asked forgiveness from Maria's mother. He subsequently joined a religious order as a lay brother, and both he and Maria's mother attended her canonization ceremony in Rome.

Emily had to admit, that up until several months ago, she had been careless with the gift of her sexuality, the virtue of chastity. Placing herself in an awkward position with Eric, then offering to have sex with Ray, even tempting her own beloved many times caused her to be ashamed and sorrowful. She had gone to confession the night before, but as she heard the organist begin to play, she made a vow to God that she would never again treat God's gift of sexual expression so callously.

As the Bridal March echoed through the church, each bridesmaid moved forward. Emily, along with her mother and stepfather, stepped forward until they were ready to walk down the aisle.

Smiling broadly, she gazed at Jason, dressed impeccably in his navy blue tux. How handsome he looked. As she moved closer, she could see that his eyes were watering. Trembling, he reached for her hand and winked, then smiled, his left eyebrow cocked. They stood before Father Ben, who would be celebrating the Nuptial Mass.

"In the name of the Father and of the Son and of the Holy Spirit. . . ." Following the readings, Father Ben stood up to proclaim the Holy Gospel (John 15:16):

> *"It was not you who chose me,*
> *but I who chose you and appointed you*
> *to go and bear fruit."*

As Father was reading these words, Emily thought of the fruit that they would hopefully bear during their marriage, not the least of which would be the fruit of children.

After the Gospel, Father began his homily. "As I looked at the weather today, I thought that we might have a 'wetting' feast." His pun was politely appreciated as a few people chuckled.

"They say when it rains on a couple on their wedding day,

that's a symbol there will be bright days afterwards. That's one point of optimism on a scattered day like today.

"I thought of the idea that what we have here are, in a sense, extended pen-pals, love at long distance, where the connection is more of the mind and spirit. Isn't that in many ways what love is primarily about?

"I was rather impressed with the cover of this young couple's marriage booklet. It says, 'Let Us Always Discover the Love in Each Other' with a simple outline — drawn by the groom — of Jesus touching a man and a woman. It's an excellent expression of the mysterious element of marriage where you see the grace of God in the marriage relationship. You see God's presence in each other, a growing, changing one, reaching out, then becoming three: you, your spouse and God as one family.

"This is the element of what the mystery of marriage is all about. It's mentioned various times in Scripture: what God has joined, man must not divide. God joins them but joins each of them to Him. If you're looking for God, then look to your spouse to discover the love in each other."

After some preliminary prayers, the priest invited both Jason and Emily to profess their vows, which they had memorized. Taking Emily's hand, with a strong, clear voice, Jason said: "I, Jason, take you, Emily, to be my wife. I promise to be true to you in good times and in bad, in sickness and in health. I will love you and honor you all the days of my life." There were no microphones, but his voice was loud and clear.

Emily gazed into his eyes and smiled. Though her voice sounded young, she spoke with the confidence of a young adult. "I, Emily, take you, Jason, to be my husband. I promise to be true to you in good times and in bad, in sickness and in health. I will love you and honor you all the days of my life." She wished that she could shout out her vows from a mountain top, but for now, the modern, in-the-round church sufficed.

After the priest blessed the rings, Jason placed the ring on Emily's finger.

"Emily, take this ring as a sign of my love and fidelity. In the name of the Father and of the Son and of the Holy Spirit."

Emily then placed Jason's ring on his finger as she said the same prayer.

The priest leaned over and whispered to Jason, "You may kiss your bride." Jason lifted the veil over Emily's head. Smiling, he leaned down and kissed her lips.

A short while later, after the newly-married couple had received Holy Communion, Jason winked at Emily, then stood up to perform the song that he had written for their wedding. They had kept this a secret until now and as he stood up, the guests started whispering to each other. She heard one elderly person remark, "Is he leaving already?" The murmuring continued until Jason picked up his guitar. With Liam, he sang the song that he wrote:

> *Here we are, close to our friends,*
> *Close friends forever amen.*
> *Gathering, before our dear God,*
> *Our God forever, Amen.*
> *Here we are together at last,*
> *Together, Forever, Amen.*

Liam sang the questions representing the voice of God and Jason responded:

> *And her hand does she give forever?*
> *Yes, my Lord, she does.*
> *And her hand do you take forever?*
> *Yes, my Lord, you know.*

> *If there are none would stand in our way,*
> *Peace, forever, Amen.*
> *And if our God would grant us this plan,*
> *Peace, forever, Amen.*
> *Here we are, together at last,*
> *Together forever Amen.*

What followed was another series of questions from God, sung by Liam, as Jason answered for both Bride and Groom. Then came a reprise of the first verse again causing a swirling overlapped effect between the two melodies:

> *And will you love Me?*
> *Yes, my Lord, we will.*
> *And will you love each other?*
> *Yes, my Lord, we will.*
> *And will you love your children?*
> *Yes, my Lord, we will.*
> *And will you love all men?*
> *Yes, my Lord, we'll try*
> *Yes, my Lord, we will.*

Emily so wished that he would keep singing 'their song.' She cherished the words that symbolized the end of their separation and the beginning of their new life together. The two men's voices echoed throughout the huge church as if each line refused to come to an end.

Oh how perfectly they are singing. She had never felt closer to Jason, or to God, than during their wedding Mass. She wished that this moment would go on forever.

The song now finished, Jason sat down next to his new wife. After Father said the closing prayer, they made their way down the aisle to the back of the church where the wedding party formed a receiving line to greet the guests, many of whom had traveled from Canada for the wedding.

Later, at the reception, as they were visiting each table of family members and friends, Emily was surprised to see Great Aunt Ruth talking with Aunt Sally. A few days before, her aunt had told her that Ruth had recently had surgery and wouldn't be able to attend the wedding.

Emily watched as Aunt Sally whispered something to Aunt Ruth and Ruth laughed out loud. She was an attractive woman, with a beautiful smile and surprisingly few wrinkles. Emily tried to calculate how old she would be now, "1982 minus 1909, that's 73, or almost 73 since she was born in September." There wasn't a gray hair out of place and her fashionable calf-length pink dress framed her still slim body well. Emily wouldn't have been surprised if her great-aunt had been a professional dancer in her younger days as she had shapely long legs and grace in movement.

Aunt Sally looked past Ruth and caught Emily's eye. She motioned for her to come and speak with Aunt Ruth.

"Hi Aunt Ruth," Emily said in her most perky high-pitched voice. She felt slightly awkward, almost like she was meeting a celebrity.

"Hi, dear, you look lovely."

"Thank you. How are you doing?"

"Just fine." Aunt Ruth slipped Emily an envelope and kissed her cheek.

"Thank you so much for coming. By the way, did Aunt Sally tell you that she gave me your parents' old ledgers from the music store?"

"Yes, she did."

"Aunt Sal told me that she was going to throw them in the trash. I'm glad she didn't."

"You know, dear, it's important to connect with one's past. There's much to be learned from discovering how your ancestors lived and what they were like, even from boring old bookkeeping records."

"Well, I think it's neat to have something that belonged to your mother and my great-grandmother."

"I think it's neat too, dear," Aunt Ruth replied, sounding out of character using Emily's vernacular.

"What was your mother like?"

"Well, she certainly had a strong-willed personality. And she was quite small, like you, dear."

"Yes, Aunt Sal told me that. And your father was quite the character too, I hear?"

"Oh, yes, my father was a remarkable man. He was quiet, but he had a loving and kind personality. I remember that he used to sit me on his knee when I was about four or five and he would bump his knee up and down and tell me that I was riding a horse. I enjoyed that special time with him."

"That's really neat." Emily was overwhelmed at the poignancy of picturing Harry with Ruth on his knee and her giggling and laughing.

"Well, dear, I know you have many people to visit and I won't keep you."

"Thank you so much, Aunt Ruth, for coming. I know you're recuperating from surgery."

"Oh, that. It was nothing, really. Besides, I never miss an opportunity to get out on the dance floor and do the Twist."

"You do the Twist?"

"I sure do. It's one of my favorite dances."

Emily laughed and kissed her great-aunt on the cheek.

Jason, who had been standing behind Emily, now came and stood beside her as they both said good bye and thank you. "Wow, that was so incredible, Jay."

"She seems like a interesting lady."

Toward the end of the reception, she stood and watched the people dancing and enjoying themselves. Many of the guests had formed a circle and were doing the "Hokey Pokey." Carrie pulled Emily's brother, Matthew, into the circle. Matt appeared to be uncooperative, but he was smiling and laughing all the same.

Rose, Evan and Liam, as well as Jason's family and the others from Canada, looked to be enjoying themselves in the large circle of dancers.

During another amusing moment, Emily watched as Jason and his brother danced the Y.M.C.A.

"Now, that was worth the price of admission," she said out loud. "I must buy my husband some dance lessons," she jokingly said to her mom, standing beside her. Jason caught her eye, walked over and leaned down to kiss her. "My wife is a beautiful bride."

"And my husband is a handsome groom."

For a moment, it seemed, amidst the loud music and chatter of the crowd, like they were actually alone, connecting in a way only a husband and wife, married sacramentally in the eyes of God, could connect.

And through it all, Emily now felt changed, for she was no longer just Emily. Her heart was filled with joy, for her soul was now joined to the one person in the world she loved more than any other human being.

All those times early in their relationship when she had questioned why they were waiting to consummate their relationship, even more recently when she was doubtful, she couldn't imagine that their relationship would ever be more intimately connected than it was before they were married. Now, they were sacramentally married, 'one' in the eyes of God, and it became so clear why they had waited to have sex. It was different. They were both changed.

Even a few months ago, she would try to rationalize and say that if they had decided to have sex, it wouldn't be any different than when they were married. Now, Emily realized that she couldn't have been more wrong. Their marriage wasn't just a piece of paper. It was a spiritual, God-given bond that now cemented her to him.

She tried to relish every moment such as that one, every comment, every smile from that day. She promised herself that she would remember the feeling of joy that radiated from everyone involved in their celebration. Nothing about the reception seemed like a 'run of the mill' family reunion. It was like everyone was united, all the guests from Canada and all those from the States, two similar but decidedly different cultures. Emily knew that she would treasure those moments forever.

Once inside their hotel room, Emily noticed that the management had left a rose and a bottle of iced champagne on their bed. "Too bad this will go to waste, eh?" she laughed.

"Yeah, too bad. That small sip at the bridal toast was enough for me. How about you?"

Emily nodded.

After getting into pajamas, they laid together on the huge king-sized bed.

"I still can't help but feel cheated out of this night. I mean, we've waited for so long."

"But we're together, Em. We're together *forever* and we never have to be apart again. What's another week or so?"

She kissed him in a prolonged gesture, wishing that they didn't have to exercise self-control. "Are you sure that you don't want to consummate tonight? Would it be so bad to conceive a baby?"

"Of course, I *want* to and no, it wouldn't be bad to have a baby. But we've been through this. We've never spent more than 25 days together at one time. I just turned 20. If you get pregnant now, you'll have to work and leave the baby or I'll have to quit school."

"I know."

Jason continued: "Think of it this way. We have the rest of our lives for sharing ourselves sexually and becoming one physically. We are going to be together forever. Hopefully, we'll have lots of kids. We have so much to look forward to. There's absolutely no reason to feel sorry for one's self."

Snuggling close to her new husband, Emily reflected on the irony that she was spending her honeymoon evening in the arms of her beloved, preparing for a night that would not include the consummation of their marriage. As a teenager, she never expected that she would be a virgin on her wedding night and now, she would remain one for at least seven more days.

17

1 Cor. 4:5

June, 1919

Katharine lifted the tuba and brought it back to the supply room. She was sure that the teenager who had just come into the store would not be buying the instrument. He had only wanted to hold it, deposit his spit in the mouthpiece, and make noise. She knew it all along and she should have just told him no. Katharine abhorred cleaning out the fluids from the mouthpiece on any of these horns, but that was part of the drudgery of this particular job.

Hearing the jingle of the little bells on the front door, she quickly finished her task, wiped her hands on her apron, and scrambled back into the store. She acted surprised to see a police officer standing at the door.

"Afternoon, ma'am." He was a tall man, but he looked like he was in high school, with a baby face and a slight case of acne.

"Good afternoon, Officer. May I help you?"

"Well, ma'am, are you the proprietor of this establishment?"

"Yes, I am. I'm Katharine Clayman. My husband and I own this music store."

"Well, ma'am, we've had a complaint about your store."

"What kind of complaint?"

"Well. . . ." he started. He was young and obviously inexperienced in calls of this nature. "Uh. . .that you have inappropriate literature available, illegal literature."

"Now, just what kind of inappropriate literature are you talking about?" she asked, hoping that it would make the young police officer feel more uncomfortable.

"Well, ma'am, I. . .uh. . .you know, the kind that talks about preventing, well, uh. . . ."

"Officer, you may look around yourself, if you'd like. I don't have anything to hide. There is nothing inappropriate or illegal on my premises, I can assure you."

He walked around the store, then looked behind the counter.

"So, ma'am, if you did have this literature, and if I was. . . ."

"Was what, Officer?"

Avoiding eye contact with Katharine, the young man continued, "Well, what I mean is, if perhaps, say, my wife and I needed this information. Sarah, my wife, has had three babies in four years. She's exhausted."

How can this young man have three children? He looks younger than Johnnie.

He stopped and quickly glanced at her face. "I'm sorry, ma'am, for bothering you. It's important to check these things out." "Just a minute, Officer." Katharine hesitated, but his awkward manner convinced her that he could be trusted. "I need to be assured that I will not be arrested."

"You can be assured, ma'am. You have my word."

Katharine nodded, then reached inside to the back of the cash box and pulled out a Family Limitation brochure. Handing it to the officer, she looked straight into his eyes. "It would be helpful if the police would just leave my establishment alone. Can you arrange that?"

"Yes, ma'am, I probably can." He tipped his cap and turned around. "Good day, ma'am."

As he exited the store, Katharine again reached into the very back of the cash box and took out the 30 or so pamphlets entitled "Family Limitation," written by Margaret Sanger.

Katharine so admired Mrs. Sanger. After all, she was trying to make women free, just like men had always been free. Ever since it was written in 1916, she kept copies of the Family Limitation brochure for women she knew who needed 'help' in that area. She didn't care that possessing this literature was illegal. Katharine realized that if she were caught handing them out, she would be arrested. She'd also had several abortions, and that was illegal as well. After her horrible experience last year, she was convinced that she needed to make this information more accessible to women, and that this was the solution.

Until then, she was grateful for whatever support she could obtain from the law, like the promise from the young police officer. Even Mrs. Sanger had been arrested countless times and that didn't stop her. Katharine especially admired her newspaper called "The Woman Rebel." The slogan under the title said, "No Gods, No Masters." The first issue printed back in 1914 talked about the "prevention of conception, the slavery of motherhood etc." She remembered thinking, what can I do to support this?

It seemed simple enough, but she agreed to always keep the Family Limitation brochure on hand for women in need. She had heard Mrs. Sanger speak in New York City a few years back. She was a small woman, like herself, but she spoke with conviction. During her speech, she gave her credo of Women's Rights: "The Right to be Lazy. The Right to be an Unmarried Mother. The Right to Create. The Right to Destroy. The Right to Love and the Right to Live."

Her thoughts turned to her son.   Now married and the father of a toddler, John and his wife Lizzie were expecting another child.

Katharine remembered the moment that Johnnie and his girlfriend had announced that she was in the "family way." Ignoring the girlfriend, Katharine winced as she looked at John's disappointed eyes and, like most mothers, wanted to erase the regret. "Johnnie, Lizzie can go to the midwife. This can be fixed, you know," she blurted out.

Lizzie's big brown eyes had widened and she had glared at John with an open mouth.

When Katharine had met Lizzie for the first time, she had remembered thinking that her son could do a lot better with regard to acquiring a wife. Though she was pretty in a plain way, Lizzie was big-boned, not fat, but certainly not slim. She came from an Irish immigrant family in a low-class section of the city.

"No, Mom, Lizzie and I have decided to get married. We love each other."

"Yes, sure you do, but if you take care of it, then you won't have to get married, not yet anyway. You're both so young."

Her thoughts jumped to months later when her granddaughter, Sally, was born. Despite her prodding Johnnie to "take care of the problem," when she held her newborn granddaughter, a flood of emotions welled up inside her. For the first time in many years, she became teary-eyed and tried to hide it by saying, "Now, just don't you two expect me to do any babysitting. I've already raised my kids." Then she had laughed.

Now, Sally was 18 months old and Lizzie was due to deliver any day. She had told John that they didn't have to keep having babies every year. John shrugged his shoulders and reminded his mother that Lizzie was Catholic and he wouldn't even discuss the subject with her.

The shrill sound of the music shop phone jolted Katharine. "Hello?"

"Ma, it's me. Lizzie's had to go to the hospital."

"What in the world for? She's just having a baby."

"No. The midwife thinks the baby is already dead. Lizzie has lost a lot of blood. I just wanted to call you. I'm rushing over to the hospital myself."

"Who's taking care of Sally?"

"I dropped her off with Pop. He seems sober. And Ruth is there too. She'll play with Sally until you get home. I need to go. Bye."

Katharine slowly hung up the phone. "This is what happens when you have babies too close together. I warned them. Oh well, what will be will be." Deciding that she should close the store early, she methodically began her nightly routine of counting cash, shutting blinds, putting instruments away.

Amidst the noise and banging of her closing ritual, there was a timid, almost weak, knock at the door. Katharine paused and listened. She had pulled the blinds down over the door and couldn't see if anyone was there. Again, she heard a quiet knock, almost apologetic.

Wiping her hands on her apron, she ran quickly to the door and opened it to find a woman in her twenties, probably from Eastern Europe, from her dark hair and features. "So sorry I bother you," she said with a thick accent of some kind. Her dark hair was partially covered by a scarf.

"I was just closing early because of a family emergency."

"My friend tell me you have paper to help me, how you say, not have baby." The woman's hushed voice continued, "Too many babies, too close, five, all under four. Please, can you help me?"

Katharine nodded, stepped outside, looked up and down the street, then pulled the woman inside and said, "Yes, I have just the paper for you." She walked over to her cash box and picked up a Family Limitation brochure. As she handed it to the woman, Katharine could see that her hands were rough and cracked, probably from washing clothes. "This will help you," Katharine said, sympathetically. "No woman should have to be a slave to her fertility."

"Thank you."

She ushered the woman back outside, finished closing up the store and hurried home.

It seemed like forever for her to walk the five blocks. She ran in the doorway and called, "Harry, Ruth? Where are you?"

"I'm up here, Ma. Sally's with me. I don't know where Pop went."

Katharine sighed. Then she caught sight of Harry's sitting chair in the corner with the spittoon next to it and frowned. Harry had obviously missed the spittoon with his last spittle and it had hardened onto the wall next to the chair. She shuddered.

"Imagine, leaving a year-old baby with an nine-year-old child. That Harry never had a brain in his head." She paused. "Have you eaten yet, Ruth?"

Sensing her mother's consternation, she timidly answered, "No, ma'am, I haven't."

Walking into the kitchen, she opened up the ice box to find some leftover ham and cabbage. She reached under the stove, pulled out a pot and plopped the food into it. "Does she need her diaper changed, Ruth? Something stinks in here."

Ruth peeked into Sally's pants and exclaimed, "It's only wet."

"Ruth, did your brother bring any diapers with him when he dropped off Sally?"

"I don't think so, ma'am. He looked pretty sad. I think he might've been crying."

Katharine sighed. *Johnnie's going to have to learn to deal with death. It's part of life.*

A few hours later, Katharine tucked Ruth and Sally into bed together. "Make sure she stays next to the wall, you hear, Ruth?"

Ruth nodded and rolled over next to the almost asleep Sally. Standing in the hallway, outside Ruth's room, Katharine gazed down at them.

Watching her granddaughter sleep, so peaceful, her lips puckered, her small hand nestled between the bed and her face, Katharine felt gratitude in a profound and deep way. In a rare moment, her face softened as she recalled how Sally called her "Da-mom." Only a year old, this toddler, her first grandchild, seemed to emanate warmth, beauty and goodness.

Hearing the front door open, then close, she walked down a few steps to the top of the staircase.

"Oh, Johnnie, you're back. I just put Sally to bed here. She's fine. What's going on with Lizzie?" she asked as she descended the stairs.

He took off his hat and forced himself to collapse on the couch. His face was etched with sorrow and his dark eyes were red and puffy. "Oh, Ma, Lizzie is so sick. She's got something called septicemia. The baby had already died and she got some sort of infection and she's very sick. The doctors told me that she may die. She's unconscious, Ma, and I haven't been able to talk to her."

"Look, Johnnie, things like this happen. Death is just a part of life. When it happens, you've got to deal with it."

"I'm so worried about her. She's my whole life." He dropped his head in his hands and started sobbing, loud, anxious crying that he had held in all day at the hospital.

"Now, now, Johnnie, get a hold of yourself. Just go home and get some sleep. I'll keep Sally here."

He nodded, pulled out his handkerchief to wipe his face, then blew his nose and stood up to leave. With his head down, he opened the door, then walked out without shutting it behind him.

Katharine closed the door behind her son. "I sure hope nothing happens to Lizzie," she said out loud. "Who will take care of Sally? Probably me." She dearly loved her granddaughter but as she got older, her energy level was diminishing and she was doubtful that she would have the stamina or patience to raise her.

Two weeks later, Katharine pushed open her son's door and let herself in. "Johnnie, you home?"

"Yeah, Ma, I'm up here with Lizzie. I'll be down in a few minutes."

Katharine took her hat off and placed it on the hat rack near the door. She looked around at the living room and sighed. *Johnnie certainly isn't the world's best housekeeper.* Clothes were strewn all over the furniture and dirty plates lay on the coffee table.

She heard him racing down the steps before she saw him. Katharine smiled inwardly. *He's still pounding down the steps even after 20 years.*

"How's Lizzie doing?"

"Still weak, but she's getting her strength back and finally starting to eat. Her heart is broken, though. We've named the baby Dorothy."

Katharine kept silent. *Naming a dead baby doesn't make any sense to me, but I guess one has to cope in any way one can.*

"The doctor told us that Lizzie shouldn't get pregnant for at least a year, maybe not ever again, after how sick she was. She almost died." Her son's voice was hushed, tired.

"Johnnie," Katharine paused. "You and Lizzie need to be responsible. You need to do the right thing here. You can't be having any more babies. One is enough work for anyone to handle."

Katharine reached into her purse and pulled out a Family Limitation brochure. "Here, take this. It's a pamphlet which outlines all the ways a couple can avoid getting pregnant."

John shifted uncomfortably in his seat, his eyes downcast. Katharine could tell that her son felt awkward, but to her way of thinking, he needed this information.

"I don't know, Ma. Lizzie's not going to like this," he whispered.

"Look, Johnnie, Lizzie's health is what matters now. You know as well as I do that if she gets pregnant again, she might die. You'd be irresponsible if you let that happen. This information is your only hope to a future."

John hesitated, then accepted the brochure from his mother's hands. He tucked it into his back pocket.

"Thanks, Ma. You're right. If I have anything to say about it, Lizzie won't be having any more babies, at least not right now."

"That is the responsible thing to do, Johnnie."

"Yeah, I guess it is, Ma, I guess it is."

18

Genesis 38:8-10

February 1984

Emily squirmed in her seat as she studied the area in the old building that the Fine Arts students had been assigned for their studios. Jason's area was always messy, with half-finished paintings, drawings, sculptures and prints standing around in a disordered fashion. Emily was afraid to sit on any of the seats for fear of getting paint on herself. She moved her arm to scratch her nose.

"Em, be still."

"I am being still."

"You moved your arm. I'm trying to paint that part of you now and it's not in the position you had it a few minutes ago."

"Can't you just make it up or change it?"

Jason rolled his eyes and sighed. "Em, I need to get this painting completed before Monday."

"Why didn't you finish it before now?"

"Come on, Em. You know I procrastinate."

Emily sighed. "Okay. I'll try to be still." Her eyes lowered to the book that she had been reading while posing for Jason. "A New Life," a pregnancy book, was Jason's gift to her this past Christmas. "Let's talk about having a baby."

"Now? Em, I'm concentrating. I can't do two things at once like you, so please be quiet and we'll discuss it tonight."

Emily sighed.

"Just let me say one more thing, Jay: I'm finding it increasingly more difficult during Phase II. I mean, it's the time I most strongly desire you and we can't have relations since we're still postponing pregnancy."

Jason stopped painting and stared at her with the 'we've been through this before' look.

"Em, babies are a huge responsibility and it would almost entirely fall on your shoulders with my work and university schedule."

"But my heart tells me it's the right time."

"Your hormones are telling you it's the right time. God gave us a brain to make a good decision here, Em. I'm only in my third year of university with two to go. You're supporting us. We both need more time."

Emily remained silent. Though they had grown closer and matured a great deal since their wedding day, she agreed that it was necessary to wait.

Recalling those first few days of marriage, she smiled as she recalled her mother calling each day to ask, "Is it legal yet?"

The physical expression of their sacrament, though awkward at first, was more beautiful than she had imagined, and in no way disappointing. But what Emily did not expect was the deep spiritual bond that she experienced with Jason when they engaged in relations which, in turn, enhanced their pleasure. It was a gradual process of getting to know each other's desires, clarifying their likes and dislikes.

She recalled Carrie's comment about sexual compatibility and the need to have experience before marriage. Even after 19 months, their sex life continued to be pleasurable and emotionally satisfying due, in large part, to their use of NFP and, she believed, their decision to wait until marriage. Abstaining for ten days out of the month definitely kept the spark alive in their sexual relationship.

However, she now began to resent the effectiveness of NFP. She found it ironic when she remembered how little she trusted the method in the first six months of marriage. Near the end of each cycle, she sometimes found herself planning where to put the crib. Then, she would get her period and part of her would be disappointed, as her heart ached to hold a baby in her arms, a child that would be the "fruit of their married love." She understood what Jason was saying about the necessity to grow in maturity, and she also knew that she didn't want to put her child in daycare. Her impatience nagged at her very soul and created this "I want it now mentality," not just about children, but about all things in life.

Once they were married and living together, her desire to be pregnant sometimes began to monopolize her thoughts and feelings. However, if they were going to wait for a baby, then her way of coping was to study every pregnancy and baby book that she could get her hands on.

She watched Jason's face as he continued to focus on his painting of her. As always, he seemed so intense when he was creating something.

"Hey, do you want to see what I've done?"

Emily stood up and walked over to the easel where Jason had worked for nearly two hours creating a piece of art, a representation of her.

She frowned as she studied the canvas. "How come you can't see my face very well?" The way that he painted her face, Emily couldn't see where her eyes ended and her nose began.

"Remember, Em, it's not my intention to create something so perfectly as to be similar to a photograph. I kind of like how the impressionist Monet created works of art. When he painted, in the back of his mind, he was trying to create a general impression, an emotional impact that would move the viewer. That's why he was called an impressionistic painter. He focused on how light reflected off of objects, not on the objects themselves."

Emily stared at him, eyebrows raised. "I love when you talk art, Jay," she said sarcastically.

"You're teasing me, aren't you?"

"Yes, I am."

"I'm just trying to explain why in some of my paintings where you're the model, it doesn't necessarily 'look' like you. In fact, sometimes, it makes you look rather strange."

"Tell me about it."

"Rodin was another example of how sometimes an artist was striving for a general impression rather than focusing on exact representation and detail. I mean, he didn't do that with one of his most famous sculptures, "The Kiss," but he did do it with other sculptures like the 'Gates of Hell.'"

Emily sighed.

"I'm boring you with art talk, right?"

"No. . .well, maybe."

"Come on. We'd better get some dinner. The Marriage Preparation Course begins tonight."

Though she and Jason had been married for less than two years, they had volunteered to help out on the weekend. Emily loved attending the Marriage Preparation Course. Listening to the more experienced couples speak on marriage allowed her to understand more fully why the Church teaches what it does.

There were about 20 engaged couples and several married host couples in attendance.

During the Sexuality talk, an attractive middle-aged couple named Jim and Peggy explained why the Church taught that contraception was considered immoral.

After the talk, a young man with a scowl on his face raised his hand.

"I don't think the Church has any business telling me what to do in the privacy of my own bedroom. It's just a bunch of old men making up rules so that they can populate the world. They're living in the Dark Ages."

The husband, Jim, took a deep breath and spoke in a clear, calm way and without judgment in his tone of voice.

"First of all," Jim was squinting to read the young man's name tag, "Frank, is it?" The young man nodded.

"Frank, let me ask you, why are you getting married in the Catholic Church?"

"Uh, well, because we were both brought up Catholic and we think that we should."

"The Church has those rules for our benefit, to help us in our journey toward holiness."

"The Church just wants us to have as many kids as possible," Frank retorted.

"No, that is not what the Church wants. The Church wants you to be responsible, but leaves the number totally up to the couple."

"You know, it's Victorian, the whole sex is wrong thing. The Church needs to get out of the 19th century."

"First of all," Jim spoke calmly, "the Church does not teach that sex is wrong. It teaches that sex is beautiful when it's within faithful marriage and open to new life."

"Yeah, right. It's like when the priests used to tell my father way back in the 1940's that masturbation will cause blindness, right?"

Jim laughed. "No, not quite. Masturbation is morally wrong, but it won't cause blindness. Perhaps the priests were just trying to give the young men some motivation."

"Look, no one gets hurt, right? And just about every guy I know does it."

As Jim was speaking, Emily studied the faces of the young couples around them. Many were looking down at the floor, some were shifting in their seats. A few of the girls' faces became flushed.

"Well, no one gets physically hurt. Masturbation can be addictive, though. The gift of sexual pleasure is designed by God to encourage procreation and bonding. However, when one takes that gift out of the marital embrace, it's selfish and self-serving."

"And the whole contraception thing is a bunch of nonsense."

"You might think it's nonsense, but it's based on 2000 years of tradition and also natural law. Did you know that up until 1930 every single Christian church taught that contraception was wrong?"

"Uh. . .no, I didn't. Really? I thought only the Catholic Church was against contraception and that all the other churches always taught that it was fine."

"That's a misconception these days. In 1930, the

Anglican Church voted to allow contraception in hardship cases. Since then, every single Protestant denomination has accepted artificial birth control and some have even allowed abortion."

"I still can't understand why you believe an institution that is so old-fashioned and out of touch with reality. Nobody listens to the Church anymore."

Emily smiled inwardly as she reflected on that statement. How many times had she told Jason that nobody listens to the Church anymore? Yet after they were married, they introduced to many couples, young and old, who continued to 'listen' to and obey the Church.

"I beg to differ. I think for you to say 'nobody' is too general a statement," Jim replied. "Besides, you're looking at two people who listen to the Church and we know quite a few more who are faithful to Church teaching." At that comment, Emily wanted to jump up and say, 'Us too!'

"However," Jim continued, "keep in mind that you have a choice to decide to follow what the Church teaches or disregard it. Following the Church's teaching is like having 'Marriage Insurance.' Couples who use NFP have a much lower divorce rate."

Some of the engaged couples began whispering to each other.

A young woman spoke up. She was probably in her mid-twenties with long blond hair and a beautiful tan, unusual for someone in Canada during the winter. "Well," she said, "can you explain again just what makes it wrong to use birth control and why NFP is so different? I mean, in both cases, you're avoiding pregnancy, right?"

"Yes," Jim hesitated again, trying to read her name. "Kathleen, do you remember the priest talking about the fact that sex has two components: the unitive and the procreative?"

Kathleen nodded.

"Let's say one couple is using the pill and another couple is using NFP to avoid pregnancy. Now, besides all the physical side effects that come along with taking the pill, that couple is essentially keeping the door shut to God. They are artificially removing the procreative aspect from their sexual union. Contraception separates a couple, whether they're aware of it or not.

"Now, let's say another couple is using NFP. This couple charts the signs of fertility and then, together, they determine when the fertile time is, that is, the time when they are very likely to get pregnant. Assuming they want to avoid pregnancy, that couple abstains for the time being and waits until they are in their infertile phase to have relations. They leave the door 'open,' so to speak, by leaving the possibility of new life there for God to work with."

Emily again studied the faces of the young couples, many of whom were already living together. She recalled, with sadness, how closed she was to the idea of using NFP and how adamantly she fought for them to use contraception. How many of these couples felt the same way? How difficult it must be for them to hear God's truth regarding married love.

For a moment, the couples were silent. Then Peggy, the wife of the speaker couple, broke the silence. "Well, it's time to disperse for a break. We'll meet back here in 15 minutes."

Emily whispered to Jason, "Let's go and talk to Jim and Peggy." Jason nodded, then followed Emily over to the speaker's podium.

"You both did a great job explaining the Church's teaching. We've spent a lot of time reading and studying "On Human Life," and "The Role of the Christian Family in the Modern World," but your talk has helped us to better understand why the Church teaches what it does."

"Thanks, Emily," said Peggy.

"Great job," said Jason, as he shook Jim's hand.

As Emily and Jason turned around, she leaned over and whispered, "It's hard to believe that I once felt that way, you know, that contraception is okay. I just want to bang it into the young couples' heads!"

"I didn't do that with you, Em."

"I know. But it just seems so simple that contraception would not be God's will. Why couldn't I see it?"

"Keep in mind that most people are influenced too much by society, and especially the media. Think about it. We watch hours and hours of television for years upon years and after a while, we just become brainwashed into that way of thinking."

"Why didn't you think that way?"

"One reason might be that I stopped watching television early on. It just seemed like too much of a waste of time. There are so many things that we can do with our free time, like writing and playing music, reading good literature, praying."

"And I know you were raised Catholic."

"Well, yeah, I was, but I really didn't know all that much about my faith. Our faith life was limited to church on Sunday. However, my mom told me that even as a baby, I had an inborn sense of right and wrong."

"Really?"

Jason laughed. "Yeah, she tells me that when I was about six months old and crawling around, when I reached the steps to the basement, I just stopped. She watched me every time and I would stop and not attempt to go down the steps. . .until I was older and able to do it."

"I'm not surprised!" Emily hesitated. "So is this a good time to talk about planning a pregnancy?"

Jason sighed and replied, "Em, we're in the middle of the Marriage Preparation Course. Couldn't we discuss this at home?"

Emily stared at the floor.

"Hey, do you want to go to a movie tonight after the course?" Jason asked.

"I don't know."

She continued to focus on the floor. How could she think about anything else when her whole body desperately ached to carry a child within her?

For three long drawn-out years, she impatiently tolerated their physical separation. Now, it appeared as if God and Jason were asking her to wait for a child.

It seemed so ironic that at first, Emily distrusted the effectiveness of NFP. Now, she resented it.

19

Psalm 139:14-15

June 1985

Emily woke to the shrill sound of the irritating clock radio. Jason, as usual, pressed the snooze button and promptly went back to sleep. She poked at him until he reached for the thermometer and handed it to her. When they had been avoiding pregnancy, a sustained first morning temperature rise meant they were in Phase III, the infertile time. After 14 days, her temperature would drop and menstruation would begin. Now, however, she knew that she had recorded 20 days of elevated temperatures. Just one more and it would confirm her pregnancy.

As she lay in bed waiting for the five minutes to register a proper temperature, Emily quietly recited the morning offering that she had begun to say a year ago. "Oh my Jesus, through the Immaculate Heart of Mary, I offer you all my prayers, works, sufferings, joys, sorrows, frustrations, in conjunction with the holy sacrifice of the Mass throughout the world, for the conversion of sinners, in reparation for my sins and the sins of others and for the intention of the Holy Father this month."

Emily recalled the celebration of their third anniversary. They had practiced Natural Family Planning to await a pregnancy for nearly three years, discussing it on a monthly basis, with Emily at times urging, almost nagging, Jason. Last year, she had come down with pneumonia requiring hospitalization then bedrest for six months. As she began to regain her strength, it became obvious that Jason was becoming less stringent about charting her cycle. It all culminated in their spontaneous lovemaking, the first time they had ever been intimate during Phase II.

It was also the first time that they had made love to a single lit candle. A few days previous, Jason had shared with her that in the 15th century, it was common for painters to place one solitary lit candle in their paintings to symbolize that Christ was present. Emily so loved the symbolism that she insisted they engage in marital relations to the soft light of a single candle to represent that Christ was a part of the physical expression of their love.

That was three weeks ago and now she was late for her period by one week. With 21 days of elevated temperatures, it would confirm that they had conceived.

Emily had known in her heart that she was pregnant, even from the beginning. In fact, she suspected that she had conceived twins because, at the time of conception, she felt ovulation pain on both sides of her abdomen. At the very possibility that they might be pregnant, at the thought that God may possibly have created a child through them, Emily wanted to jump for joy.

Now the five minutes were up. Emily checked the thermometer and yelled, "Yes! 21 days of elevated temperatures!"

Emily showed her semiconscious husband the thermometer and he smiled. "Looks like you were right, Em."

In awe, she realized that their love was so real and so sacred that not just one but, she believed, two tiny human persons were beginning their lives in the loving safety of her womb. Their love had become fruitful. God had created these human beings through *them*. Emily was filled with so much happiness that she wanted to share her news with everyone.

She thought, with anticipation, about the fact that her family tree album, which began as a high school project, had turned into a lifetime hobby and with this pregnancy, she and Jason were beginning their own branch. Emily wondered what the future would hold for her unborn children.

When Jason arrived home that evening, she complained of being nauseous. "What a wonderful feeling this is. And by the way, I'm sure it's two."

Jason, left eyebrow raised, with doubt in his eyes, said, "Em, how could you possibly know that?"

"I just know."

He smiled. His young wife was absolutely beaming.

"How can I possibly wait eight more months to meet our children?" she complained again.

Emily was excited about this unique new oneness she now felt with her husband. "Our love is no longer abstract, but *real,* and we'll be holding them in our hands in eight months!" she exclaimed.

Her excitement continued and, over the next week, they began sharing the news with close relatives and friends.

One night, several weeks later, Emily woke up to a feeling of wetness on the sheets. She reached down to touch her nightgown and held her hand in front of her face. The moonlight lit up the room enough to reveal that there was blood on her hand.

"Oh, God, no." Her heart dropped. Though she tried to remain calm, she pushed the covers off and rushed to the bathroom to see how much bleeding there was. As she sat on the toilet, more blood came out, at first a trickle, then a gush.

"Em, you okay?" she heard Jason say.

"I don't know. I think I may be having a miscarriage."

It felt like a vice was gripping her uterus. As the bleeding became more heavy, Jason stood vigil next to his wife as her body attempted to expel a newly-conceived child.

"We should go to the hospital, Em."

"No, they'll want to do a D and C. I'm positive that we conceived twins."

"But you're bleeding so heavily."

"I'm not losing hope that perhaps one of our children has survived."

After sitting up all night with Emily, Jason pleaded with her to go to the doctor's office. The next morning, after heavy cramping and bleeding, she finally agreed. In tears, she told the doctor, "I'm six weeks pregnant and I may be having a miscarriage."

The doctor's words were not very consoling. Instead, the words were patronizing, "My dear, don't worry, you're probably just having a heavy period."

"I'm not having a period. I already have 35 days of elevated temperatures and I *am* pregnant." He agreed to do a pregnancy test but it came back 'atypical,' not positive and not negative.

Though the bleeding had slowed down, the abdominal pains and cramping continued over the next several days. After missing three days at the courthouse, Emily forced herself to get dressed and go to work. As she sat in court, she felt another gush and silently groaned. She knew that she wouldn't be able to stay much longer.

During a recess, Emily revealed to the court administrator why she needed to leave, then drove to her doctor's office. Her doctor wasn't available so a younger, more receptive doctor gave her another pregnancy test. When the test came back positive, he ordered an immediate ultrasound and, after having Emily drink three large glasses of water, she was sent down to the basement of the large hospital.

In the small dark ultrasound room, Emily lay on the examining table as the stone-faced technician moved the wand across her abdomen. Images of her uterus and abdomen were being displayed to the technician, with the screen away from Emily. Desperately searching for some hint of optimism in the young woman's eyes, Emily finally asked, "Can you see my baby? Is everything all right?"

The woman frowned and said, "I can't tell you anything. Ask your doctor."

Emily's eyes began to water. The indifference and coldness in the woman's voice was like a sword piercing her heart. She felt so alone, so lost. She urgently needed her husband's presence and wished that she had tried to reach him at the university.   Moving along the damp concrete corridors of the hospital's basement, she walked but didn't have any consciousness of doing so. She climbed the stairs but as she reached the top, she couldn't remember maneuvering them. Reaching the doctor's office, she stood there, feeling numb.

She finally opened the door and, when the nurse saw her, she was immediately taken inside an examining room, where she nearly collapsed in a chair near the door. The young doctor walked in and pulled his seat next to her. At first, she kept her head down and avoided eye contact with him. Then, she could see that he had the ultrasound photos in his hands. Looking at his face, she watched as his eyes became sympathetic. He spoke in a calm, quiet tone of voice. "Emily, there's no sign of an embryo in your uterus. At this stage it would be the size of a bean in the middle of your uterus. You've probably already had a miscarriage."

Her voice pleaded with him. "But my pregnancy test is still positive."

"It can remain positive for weeks after a miscarriage."

"I have a strong feeling that I conceived twins."

His eyebrows formed a frown. "That could very well be. If there is another embryo, we should be able to see it.   Right now, there is no sign of anything in your uterus."

"Maybe with all the bleeding, it can't be seen."

"Emily, what concerns me is that the ultrasound shows internal bleeding, and it could be from the miscarriage.   Your blood pressure seems like it's on the low side. It's likely that you will need a D and C (dilatation/curettage.)"

Knowing that a D and C would scrape out the contents of her uterus, Emily blurted out, "No! I haven't lost hope for the other child I've conceived.   Having a D and C would destroy that baby."

"I strongly advise you to get that procedure done." He looked down into her pleading eyes and said, "Just promise me that if the bleeding gets worse, you'll come to the emergency department immediately."

She nodded.

As she was driving home, she felt lightheaded and nauseated. She walked into the main door of her building, then she ran to her apartment just as another gush of blood came from her. Now, Emily felt weak and disoriented. The cramps were turning into unbearable pain. It now became necessary for her to remain on the toilet. *How could I have that much inside of me?* The room began to spin. "I'm not fainting here on the toilet, that's for sure," she mumbled.

She stumbled out of the bathroom and tried to walk toward the phone, but Emily felt as if every ounce of energy had just been sucked from her being.

Collapsing on the floor of her bedroom, she felt someone patting her face as she woke, staring at the ceiling. "Did I just faint?" she asked herself out loud. "And who was touching my face?"

Still alone, hopelessly weak, and knowing that Jason wouldn't be home for another two hours, she realized that she needed to phone someone to take her to the hospital. Mustering every ounce of strength that she could, Emily dragged herself over to the phone at the bedside table. Looking back, she could see that she had left a light blood trail on the hardwood floors of their bedroom. She tried to take a deep breath, then yanked the phone down onto the floor. Emily carefully dialed a friend's number and silently prayed that someone would answer. One, two, three, four, five, six rings. *Please, someone pick up.* She hung up the phone, lay on the floor and drifted in and out of consciousness.

"Oh my God!" She opened her eyes to find Jason leaning over her.

"Emily, we need to get you to the hospital."

"I know."

He leaned down and carefully lifted her in his arms.

"I can walk."

"No, you can't. I'll carry you."

"But there's a lot of blood. We'll need to get a towel for the car."

"Screw the car's upholstery, Em." He was raising his voice, something he rarely did. "You need to get to the hospital now and I don't give a damn whether you get blood on the car."

She sighed and laid her head on his chest. Nodding off, the next thing that she remembered, he was carrying her through the emergency room door, then into an examining room. A youthful-looking resident approached her to take her blood pressure. "Hi. I'm Dr. Preston." Emily felt comforted by his young looks and his caring, soft-spoken manner. He approached Jason. "Are you her husband?"

"Yes. My wife needs immediate medical attention, but I need to move my car. I'll be right back."

The resident turned his attention to Emily. "Are you always this pale?"

Emily replied, "Well, my mother tells me that I need to use more makeup."

He laughed and took her blood pressure. With concern on his face, he took it again, then yelled "I need a nurse stat!"

Two nurses came running into the room. The young-looking intern was now shouting at them. Emily, now semi-conscious, heard something about "intravenous." Still weak, she moaned as one nurse tried to insert the intravenous needle in one hand and failed to get it in the right place. A few more painful attempts and the nurse finally succeeded.

After giving Emily a quick pelvic examination and taking a urine sample, the young resident told her that he would be bringing her to the ultrasound room to check on the status of her pregnancy.

"My husband. Where is my husband?"

"We'll find him and he can come with you to the ultrasound room."

Jason walked in as they were beginning the scan. In the darkness of the small ultrasound room, as the young resident prepared to perform the procedure, he told them exactly what was going on. As he was moving the wand over her abdomen, he turned the screen so that both Jason and Emily could see it.

"Emily, there is no evidence of a fetal sac in the uterus. But you do have a significant amount of internal bleeding in your abdominal cavity, as evidenced by this dark area all around here. I have a strong suspicion that you have an ectopic or tubal pregnancy. Do you know what that is?"

Emily groaned. She knew exactly what that was. She remembered Aunt Sally telling her that both her great-grandmother, Katharine Clayman, and her great-aunt, Ruth, had endured tubal pregnancies.

Emily was wheeled back into the examining room and prepped for emergency surgery. Dizzy, weak and feeling like she was going to lose consciousness again, Emily listened as the young intern ordered an oxygen mask for her, then, in a calm and gentle voice, he explained what was going to happen.

Emily heard "abdominal surgery," then she slipped into unconsciousness. She woke up to hear him say "laparoscopy," then a few seconds later, "internal bleeding, and pregnancy test positive."

She opened her eyes as Jason squeezed her hand again, then watched as Dr. Preston handed a clipboard to Jason.

He scanned the forms and signed them. He handed the clipboard back to the doctor and, his face drawn, looked down at his wife. Her eyes were partly closed.

He tentatively placed his hand on top of hers, careful not to disturb the intravenous line. Emily opened her eyes and tried to speak, but with the oxygen mask, it was impossible.

"Doctor, can I take this mask off for a minute? My wife wants to say something."

"Sure," he said, as he removed it. "We're taking her to surgery in a few minutes."

"I'm so glad you're here," she whispered. He could barely hear what she was saying. "I love you so much," she said, as she squeezed his hand as tightly as her weakened body could.

He had to fight to keep his eyes from starting to tear, "I love you too, Em. You're going to be all right." His voice was cracking.

"I'm scared," she whispered, but he wasn't able to hear her. Leaning down right next to her, she whispered it again. "I'm scared. I don't want to die."

"You're not going to die. Not with me, St. Jude and Our Lady praying to the Boss for you," he reassured her. "While you're in surgery, I'll be praying the whole time. I have my rosary right here." Though his expression was full of uncertainty and worry, he forced a smile. Emily closed her eyes. He leaned down, kissed her forehead, and very softly whispered, "You need to get well again so that we can have those ten children you've been hoping for."

Her eyes opened slightly and she nodded. At that moment, the doors banged open with a stretcher to take Emily to the O.R. With her oxygen mask in place, she managed a small wave to Jason. He replied, "I'll be here for you when you come out of surgery."

"There's a waiting room down the hall and the surgeon will come out to talk to you when surgery is completed," Dr. Preston told him, as he shook his hand. "I wish you and your wife all the best."

As Emily was being wheeled to the operating room, she watched the ceiling lights pass over her. She felt so weak, so tired. She just wanted to fall back to sleep. *Oh, God, all I wanted to do was have a baby. Why is this happening? Is this some kind of punishment for something?* Her glimpse of happiness seemed short-lived.

The operating room was green and sterile. Several doctors and nurses were preparing for the surgery. The surgeon leaned over to talk to Emily. He was a tall, balding man with an English accent. "We're preparing you for a laparoscopy. I'll make a small incision in your navel to look around, then I may need to do abdominal surgery, dear." He said "do" as if it was pronounced "due," almost a royal inflection.

She was moved to an operating table and all at once, two nurses were taking Emily's arms and placing them on two small boards to either side of her head. As her arms were outstretched, she immediately envisioned Christ on the cross and how he suffered, his arms outstretched, for us.

Everything was happening so fast. A kind-looking, grandfatherly physician approached her and patted her hand.

Emily must have appeared to be afraid, because he spoke to her in a calm, soothing voice. "Now, now dear. You're in very capable hands. We'll have you fixed up in no time." Emily wanted desperately to believe him but wondered perhaps if he said that to all his patients. *You can't very well have the patient hysterical.* Then again, Emily didn't have the energy or strength to be hysterical.

"We're going to give you some blood before your surgery and that'll take a few minutes." Emily, weak and tired, glanced over as they hung one, two, three, then four bags of blood on the intravenous pole. The blood was cold as she felt it going through her veins. It all seemed like a horrible nightmare.

He placed a mask over her mouth and nose and said, "Now, dear, I need you to count back from 100. . . ." A calm settled over her as she started counting, "100, 99, 98. . . ." Emily tried to mouth 97 but in seconds, she was unconscious.

Emily gradually became aware that a nurse was changing something on her intravenous pole and throwing the small tabs on to the side of the stretcher she was lying on. All of a sudden she could feel it, the sharp, stabbing pain in her abdomen. Emily had never before endured such an excruciating pain. It felt like someone had just ripped her stomach open. She let out a gasp.

She tried to say "pain" but all she could do was mouth it.

The nurse responded quickly. "I've given you some morphine in your IV. It should help with your pain."

The grandfatherly physician stood beside Emily's stretcher and again patted her hand. "You had a right tubal pregnancy and it had to be removed. But they were able to leave the tube in place. It was a miracle you didn't lose that tube. The surgeon also did a D and C, and found fetal tissue there as well from your miscarriage. It means that you had conceived twins, young lady. Two embryos. But you'll make a complete recovery, my dear. You were very, very lucky."

Emily closed her eyes and sighed. All along she knew that there were two babies, two little eternal souls who represented the love that she and Jason shared. And now they were gone. She would never give birth to them or nurse them or watch them go off to their first day of school. *Oh, God, why did you allow those babies to be conceived when you knew they would die?* Though her abdomen was excruciatingly painful, her heart held a far more agonizing pain.

An announcement came over the PA system, "It's now nine o'clock and visiting hours are over. All visitors must leave the hospital."

Oh, God, please don't let Jason leave, she silently begged. *I need him. I have to see him.*

Within minutes, a nurse stood by her cot and told her that she was being moved to a regular hospital room. As she passed by the hospital's nursery, she could hear a baby crying. Knowing that patients who miscarry normally recover in obstetrics, she prayed to Our Lady to please make her room not be in the maternity ward. She couldn't bear to be near any newborn babies right now.

"We've had to put you in the cancer unit, dear. There's no room in maternity right now."

Emily said a mental thank you to Our Lady for her intercession. The left side of her bed lined a wall in a small three bed ward. She closed her eyes and desperately tried to find some way to be more comfortable. She fought the impulse to ask God to take away her pain. Then she remembered her morning offering, to offer up her suffering for the conversion of sinners and the reparation of sins.

After a few minutes of experimenting, she found if she pulled her knees up slightly with her feet flat on the bed, it took the pressure off her stomach and allowed her pain to be somewhat bearable. She closed her eyes again, then heard the quiet sound of footsteps in the room. She opened her eyes to find her husband on the right side of her bed, leaning over her and smiling.

"Hey, Em, I've been waiting such a long time for you." His hazel eyes held a mixture of relief and sadness.

"Twins," was all she could say.

Jason smiled. "You were right, Em. The surgeon told me that we had conceived two babies. Pretty neat, eh?"

She nodded. "It hurts."

"I know."

He took her hand and, careful not to disturb the intravenous line, gently kissed her fingers. Jason leaned over and stroked her hair, "I love you, Em. I hate to see you in such pain."

"It hurts, but at least I'm alive."

As she dozed off, he sat patiently by the side of her bed. She woke up and saw that he had fallen asleep and his head was lying beside her shoulder. With her left arm, she caressed his curly hair and smiled. Even without her glasses on, she could see several flecks of gray amongst his dark brown hair.

She kissed the top of his head and whispered, "You look tired. You need to go home and get some sleep."

Half asleep, he nodded. Leaning down, he kissed her forehead in a prolonged gesture and whispered, "I love you, Em. I'll be back in the morning."

Emily woke up to the familiar excruciating pain in her abdomen. She had been able to sleep for four hours, grateful for the morphine injection given to her five hours previous.

Now morning, Emily opened her eyes as a woman was bringing her a tray of food. "Breakfast, Sweetie," she said, as she placed the tray onto Emily's side table. The strong smell of coffee filled the air and she could hear the banging of trays as other patients received their breakfast. As she tried to roll over, her already sore incision site felt as if it was ripping open.

A tall, young-looking nurse came in. "Oh, I see you've

gotten your breakfast." She stood by the bedside table and positioned it over Emily's bed. When Emily tried to sit up, she winced.

"Do you need something for pain?"

"No, thanks. I really don't want to become addicted to drugs or anything."

"Addicted? Hun, you just had major abdominal surgery ten hours ago. You need pain medication just to move around. I'll have to check your chart to see what the doctor ordered for pain."

She moved to the bottom of the bed where Emily's chart was kept and said, "Morphine, IM. I'll be right back with your shot."

While Emily was waiting, she lifted the metal top of the plate to see that she had a small bowl of jello, a small container of some kind of broth, a cup of apple juice and a cup of black coffee. She was still somewhat nauseous, but felt surprisingly famished.

"I'm back with your shot," the nurse called to her. Emily leaned over as the young woman gave her the shot in her buttock. All at once, Emily became dizzy and euphoric. It was as if the medication went right to her incision and made the pain bearable. "Gee, no wonder people get addicted to this stuff. It sure does make you feel good."

"You bet. Oh, good, you haven't eaten yet. I need to take your temperature." She slipped the thermometer under Emily's tongue and in a few minutes, removed it.

"Can you tell me what my temperature is?" she asked the nurse.

"It's 36.5." Trying to do the mental calculation, Emily calculated the temperature using her NFP knowledge and figured out that it was approximately 97.8.

Emily's heart ached. This was the first day her morning waking temperature was low. For nearly five weeks, she took her temperature every morning, despite the heavy bleeding at times. It continued to be somewhat high, until this morning.

Her eyes now starting to tear, she focused on the fact that

she was no longer pregnant. She was only considered six weeks pregnant and yet, she had bonded with her two children, already felt a maternal connection with them, a mother's love. She knew that she should feel grateful for her life, but all she could think about were the two newly-formed lives who were now gone.

She wiped her eyes as the surgeon walked in with seven young interns. He began speaking as if she wasn't there. "Patient is a 26-year-old nullipara who presented last evening with right side pelvic abdominal pain, bleeding and a positive pregnancy test. Blood pressure on admittance was 60 over 40. Last menstrual period, May 12, 1985. In the O.R., after giving patient 4 units of blood, laparoscopy showed right ectopic pregnancy, of which the products of conception were surgically removed and tube was washed with saline solution. D and C showed evidence of fetal remains as well. No apparent tubal scarring. Now, who can tell me what this young woman's chances of having another ectopic pregnancy are?" He pointed to a young intern who seemed like he was young enough to still be in high school.

"Yes?"

"Fifty percent?"

"That's correct. Many women who have ectopic pregnancies will suffer from infertility as well."

"Doctor," Emily interrupted, "What happened to my baby's remains?"

"What baby?"

"The baby that was removed from my tube."

"Oh, the products of conception."

"No, the baby, the perfectly formed baby, who just happened to be in the wrong place."

"My dear, the products of conception were disposed of." His words were so cold, so unemotional, so hard.

Emily felt her eyes start to water again. "What are you talking about, the products of conception?"

"That's what was in your tube." He said "tube" as if it had an extra 'u' in it.

"No, that's not what it's called. It's called a baby, certainly not the products of conception. Why couldn't I have the remains?"

"Because that's simply not allowed." His patronizing Oxford English accent was starting to irritate her.

Emily could see the interns shifting their eyes to avoid eye contact with her. "I should have been able to have the remains for burial."

"Well, dear, that kind of thing is not allowed."

It was too much for Emily to bear: products of conception, remains disposed of, likely infertility.

"Look," she tried hard not to cry, her voice cracking, "I've just lost two very wanted children, not products of conception. My stomach has been cut open and my heart is breaking. So, if you don't mind, I'd like to be left alone. *Please.*"

As he was walking toward the door, the surgeon moved his head in a motion to communicate to his interns to leave the room. He followed behind, then Emily was left alone. The room felt cold and lonely. Though there was another woman in the room, she was unconscious and hooked up to some machines. Besides, Emily just couldn't concentrate on anyone but herself. Her grief, her loss, her needs seemed to be the only ones that mattered right now.

Oh, God, why did you allow those two babies to be conceived when you knew they wouldn't be born? Her eyes filled with tears when she thought of what they may have looked like had they been born.

Then her mind wandered to her great-grandmother and she wondered if she had experienced the same heartbreak that Emily was feeling. It must have been disappointing for her ancestor to lose a child in that way. Again, Emily felt an affinity, a deeper connection, to a great-grandmother she never knew.

Now, she began to welcome the self-pity again. She had always wanted to have children, even as a teenager. Once she met and fell in love with Jason, she desired children even more deeply. It was difficult for Emily to wait for three years. She had been so ecstatic that her time had finally come. Never would she have expected something as devastating as this.

She allowed her eyes to close and drifted off to sleep. "Em?" she heard, then opened her eyes. Her father stood next to her hospital bed with two sleeping babies in his arms. He said nothing, but there was a pleasant, content expression on his face. She could smell his Old Spice aftershave.

"Dad?"

Emily woke with a start. "That seemed so real."

A few hours later, the young intern who admitted Emily, Dr. Preston, came to visit her, pulling the curtain around her bed. "Hey, you're looking a lot better," he commented. *Gosh, he looks so young, probably around the same age as me.* She was grateful for his caring, sensitive bedside manner.

"Yes. I want to thank you for all that you did for me."

"Hey, don't mention it. I was only doing my job. I'm glad everything worked out all right for you."

"Me too."

"By the way, I wanted to ask you about something. It's noted on your history that you have never used contraception."

"That's right."

"What have you done in the past to prevent pregnancy?"

"My husband and I use Natural Family Planning."

"Oh, is that like rhythm?"

"Actually, it's quite different from calendar rhythm and very effective in preventing pregnancy. It's based on scientific observations."

Emily never missed an opportunity to be a commercial for NFP. After all, how were doctors and the general public to find out about NFP without lay people, like Emily, promoting it.

"Really? I've never heard of anybody using that method effectively. That's great. I'm just stumped as to why you had an ectopic pregnancy, because you've never used any form of contraception. You've never had any sexually transmitted diseases, have you?"

"No, I haven't."

"It doesn't make sense as to why this would happen. Usually these things occur to women using intrauterine devices or the pill. Women who have sexually transmitted diseases tend to have more of these too. I guess it was just bad luck."

"It's very disappointing."

"I'm very sorry for your loss. I'm just happy that you came in when you did. You may not have survived had you waited."

Emily nodded. As the young intern was saying goodbye, Jason walked into the room with a bag full of books and magazines. He smiled at Dr. Preston and walked over to the side of the bed.

"Hi, Em." He leaned down to kiss her lips. "You look amazing this morning. There's a lot more color in your face."

"What have you got there?" she asked.

"Oh, I brought you some magazines. Also, I was cleaning out the bedside table and noticed this old ledger in the pile too. I'll take it back, if you want."

"No. Just leave it all on the table next to my bed."

Jason leaned down to kiss her again. "You've been so brave throughout all this, Em. I'm very proud of you."

Emily nodded. "I'm still sad. I keep thinking about those two tiny persons that we'll never get to know."

"I know. But we'll have more children. Oh, remember that I have to drive to Arrandale today. I'll be back tomorrow morning."

He kissed her forehead. "See you later. I love you," he whispered.

"Love you too."

He walked out the door and the loneliness and self-pity returned. *All I wanted to do was have a baby. This just seems so unfair.*

Emily reached over and picked up a magazine, then her eyes were drawn to the ledger. It had been several years since she studied this book. She picked it up and began familiarizing herself with it again.

She remembered the beautifully-handwritten sections with words, *"Michael moves in,"* and *"BPO, Midwife,"* occurring every so often.

"That's interesting," Emily mumbled out loud. "This 'BPO, Midwife' is in here three different times within 18 months."

Then she came upon, "*Ruth born at home, September 9, 1909.*"

Scanning through the next 20 pages or so, Emily came to a month's period of time where the handwriting was different, more scratchy, and barely legible. The poor handwriting ended on April 18th, with the beautifully handwritten words, "*Michael left today.*"

Why would Katharine write that her boarder had left? Perhaps because he was the source of some income? And, assuming the messy handwriting was not hers, why would she not have made notes in the previous month? Who could have been the person with the illegible, almost indecipherable writing?

As she was contemplating and trying to decode her own family's mystery, the phone rang and interrupted her train of thought.

She reached over, moving slowly so as to not disturb her painful abdomen, before it rang a third time and answered, "Hello?"

"Oh, Tootsie Roll, I hope Aunt Sal didn't wake you."

"Oh, no, you didn't."

"How are you feeling?"

"Oh, I'm sore, but okay, I guess. Feeling sad too."

"That's natural."

"Jason brought in some magazines and the ledgers. Can you believe just as you called that I was paging through the ledgers you gave me years ago?"

"Really? You've had them for so long. Are you finding anything interesting in them?"

"Well, I wanted to know if you might be able to help me figure something out."

"Sure."

"Well, most of the ledger entries and words are written in beautiful script handwriting. But for a month or so in March and April of 1912, I can barely read the writing and the numbers. Was your grandmother away or something?"

"You know, Tootsie Roll, Aunt Sally thinks that may have been when Grandmom was in the hospital for a tubal pregnancy, just like you just had."

"Really?"

"Yes. My father told me he thinks that it took place right around the time of the Titanic disaster."

"Wow, that's interesting."

"I think Grandpop managed the store until Grandmom was well enough."

"Really? Would he have been the one with the poor handwriting?"

"That would be Aunt Sal's guess, Tootsie Roll. To be quite honest, Aunt Sal didn't think he was literate at all, but perhaps he could write a bit."

"That's helpful, Aunt Sal."

"So when do you think you'll be out of the hospital?"

"I don't know yet."

"Aunt Sally will be praying for you, Tootsie Roll. Love you." "Thanks, Aunt Sal. Bye. Love you too."

Emily studied the words, *"Michael left today,"* and noticed that, though it was beautifully handwritten, it was more shaky and less precise than the other entries. She must have been still quite weak from the surgery, Emily figured. She again felt the connection to her great-grandmother, a bond that appeared to reach out through the generations.

"No, no, please, no!" A commotion was going on in the hallway outside her room. It sounded like someone, perhaps a girl, was crying hysterically. There was something in the young woman's voice which reached out and touched Emily's soul.

She shifted uncomfortably in her bed as she endured the screams, now filled with uncontrolled sorrow. The girl's voice became distant and it sounded like she was being taken away.

That poor woman. I wonder what was wrong with her. She silently prayed a Hail Mary for her.

A few minutes later, Emily overheard two people

speaking in hushed tones. Though the curtain around Emily's bed hid her from the hallway, she could hear everything they whispered. It reminded her of those times as a little girl when she used to hide away in her family's wicker hamper and eavesdrop on conversations.

"Mrs. Jamieson is going to need some time to accept the news that her husband will likely be dead from cancer in just a few months."

"It's a real shame."

They stopped talking and Emily assumed they had walked away. "Oh, God. That poor girl."

A nurse approached her to check Emily's temperature, blood pressure and pulse.

She took off the cuff, then checked Emily's incision. She carefully and slowly peeled the gauze bandage off. Emily winced as the entire area was still so sore. When the bandage was off, Emily glanced down. It appeared as if they had cut her from hip to hip. Her baby must have been so small, why did they need to make such a long incision? Holding her skin together were small metal clips or staples. *Didn't Frankenstein have metal clips holding his brain in?* This was certainly the largest incision she had ever seen, though admittedly, she hadn't seen too many in her life.

"Your incision looks great," the nurse said as she applied a fresh new gauze bandage. "Great?" Emily said. "If that looks great, what does horrible look like?"

After the nurse left the room, Emily began to reflect on her own situation. That young, grieving woman helped to put things into perspective for Emily. She began to feel remorse about her self-pity. She quietly prayed, "Thank you, God, for allowing me to survive this ordeal. Thank you for the gift of my husband. Help me not to feel sorry for myself, but to be grateful for my life. And please take care of my children in heaven.

20

Isaiah 13:18

June, 1926

"It's blasted hot today, Ruth. Why did you wear that woolen dress?"

"Oh, Mother, you just don't understand these things. It's uncomfortable, to be sure, but it's a beautiful dress and the boys always stare at me when I wear it. Besides, it's not all that hot anyway."

Katharine shrugged her shoulders and rolled her eyes. Though she was thankful to be past childbearing, she despised going through the womanly change. She felt hot even in the winter when it was bitterly cold outside.

Sitting next to her teenaged daughter on the streetcar, Katharine nonchalantly glanced out the window to see the ever-growing, ever-changing bridge to the right of the trolley. From her position, she could see the gigantic cranes carrying the massive steel tops of the new suspension bridge which would soon allow cars and buses to cross the Delaware River into New Jersey.

The streetcar came to a stop with its clanging sound. "Come on, Ruth, let's go."

Ruth stood up, now nearly a half a foot taller than her mother, waited for some passengers to clear the aisle, then allowed Katharine to move in front of her. They stepped off the trolley and followed the crowd for a few blocks, at the same time, staring in wonder at the majestic bridge nearing completion. She and Ruth enjoyed spending their afternoons with the other spectators, watching the various stages of construction of the Delaware River Bridge, beginning with the stone foundation on the Philadelphia side to the huge pieces of metal being hoisted to the sides and top.

Katharine and Ruth sauntered over to a shaded section toward the rear of a small stretch of land which had been converted to an informal viewing area for Philadelphia residents. Katharine studied the enormous stone foundation close to where she and Ruth stood. She found it difficult to believe that, in a short while, the bridge would actually be in use with cars and buses driving and pedestrians walking across the large suspension bridge.

"Aahh. . . ." Katharine jumped as a small child screamed.

"Why can't they just leave their children at home?" she commented to Ruth.

Ruth smiled and leaned closer to her mother. "Because families enjoy being together, Mother. After all, you brought me, didn't you?"

"That's different, Ruth. You're a teenager and a well-mannered young woman at that."

Katharine studied her daughter, now 17, who was taller than she by six inches. She was convinced that she resembled herself more than Michael but every so often, Ruth would laugh or look a certain way and Katharine's heart would ache. And her eyes: occasionally, Katharine would peer into her daughter's eyes and see Michael staring back at her.

She sometimes allowed herself to wonder what he was doing; if he was married, if he had children. *Does he ever think of me?* For a moment, she felt a pang of jealousy and envy at the thought that some other woman might be enjoying his quiet-mannered personality, his gentle voice, his sensual touch.

"Mother, look at that handsome boy over there." Katharine's eyes formed a frown as she studied a tall, well-dressed boy in his late teens, with black hair and dark eyes.

"He looks like Rudolph Valentino, don't you think, Mother?"

Katharine rolled her eyes.

"Doesn't he, Mother?"

Katharine shrugged her shoulders and replied, "I thought you wanted to accompany me to watch this historic event. Besides, that boy is too old for you."

"Posh, Mother, he's probably younger than me."

Katharine realized that it was just a matter of time before Ruth was regularly bringing home suitors. She continued watching the cranes carry another piece of metal and attach it to the suspension arch closest to the viewing area. "Aaaagh. . . ." She jumped again as a small group of boys in knickers and caps ran past them.

"Nuisance," she mumbled.

"Excuse me?" Katharine heard, then looked over to see a young woman in her twenties, dressed in ridiculously bulky clothes for the warm weather.

"Yes?" she replied as she studied the young woman. She appeared to be no more than 23 or 24, yet her face was worn, pale. Her eyes seemed haunted by some inner torment that Katharine couldn't explain and for a brief moment, without knowing her, she felt sorry for her.

"Are you the owner of the Parlor Music Shoppe?"

Katharine nodded, a bit annoyed. "Did you want to order some musical equipment?" *Why didn't this woman just come to the music store instead of bothering me here?*

The young woman shook her head. She hesitated, then whispered, "I need information."

Katharine smiled at her, a knowing smile, then realized that Ruth was still standing next to them. "Ruth, would you be so kind as to buy me a cool drink over there at the vendor?" She reached into her purse and pulled out a few coins. "This should be enough for two. Get one for yourself."

Ruth walked off as Katharine focused her attention on the woman.

"Now, what kind of information do you need, ma'am?" Katharine whispered.

The woman leaned closer to her and spoke in short quiet fragments. "I have missed my period. I have four children already, all very close together. . .and my husband beats me. I need to have someone bring my period on. I can't have another baby right now. I just can't." There were tears in the young woman's dark eyes.

"Have you tried the midwife, Annie Gliddon?"

"No, I haven't. I didn't know where to go, but I've already felt movement."

"I'm sorry, dear. I think it's too late for you to have your period brought on. But I'll give you Annie's number and you can contact her yourself. Do you have a telephone?"

The woman whispered, "Yes."

"Do you think you can remember the number?"

The woman nodded, then Katharine gave her the midwife's phone number.

"She's a busy woman, but perhaps she can help you. Haven't you heard about ways to prevent this?"

The woman appeared confused. "There are. . .you mean, not. . . ."

"No, no, I don't mean that at all."

"My husband would beat me even more."

"No, dear. There are devices that prevent this."

Katharine hesitated before speaking again.

"Look, if you come to my music store at 15th and Ritner tomorrow, I will give you a paper with that kind of information on it."

"Yes, yes, I will come tomorrow. Thank you."

Katharine smiled as she realized that the young woman's eyes now held some relief. But the sadness hadn't disappeared. It remained entrenched in her dark eyes as she glanced back at Katharine.

"Here's some lemonade, Mother," Ruth said, as she handed her mother the cup and the change.

Katharine took a sip and felt refreshed.

"Mother, I can't wait to be an aunt again."

Katharine's eyes formed a frown as she realized, with dread, to what Ruth was referring.

"Well, I think they're being irresponsible. Lizzie almost died last time. How do they know that won't happen again?"

"Oh, Mother, sometimes you can be so dramatic. With all the modern medical procedures, childbirth is becoming much safer. Besides, it wouldn't be fair for Sally to grow up without any brothers or sisters. Johnnie and Lizzie want more children." Ruth sounded so grown-up, too mature, in Katharine's opinion.

"Yes, well, who would ever want more than one child? One is enough for any parent to handle."

"But you only had one child when you had me, right?" Ruth paused. "You. . .didn't want me?"

The sun was beaming down on both of them and Katharine was now sweating profusely. "Ruth, if you don't cover yourself, you'll get burned. You know you get burned easily. You're so fair, just like me." Katharine pulled on her daughter's sleeve as she walked over to a more shaded spot in the viewing area.

"Yes, I'm so much like you, Mother," she responded, somewhat agitated.

"Ruth, keep your voice down. You're making a scene."

"No, Mother, I'm not."

"Just keep your voice down," she whispered nervously.

Katharine tried to act nonchalant, but she had failed. She knew that Ruth was looking at her and she ignored her daughter, pretending to stare at the bridge. After several minutes of silence between them, Katharine glanced at Ruth, who was now staring at the ground.

"Why am I so fair, Mother?" she asked, her eyes remaining downcast.

"Look, Ruth. . . ."

"Why?"

"Because you. . .ah. . .well, you resemble me, Ruth." She stuttered the words, hoping that her daughter wouldn't put the pieces of the puzzle together.

"Why would I not look anything like my father?"

"Because that's the way. . .it happens. . .sometimes, Ruth.

And keep your blasted voice down. People are staring. You just look like me."

"That's not totally true. I'm fair, but I have dark eyes and hair and a strong jaw. That's what you said. Why is that?"

"I. . .ah. . .my. . .mother's brother had a strong jaw."

Ruth stared at her mother, an accusatory look that made Katharine uncomfortable.

"What do you want me to say, Ruth?"

A crashing sound distracted them as they glanced toward the area of the towering crane. A gigantic piece of metal was still rocking in the water several hundred feet in front of them.

"Hey, Ruth. That boy over there, the one that looks like Rudolph Valentino, is talking to a young girl. She's not nearly as pretty as you."

Ruth's head jerked up and she studied the girl next to the handsome young man. "You're right."

"Let's go home." Katharine took hold of her daughter's shoulder and, relieved, walked toward the trolley stop.

A week later, as Katharine was beginning the routine of closing down the store, she heard the bells jingle and looked up to see the young woman who had approached her at the bridge building site.

"Oh, I'm glad you came. Are you looking for some information?"

The young woman, head down, finally looked up at Katharine.

"I. . . ."

"What's the matter, dear?"

"I don't. . .feel. . .well."

"Did you visit Annie?"

"Yes, but she said she couldn't, that I was too far along."

"Oh, I'm sorry."

Katharine studied the young woman, whose pale face appeared more drawn and gaunt than a week ago.

"So I tried to do it myself."

"Oh, dear," Katharine replied.

"And I'm bleeding." She lifted part of her skirt up to show Katharine that it had already seeped through.

"How long have you been bleeding?"

"Several days." The woman paused. "And it doesn't seem to be stopping."

"Come here. Sit down a moment." Katharine pulled the stool from behind the counter to the front and gently guided the young woman on to it."

"I can't go to the hospital. They'll know. Do you know of anyone that could help me?"

"I'm going to call Annie. Just wait right here."

Katharine walked behind the counter area to the wall phone and dialed the midwife's number. One, two, three, four, five rings. *Annie, pick up.*

Katharine heard a large thump, then turned around to see that the woman had fallen to the floor.

She rushed to the woman's side. "Are you all right?"

"No. I feel so. . .weak. I. . .I don't feel. . .well."

"Wait. I'm going to call the hospital."

"No, please. . .don't."

"What is your name?"

"Hannah," she replied, her voice barely above a whisper.

"Look. . .uh, Hannah, you're going to be fine. We'll tell them you're having a miscarriage."

Katharine quickly reached the phone and dialed the number of the hospital."

"Yes, I need an ambulance to come immediately to my music shop at 15th and Ritner." Katharine hung up the phone.

"They're on their way, Hannah. Everything will be fine."

Katharine leaned down. "Did you hear me, Hannah? Everything is going to be. . . ."

The young woman's eyes were closed, her face still, and Katharine could see a large puddle of redness coming from beneath her long skirt.

"Hannah?" Her hand shook the young woman's now limp arm, her body still.

Katharine knew that she was gone.

21

1 Samuel 1:27

November 1986

Emily had felt the familiar cramping all day, and when she went to the bathroom, she discovered the seemingly telltale sign that told her that she had not yet conceived. *Oh God, why will you not give me a child, a baby I so desperately want?*

Her eyes watered and she began to cry quietly. After trying to conceive for six months, Emily was convinced that this month a child had indeed been created. Her basal body temperature remained elevated, but as it got closer to when her period was due, she began to experience cramping. She became moody and restless: all indications that her period was, in fact, on its way.

She remembered the saying that a woman's period is actually 'tears of a disappointed uterus.' *How fitting.* She questioned God, "Why will you not give me another child?" She repeated the question, thinking that perhaps God would verbally answer her in her despair. Emily continued to cry, her tears now becoming long, hard sobs. Then she became haunted by the doctor's comment that women who experience ectopic pregnancies tend to be infertile.

"What if I have another tubal pregnancy?" she whispered out loud. She couldn't bear the thought of losing another child because her body didn't work properly.

Loneliness consumed her. Jason was at work, at his new job teaching art at Arrandale High School.

Now retired from court reporting, Emily wandered around their new apartment, anxious and alone. Part of her was relieved that Jason wasn't home because she was sure that her tone of voice would be abrasive and hurtful to him, as he seemed to accept the fact that they weren't conceiving so much more willingly than she did.

As always, when she was feeling depressed, she found it difficult to be grateful for the blessings and gifts that she did have, like her relationship with Jason.

At that moment, all she could think of was, why? With all the abortion, child abuse and promiscuity out there, why would God withhold a child from her?

She peered out the living room window. Although it was November, it was a beautiful spring-like day. Opening the small window, she inhaled the fresh air and immediately felt comforted. She found it ironic that the scent of air helped her. She recalled those times when she was younger and saddened, like at the time of her father's death. In order to distract herself at that time, she had watched even more television than normal. Today, she used the intoxicating scent of the cool air to distract her from her loneliness.

She turned around and, walking over to the sofa, picked up the book that she had been reading entitled "Breastfeeding and Natural Child Spacing," by Sheila Kippley. Both she and Jason had read the book when they were studying to become teachers of Natural Family Planning and she was reading it again in the hopes that she would soon become pregnant and be able to use the information after she gave birth. Just the sight of the mother and baby on the front of the book was enough to remind Emily that she was not yet pregnant. Her depression enveloped her and she found herself overwhelmingly tired. Emily sat down on the couch, thinking she would merely relax for a few moments. Instead, she fell asleep for four hours. Upon awakening, she discovered that the spotting had stopped. By the time Jason came home from his job, Emily was trying to keep what little remained in her stomach.

"I'm not sure what's going on here, Jay. My temperature is still elevated and I had some bleeding earlier on, but now I'm throwing up and I can't seem to keep my eyes open."

The next week at her doctor's appointment, she was given a urine test to determine if she was, in fact, pregnant. The test was positive, so the doctor sent her for an ultrasound a short while later to confirm that their child was safely growing in her uterus. Jason accompanied her. On the way to the hospital, Emily, nervous but excited, began talking rapidly.

"So if the baby's in the uterus, then we'll be home free, right?"

"Well, Em, we have to be open to any possibilities. We are not in control here."

"I know. But I'm so anxious. I have this feeling that everything's all right. I mean, I'm so sick. It's a good sign, isn't it?"

"I guess so."

"You're not being helpful here, Jay."

"Em, you need to calm down."

"I am calm."

"Right."

They reached the hospital and eagerly waited for the scan to begin. In the darkness of the ultrasound room, with Jason holding her hand, Emily had flashbacks to the previous ultrasound over a year and a half ago when the female technician would not speak with her, would not reveal the information that Emily couldn't bear to hear. Now she hoped, then begged, God that the news would be different.

The young female technician began moving the wand back and forth across Emily's abdomen, pointing the screen toward her and Jason.

"There's your baby," she said, as she pointed to a dark bean-shaped figure in the middle of the screen.

"Really?"

"Yes, it looks to be the normal size of a 30-day-old embryo."

Emily's heart filled with joy as she studied the scan of her tiny child nestled in the loving safety of her womb.

"This one made it, Jay. He made it to the right spot."

"He sure did, Em," he said, his mouth upturned in a smile.

Five months later, Emily felt so wonderful to have energy again. After six months of throwing up day and night, she was finally able to get through a day with minimal vomiting. Each time she felt nauseated, she thanked God for the opportunity to be carrying this little person inside of her.

She walked around the small-town grocery store, and out of the corner of her eye saw an elderly woman looking at her. *Another person staring at me, thinking I'm a pregnant little girl.*

As Emily watched the woman, she noticed that she was avoiding eye contact and instead, she appeared to be studying Emily's hand. *I wish I wasn't so bloated, then I could wear my wedding ring and people would stop staring.*

The woman then glanced at Emily's face and when she saw that Emily was watching her, she looked away. *Why do people have to be so rude?*

"Hi, Em!" She turned to find Rose smiling at her.

"Hi, Rose. How are you doing?"

"Oh, fine. Hey, you're looking good, getting bigger, eh?"

"Yeah, I sure am. But I hate when people stare at me because they think I'm a pregnant little girl."

Rose laughed. "You do look awfully young, Em. I mean, you can understand why people stare, eh?"

"I suppose, but people can be nicer about it."

"You're right about that."

"How are your mom and dad doing?"

"Oh, fine. Kevin's getting married next year."

"Really? That's great, Rose."

"Well, I have to run. Let me know when the little one arrives, eh?"

"Sure thing, Rose."

Emily arrived home and decided that it was time to do some spring cleaning. With renewed energy, she felt like she was able to do a job that would make even Aunt Sally proud.

Starting on the second floor, she began sorting through a pile of papers and books next to her bed, in anticipation of her baby's arrival. She and Jason had decided to keep the crib in their bedroom, next to their bed rather than have the baby in his or her separate room.

Several minutes later, Emily was delighted to rediscover the ledgers from her great-grandparents' store. She had almost forgotten about them and had again neglected her family tree project for over a year. What better time to get reacquainted with her ancestors than during the time that she awaited this child's birth.

Emily sat with her legs crossed and began reading one of the ledgers again.

Scanning the pages again, she came to the last page she had read, *"Michael left today."*

Emily picked up another ledger and began paging through the book, this time, searching for more entries which read, *"BPO, Midwife."* "That's strange," Emily reflected out loud, "there are no more BPO Midwife entries from 1914 to 1918. In 1918, again, was the scratchy, illegible handwriting, she assumed, of her great-grandfather. Katharine must have been ill again during that period. Wasn't that the year the Great Flu Epidemic occurred? She had read that Philadelphia had been hit hard with the epidemic. Emily made a mental note to ask her mother or Aunt Sally if they knew what happened in 1918.

A few days before Mother's Day, Jason surprised her with a bouquet of red roses.

"Happy Mother's Day, Em."

"These are beautiful, Jay. But it's not Mother's Day yet."

"I know, but I wanted to give these to you before we went to the Walk for Life. Read the card."

Emily picked up the small card and read the words written by her husband, "May our child someday be thankful that he or she was wanted. Happy Mother's Day."

"I hope you like them."

"I do.   And I especially love the card.   Thank you so much." She leaned up and embraced him.   Their unborn child kicked within her so strongly that Jason pulled away as he could feel their baby's movements.   He placed his hand on her protruding stomach.

"Wow, this kid is strong."

She repeated the words from the card, "And may our child someday be thankful that he or she was wanted."

"Come on. We have to get going."

Emily and Jason arrived at the Walk for Life in Ottawa. A beautiful sunny day, it was the first time that she had attended a pro-life event since becoming pregnant.   The whole abortion matter became ever more personal now, as Emily continuously felt her child kick and move within her.

As she stood with the thousands of other demonstrators, she wondered why it was considered legal to kill an unborn child for the plain and simple fact that the parents did not want it. Though she realized that a small number of women have abortions for perceived health reasons, she also knew that the majority have abortions for other motives, like inconvenience.

Her child again moved within her, as he or she did frequently, and the abortion rights issue became even more clear and resounding. Her blood flowed frequently through this small person. The food she ate became nutrition for her unborn child. The air she breathed gave oxygen to this fellow human being.

"Hey, Em, look over there," Jason had whispered.

Emily   noticed   a   small   group   of   pro-choice demonstrators, perhaps 20 or so, who were chanting, "Holy Mary, mother of choice."

"Oh, God, Jay, that's horrible."

"Yeah, I know. It's one thing to be demonstrating for abortion rights. It's quite another to be using Our Lady for their cause. How could they ever convince themselves that Mary would ever be a proponent for abortion rights?"

"I don't know. Hey, look, television cameras."

"Do you remember when we attended that pro-life rally a few years ago when you were attending university, Jay?"

"Yeah. Weren't there about 4,000 people there?"

Emily recalled that when they had turned on the news, they had heard,   "Today at the university, a few hundred protesters attended an anti-abortion rally. . . ."

Both Jason and Emily had been shocked as they had watched the cameraman spend the next three or four minutes interviewing the members of a pro-choice group, giving limited air time to the pro-lifers.

Now, standing amongst the thousands of protesters, they hoped for a more reasonable account on tonight's news.

Emily lay on the stretcher staring at the ceiling lights as she was being wheeled to the operating room. Two years ago, she had, in despair, prepared to have surgery for an ectopic pregnancy. Now, she was nine months pregnant, preparing to have a Cesarean section. The nurse wheeling her to the O.R. began some small talk with her.

"Is this your first baby, hun?"

Emily nodded.

"That's too bad you have to have a C-section. But you're such a little thing, aren't you?"

Emily smiled, then turned her attention to her unborn child. She held her hand to her large stomach. "We'll get to meet you in just a few minutes, little one," she whispered. Part of her was disappointed that they would not be able to have their baby the natural way. She had been in labor for 16 hours with no progress and the doctor's pronouncement that the baby was just too big for Emily's narrow pelvis.

The nurse wheeled the gurney to the area just outside of the operating room. She glanced up to see Jason dressed in green scrubs. He was smiling with his left eyebrow cocked.

"You look sexy in those scrubs, Dad!" she exclaimed.

"You think so?" he asked, playing along.

"Absolutely."

The nurse stepped forward and directed her comment toward Jason, "You'll need to wait here while your wife is given a spinal anesthetic." He nodded and leaned down to kiss Emily. "I love you," he whispered.

Several minutes later, gowned and wearing a surgical mask over the bottom of his face, Jason was escorted into the operating room, to a chair situated near Emily's head.

"Sit here," he was told. "And don't move."

He held her left hand and when he looked down he could see both her arms were outstretched on long narrow extension tables on either side of her shoulders. One arm had an intravenous tube attached and the other had a blood pressure cuff. There were little round patches with wires at the top of her chest. For a moment, with her arms outstretched, Emily again pictured Christ on the cross. Despite her disappointment at having a C-section, it became difficult for her to focus on the passion when her heart was overflowing with the joy of the impending birth of her child. Emily whispered to Jason, "This sure is a complicated way to have a baby."

One of the doctors had turned on a radio station playing elevator music. With all the equipment and the green, sterile environment, the slow music made everything seem surreal to Emily. The anesthesiologist, a young doctor in his mid-thirties, began singing along with a Frank Sinatra tune. She listened as he sang, "Doobie doobie doo. . . ." Emily cracked a grin. His voice wasn't half bad. He was on key most of the time and appeared to be enjoying himself as he sang.

Jason lifted his head over the curtain placed in front of Emily's head to observe the surgeon.

Though he sounded concerned, there was excitement in his voice as he whispered, "He started cutting, Em." Thankfully, the spinal anesthetic had taken full effect and Emily couldn't feel a thing.

Jason leaned down and kissed her hand, now strapped to the table. "You doing okay, Em?"

She hesitated, then nodded.   She knew that they were cutting her at this very moment and prayed that the surgery would be over soon.

A few minutes later, Jason leaned over and with the excitement of a kid at Christmas, said, "I see the head," and in another minute, all but Emily cried out, "It's a boy!"

Emily's eyes filled with tears of happiness and relief. Filled with joy, she looked over to see Jason's eyes were watering, "We have a son, Em."

She could hear her newborn son wailing as they cleaned him. A few minutes later, one of the operating room nurses brought their baby to Jason. Their son was still crying, a bit blue, and his skin had a wrinkly appearance like it had been under water for a long time. To Emily and Jason, he was the most beautiful sight in the world. Their love had been made real, was now breathing and crying and had to be given a name.

Emily's long wait for children was finally over. Through the heartache of losing two babies was now the joy of giving birth. *Life does not get any better than this.*

"Congratulations," one of the nurses said to Emily and Jason, "on your firstborn child."

"The first, I hope," Emily replied, "of many."

"Have you decided on a name for your baby?" one of the O.R. nurses asked.

Jason spoke up. "Jacob. We've chosen the name Jacob."

A short time later, Emily was wheeled back to her room, Jason following close behind. The baby's bassinet was placed alongside her hospital bed. The spinal was still working and Emily couldn't as yet feel any sensation below her waist. She remembered a few years ago how painful her first abdominal surgery had been, physically and emotionally. She was thankful for the short-lived relief that she had no feeling in her abdomen or legs.

"Can you help me try to nurse him, Jay?"

He reached in, picked up his new son and gently placed him beside his wife. Emily lifted up her hospital gown to nurse her baby. As she tried to latch him on, he screamed and pulled his head away.

"I guess we should try later. I read that the best time to begin breastfeeding is as soon after the birth as possible. That's when the sucking reflex is the strongest," she said. "I hope he nurses soon."

Jason nodded as he cradled his newborn son. The new father began moving and rocking to calm him down. He swayed back and forth as if there was music playing. Within minutes, the baby had settled and was asleep on Jason's shoulder.

"Add another one to your list of many talents," she observed.

He pulled his small sleeping son off his shoulder and held him next to Emily. They studied his calm face, his lips puckered.

When she looked up at Jason, he was gazing down at her with his left eyebrow raised and a smile so wide, she was sure that his face would burst.

"We made him because we love each other," she said.

"I know, pretty awesome, eh?" he replied.

She nodded.

Jason carefully laid his son in the bassinet.

"Let's say a prayer, Em. I feel so blessed to have a son. We need to pray."

They both did the sign of the cross, then Jason began quietly praying: "Oh, God, we thank you for the gift of parenthood, for the gift of this new life, for the safe delivery of our baby, Jacob. We pray for a speedy recovery for Emily. Please help us to raise our child to be a disciple of Christ. Give us the grace to be exceptional parents. In the name of the Father and of the Son and of the Holy Spirit."

"That was beautiful."

"Well, I better let you get some rest. I'll be back later. I love you." He leaned down to kiss her lips, then placed a gentle kiss on his newborn son's head.

He left the room and within about 20 seconds, the baby began crying, not whimpering but full screaming. Emily, still paralyzed from the waist down, could only watch as he bellowed out a high-pitched cry, his small face becoming red.

A nurse rushed in, picked him up and handed him to Emily. "Here, hun, I'll help you, if you want to try to breastfeed."

Emily nodded. When the baby was near her breast, he started rooting and in an instant, latched on. It was a sensation that Emily had never felt before. Now she knew what the term "strong sucking reflex" meant. After a minute, his tiny lips broke the suction and he started screaming again.

"Looks like you've got a live one, that's for sure. He's angry!"

She hated to hear him cry, but at the same time she relished the sound of a baby wailing, for it became the physical manifestation that she was a mother and responsible for another human being. The nurse patted his back and after several minutes of back pounding, he let out a loud burp. She continued to rock him until he fell back to sleep. As she was preparing to lay him in his bassinet, Emily said, "Oh, I'd like to hold him, if you don't mind."

"Just make sure that you don't spoil him. He's going to have to learn how to sleep on his own."

Emily ignored her comment and whispered to her son, "I waited a long time to hold you. You can learn to sleep on your own when you're older."

She gazed down at her child as he was sleeping. In her last month of pregnancy, she had read John Paul II's The Role of the Christian Family in the Modern World again. One section of that encyclical so affected her that she decided to write it down and stick it in her suitcase for the hospital.

Before she had been wheeled down to the operating room, she had asked Jason if he would get the little slip of paper with the quote and display it on her bedside table so that she could read it when they returned to her room with their new baby.

"The child is the living testimony of full, mutual self-giving on the part of husband and wife. The child comes from the couple's most intimate act of love and becomes a kind of seal of the covenant of love. Even physically, the child is a reflection of the union of the parents and carries certain features. . . ." She stated it out loud: "Our child is the seal of our covenant." *Such an appropriate description.*

It seemed to make perfect sense now, especially staring into the face of the child that God created through them. Emily had initially yearned for children more from a selfish standpoint than from a selfless one. Her whole life, all she could think about was how much joy she would receive from holding her child, not how much she could serve God by conceiving, giving birth to and raising a godly child.

Gazing at his face, she concluded that he was, in fact, the most beautiful baby that she had ever seen, with small fine features and blonde peach fuzz on top of his head. What a tremendous blessing it was to have a child, to be able to gaze down upon the face of your child and know that he is the product of God, you and the one you love. Emily had waited for this moment for five years and for most of the time that she and Jason had dated. It seemed that no words could possibly describe the feeling, the abundant joy and happiness that surrounded her very being with the realization that God had entrusted them with this child. *Thank you, God, for the gift of our baby.*

Three weeks later, Emily roused from her sleep as baby Jacob started to cry. He lay next to her in bed and she tried to placate him by putting her nipple in his mouth as quickly as possible. At least once a night, he would refuse the breast and just scream at the top of his lungs. Sometimes it would be several times a night that he would cry. The doctor said there was nothing wrong with him, that he just had 'colic.'

Frustrated, she picked up the baby and began walking with him. She glanced over at Jason and could see that he was sleeping through the whole screaming incident. Over the last few weeks, she had become exasperated with him that he could sleep through noise like that.

As she walked back and forth with her baby, she heard echoes of the well-meaning comments of relatives, "You're spoiling your baby," and "You shouldn't be sleeping with your baby," and "Just let him cry it out." Right now, she wondered whether that was the right thing to do. Rocking and nursing sometimes didn't settle him. Letting him just cry, she felt, would be a cruel thing to do.

After she spent an hour of walking with the baby, Jason finally sat up in bed and asked Emily if she wanted a break. "Yes," she answered over the ear-splitting cries of the baby, "but I won't be able to sleep knowing that he's fussing. Thanks anyway."

He lay back down in bed and within minutes she could see him breathing heavily. "How in the world can he sleep through all this?" she said out loud.

After another hour of walking in the hallway with her bawling infant and not having had proper sleep in three weeks, Emily's patience was gone. Still sore from the C-section, her ears were ringing from the constant screaming. She walked into the bedroom, sat on the edge of her bed and began sobbing herself. "I can't take this anymore. I have to get some sleep."

Jason, roused after hearing the baby cry right next to him, dragged himself out of bed and stood in front of Emily. He looked down at her with what appeared to be a sympathetic expression. Expecting that he might say something like, 'You poor little thing,' instead she heard, "Welcome to Motherhood, Em."

She stopped crying and glared at him. *Honestly, if I could slap him, that would make me happy.* "Thanks for the empathy," she replied in a somewhat caustic tone.

"Look, Em," he tried to say over their screaming infant, "parenthood is not all cute sleeping Gerber babies. Being a mother in real life is not like it is on television. Most of the time, it involves this kind of thing."

"I need sleep."

"I know you do, and I offered to take him for a little while. Try to nurse him again and if he continues to fuss, I'll put him in the Snugli and walk around with him downstairs."

She tried to coax the baby to latch on one more time. "I just tried a few minutes ago and he wouldn't nurse."

As she put her breast near his mouth, he eagerly latched on and began to suckle. "Thank you, God," she whispered.

She carefully lay down on the bed and turned to her side so she could nurse him and fall back to sleep. Jason cuddled up behind her and held her close. As she became drowsy, she thanked God that, even if it was for a few minutes, she could drift off to sleep.

22

Psalm 43:3

December 1929

Katharine pulled her wool coat closer to her body as she waited for the streetcar to arrive. She hadn't realized it was so frigid when she had left this morning. Two of the buttons were missing from her coat and she had professed on many occasions that she wasn't going to waste her time sewing on two more. After all, it was usually not that cold this time of year. Besides, many people these days wore coats with no buttons, or even worse, with holes in them.

The stock market crash five weeks ago would make this a dreary Christmas. Katharine felt overly smug about one thing, though. She and Harry never invested anything in the stock market and didn't believe in using banks. Their money was still safely tucked away, stored in a cigar box in her bedroom closet.

On the other hand, business was certainly down at the store. Far too many people were out of work or out of money and were not going to buy frivolous sheet music or instruments.

Despite her discomfort, Katharine found herself the most excited she had been in years in anticipation of seeing her favorite artist's works in person. She regretted missing the grand opening of the Rodin Museum here in Philadelphia last month because Lizzie had given birth to yet another son. Even though she did not agree with their decision, she felt obligated to be available, in case there were problems.

A few years before, when Johnnie and Lizzie had revealed that they would be having another child, she shrugged her shoulders, somewhat annoyed that they had decided to have more children. After all, she had helped countless women prevent unwanted births by giving them valuable information. Why wouldn't her son and his wife continue to accept this assistance from her?   Now this new son would keep Lizzie quite occupied, though she knew that Sally, at 12 years of age, would be a huge help to her mother.

The trolley followed its normal route, its wretched stop and go motions and irritating clang becoming a bane to her comfort.   She knew that her stop would come quickly and when it did, she descended the steps.   She walked the remaining 12 or so blocks up the newly-paved parkway to the museum. Getting closer, she could make out the beautiful marble entranceway and a large cast sculpture of the original "Thinker."

Katharine quickened her pace at the excitement of seeing Rodin's works in person. She stopped at the massive reproduction of "The Thinker," situated in front of the entrance.   Glancing around, she was surprised that there were no other patrons visiting the museum. It seemed so quiet that she wondered whether it really was open for business.

She strolled around the outside, ignoring the cold temperatures, then she casually walked over to the huge marble gate area. Two bronze sculptures, one Adam and one Eve, situated rectangular openings on either side of the gate area. She walked to the left side opening which housed the sculpture entitled "Eve." Eve appeared to be twisted and ashamed, bending her body to cover it.   In the other opening was the sculpture "Adam," again twisted, tense and ashamed. She then sauntered to the entrance, just beyond the small garden created at the front of the museum, surrounding the sculptures.

Before entering, on the outside wall of the building, she stopped and studied one of the early large-scale models for the "Gates of Hell."   Katharine had read that the original "Thinker" was a man contemplating his life as he sits over the door to the gates of hell. She knew that her favorite artist was a free-thinker so why would he waste his time building the "Gates of Hell?" Feeling torn, she stood in awe and wonder at Rodin's exquisitely expressive creations, struggling to understand why this free-thinking artist would apply his talents to religious subjects like Adam and Eve, heaven and hell. However, she also realized that artists sometimes tended to be a strange bunch.

This sculpture, the "Gates of Hell," seemed so massive that it was almost too much to try to comprehend. Just to the left of the miniature Thinker and below him was what appeared to be a naked man, twisted in agony. In fact, it looked like he was trying to escape, but was being pulled back inside the gates.

She paused to analyze these twisted figures, reaching out a hand to trace the lines of tension on one of the bodies bent in shame. Abruptly, she drew back and thrust her hand into her coat pocket.

Katharine turned away for a moment. Why would this make her uneasy? She glanced back again at the sculpture and studied for a moment the miniature "Thinker's" face. What would any man be thinking about if he was about to enter the gates of hell? To Katharine, it seemed to be such a waste of time to be wondering about that. Hell didn't exist. Isn't it bad enough that when a person dies, he or she simply dies?

Shaking her head, Katharine walked into the warmth of the museum.

"This looks interesting," she said out loud, as she began reading quotations by Rodin: "Nothing is a waste of time if you use the experience wisely." She frowned, then stood back and read it again, "Nothing is a waste of time if you use the experience wisely." Relaxing her shoulders and unbuttoning the rest of her coat, she reflected on this idea. The images of the "Gates of Hell" were fresh in her mind. She realized that 'waste of time' came often to her lips. Throwing away life and its experiences. . .was that part of Rodin's hell?

Katharine scrolled down and her eye caught another quote, "To the artist, there is never anything ugly in nature." *I can't understand that one.* She thought of her husband's face, with his big nose and harsh features. She remembered the son of one of her friends coming back from the Great War with one arm and one leg missing and his face mangled beyond recognition.

Land mine, they said. Her mind wandered to the image of the young woman who had tried to take care of the problem of her unwanted pregnancy and the sunken, gray face of her newly-dead body. She had a difficult time thinking those things wouldn't be ugly to Rodin, or to anyone, for that matter.

She walked into the larger open area which housed the gigantic Burghers of Calais sculpture. Katharine was confronted by a museum worker, dressed in a blue uniform coat. Other than this man, it seemed to Katharine that she was the only other person in the museum.

She nonchalantly strolled further into the museum and was overwhelmed by the smell of fresh paint. The odor seemed to hit her like a blast of air when she walked into one of the smaller rooms and made her feel lightheaded.

She came to a sculpture of a priest and Katharine remembered that she was surprised when she had read in one book that Rodin had studied with a Catholic order. Knowing that he had a companion for many years who served as his model, as well as various mistresses, it appeared to Katharine that Rodin's philosophies were extremely contradictory. She had read that he married his long-time companion at the end of their lives together, only a week before his companion died and 10 months before he died. *Better late than never.*

She moved on to another bronze sculpture, this one entitled "Hand of God." This particular piece was too abstract for Katharine's liking yet she still lowered her head to read, "The Hand of God. . .now holding two small figures, conveys the omnipotence of God and becomes a symbol of creation, both of God's power to create and of the creativity of the sculptor." Impatiently, Katharine stepped back to scrutinize the work. Where did God's hand begin and the human beings held within it end? She scratched her neck where her wool coat grazed her skin. Where was God when that young woman died on her shop floor?

God's omnipotence? Again, it seemed so out of character for Rodin to create sculptures which seemed to illustrate a strong faith when she considered his life, one that included living with a woman without benefit of marriage, as well as various other mistresses. That kind of situation was unheard of, even in these modern times. It was, in fact, the kind of behavior which endeared Rodin to Katharine's way of thinking.

She gripped her handbag and pressed on, finally slowing as she reached some of Rodin's nude sculptures. Like "The Kiss," she considered these images erotic and appreciated that they were now publicly displayed for Katharine and others to enjoy without fear of the police seizing them for indecency. Unbidden, Michael's voice echoed softly in her mind. *For you, Katharine.* His gift of the small reproduction of "The Kiss" was so precious to her, yet she'd had to keep it tucked away, out of sight.

"Mrs. Clayman, are you unwell?"

Katharine brushed the back of her hand across her eyes and turned around. Disconcerted, she recognized a customer from her store. He was always impeccably well-dressed, today wearing an expensive tailored coat. His gray hair was covered by a derby hat and his still dark beard suited his long face. She had always considered him quite handsome, but if Katharine had to use one word to describe him, 'pompous' would be her choice.

"Thank you, Mr. Blake. I am just fine, perhaps a little warm after stepping in from the cold." Katharine now became self-conscious about the two buttons missing on her coat and tried to casually shift her purse to conceal them. Still vexed at being caught unaware, she continued, "A fine exhibition, don't you agree?"

"Exquisite. I have appreciated Rodin's art works for some time now. I have been to the Rodin Museum in Paris."

Eyebrows raised, she kept silent and wished that she could tell Mr. Blake what she thought of his self-important airs.

"You're looking lovely today."

"Good day, Mr. Blake."

He tipped his hat and walked on.

Suddenly feeling drained and somewhat claustrophobic in the dim museum rooms, Katharine made her way to the nearest exit, almost walking by a sculpture entitled "Hand of the

Devil Holding Woman" in her haste. Rodin's signature, obvious on the lower right hand side of the piece, caught Katharine's eye and kept her from moving on. She studied the piece at first from the front, then she moved to either sides. A hand, laying almost flat, cupped the body of a nude woman in a fetal position. The clearly-defined outlines, the separateness of the hand and the woman moved Katharine in a way that she couldn't explain. It was one of those pieces that plainly and simply displayed Rodin's genius.

As she began reading about the piece, she caught her breath. "In his early life, Rodin distrusted women and, like so many other intellectuals of last century, often associated them with the devil."

Katharine's face formed a frown. *What a ridiculous theory.*

Sometimes, she was convinced that it was men who were Satan's associates. Debating with herself was a waste of time when she didn't even believe in any God or devil, heaven or hell. At least her beliefs came without contradictions.

23

Song of Songs 5:16

May, 1989

Emily dragged herself out of bed and sighed. It was difficult trying to deal with young Jake's sleeping problems and nightmares, then waking up the next morning with only a few hours of sleep. Thankfully, Jason took him often in the night. However, it was more frequent that she comforted him as Jake sometimes would only accept soothing at the breast. In the early months of this newest pregnancy, she hardly had time to think of the little person growing inside of her. With the initial nausea gone, Emily was thankful that she could at least have enough energy to complete her household duties of dishes and laundry. As well, she had gotten out her great-grandmother's ledgers and had begun the job of trying to decipher them again.

Despite her pregnancy and weight gain, at 30, Emily still enjoyed her youthful looks, her brown hair once again waist length.

With two-year-old Jake playing with a Lego set in the living room, and with one of the ledgers in front of her, Emily telephoned her mother.

"Hi, Mom."

"Hi, Em, feeling better?"

"A bit. Jake had another bad night and yet it doesn't seem to affect him during the day. I mean, he seems to deal well with his own lack of sleep."

"Kids are resilient."

"Tell me about it. Mom, remember that I asked you about your grandparents' ledger entries?"

"You did?"

"Yeah, around two years ago when Jake was a baby. I asked you if you knew anything about what 'BPO, Midwife' meant and why your grandmother would've been away from the store in 1918."

"Oh, yeah, I remember."

"You told me that you didn't know what BPO meant but that you did know that your grandmother definitely didn't have the bad case of Influenza that spread through Philly in 1918."

"Yes. I'm not sure why she was gone from the store. Did Aunt Sally know?"

"Aunt Sal wasn't sure, but she agreed with you, that she definitely didn't have the flu during that time, that it must have been something else. Aunt Sally would've only been a year old then. She did tell me that your parents had another child and she died during that time, or the next year, so maybe she was helping to take care of Sally."

"I don't think that was it. Grandmom wasn't that kind of a grandmother."

"It's hard to believe that I've been researching this family tree stuff for 12 years. You would think that I could've discovered what some of these codes mean before now. Then again, I just wish I had more time to spend on this project. Jake takes up so much of my time and once the new baby comes, I'll be busier than ever."

The next morning, at breakfast, Jake was his usual rambunctious, active self, fidgeting in his seat, slurping large, dripping gulps of his Rice Krispies. Jason walked into the kitchen and reached up into the cupboard for some cereal. Emily was standing close to him at the sink in their large kitchen, looking out the small window. "Jay, it's going to be a beautiful, sunny day. It's hard to believe that in six weeks, you'll be home for the summer."

Jason moved closer and stretched his arms around his pregnant wife's growing belly and leaned down to kiss her neck.

Emily turned around and reached up to return the kiss. As she broke off the kiss, she studied her husband. His dark curly hair now had generous flecks of gray and it created the impression of his being much older than 27 years.

"I'm so thankful we live close to the school where you teach," Emily said. "It's great to have you home every day for lunch. After all, I'm making your favorite lunch today. It'll be ready when you come home at noon."

"Uh-oh. I hope you're not making cream of bag clipping soup, Em."

"Very funny. Am I not going to hear the end of that?"

"Come on, Em. It's hilarious."

"I suppose it is," she admitted.

He was referring to the time that she had made his favorite soup, homemade cream of celery. Unbeknownst to her, she had cut off the edge of a milk bag and it had fallen into the pot. A short while later, when Jason began to eat the soup, he discovered the clipping and refused to tell Emily. Later, he told her about it and they both had laughed.

Ever since then, whenever Emily offered to make homemade soup, Jason couldn't miss an opportunity to tease her about the bag clipping incident.

"I'm making blueberry pancakes with maple syrup."

"Ah, then I'm safe, unless, of course, you use milk to make the pancakes."

"I'm using a mix, happy?"

"Relieved."

"Listen, Jay, would you mind if. . . ."

She was interrupted by a crashing sound. "Aaaah," screamed Jake, as they looked over to see Jake's bowl of Rice Krispies splattered all over the floor and wall. Their son's voice was piercing as he was yelling and pounding his hands on the table. "Want Kispies, want my Kispies!"

Emily sighed.

"Here, Em. I'll get the mess," her husband offered.

"No, no, I'll get it."

Her son's screeching made her ears ring. Walking toward the milk-covered floor, she crouched down in a somewhat awkward position, her protruding middle making it more difficult to accomplish the simple task. "I hate when this happens first thing in the morning," she grumbled and threw the towel on the floor. While she grudgingly wiped up the mess, Jason leaned down and in Jake's ear said, "I'm Kermit dee Frog and I love Miss Piggy," in his finest Muppet voice.

Jake became quiet and, distracted, started giggling at his father's impeccable Kermit impression.

Emily stopped cleaning for a moment and watched them. "Is there no end to your talents?"

Jason looked up at her, his mouth upturned in a smile and replied, "Wait till you hear my Big Bird."

As she watched her husband interact with their son, her heart softened. That kind of behavior always made her fall more in love with him.

She remembered a recent telephone conversation with her friend, Carrie, who was complaining that her husband didn't 'turn her on' anymore, that she no longer found her spouse attractive. Carrie had asked Emily what Jason did to 'turn her on.' Emily's answer had probably shocked her friend: "I get turned on when I watch my husband playing with my son, or making breakfast with an apron around his waist, or cleaning up a mess on the floor. There's nothing like the sight of your husband rocking a newborn baby and singing a soothing lullaby to put a wife in the mood for marital intimacy."

Her friend had replied, "You are kidding, right?"

"No, I'm not."

"How in the world can those things turn you on? Me, I need to read a explicit romance novel to get in the mood."

"That, in my eyes, is missing the point," Emily had said. "Sex is much more than just pleasure. Part of desiring my husband is wanting to join with him in the celebration of our covenant."

Carrie had been silent for a few seconds.

"Right, it's all this spiritual stuff and no pleasure?"

"No, no. I didn't say that. But without the spiritual stuff, the physical aspect is empty pleasure."

"Look, Em, I know you mean well, but all this religious talk makes me uncomfortable."

Jake's loud giggle interrupted her thoughts. Watching her son and her husband interacting, her heart filled with love for the two people in the world that she cared most about.

Jason glanced at the clock. "Hey, I've got to get going. See you in a few hours." He leaned over to kiss Jake and Emily, then planted a soft kiss on her stomach and rushed out the door. As her son played again with toys on the floor, Emily picked up a pen and began writing:

Jay,

I feel emotional today, perhaps from the pregnancy or maybe it's just an overwhelming need to tell you how much I love you and appreciate your presence in my life, your unconditional love despite my negativity and complaining.

God has blessed us with so much, not the least of which is this rambunctious "walking representation" of our love.

Thank you for loving me when I'm grumbling and complaining. . . .

"Waaaah," Jake cried. He had begun to build some kind of fort with large Lego blocks and it had fallen apart.

Emily sighed, then crouched down to comfort her son. "Fort fell, Mommy."

"Yes, honey, I know. I understand why you're sad."

He stopped crying, then looked up at her. "Mommy, help?"

"Sure, I'll help you build another."

With that, she stooped down and began picking up the Lego pieces.

24

Psalm 73:21-22

December 6, 1941

"My dogs!" Katharine yelled at her son as he watched his daughter, Becky, playing in his mother's small front yard. The youngest grandchild was now seven and constantly pestering her Lhaso Apso dogs.

"She's not going near the dogs, Ma," John said.

Katharine, 62, frowned as she watched young Becky. After all the trouble that Lizzie had gone through, she still couldn't believe that they had three more children. More kids meant more people for Katharine to worry about.

She smoothed out the apron on her dress. Though she had remained quite thin, in the last few years, she had started to lose a rotten tooth just about every year. That hadn't happened to her since she was a young child. Her new dentures felt like horse teeth and she was always biting her lip. Her mostly gray hair was tidily gathered into a low-netted bun.

"I thought you were going to bring the boys to help me move some furniture. Your father's about as much help as a two year old and Charlie's got a bad back."

"I told you that the boys had band practice," he replied.

"They're getting too old for that kind of stuff. They both ought to be getting a job to help out."

John sighed. "Ma, you certainly have your priorities, don't you?"

"What's that supposed to mean?"

"You know, there's a war raging over in Europe. It's only a matter of time before we're involved in that."

'That type of thing doesn't interest me, Johnnie. After all,

I don't have any sons who would have to fight."

Sally was walking up the street from her apartment a few blocks away. When she was close enough, she said, "Hi, Dad, Grandmom."

"You're looking awfully chipper, Sal," Katharine observed.

"I have some great news, but I want to tell Mom first," Sally said, as she walked quickly toward John and Lizzie's house.

Katharine watched her oldest granddaughter with pride. She had grown into a lovely young woman and now seemed to be enjoying married life.

A few minutes later, Katharine could see Sally almost running up the street toward them. As she got closer to her father and her grandmother, she said, "I've got wonderful news. Bill and I are expecting a baby!"

Katharine sighed. *No wonder she has such a smirk on her face.* "I hope you're not going to have a pile of kids like your mother."

"Ma!" John said. "Honey, that's great news. I'm going to be a grandfather."

Sally looked down, then over at her grandmother. "I'm very happy, Grandmom, and I hope I can have a pile of kids, just like my mother."

Katharine rolled her eyes. "Look, Sally. . . ."

The distant sound of the phone ringing inside the house interrupted her.

"Keep an eye on the dogs, Johnnie, while I go in and get that blasted telephone."

Sally and John listened as they heard, "Yes. . .yes. . .when . . .no. . .all right."

She rushed out the door and yelled at her son. "John, Ruth's in the Pennsylvania Hospital. She's just had surgery. I'm not sure what the hell is going on. All I know is that Howard called to tell me she's had an operation and is recovering. My car's in the shop, so I need you to drive me to the hospital."

"Sure, Ma. Sally, will you take Becky home?"

Sally nodded as she took her sister's hand and walked down the street to her mother's house.

John ran around to the area behind the row houses where his car was parked, hopped in, and was pulling up to the back of his mother's place just as she was closing and locking the back door. He watched as she quickly maneuvered the somewhat rickety wooden steps.

"Pop coming?" John asked.

"No. He's been drinking all night again and I couldn't budge him."

Katharine got in the car and they began the short drive to the hospital.

"I can't imagine what in the world she could be having surgery for. I hope she's all right, Johnnie."

"She's young, Ma. I'm sure she'll be all right."

John pulled up to the entrance, allowed his mother to get out, then parked the car. Not knowing whether he would be allowed to visit his sister, he sat in one of the comfortable chairs in the lobby and picked up a Saturday Evening Post magazine with a Norman Rockwell picture on the cover.

At the registration desk, Katharine was told her daughter's room number. She stepped into the elevator that would take her to the room. Tapping her foot nervously, she wondered why the elevator took so long. She rolled her eyes as she listened to the operator humming some kind of jazz-type tune. "Here we are, third floor, ma'am," she heard him say.

Katharine sighed as she exited the elevator. "347," she kept saying as she was searching for the room. "Ah, here it is." She walked in and saw Ruth's husband, Howard, sitting in a chair beside his wife. "What in the world is going on here? Why did she need surgery?"

"They tell me she's had an ectopic pregnancy. That's where the pregnancy is in the tube, instead of her womb."

"I know damned well what an ectopic pregnancy is."

"Well, she's lost a lot of blood and she's very weak, but she's going to be heartbroken when she wakes up."

"What in the world for? She's not going to die, not in this day and age."

"No, no.   But now she. . .won't be able to have any children. . . not with this operation." Howard's voice was cracking.

"What are you talking about?"

"She's already had one of these, a few years ago.   It happened while you and Harry were down at the shore.   She didn't want to tell you. She didn't want you to worry about her."

"Well, it's not really that big of a deal anyway. You can get along fine with no kids. Besides, that's even better. You can have fun and not ever have to worry about getting pregnant again. I'd say she was darned lucky. I would've given anything to be in her shoes."

Katharine then watched as her son-in-law's eyes became downcast.   There was an awkward silence between the two of them.

Howard motioned for Katharine to come sit in the seat next to Ruth's bed.   She studied her daughter's face, pale and calm.

"Did you want some coffee, Mrs. Clayman?"

"No, thank you, Howard."

"I'll be back shortly."

"She's going to be just fine, Howard, just fine. Don't you worry."

"Of course, she is," he said, then he walked out the door.

The next day, Katharine was relaxing in the living room, listening to the radio and Glenn Miller's orchestra playing "Pennsylvania 6-5000." During the chorus, as the band was singing the words, "Pennsylvania six five oh, oh. . . ." the music stopped and an announcer came on.

"We interrupt this broadcast to bring you a live bulletin. The Japanese have attacked the naval bases at Pearl Harbor, Hawaii. . . ." Katharine then listened to several minutes of news concerning the attack.

"Did you hear, Mom?" she heard, as John walked into her house. "We're at war."

"Yeah, yeah. I heard. I wish they would put the music back on. Listen, do me a favor and go tell your father. He's been down in the basement again. And throw some coal on the fire while you're at it." Katharine walked with John to the kitchen, then listened as John rushed downstairs. "Pop, wake up."

"Yeah, Johnnie, what is it?" she heard her husband say.

"We're at war. The Japs have attacked Pearl Harbor in Hawaii."

"They what? What are you talking about, Johnnie? What the hell do the Japs want to attack us for?"

"Don't know. I was hoping that we would keep out of the war."

Katharine couldn't hear her husband's response, if any. "I should go home before Lizzie and the kids return from church. By the way, you probably haven't heard, but Ruth is in the hospital. She's just had surgery."

"She what?"

"Yeah, Pop, I have to get going, but Ma can tell you about it. Some kind of woman problems or something. It looks like she's going to be all right."

John ran up the steps and past his mother in the kitchen. "See you, Ma. I've gotta go home before Lizzie and the kids get home from Mass."

Katharine waited in the kitchen for a few moments. She couldn't explain why, but she felt on edge, especially hearing the news of the attack. Katharine listened at the top of the steps. It appeared to be quiet again in the basement. Her husband had obviously fallen back to sleep.

In the living room, she walked by the bookcase, picked up a book from the table and placed it on the shelf. She caught a glimpse of the boat Harry carved for her. *If that thing wasn't there, I'd be able to store more of my books.*

She climbed the steps, turned and walked toward her bedroom. As she opened the door, she could see that Charlie was sitting on the side of her bed.

"What are you doing in here?" Katharine studied her

boarder. After ten years, she was beginning to tire of him, despite the fact that he was ten years younger. Though he was a fairly handsome man with an exceptional physique, his bodily hygiene certainly left a lot to be desired and his breath smelled like chewing tobacco. However, she reasoned that he had been a mediocre lover.

"It's Sunday, Katharine. You know what that means."

She frowned. "You're not supposed to come into my bedroom without my invitation."

"I thought you forgot, Katharine. I've been looking forward to this all week."

"All right," she said, as she pushed the door closed.

As they became involved in their growing pleasure, Katharine sat up abruptly in bed.

"What was that sound?"

"Nothing, Katharine. Shhh," he whispered.

"Get up, Charlie. I need to get dressed." Katharine reached for her dress.

"But we're not finished yet."

"Get your damned pants on," Katharine ordered, as she began to button up her dress.

Charlie lifted himself off the bed. "Gee, Katharine, the least you could do is. . . ." As he was pulling his pants on, Katharine looked up in horror to see her husband opening the door, a shotgun in his hand. For a few seconds, her open mouth couldn't speak. Everything seemed to be happening in slow motion.

"Harry! What. . .what the hell are you doing?"

Harry's eyes were bulging and the gun was pointed straight at the boarder.

"Get outta my wife's room, Charlie."

"Now, now, Harry. No need to get all upset."

"I don't want to mess up my wife's bedroom with your blood, Charlie. Get out, now!"

"Sure, Harry, sure, sure. Whatever. . .you say."

"Put the damned gun down, Harry. You're being an idiot," Katharine yelled.

Ignoring his wife, he continued pointing the gun at Charlie and forced him down the steps, the gun at his back.

Katharine wanted to run after them, but like in a bad dream, it felt as if her feet were nailed to the floor. A few seconds later, she was able to move. As she descended the stairs, she desperately tried to fasten the last few buttons on her dress, her hands shaking. Halfway down, she watched as Charlie escaped out the front door.

"Damn it, Harry, put the gun down," she screamed.

Katharine had never seen such rage in Harry's eyes and for a brief moment, she was afraid. It was as if someone had taken over her husband's body. She watched as he ran out the door, knocking over the hat rack beside the doorway. Katharine rushed through the living room and onto the porch in an attempt to reach her husband as he chased after Charlie.

Outside, Katharine could see that Harry had stopped in front of Johnnie's house at the end of the street, the gun pointing at Charlie's chest. Ten feet behind him, Katharine watched her son calmly approach his father. John stood beside him, and she could see her youngest granddaughter on the porch, wide-eyed and confused.

The scene appeared frozen in time. Several onlookers from the neighborhood had gathered across the small street. "I'm gonna kill him, Johnnie. I'm gonna kill him, once and for all." Harry was yelling, his usually deep voice at a high pitch.

"Pop, look at me."

As Harry fixed him with a fiery glare, Charlie shuffled backward against a fence, face pale and fists clenched.

"Pop," John was yelling now. "Look. . .at. . .me."

Harry finally took his eyes off of Charlie and, with a haunted expression, stared at his son.

"Give me the gun, Pop. This won't solve anything." John tried to speak as calmly and slowly as possible.

Harry released the weapon to the ground and dropped to his knees. With his hands covering his eyes, he started to cry, long, hard sobs. John let out a deep sigh of relief and picked up the gun.

"Come on, Pop." He gently pulled his father to a standing position and began walking up the steps to his home. Looking back at Charlie, John tilted his head, indicating that he should take the opportunity to leave before Harry changed his mind.

Charlie rushed past Katharine, shoving her out of the way. "Charlie, wait," she yelled.

He turned around. "No, Katharine, I'm not waiting. I'm gettin' outta here before your madman husband shoots me."

"He wasn't going to shoot you. He's not like that."

Charlie's jaw dropped and his eyes widened.

Katharine tentatively walked up to her son's porch, remaining hidden as she stood outside, listening to her husband's sobbing.

"I love her so much, Johnnie. I knew what she was doing with him. But I had never seen it happening. This time I did. Just watching them set me off in a rage I never knew. I just wanted to kill him, I did. I wanted to kill him."

"I know, but you didn't."

The aroma of cinnamon buns filled the house and porch. It was Sunday morning and Katharine knew that Lizzie would be baking after Mass.

Katharine stood awkwardly on the porch, unnoticed by her son and husband. She began to shiver in the cool air. In her haste to catch up to Harry and Charlie, she had forgotten to grab her coat.

Part of her wanted to smack Harry across the face. Another part of her felt regret. She realized that Harry knew about the boarders and for the most part, she didn't care. But for one brief moment, she wondered whether someone could have been killed because of her actions. No, she told herself, Harry wouldn't ever hurt a flea.

The door opened suddenly and Katharine, caught off guard, jumped back.

"Hello, Grandmom."

"Shhh, be quiet, Becky." She pulled her seven-year-old grandchild away from the door.

"Want me to get Grandpop? He's sad. I don't like seeing him cry."

"No, no, just be quiet," she whispered.

She listened as her husband continued his sobbing.

"I think Grandpop needs a hug, Grandmom."

"Yeah, well, that would be a good thing for you to do. Give him a hug."

Becky smiled, her little curls bouncing like Shirley Temple's, as she opened the screen door. Katharine, still hidden from sight, watched as Becky climbed onto her grandfather's lap. She wondered why her husband had to make such a scene.

"Becky, honey, Grandpop's real sad," Harry tried to say through his tears.

"Grandmom said to give you a hug."

Katharine's eyes widened, then she stepped away from the door to avoid being discovered.

Within seconds, her son opened the door and stood on the porch. "Come inside and talk to him, will you, Ma?"

"No, Johnnie, I'm going home. If he wants to talk to me, he can come there. That was a foolish, stupid thing for him to do and you know it."

"That was a real smart thing that you did, Ma," he said sarcastically.

"You mind your tone with me. I'm still your mother. Have some respect."

"And you?" his voice was quiet, but it had a sharp edge to it. "What about respecting your husband?"

It was the first time Katharine had heard her son speak in a cross manner to her. Shocked, she stared at him with an open mouth, unable to respond.

John shook his head and walked back inside the living room. Katharine rushed down the porch steps and hurried home.

She opened the door, then listened. She could hear banging noises coming from upstairs. Walking slowly to the bottom of the stairs, she yelled to her boarder, "Want some coffee, Charlie?"

Hearing no answer, she stood silently, listening to the sounds emanating from the upstairs. If she didn't know better, she would swear that he was rearranging furniture. Katharine decided that despite her boarder's refusal to answer, she could really use a cup of black coffee.

In the kitchen, she plopped herself onto the chair. The seat felt ice cold and for a minute, Katharine shivered, but she was determined to wait there until Harry returned. She refused to apologize. It was her husband who needed to say he was sorry to Charlie. She couldn't imagine ever holding a gun to someone's head and chest like Harry did.

A few minutes later, Katharine heard the door open.

"Is that you, Johnnie?"

"Yeah, Ma, it's me."

Katharine yelled, "I'm in the kitchen. You got your father with you?"

"Yes, I've got Pop with me."

She attempted to appear calm, but the truth was, she was madder than hell at Harry. Her teeth clenched, she glanced up to see her husband's hang-dog expression, his eyes avoiding hers.

"What the hell did you think you were doing, Harry? What a stupid thing to do!"

John interrupted her. "Oh, and what you did was smart, Ma?"

"I told you to watch your tongue." Katharine refused to let her son show any disrespect to her.

John replied, "Look, Pop feels bad enough about it. I think something needs to be done about Charlie."

"Listen, Johnnie, you keep your nose out of our affairs. Charlie's got no place to go but the street. He's got feelings too, you know. He's been here for nearly 10 years. Besides, we need his rent money."

"A man could've died today, Ma," he said in a soft-spoken tone of voice.

"That's nonsense. I knew Harry wouldn't kill him."

"Ma, do you hear yourself? A man could've died today.

Why can't you see that?"

Katharine stared straight ahead, then her eyes focused on the table.

After a few minutes of awkward silence, Harry finally spoke up, his voice timid and cracking, "I'm. . .I'm. . .sorry, Katharine."

She studied her husband's face. He stared at the floor the entire time.

"Just don't do it again, Harry. That was really stupid."

"Look, Pop, I'd better go home. You gonna be all right?" John turned around and began walking to the living room.

"Yeah, Johnnie, I'll be fine. Going downstairs."

Katharine watched, then listened as her husband's footsteps slowly maneuvered down their steep staircase to the cellar. Her attention was drawn to the living room as she heard Johnnie speaking to someone.

"Does Mom know you're leaving?"

"I'm not figuring on telling her neither. I'd be grateful if you told her I said goodbye."

"I think you ought to do that, Charlie. I have to go."

Katharine sighed, but made no attempt to move as she heard the door open and close, then a few seconds later, listened to the door open and slam shut again.

A man could've died today, Ma. Her mind replayed the scene again: Harry's face and eyes full of uncontrolled rage, the gun staring at Charlie's frightened form, Johnnie's worried expression, the neighbors' stares, her granddaughter's wide eyes, her husband's sobbing.

Katharine's hands shook almost uncontrollably as she took a sip of her coffee, now lukewarm. Setting it down, she realized that the top two buttons of her dress were undone.

She began fastening them, then stopped.

A man could've died. She clutched the top of her dress, then stood up. *Either way, he's gone.*

She slowly walked into the living room and opened the screen door.

Katharine stepped out onto the porch and, eyes watering, stared down the street at Charlie's figure, now a speck in the distance.

25

Psalm 25: 16-18

July 1991

The quiet sobbing echoed throughout the house. Emily, absorbed in sadness, cried for an entire day. The physical pain of her last miscarriage, the second loss in three months, was almost gone. The emotional distress, the gut-wrenching despair, seemed to consume her and she welcomed it.

Jason was in the next room, sleeping with his two young sons, Jake, now four and Nate, almost two. Emily's husband was known for his ability to sleep through major explosions. And yet, he made himself present in their bedroom, positioned himself on the side of their bed, and gently cradled her in his arms.

"All I wanted to do is have another baby."

"I know, Em." He allowed his wife to simply cry and grieve.

Later that morning, the phone rang and Emily hesitated. She refused to talk to anyone, even Jason at that moment. However, the person on the other end was persistent. After listening to the phone ring many times, she figured that she might as well answer it.

"Hello."

"Yes, Em, this is Aunt Sally."

"Hi, Aunt Sally."

"Aunt Sally's been so worried about you, Tootsie Roll. I've rung your phone several times today. Your mother and Susan have also been trying to reach you."

"I don't really feel like talking to anyone, Aunt Sally."

"Now, look here, Tootsie Roll, Aunt Sal knows how hard it is to lose a child. You've got to pick yourself up and carry on. After all, you've got two babies who need you."

"I know you mean well, but I'd better go," she said as she hung up the phone. She was just going through the motions, keeping the television on for the boys and trying to avoid the inference that God was saying no to her.

Another week went by and Emily continued to welcome her depression. Whenever she saw a pregnant woman, her eyes watered. Whenever she heard of a woman getting her tubes tied or a man having a vasectomy, she became angry. *All I want to do is have another child. These couples who are destroying their fertility don't want any more children and yet I do. Oh, God, why won't you give me another child? Why do you allow so many couples to destroy their fertility? Why do you allow teenagers to get pregnant, when you know some of them are going to have abortions?*

Four-year-old Jake came up to Emily that evening, stood by her side until she looked at him, then asked, "Why are you sad, Mommy?"

Not seeing the point in explaining her emotional state to her young son, she ignored his question.

"Mommy, please," he persisted, "Why are you sad?"

Eyes downcast, she continued to ignore his question.

Emily's husband, unusually patient and tolerant, finally approached her. "Em, I know you are still grieving, but you have two young sons who need you."

"But all I want to do is have another baby."

"I know you do, but you have two children here, now."

"Why won't God allow me to have another child?"

"Em, we have to be open to God's will, whatever that is. Perhaps His will for us is to have a smaller family than we anticipated."

"No! It can't be! It's not fair."

"I know that it's hard right now, but you need to focus on God's will, not yours. Our boys need their mom."

Emily began to weep, not quietly, but hard, loud sobbing. Jason simply held her, rubbing her back, stroking her hair, consoling her.

"God, please help Em to deal with her grief," he whispered.

The next day, after Jason had gone to work, she sat on the couch with her two young sons as they watched a video. She studied them, Jacob, her four year old, blond and blue-eyed and her toddler, Nathaniel, with brown eyes and dark curly hair like his father's.

She remembered Pope John Paul II's quote from The Role of the Christian Family in the Modern World where he referred to children as ". . .the fruit and sign of conjugal love, the living testimony of the full reciprocal self-giving of the spouses."

During the last few weeks, she had been angry with God for allowing the most recent miscarriage. Now, she felt an overwhelming need to be closer to Him. She picked up their bible from the end table. She opened it to Isaiah 49:15 and found the words:

> *"Can a mother forget her infant*
> *be without tenderness for the child of her womb?*
> *Even should she forget*
> *I will never forget you."*

She allowed the words to take hold of her and they gripped her like a vice on her heart. "Oh, God, how could I forget my two beautiful children? How could I be so self-centered?"

She was immediately filled with remorse. How could she have allowed herself to become so self-absorbed in her grief that she couldn't love and pay attention to her sons? They were, after all, great gifts from God and He trusted her to take care of them.

Next, she opened it to Romans 8:31:

"If God is for us, who can be against us?"

It occurred to her that God had always been on her side, that He loved her unconditionally, that He had never forgotten her.   She realized that God did not allow these losses to hurt her. Emily understood that she needed to let Him have control over her life and her responsibility would be to deal with whatever happened.

She walked over to the television and turned it off. Jacob began screaming and Nathaniel started crying. "Come on, boys, let's   make   some   'playdough.'   Jake,   how   about   you   do   the mixing?"

"Yay. I love to mix it!"

"Me, me," cried Nate.

She leaned down and picked up her toddler and studied his face and his dark curly hair. "He looks so like his dad," she said out loud, "a living reflection."   Walking into the kitchen, Emily sat him in the high chair and helped Jake into his booster seat at the table while she retrieved a bowl from the cupboard. They spent the next several hours mixing and coloring 'playdough,' then creating miniature sculptures.

"Mommy, look at my dinosaur," Jake said proudly as he showed her his creation.

"My, what a scary-looking dinosaur."

"Yeah, it's a T-rex. It can eat people."

Emily's eyes focused on young Nathaniel and marveled at his concentration.

"What are you making, sweetie?"

He babbled in his own language, "doo sah, Mamma."

Emily's heart was full of love for her children and again she felt immense gratitude for the tremendous gift of motherhood.

How could she forget about that in a self-centered quest for more children? Why was she looking for something that she already had?

"I'm glad you feel better, Mommy."

"Yeah, me too, Jake."

With renewed strength, as the boys were playing with the 'playdough,' Emily began cleaning the several days' worth of dishes still sitting in the sink and on the counter. Under a pile of junk mail was a single ledger from her great-grandmother's music store. She dusted it off and placed it on the corner of the counter to remind herself to page through it again. She found a note to call local midwives to ask them if they knew what BPO could possibly mean. After all, Katharine had written it next to the word *midwife*.

When Jason returned home for lunch, he found a reborn Emily. When he gazed down into her eyes, he saw joy rather than depression; hope rather than pessimism. His expression was one of relief.

"I've been praying a lot this morning, Jay."

"Apparently," he said.

"I'm going to be okay. If it's God's will that we only raise these two beautiful boys, then I accept that. I keep thinking what a great gift these children are and I am so grateful that I am able to be their mother."

He embraced his wife. "I've been praying for you almost constantly, Em."

"I know you have, Jay."

Later that night, the two of them prayed the rosary with their two young sons. There were many interruptions, but their family unity was preserved. Emily promised God that no matter what happened in the future, she would trust His Will, whatever that was.

26

Rom. 5:3-5

June 1993

The pain in her abdomen became more excruciating with every passing moment. She sat on the sofa and dialed the number of the high school. It seemed like an eternity for the line to connect. One, two rings. *Please, someone pick up*, she silently begged. Hearing the secretary's voice, Emily could barely speak, but she uttered enough to make it clear that she needed her husband. She dropped the phone and tried to take a deep breath. Feeling an overwhelming need to vomit, she rushed to the bathroom just in time to spill the contents of her stomach. She gripped the cold, hard toilet, as if in some way, it would make her pain bearable. Disoriented, she thought of her baby and quickly glanced over at his smiling, inquisitive face, oblivious to his mother's pain.

I've got to stay conscious for my baby, she repeated over and over again in her mind. She thought of her two older sons, Jake, six, and Nate, four, safe at school. She moved back to the floor next to the sofa, trying to sit upright with young Thomas next to her, while drifting in and out of consciousness. Keeping a death grip on him, she woke up as the paramedics were prying her hands off her toddler and placing her on a stretcher. It all seemed like a dream.

Too weak to make a sound, she wondered where her young son was. She caught a glimpse of her husband holding their young son at the back doors of the ambulance.

His right arm cradled their son's little body, while his left hand clasped his small head to his chest as if to shield and protect him from the turmoil that surrounded them both. But her husband's face. . .his face was so broken and distraught and Emily felt the anguish of a wife and mother abandoning her family. Tears welled up in her eyes and for a moment, Emily forgot her pain.

Then his eyes caught hers and he realized that she was watching him. Everything changed. His chin lifted as if for courage and penetrated her being with a look of tenderness, of confidence and reassurance. *Whatever happens, I will be strong for you and for the sons we both love and for God, who has asked so much of you.* He seemed to say all of this with his eyes, all of this and more. As his love reached out to her through the shouts of the paramedics and their frantic procedures, the beeping of machines and the overwhelming wail of the siren, its light already flashing, her terror began to fade and her heart surged within her. Now reassured, she allowed herself to fall back to sleep.

Emily's eyes opened again this time as the paramedics were inserting an intravenous needle in her arm. Although it felt like they were stabbing her with an ice pick, all she could manage was a wince and a quiet moan. It seemed as if every ounce of energy had been sucked from her being. *This is what it feels like to die.*

She imagined her three little boys' faces and suddenly, the possibility of dying weighed heavy on her heart. *Please, God, I can't die*, she silently prayed. *I don't want my boys growing without a mother.* All at once, a feeling of warmth surrounded her, then she felt at peace. There was no bitterness, only acceptance, a calm that was huge enough to quiet an ocean. She silently recited a Hail Mary. ". . . *now and at the hour of our death. Amen.*" Those last words took on powerful meaning with the possibility that this could be her hour. She trusted that whatever happened would be God's will, and she would submit to that, whatever it was.

Drifting into unconsciousness, the last thing she heard was "We're losing her. . . ."

A bump in the road jolted Emily awake. *Oh God, the pain is so unbearable.* It felt as if something was going to burst inside of her abdomen. Her whole body felt weak, tired. Too stubborn to give up, she again imagined her three small boys' faces and her will to live became strong.

She woke up inside the brightly lit, sterile, clean-smelling environment of the emergency room.

With the cold intravenous fluid going through her, Emily began to shiver. One of the nurses approached her. "Here, I'll get a blanket for you, dear," she said, walking away.

Too weak to say thank you, she realized that she was shaking not so much because she was cold, but because she was frightened. "Please, God," was all she could manage to say. Instantaneously, she felt warmth all around her, almost as if someone was holding her, cradling her entire body and bringing His warmth to her. Her soul now filled with gratitude, she prayed, "Thank you, God," then she slipped into unconsciousness again.

"Emily, wake up, hun." *Please, just let me sleep*, she wanted to say. It seemed like she was in a long, deep and dark tunnel and the woman sounded like she was at the end of it.

"Come on, sweetie. You need to wake up." She tried to open her eyes, but it felt like they were taped shut. Finally, she accomplished the task and felt the familiar excruciating pain in her abdomen. She no sooner thought, "I'm alive," when she vomited down the side of the stretcher. Her abdomen felt like it was splitting open. "Oh, God," was all she could mutter. Then her body convulsed again.

Visions of Christ's passion filled her soul and her mind. Each time her body convulsed and she experienced agonizing pain, she tried to think of the stinging pain that Christ felt with each blow of the scourging at the pillar or the pain He experienced when the long stakes were pounded into his hands and feet.

Her small body, already overwhelmed with the toxicity of the general anesthetic, her abdomen so sore from being operated on and her loss of blood left her weak, hurting and feeling sick. After ten minutes of constant vomiting, Emily buzzed the recovery room nurse.

"Yes, dear," she replied.

She tried to mouth the word "Gravol," then managed to blurt out, "Need something for," as she vomited again.

"I'm sorry, dear. I just gave you a shot for nausea. I can't give you anything else."

"But it's. . .not. . .work. . . ." and though her stomach convulsed, nothing came up.

She was wheeled back to her room and her long night's journey began. She had already used the small green pan several times on the way to her room. "Oh, Lord, please."

Every time her stomach convulsed, it felt like it was ripping open. "Oh, God, I can't do this, please."

Where is all this stuff coming from? Surely, she hoped, there was nothing left. However, it seemed like there was a never-ending supply and as if something had taken over her entire body and there wasn't a thing anyone could do for her.

Hoping that it had been at least a few hours, she buzzed the nurse again.

A young-looking nurse came in, "What do you need?"

"More Gravol, please." Emily was desperate. "I can't. . . ." Again, she spilled a meager amount into the small green pan next to her mouth.

"I'm sorry, hun. It's only been 20 minutes since you had your last shot for nausea."

Emily's eyes pleaded with her, and she began sobbing again. The nurse gently took hold of her hand, saying, "you poor thing." Then, as Emily was again filling the small pan, she listened as the young nurse began to pray, "Dear Jesus, please help this young woman get through this horrible experience. Help her to unite her suffering with yours."

She tried to look up at the young nurse, to somehow thank

her, then felt her body convulse yet another time. "Please God, I can't do this anymore. Can't you just take this away? Can't you just. . . ."

For Emily, time seemed to be crawling by. Minutes felt like hours. She checked her watch and was surprised to find it had been only an half hour since she had woken up in the recovery room.

Convulsing again, she felt as if salt was being poured into the wound of her incision.   She tried to focus on Christ's passion as the pain became unbearable.

A few minutes later, Emily nodded off. She could smell flowers and she was walking in a beautiful field with plentiful daisies and sunflowers. Far away, she could make out the image of a man and three small children. As she got closer, she could see that it was Jason and their three young sons. Running as fast as she could, Emily reached Jason and the boys and they all embraced. A euphoric feeling flooded her being.

She woke up just as her body was convulsing yet another time.

She glanced at her watch at the bedside table, hoping that it would have been hours that she had been sleeping. She groaned when she realized that she had been asleep for less than eight minutes.

"How can I get through this night of pain? Can't you just take it away?" she pleaded with God.   At the same time, Emily knew that she needed to pray for the grace to endure the suffering.

Within minutes, she found enormous strength and a renewed sense of peace. Accepting and embracing this particular cross was not something that came easily or naturally to Emily. She recognized that her whole life had been spent trying to rid herself of suffering, to increase her comfort.   Now, she had no choice but to accept her pain. The real challenge was to be at peace with it.

The next few hours were spent in and out of consciousness, her body convulsing as she woke up.

A new, different and older nurse approached her to check

her blood pressure. "Oh dear," Emily heard her say, "You've thrown up all down the front of yourself."

Emily felt the front of her hospital gown, now soaked. Her heart ached when she realized what it was.

"No, no," she responded. "It's not vomit; it's breast milk. My breasts are leaking because my baby hasn't nursed since before the surgery." With the agonizing pain and the constant vomiting, Emily hadn't realized that her breasts were engorged.

She heard the woman say, "You're still nursing?"

Emily nodded. Trying to say it as quickly as possible, Emily answered, "He's only nine months old and I nurse my babies until they wean themselves."

Without her glasses, Emily couldn't see, but she could sense the woman's raised eyebrows. "I'll see if I can find you a pump."

Her breasts heavy and her heart aching, she thought of her youngest child, Thomas. She knew that he was probably crying, missing her presence, asking to be nursed.

It became difficult to focus on her child when an overwhelming odor of vomit surrounded her. She laid still, sore and weak. An hour later, her body exhausted, she convulsed again.

As the sun began to rise, Emily realized that two, then three hours, had passed. Her painful incision, sore abdominal muscles and vomit-burned lips left her feeling battle weary. If someone had handed her a mirror at that very moment, Emily would have been shocked to see how war-ravaged she actually appeared. Her hair tossed, her lower lip burned almost beyond recognition, her skin white, pale and clammy, dark circles under her eyes. Indeed, it felt like she had been to hell and back again.

Exhausted and aching all over, Emily was finally able to drift off to sleep. She was alive. . .suffering, but alive, and grateful to God for her life and for the relief that had come in the form of much-needed sleep.

"No, don't wake her." Emily could hear her spiritual director's voice. She called for the nurse to bring the priest in. "It's okay. I'd like to see Father Dominic."

He came around the curtain which hid Emily's bed and sat down next to her. "I brought the Eucharist for you, Emily, and I can also give you the Sacrament of the Sick."

It was comforting to see her spiritual director. Father Dominic was a friend of Emily's and Jason's. They had first been introduced to him a few years back while attending a nearby parish's mission week. His short, balding and bearded appearance made him look like he belonged in New York's Little Italy. Emily was drawn to his calm and loving approach and she was thankful that his parish was closeby.

"What time is it?"

"It's seven o'clock at night."

Thankfully, Emily realized that she had slept practically the entire day. The nausea had stopped and though her abdominal incision was throbbing and painful, it was bearable.

"Jason called me and asked me to come and give you Communion. He's very worried about you, Emily. He told me that he came to visit you earlier and you were sleeping so soundly that he didn't want to wake you."

Emily nodded.

Father Dominic anointed her. They prayed a reverent Our Father together, and he gave her Communion.

"What happened, Emily?"

"The surgeon came in this morning and told me that I had another ectopic pregnancy in my right tube. The baby had died, but there was a trophoblastic tumor and it burst the tube and was wrapped around my bowel, ovary and part of my uterus. I've lost a lot of blood and they tell me that I'm lucky to be alive."

"You've been through a lot, Emily."

"I feel horrible about the baby being in the wrong place again. I love our baby and mourn her loss. More than that, I feel betrayed by my body."

"Emily, you made the best decision possible in your situation, the decision to be open to life."

"I know, but my heart aches for my child, and I'm starting to think that perhaps we should never have been open to another pregnancy. That's hard for me because I deeply desire more children."

"Then you should be open."

"Only to have them die, Father?"

"No, Emily. Whether your child survives or whether he or she dies, his or her life is eternal and still a great gift. Have you named your baby?"

"Yes, we've decided on Mary after Jason's grandmother and Elizabeth, after my grandmother. I feel awful about losing another child."

"Emily, your child, Mary Elizabeth, isn't lost. She is now in heaven, waiting for you, praying for you. And isn't that your goal as a parent, to get your child to heaven?"

"Of course it is."

"Then be assured that your child is in heaven, with your other children who have died before birth."

"What about the risks of another pregnancy? I mean, I deeply desire more children and yet some of our relatives are telling us that we're being irresponsible, that we should stop having children."

"Emily, that decision can only be made by you, Jason and God. You need to consider the risks, but it's also important for you to do what you believe is God's will. If you feel it is God's will for you to be open to more children, then it is your duty to do so. If, however, you feel that perhaps it is too risky, then using natural methods to limit your family would be completely moral. I recommend that you prayerfully spend time in front of the Blessed Sacrament to try to discern what God's will is for you."

Emily nodded, then smiled. She and Jason had been getting negative comments from relatives all through her last short pregnancy. She heard comments like, "You're just being selfish, Emily. You're irresponsible."

She was comforted by Father Dominic's presence. He always knew how to put Emily at ease. She trusted his wisdom and guidance.

"Emily, have you ever heard of a woman named Gianna Beretta Molla?"

Emily shook her head.

"Right now, there is cause for her canonization. She was an Italian doctor, pregnant with her fourth child when it was discovered that she had a tumor on her uterus. The doctors insisted that she have an abortion but she refused any treatment until her second trimester, to protect the baby. She died just a few days after her baby daughter was born. She gave her life so that her daughter would live. Perhaps you could pray for her intercession."

Emily nodded.

"Well, I should be going. You need to get some rest. I'll keep praying for you."

He patted her hand and blessed her. "May the Lord bless you and keep you, May He make His face to shine upon you. . . ."

No longer distracted by her visitor, the throbbing in her abdomen became even more pronounced. Strengthened by Communion, the very Body, Blood, Soul and Divinity of Jesus Christ, Emily knew that God's grace would make it possible for her to endure any further suffering. She remembered her daily morning prayer, to offer up suffering for the conversion of sinners and the reparation of sins. She knew that if Jesus could hang on a cross in horrible pain for three hours in reparation for her sins, then she can certainly cope with the rest of this suffering for whatever intention He chooses.

27

Psalm 88:19

September, 1950

Katharine stared at the open casket containing her husband's remains. At 71, her now-thinning gray hair was pulled back into a netted bun. A hat she wore only to funerals, a black pillbox type, covered her head. Harry looked like he was asleep. *That's what he did most his life so he'd be pretty good at it by now.*

She recalled a few nights ago, her husband coming into her room, waking her up in the middle of the night, gasping for air, "Katharine, I don't feel so good."

"Harry," she had said, "just go back to bed. Don't bother me now."

"But Katharine, my stomach. . .my chest. . .is. . . ." Then she had watched as he collapsed on her bedroom floor.

"Come on, Harry." She had leaned down, the blackness of the night surrounding them both, no moonlight offering even the slightest amount of illumination.

When she had touched him, he seemed so still. Katharine had immediately telephoned her son and Johnnie was there within a few minutes, confirming that Harry was no longer alive.

Katharine continued staring at her husband's dead body unusually dressed in finery, his now old and wrinkled face peaceful in death. It was peculiar seeing him in such formal clothes. He had one pair of overalls that he wore for nearly 40 years, faded and slightly yellowed with age.

She wasn't sure how to feel at that moment. Sadness and grief were both words that came to her mind, but those were not the emotions she was experiencing. People were crying and sobbing over his death, but she kept stoic and silent.

She sighed as she thought about her life with him. He always seemed to get in her way, to annoy her, like a mosquito buzzing by the ear.

She admitted that in her own way, she would miss him. He drank far too much of his homebrew but he was a kind man, one that didn't get angry often.   Of course, there was the time that he chased Charlie with the shotgun. *A man could've died today, Ma.* She shuddered when she thought of Johnnie's words.

Up until that point, she had never seen rage in his usually complacent eyes.   She had rarely heard a raised tone in his normally unobtrusive voice. After reflecting on it for many years, Katharine had come to recognize his outburst as the one act of masculinity her husband had ever shown. She recalled that he had drunk himself to a stupor the entire week after the incident. As was her custom, Katharine placed a 'room to rent' sign in the window when her boarder left.   Then, a week later, in Harry's presence, Katharine removed the sign from the window and tore it up.

The long, tedious memorial service ended and many of the people gathered back at her son's place for the luncheon. Katharine dreaded going there and listening to everyone reminisce about her husband.   She just wanted to return to her home and be left alone. However, as Harry's wife, she realized that she would be expected to make an appearance. She hated the idea of everyone talking about him, making a fuss over him. In one sense, it seemed like he was still bothering her, despite his now permanent absence.

At her son's house, she stood by the food table listening to her son and daughter-in-law tell a funny story about Harry. She glanced over and saw her four grandchildren, huddled around each other, laughing and teasing one another, two grandsons, tall and handsome men in their twenties, and two granddaughters, Sally, now in her early thirties, and Becky, a giddy teenager.

Katharine could not understand what her son and his

wife were thinking bringing all those kids into the world, each of them, just another problem for her to worry about.

Sally stepped back from her siblings, picked up a piece of cheese from the table, then stood alone in the corner. Katharine walked over to stand beside her. "You all right, Sal?"

She nodded. "I guess so. Feeling sad about Grandpop. I'm going to miss him. He always made me laugh. When my first baby died, he was the only one who could make me feel better. And. . . well, after my second son was born dead, he just held me. When the doctors told me that I would never have a child of my own, he was there for me, probably more so than my husband."

Katharine shrugged her shoulders. How a man who spent most of his life drunk on the cellar floor could affect so many people was just beyond her comprehension. And yet, for all his drinking, it was obvious that there would be many people who would miss him.

Sally walked back to the area where her brothers and sister were standing.

Katharine stood alone for a few moments. A man whom Katharine vaguely recognized approached her.

"Mrs. Clayman, my name is James Colbert. I used to frequent your music shop on Ritner Street many years ago when I was newly married. I'm sorry to hear about your husband. He was one of a kind."

"Thank you."

"By the way," he spoke in a whisper, "you. . . ." Mr. Colbert hesitated, biting his bottom lip. "Well. . . ." he started saying.

"Well what, Mr. Colbert? As you can see, I'm busy. This is, after all, my husband's funeral."

"Yes, I understand that. You see, my wife came into your music store many years ago and you gave her a pamphlet on how to prevent pregnancy. . . ."

"Yes, so? Have you come here to thank me? I took great risk offering information to women back at a time when I could have gotten arrested."

"Yes, I realize that."

Katharine became irritated. She wished that he would just blurt out what he wanted to say.

"You know, we were young and in love and already had three babies all very close. We thought that information would help us but there we were six months later with Ellie pregnant again and we still had three babies."

"Look, Mr. Colbert, I'm very busy."

He shifted, bit on his lip again, then looked down at the floor. "You. . .recommended the name of a midwife who would bring her period on; do you remember?" He now leaned down and whispered very close to her ear.

"No, not really, Mr. Colbert," she answered curtly.

"Well. . . ." he paused again.

Katharine's pulse quickened and she gritted her teeth. "Well, what?"

"Well, it turned out real bad. We never let anyone find out about it, because we didn't want to get arrested. Ellie was so sick, she never quite recovered. We moved out of town where she died a short while later. She had lost so much blood and had an infection. Then I had three little ones to take care of. If I could have, I would have taken back what we did, but I couldn't and she was gone. I don't mean to be telling you this while you're trying to deal with your own husband's death, but I moved back to town a few years ago and I've been meaning to come and talk to you."

Katharine continued to grind her teeth and she stared at him stone-faced as he finished his soliloquy. What exactly was he trying to tell her? So his wife died. Things like that happened. *I almost died myself from a mishandled abortion*, she silently retorted.

"I just want to let you know that. . .well, that I forgive you for telling us the name of that midwife and for giving us that information. It took me a long time to forgive myself for what an awful thing that was. I mean, if we hadn't gone to that midwife, my wife would have lived a lot longer than she did."

Any other day, Katharine would have been screaming swear words at this man, but today, she sat stiffly and listened.

He tipped his hat and said, "Good day, Mrs. Clayman." He turned and left the house.

Katharine stared toward the door, then walked over to the sofa and sat down. At her age, she was too tired to argue with anyone, let alone a man who blames her for his wife's death. Besides, her feet were almost numb from the black pump shoes she wore. Her son sat down next to her. "Hey, Ma, you don't look so well. You all right?"

"Sure. I'm fine. Just tired, that's all. Look, Johnnie, I think I'm going to walk back to my place. I think I just need to be alone."

John nodded and helped his mother off the sofa. He leaned down, kissed her cheek, now wrinkled and rough. Without saying goodbye to anyone else, she quietly opened and closed the door, stepped on to the small porch, down the steps, and walked the 50 or so feet to her own home, the home in which she had lived for the past 45 years.

There was a soft mist in the air, minute droplets, enough wetness to make her face and hands moist, but her clothes remained dry.

She slowly opened the door amidst the yapping and barking of her pets and went inside. Katharine greeted her little Lhaso-Apso dogs with much love and affection. She took her hat off and placed it on the rack near the door. Sitting back in her favorite green wing-backed chair, the two small dogs jumped onto her lap and began licking her hands. She knew that her black dress would be covered with white dog hairs, but she could care less. Katharine welcomed the interaction.

The peaceful solitude of her living room was a pleasant contrast to the noise of the reception.

While the dogs continued to lick her hands, her eyes gazed around the room.

The now faded and peeling wallpaper contributed to the somber, gray mood of the day. She recalled when Harry and

Johnnie had papered the living room in 1929, just before the stock market crash. Katharine had been given the gift of several rolls of wallpaper from one of her customers at the store: soft pink flowers, nestled in a cream-colored background, now looking faded and cracking at the corners.

Her eyes stopped when she saw the boat inside the glass casing, sitting high above on the top shelf of the bookcase. Harry had built a beautiful model boat made out of fine carved wood, intricately designed and hand painted. He named the boat "Katharine," and built a glass casing around it.

Her mind wandered to about a year before her wedding. Katharine used to sneak out to the Philadelphia harbor to watch the boats. So enamored with the majestic ships, she neglected to notice one of the workers staring at her. Harry told her later that he had fallen in love with her the very first moment he laid eyes on her at the dock.

Staring at the boat, she recalled the warm summer day that he had given it to her. His eyes had been wide with excitement when he had proclaimed, "For you, Katharine."

She remembered looking down at it and thinking, "Why in the world would he waste his time working on that for so long?" Then she had said, "It's nice, Harry," set it down and never studied it again. Until today.

She pushed the dogs off her lap and got up out of her chair. Walking over to the bookcase, she reached up and attempted to yank the boat down. "Damn," she muttered as she realized that she was just too short to retrieve it. She dragged the small stool over to the bookcase, stepped on it and was finally able to pull the model down. She began to notice and appreciate the intricate design of the boat through the glass casing. The top of it was covered with dust, but the rest of it was as bright and beautiful as the day that he had given it to her.

She studied the 'water' he created for the boat. He had painted it green, and for one brief moment, she thought that she saw it move. The boat itself was exquisite and she could now comprehend that he had spent long hours making every detail realistic, no matter how small, from the miniature life preservers to the tiny ropes. Then her eyes glanced down at both the front and back of the ship where he had printed the word, "Katharine." She pictured his large, callused hands trying to write her name in small white letters, then she smiled as she wondered how many times he had to print it. Her husband's literacy was limited and his handwriting barely legible. And yet her name was written almost as if a machine had done it. It seemed odd how she never noticed all the little details before.

She continued to study the boat and the beautiful craftsmanship it displayed. How ironic to think that this man that she had been married to for 55 years, who spent much of his life drunk, possessed a capacity for creating art work, not unlike Rodin's, which was capable of moving and changing a person's soul. And yet for her entire life, her perception was so limited and so superficial that she refused to see him as anything else but the drunk on the cellar floor, the mosquito buzzing in her ear.

Still, it was beyond her understanding why anyone, especially Harry, would spend so much time working on a model boat simply for her.

Despite her love for Rodin, Katharine remained logical and rational when it came to her husband. Harry must have realized that she would have little use for a boat that sat on the shelf. Over the years, many people had commented on the exquisite job that he had done, but it was difficult for her to be grateful for something that she rarely looked at or appreciated.

And yet, in one sense, she could understand that the boat actually did serve an important purpose. She recalled the summer that he worked on it. Johnnie was just a baby, about two years old. She remembered feeling surprised that since he worked so long on the boat, he seemed more pleasant and less annoying than normal. She didn't pay much attention to him either way.

Katharine walked over to replace the boat on top of the bookcase. As she tried to place it firmly against the wall, she became frustrated when something prevented her from doing so.

Using the stool, she stepped up one more step and, holding the boat on the bookcase with one hand, she reached back to retrieve the small box that had lodged itself between the top of the bookcase and the wall.

Pulling it out of the way, she was now able to move the boat smoothly against the wall. Stepping down, she took the small container to her favorite chair. Her hands began to tremble as she realized what it was. *For you, Katharine.* Michael's words echoed in her mind. Pulling the small sculpture replica out of its box, she stared at it for several moments, recalling the time that Michael had given it to her.

Even after all these years, "The Kiss" was still her favorite sculpture. How could one miniature sculpture create so many memories for her? How can something like this move her soul? Memories of Michael first giving it to her, of her keeping it hidden when the police came, trying to explain to Harry why she kept it at the store. It seemed like a lifetime ago.

When she thought of all the lovers who shared her bed, it was Michael who had truly captured her heart, not by physical intimacies, but by his soft-spoken, sensitive personality and caring manner. Most of her paramours were only interested in one thing and in one sense, they all became the same person. But Michael was different. He would talk with her for hours about Rodin and things that Katharine enjoyed. His selfless way of doing things endeared him to her.

Then her mind wandered to their daughter, and of having the midwife attempt to bring on her period while she was pregnant with Ruth. She remembered being so angry that it had failed when she felt the first movements of the child within her. Even at Ruth's birth, her heart was hardened and all she could think of was the tremendous work involved in raising another child.

Now that child, their daughter, was 41 years of age. It was the only piece of Michael that remained with her. Suddenly, she felt abundant gratitude that her attempts at ending that pregnancy had failed.

She wondered, with a tinge of sadness, if Michael was gone now or if he was still alive.

Placing the sculpture back into its box, she glanced up at the boat again.   All those years, she barely noticed that gift which had taken up such a large section of her bookcase.   She stared at it and strangely, her eyes began to water.

Now he was gone, never to bother her again. Drying her eyes, she refused to sink into melancholy musings about death. *No point to it, really. We live our lives, then we die and that's the end of us.*

28

Isaiah 60:20

May, 1997

Emily picked up the grocery bag and handed it to her toddler to bring inside. She watched Andrew, her fourth son, struggle to carry the bag.

It was a warm and sunny spring afternoon. The flowers were in full bloom, their scent permeating the air.   It was one of those beautiful days that one was glad to be alive.

Emily thought of her near-death experience four years ago with her second ectopic pregnancy. The surgeons had told her that she had minutes to live once the baby and tumor had burst her tube and had caused her to hemorrhage internally.

After her brush with death, her spiritual life became more intense.   Her trust in God's will strengthened.   At a Catholic conference, she stumbled across a book called "Divine Mercy in My Soul" by Sister Faustina Kowalska. In this book, Emily discovered a prayer which focused on Christ's passion and on God's mercy. She began saying this Divine Mercy Chaplet every day at three o'clock, an appropriate time referring back to Christ's hour of death.

As well, Emily began spending more time in front of the Blessed Sacrament at her small country church. Just sitting in Jesus' Real Presence supplied fuel to Emily's own soul. It gave her peace and serenity to accept the challenges that came her way.

One evening, she was praying before the Blessed Sacrament in the quiet solitude of the first pew. For an entire hour, she felt alone. As she blessed herself to leave, she sensed someone nearby. Emily looked around and, as she suspected, no one was there. Memories flooded her mind of times in the past when she felt support from an invisible helper.

One incident occurred several years back when she was five months pregnant with her fourth son. It had snowed and there was a great deal of ice on the walkway to her house. When she had gotten out of the car, she started walking but suddenly slipped and began falling forward. In an instant, she was convinced that she had felt someone hold her to keep her from landing onto her stomach.

Seen in this light, many past incidents began to make sense to her. She remembered the tapping of her shoulder which kept her and Jason from consummating their relationship before marriage, those many years ago, then the patting of her face to keep her conscious during her first pregnancy loss.

Finally, in the peaceful silence of the church, it also occurred to her that it must have been her angel at that busy intersection when she was 17 who pulled her to safety when a van sped around the corner.

She continued in prayerful meditation, pondering the supernatural experiences that had just returned all at once to her. Emily treasured these moments of reflection.

Emily's quiet time at home, however, decreased when she and Jason had made the decision to homeschool their boys. From the beginning, it became apparent that their oldest son was not flourishing in the classroom environment. Although he had some wonderful and dedicated teachers, it seemed to be the only reasonable option. Their experience was so successful that it became the natural thing to do when their second oldest was ready for first grade. Emily recalled an acquaintance's remark, "How can you stand to be with your kids day and night? Gee, I need a break from mine." She had replied, "It's challenging, but for the most part, I thoroughly enjoy teaching and spending time with my children."

She and Jason's prayer life had deepened as well. They had a nightly prayer time with the family which included saying the rosary and reading scripture. They had also become involved in Catholic apologetics, or defending the Catholic faith.

After nearly a year of trying for another pregnancy, one night when they were in bed together, Emily said, "I have to admit that I'm disappointed that God hasn't blessed us with another child. I mean, it's been almost a year. . .that's 15 cycles."

"I know, Em, but remember, we're not the ones in charge here." He certainly had changed since they first met 18 years ago. His hair was now almost fully gray, not just the normal flecks at the temples but unrepentant silver that dominated his dark curly hair. His strong jaw sported a graying beard and moustache. Emily thought that it was amusing how he was often mistaken for her father, despite the fact that he was three years younger.

"I know. It's God who opens and closes the womb."

"And don't lose hope. It may take two years to conceive again, and we might as well enjoy it. Kind of different from our honeymoon, eh?"

"How could I forget? How many couples don't consummate on their wedding night?"

"Probably more than we can imagine." A decade and a half of marriage certainly had changed Emily's understanding of the marital act.

Several days previous, she had listened to the "Life-Giving Love" tape set by Scott and Kimberly Hahn, Catholic speakers. She remembered Scott's quote, "Sex is not good like Campbell's soup is good. Sex is not grrrreat like Frosted Flakes are great. Sex is holy." He seemed to be able to sum up, in just a few words, the status of sexual expression within the Catholic Church.

Emily had discovered that sex, when lived and enjoyed with the right attitude, during marriage and with no contraception, actually facilitates a couple on the road to holiness. Emily then thought of how satisfying, passionate and exciting their sex life had become, with no masturbation, no contraception, no pornography and no adultery. She couldn't think of a more enjoyable way to sanctification.

"I love you so much, Jay. And if it's God's will for us to raise only these four children, then I will gladly accept it."

The next morning, as Emily began to rouse, she realized that she probably should have gotten her period by now, but in reality, hadn't kept track.   For the last several months, she hadn't bothered to take her temperature.   Since she knew that she should be getting her period any day, she decided to pop the thermometer in her mouth, wait the five minutes and see what it was. She took it out of her mouth and looked.

What she saw made her sit up in bed. "Jason, wake up! My temperature! Look at my temperature!"

Not a morning person, Jason strained to lift his head and squinted his eyes and said "What," in his default, waking voice. "Is that 99.1?"

"I can't believe it. We're pregnant! After a year of trying, we are *pregnant*!"

"Looks that way, Em."

Filled with joy, Emily echoed the words of Kimberly Hahn, "We've gotten a promotion from the Lord!"

His head flopped back on his pillow. "It's going to be hard with homeschooling, though."

"I know, but I won't let you or God down. I can do this. I know I can."

Over the next few summer months, she began to experience excruciating migraine headaches every third or fourth day of early pregnancy. During the most difficult times, she tried to remember Mother Teresa's words, "Suffering is but a kiss from Jesus."   Through every headache, she prayed for the grace to endure and to accept her suffering.

Several months later, Emily's second oldest son, Nate, pulled on her sleeve. "Mommy, Mommy, come on, it stopped raining. Can we go for a walk now?"

Emily peered out the window at the still threatening sky. "We'll have to wait a little while, sweetie, just to make sure that we don't get caught in the rain."

"Aw, come on, Mom, it's fun getting caught in the rain. It's just like having a great big sprinkler."

Emily was thankful for the childlike tendency to look at negative things positively. It was somewhat of an irony that parents probably learned just as much from their children as their little ones learned from them. How many years had Jason been telling Emily that she tended to look at things pessimistically?

"Well, okay, Nate." Glancing out the back window, Emily could see the sun breaking through the clouds. "Come on, boys. Let's go for a walk. Jake, can you help Andrew with his shoes?"

Jake, now aged 10, crouched down and spoke softly to his younger brother. "Here, buddy, I'll help you."

Andrew gazed adoringly at Jake and smiled.

"Come on, Mommy, hurry up," Nate yelled, with his hand on the front door.

Emily finished zippering Tom's coat and said, "Patience, Nate. Mom doesn't move as quickly with her growing tummy." At that moment, Emily felt a flutter of movement as it seemed like her unborn child executed a somersault inside her. She placed her hand firmly on her stomach to determine whether it could be felt from the outside. Disappointed, it was still too early.

She watched her four boys anxiously prepare for their walk. Since they had moved to the country, hikes had become their favorite pastime: searching for wildlife, throwing pebbles in the small, shallow pond, exploring in the woods.

"Okay, boys, let's go."

"Yeah," they yelled in unison.

They all pounced out the door and onto the bedrock, toward the dirt road near their house.

"Stay close," Emily reminded them. "Jake, you hold on to Andrew's hand."

He rolled his eyes, then nodded. Tom, aged five, yelled, "Mommy, a rainbow!"

Emily's eyes were drawn to the sky where the beautiful half-arc of a rainbow began to appear in the distance, separating the dark clouds at the right from the clearing sky to the left.

"Pretty, Momma," said Andrew, in his high-pitched two-year-old voice.

"You can say that again, sweetie."

"Mommy," asked Tom, "how does God make a rainbow?"

"Well. . . ." Emily paused. She relished teaching moments such as these. It was definitely an advantage of homeschooling and one of the reasons she enjoyed it so much.

"Do you remember the first time God made a rainbow, Tommy?"

"Oh, oh, pick me, Mommy, I know, I know," Nate yelled, with his hand in the air and sounding more like Horshack from Welcome Back Kotter.

"Let Tom try, Nate."

Tom stopped walking and stood silent on the dirt road. His eyes formed a serious frown and he bit down on his lip.

Nate, who was eight years old but the same size as his five-year-old brother, leaned over and said, "Think water, Tom."

"I've got it, Mommy, the flood. Noah!"

"That's it, Tom. God gave us a rainbow as a sign that he will never destroy the earth by flood again."

"Yeah, Mom, but what's the scientific definition of how a rainbow is made?" asked Jake, typically interested in how the world works.

"Well, Jake, I'm not too sure about that, but that can be your science project for the week. Research how a rainbow is made and make a presentation to the family."

"Great," he said, sounding a little annoyed.

Emily glanced up again at the rainbow. It now formed a full arc completely across the sky. The fresh scent of grass and the invigorating country smells after a rainfall filled Emily with a sense of well-being. Despite the boys jumping in every puddle, water splashing everywhere, she was thankful that Nate had pestered her into a walk.

She thought of Catherine Doherty, the foundress of Madonna House, a spiritual retreat center a few hours from their home. In one of her beautiful writings, she once said, "Give me the heart of a child and the awesome courage to live it out." Why do adults have to carry so many burdens and worries? Why can't they just stop worrying about the rain and enjoy a beautiful walk and a stunning rainbow?

Several feet ahead of them, Andrew and Jake were crouching down and studying something on the dirt road.

"Hey, Mom, a frog. Cool," Jake said as he reached over and picked it up.

Emily cringed. "Can't you just admire it from afar, Jake? I mean, don't frogs give you warts or something?"

"Come on, Mom, that's not true. I've picked up hundreds of frogs and never got a wart."

That's an obvious difference between girls and boys, or at least between me and my boys.

Jake showed the small frog to his brothers, then leaned down and allowed it to hop away.

"Bye, bye, fwog," Andrew waved.

"So, Jake and Nate, is this tree here a deciduous or coniferous tree?"

"Come on, Mom, ask a hard question," Jake complained.

"Let Nate answer it, Jake."

"It's the cone one, Mommy," Nate replied.

"You got it, Nate."

They walked in silence for another hundred feet, then they turned around to start the journey home. As they were walking, Emily kept turning around to enjoy the sight of the rainbow, now fading in the distance.

Then Emily felt an unfamiliar gripping of her uterus, a pain low in her abdomen, different from the usual Braxton-Hicks contractions. It became difficult to walk, but in a minute, the pain subsided.

The next day, as Emily tried to wake herself for the day's activities, she said out loud, "A pregnant woman never gets enough sleep, or at least that's how it feels."

She pulled her pregnant body off of the bed and again felt an unfamiliar tensing in her lower abdomen, a painful cramp unlike the normal Braxton-Hicks contractions she experienced frequently at this stage. Unshaken, she continued over to the bathroom. She frowned as she saw that Jason had left several pairs of socks sitting on the floor of the bathroom, right where he had taken them off. It was certainly difficult for her to understand how a guy who could paint a set of the Stations of the Cross, write a pro-life song and carry on intellectual conversations about the Catholic faith, couldn't quite figure out how to get his socks to the hamper.

Before making it to the toilet, she felt liquid trickling down her legs. *Did my bladder just burst or what?* She changed her clothes and as she was walking to the kitchen, she felt another more painful gripping in her lower abdomen and back. "Now, that one hurt." It finally dawned on her what might be happening. "Oh God, please."

Rushing into the bedroom, she pushed Jason awake with no sensitivity to his poor waking skills.

"Jason, wake up *now*. I think I may be in pre-term labor. I just had a gush of fluid and I think I have labor pains. It's really hurting and I need to get to a hospital as soon as possible."

He jumped out of bed and while Emily called her mother-in-law to babysit the boys, he quickly got dressed and started the car.

Several hours later after an initial exam at the hospital, it became apparent that Emily was indeed in premature labor. After trying several drugs to stop the labor, she found out that this baby would be born today. "I'm sorry," said the doctor. "Your cervix is already dilated. I'm not sure how much we can do to save your baby, not at 20 weeks."

The words tore through Emily's heart like a knife. Another contraction, more pain, more breathing. Even though she had given birth by Cesarean section to four babies, she would now give birth to this child naturally, this child destined to live only a short time. In between contractions, she knew that her child was still alive, kicking and moving within her.

Emily looked at Jason's tear-filled eyes. "We need to get some water, Jay, to baptize our baby, please!" The tone of her voice was sharp as she tried to breathe through another contraction. He nodded, rushed over to the small sink, grabbed a small paper cup from the dispenser and filled it with water.

Another painful contraction and she tried desperately to remember her Lamaze breathing techniques, but after having four C-sections, she hadn't used them in a very long time. Her previous miscarriages were before 12 weeks and not as painful.

Within minutes, she felt an urge to push. "Wait a minute, dear," the nurse said. "Let me check you."

Jason sat on the bed beside Emily, his hand tenderly holding hers, trying to support her through the last agonizing contractions.

"I need to push." She wanted so desperately not to push, to allow her baby to stay inside of her, and for her to continue to nourish and nurture her child, but her body wouldn't allow that. She pushed only twice and her small child was born. Emily heard a sound like a kitten crying, then realized that her baby had let out a small, soft, weak cry.

As soon as the umbilical cord was cut, the nurse immediately carried the baby across the room as the pediatric staff attempted to work on their child. Emily and Jason sat quietly, their hearts heavy with emotion. A few minutes later, she felt another contraction and her placenta was delivered. She could hear a nurse referring to "him," and realized that their child was another boy. After a few minutes, the doctor brought him back, his small form still hidden in the blue hospital blanket. He spoke in an hushed, almost apologetic voice, "There is nothing we can do for him."

He handed the tiny one-pound baby boy to his mother. Jason held on to Emily's shoulder and watched as she cradled the smallest baby they had ever seen. He was so perfect and looked identical to their oldest son, Jake. His small body was covered with minute white hairs. He was perfect as he struggled to breathe. He was perfect as he opened his mouth to cry.

Emily held her new son as gently as she could. Jason reached over and poured a few drops of water on him and said, "I baptize you in the name of the Father and of the Son and of the Holy Spirit." Emily could feel the vibration of his tiny heart beating so fast.

The nurse came in with a Polaroid camera and asked if they wanted her to take a photo of their child. Emily nodded as the nurse took a photo of her and Jason and their tiny son.

She gazed in awe at this miniature human being and marveled at the fact that even though he was tiny, he was so perfect. His little hands looked like a doll's hands. She removed the baby blanket and laid his small, warm body on her chest. She could feel his heart beating rapidly. After several minutes, she wrapped him again in the small blue blanket.

"Here, you need to hold him," Emily whispered. "He's so light."

Jason held his new son with such care that it looked like he was afraid that he would break their baby.

He moved over to the rocking chair next to the bed and began to rock him. Jason began humming a tranquil melody that he had composed on the spot.

She gazed down at her tiny infant and he seemed to be calmer, more at peace as he heard his father's quiet, soothing melody. Jason handed their child back to his wife. She unwrapped him and again laid his small body on her chest, then pulled her nightgown over top of him.

One hour went by and he continued breathing. Two hours went by. *Oh God, he has already lived longer than they predicted. Could it be that perhaps he will make it after all?*

Then, in an instant, he was still. She could feel that his heart had stopped and he wasn't breathing, but he continued to feel so warm and so soft. He looked like he was sleeping peacefully.

"He's so beautiful, isn't he?" Emily's eyes were filled with tears.

Not able to speak, Jason nodded.

She lifted their son off her chest, wrapped him in the blanket, and handed him to Jason. Glancing up at the clock, she could see that it was 3:10. *Seems so fitting for him to die at this time.* "Have mercy on us and on the whole world," she echoed the words of the Divine Mercy prayer.

Her heart was aching as she realized that just a few minutes ago, he was still alive and a few hours ago, he was safe inside her, continuing to grow and to be nourished by her. Now, he was dead and he was in heaven.

"We should name him." Her voice was quiet and hushed.

"What do you think?" His voice was cracking.

"I like the name Seth." Like their other sons, she chose a strong biblical name.

"Seth it is. I can't believe how perfect he is, but he's so small, so still."

"This is so hard." Emily started to weep. Jason leaned over and kissed her forehead. He handed his tiny son back to his wife and sat quietly, listening to her cry.

"Oh, God," Jason prayed, "please take care of our son in heaven. Give us the grace to deal with the grief of losing another child. . . ."

He couldn't finish because, like his wife, he began sobbing quietly.

The nurse walked in and asked if they wanted more time with their child.

Without speaking, they both nodded. Emily continued holding and rocking their child, still warm to the touch. It occurred to Emily that, though her heart ached, she was tremendously blessed to be able to spend two hours with her son, getting to know him, talking to him, holding him, rocking him. Their little son seemed so peaceful and calm in those two hours.

Emily felt God's grace working abundantly in her at that very moment as she felt privileged to be able to experience her son dying in her arms. The vision of Our Lady holding the crucified Christ came to her mind and what a grim task it must have been for her to hold her dead son, her only son, bruised and beaten, in her arms. Emily understood more deeply how difficult it must have been for Mary to deal with her son's death. She could now grasp just a tiny portion of what Mary had to endure.

She and Jason waited another hour and when the nurse came in, she kissed their baby goodbye, just as she did to her father at his wake. Her father was cold and hard, but her baby, now grayish in color, was soft. He was so tiny and so young. Emily wished that she could hold him all day. Her heart ached when she imagined that their child would soon be placed in the ground, never to be nursed or grow up or play with his brothers.

Jason kissed his little forehead as he gave their son to the nurse. There would be burial arrangements to make and duties to perform at home.

Though the doctors had insisted that Emily spend the night, she pleaded with them to allow her to return home to her four younger children. They relented, so she and Jason left the hospital and returned home.

Her younger sons now were yelling, "Where's the baby, where's the baby?"

With tears in his eyes, Jason took his young sons aside and explained that their new little brother was now in heaven. Emily's heart was breaking as she listened to her young sons begin to weep. Nate kept saying, "No, Daddy, no." Jake and Tom sat quietly, softly crying. Her youngest son seemed almost disoriented. Little Andrew looked up and said, "I miss Mommy."

She sat on the sofa and cradled him in her arms. "Nin-nin, Mommy?" he asked.

She lifted up her shirt and he latched on eagerly to her breast. What an overwhelming comfort for Emily to be able to nurse her two year old. Despite the fact that she had breastfed all her sons until they were three or more, she had gotten pressure from relatives to wean him during her difficult pregnancy with Seth. She looked down at his body which now appeared enormous compared to his miniature younger brother. Little Andrew had whined in the last few weeks, "Milk all dawn, Mamma," in his sweet voice. There was no complaining now. Though he was only getting colostrum, it seemed that the breast served more as a soother. And the 'first milk' that was to be Seth's first dinner was now young Andrew's comfort.

A few days later, Jason approached her with a package from Morning Light Ministry, a Catholic organization for bereaved mothers and fathers who have experienced ectopic pregnancy, miscarriage, stillbirth or infant death. Emily opened it and studied the small prayer card with the picture of Jesus holding an infant. Her eyes began to tear and her breasts felt full. At the sight of Jesus holding the baby, her milk let down and she began to leak milk.

There was a small white and blue cross, a card with Seth's name on it, a small Miraculous medal and Divine Mercy medal, and a prayer card which said, "With you, O Lord, You have," and a blank for the baby's name, "whose little heart is joyful within your loving embrace." She was comforted by the fact that her child was in heaven with Jesus and was now praying for her. She remembered Kimberly Hahn's statement that when we suffer a pregnancy loss, our child is in heaven before the throne of grace and what better way to store up treasure in heaven. Our job as parents is to get our children to heaven and now, Emily thought, there were six children waiting, praying for her, in heaven.

"Mamma, nin-nin?" Andrew climbed onto her lap and she lifted her shirt to allow him to nurse.

Studying the cross and prayer card and little mementos from Morning Light Ministry, she was reminded of the story that a friend of hers told her many years ago when Emily had experienced her second miscarriage. This friend had said that when her mother was dying in the hospital, toward the end, she kept saying, "They're singing to me, they're singing to me." Her grown children asked her, "Who's singing to you, Mom?" She replied, "My children in heaven." This friend went on to say that her mother had had four miscarriages before she was able to give birth to three children. The story always gave Emily a great deal of hope, not only for her unborn children's eternal destinies, but for her own destiny as well.

With Andrew still on her lap, in the loving comfort of his mother's embrace, she glanced outside at her three older boys playing in the back yard and her eyes began to tear again. Emily was in awe of God's gift of parenthood. It still seemed so miraculous that she was able to have four children to raise. What did that doctor say many years ago after she had experienced her first ectopic pregnancy: "chances of infertility, 50 percent?" Many women who experience ectopic pregnancies tend to be infertile, and yet Emily was blessed with four beautiful little boys. Even with the loss of little Seth, her heart yearned for and remained open to more children.

Emily realized more fully that even in a much-desired pregnancy, we do not have control over what happens. She silently prayed to God that He would give her the grace to deal with her grief, and that she could eventually bear more children, if that was His will.

29

Prov. 13:12

January, 1955

From her seat near the door of the reception hall, Katharine watched as the bride and groom danced their first dance. At most weddings, this was considered to be a poignant moment. Yet, for Katharine, it was at this time that she longed to be home with her little dogs. Weddings were supposed to be happy, festive affairs. Katharine felt they were a reminder of her advancing years.

She watched as the other members of the wedding party stepped out on to the dance floor with their partners. Sally, now in her late thirties, still looked radiant to Katharine. She was dancing with one of the groom's brothers, a tall fellow, much taller than Sally.

Katharine studied Becky as she danced with her new husband, Phil. Becky's eyes were full of love and joy.

"Ma, doesn't Becky make a beautiful bride?" she heard Johnnie whisper in her ear.

Katharine nodded, then turned around to face her son. He pulled out the seat next to hers and sat down. John's face held a smile so wide, bursting with pride as he gazed at his daughter. "It's hard to believe my little girl's married."

Katharine kept silent.

"You know, Ma, with Becky gone, that means we have a lot more room at home. Lizzie and I were thinking perhaps you should move in with us. It'll make things easier for you."

Katharine ignored her son for a moment, staring at the dancers.

"Ma, did you hear me?"

"Huh, what did you say, Johnnie?"

"I think you heard me. Why didn't you answer me?"

"Because it's absurd. I'm doing fine living alone."

"Yeah, Ma, but I do just about everything in the house for you. It would make things easier to have you come to live with us."

Katharine remained silent. *Yeah, easier for you.*

"Look, Ma, the other day, you left the gas stove on. A month or so ago, you left the water running all day and there was a flood in the kitchen and cellar. It took me all day to clean up the mess."

"What are you trying to say? I can't take care of myself?"

"No, Ma, that's not what I'm saying. I'm just saying it would make things easier if you came to live with us."

Katharine's eyes focused on the floor.

"I don't want to move in with you and Lizzie, not comfortable with her, that's all."

"What about the rest home near Sally?"

Katharine shrugged her shoulders.

"We could come and visit you every day."

"That band is too loud."

"Ma, that's why we put you back here close to the door. That's what you asked for."

"You should've put me in the hallway. That music is atrocious. It's too loud."

"Ma, you're changing the subject."

The music stopped and the dancers dispersed.

"Johnnie, I'd like to go home now."

"All right, Ma. I'll take you. We'll go and tell Becky and Phil that you have to leave."

He helped Katharine up and together they walked over to where the bride and groom were standing.

"Oh, Grandmom, getting ready to dance?" Becky asked playfully, her tone lively and giddy.

"No, Becky, you know I don't dance. I'm going home."

"Oh," Becky responded, her eyes darkened with

disappointment. "Well, I'm so happy that you were able to come to our wedding," she responded, in a softer tone of voice.

"Nice to meet you, Mrs. Clayman," Phil held out his hand, which Katharine shook politely.

"I'll be back in a few minutes, Beck," John said, then kissed her cheek. "Come on, Ma."

At the cloak room, John acquired his mother's coat, then helped Katharine into it.

As they left the reception hall, a waft of cold air almost knocked Katharine over. "I hate this damned cold weather."

Katharine pulled on John's jacket.

"What will happen to my dogs if I go to the rest home?"

"Uh. . .I don't know, Ma. I forgot about the dogs."

Katharine's heart ached. *How could he forget my dogs?* Those two pets were more than animals to her. They were her friends, her loyal confidants, the ones who kept her from loneliness.

"I suppose either Ruth or I can take them, if it will make you feel better. Besides, they're getting on in years too."

Katharine again pulled on John's coat. "Wait, Johnnie. I don't have my pocketbook. I need my pocketbook. It has all my important papers. It must be back inside the hall."

"Mom, look, it's on your arm." John was pointing down at his mother's arm.

Katharine glanced down, then she breathed a sigh of relief.

The drive to Katharine's house was spent in silence. What more could be said? She really didn't have any choice. She knew that she was becoming more forgetful and it wasn't fair to Johnnie to burden him with her for much longer.

They reached her house and John helped Katharine up the steps.

"Be quiet, you two," John said to the dogs, now yapping and barking, excited that Katharine had returned home.

"Thanks, Johnnie. You go and enjoy the rest of the reception."

He nodded and let himself out. Katharine settled back in her favorite chair and her little dogs jumped on her lap. What else was there in this world but the friendship of these two animals and now Johnnie wanted to take that away from her? Her heart was heavy as she looked down into their little faces. The two of them were licking her hands as if it was the most important job in the world.

After a few moments, they stopped licking her and settled comfortably on her lap. As she patted their heads, Katharine studied her hands, now brown-spotted and wrinkled with age. *My skin looks like an old woman's.*

She sighed, then recalled the way Johnnie looked at Becky and how happy he had been for his daughter. Even Harry had been a wonderful father to Ruth.

She thought back to her own wedding. Harry had been so nervous, he had sounded ridiculously silly when he had recited his vows. Katharine, on the other hand, had said her vows clearly and without hesitation. *If someone is going to do something, they ought to do it properly.*

With that, she continued to stroke the dogs' smooth, white fur.

30

Psalm 36:10

July, 2000

"How many children do you have now, Em?" Carrie, her long-time friend, asked, as they spoke over the phone. Emily, Jason and their boys were visiting her mom's place in New Jersey. She hadn't talked to Carrie in over 10 years.

"I've got five boys. My youngest is a year old and my oldest is 13."

"Holy smokes!" she responded. "Gee, haven't you and your husband heard of birth control?"

"We've heard of it. We just don't believe in using it. Besides, you know that I have always wanted a large family."

"I know that, Em. What's wrong with it? I mean, I understand why abortion is supposed to be bad, but what could possibly be wrong with birth control?"

Emily said a mental prayer to the Holy Spirit to help guide her words. Never missing an opportunity to evangelize, she answered, "Well, first of all, when a married couple have sex, they are renewing their sacramental marriage covenant or vows. Contraception separates a couple during sex so that they are not truly one."

"What do you mean separate? Certainly when I use the pill, it doesn't physically separate me from my boyfriend."

"Let me state it this way: marital sex has two essential dimensions: a couple's unity, or oneness, and the life-giving, or as Jason likes to call it, the 'baby-making' aspect."

"Marital?" Carrie paused. "What about premarital sex?"

"Okay. When a couple who is married sacramentally have sex, they renew their marriage vows. If there have been no vows, there can be no renewal."

"Yes, but what if we love each other?"

"That's nice, but love is not the 'permission slip' by which a couple can morally have sex. Marriage is."

"Well, I guess you're entitled to your opinion."

"It's not just my opinion, Carrie. I believe it's the truth."

"Whatever. You were talking about how birth control is wrong."

"Right. So marital sex encompasses two aspects. The unitive, or oneness, is meant to bring the couple closer spiritually and physically. The procreative aspect is meant to bring forth new life. Contraception basically says, 'I want the pleasure but none of the responsibility of sex.' Natural Family Planning, on the other hand, says, 'If we're avoiding pregnancy, then we will abstain from marital relations during the fertile phase.'"

Carrie interrupted again. "Wait a minute. Are you saying that you have to tell your husband, 'Not tonight, honey, I'm fertile?'

"Well, Jason would already know since he takes a big part in the responsibility of charting."

She laughed. "So, I guess you guys don't have sex very much?"

"On the contrary. You know, statistically, North American couples have sex an average of eight to ten times a month. Couples using NFP fit well within the average."

Carrie laughed again. "I'd much rather just take my pill and forget about it. Besides, I'd also prefer to have sex whenever I want to, instead of a few times every month, like you."

"As I said, it's more than a few times a month. But that's basically up to each couple to decide. Besides, during times of abstinence, we find that it's almost like dating again. When we're abstaining, it doesn't mean that we stop loving each other."

"Even so, it seems like a big inconvenience to me."

"By the way, Carrie, were you aware that the pill can act as an abortifacient?"

"A what?"

"Well, the pill works in three different ways: it suppresses ovulation, thickens the cervical mucus and makes the lining of the uterus such that the newly-formed life, if conceived, couldn't implant. That's considered an early abortion."

"No, I haven't heard that, but really, I don't think that would be considered a baby anyway, Em. I mean, it's only a few cells at that point, isn't it?"

"We were all that small once, Carrie, and it doesn't make the baby any less a baby because of how many cells he has."

"Whatever."

Her friend was silent for a moment. "You know, I really should have told you that Bob moved out a few weeks ago."

"Oh, I'm sorry, Carrie."

"So for now, I'm celibate. But you've got me thinking. No one has ever told me these things before. I just find it hard to believe you've never used birth control and you have an active sex life. You must have had a few unplanned pregnancies then, right?"

"We've been pregnant 10 times with 11 babies and not one of them was unplanned, though, if we had a surprise pregnancy, we would certainly be open to that. I hate when people call an unplanned pregnancy an 'accident.' I mean, there are no accidents when it comes to God's plan. Besides, we're talking about another human being here."

"Are you trying to tell me that you've never used any kind of birth control, only this natural method, and you haven't had any unplanned pregnancies?"

"That's right."

"That's certainly extraordinary. Well, I guess this is all a moot point for me since I'm now unattached."

"I didn't mean to be insensitive, Carrie, but it is my firm belief that the Catholic Church is proclaiming the truth through its teachings on contraception and marital sex. And I've certainly never had to deal with any of the side effects of the other methods. By the way, Carrie, have you ever read the insert that comes with the pill?"

"Who has time to read stuff like that?"

"Well, you really should. There are many side effects to hormonal contraception, some of them dangerous."

"You know, to be quite honest, I feel a heck of a lot better since going off the pill. However, that NFP method you talk about sounds a bit too inconvenient for me either way. If I ever do go back on the pill, I promise I'll read the insert."

"You owe that much to yourself."

"So what will you tell your sons when they become teenagers? To just not do it? I mean, that's asking a lot, isn't it?"

"I don't think it is, Carrie. We have already begun teaching our boys about chastity and courtship. We're definitely going to be discouraging them from dating until they're much older."

"Are you kidding?"

"No, I'm not. I mean, what's the point of 'dating' anyway? One of the main purposes is to find a lifetime mate."

There was an awkward pause on the other end of the telephone. "Uh. . .listen, Em, I've got to run. It's always an interesting experience talking to you. By the way, I'd love to see you at your mom's. How long are you going to be there?"

"For a week. I'd love to see you too. Come any time."

Emily said goodbye to her friend and hung up the phone. *Carrie must have thought I was a bit of a fanatic.* Over the years, Emily carried on quite a few conversations like the one that she had just had. Carrie seemed open to what she had to say, though Emily realized that it's difficult trying to convince someone in one conversation. In her experience, some people, even relatives, had not responded positively when she tried to share the truth.

She relaxed and tried to enjoy a rare quiet moment. Jason had taken all the boys to the Philadelphia Zoo along with Emily's younger sister, now 19.

Her mom walked into the room and commented, "You sure do go on about contraception and NFP, Em."

"I guess I do."

"By the way, Matt and Sue and their families are coming for dinner. They won't believe how much the boys have changed in only a few months, especially the baby."

"Yeah, I know."

As Emily sat on the couch in the living room of her mom's house, the home in which she had been raised, she noticed an old photo album on the end table.

"Is this one of Aunt Sally's photo albums, Mom?"

Becky nodded. Aunt Sally had been dead for eight years and Becky had inherited all the old albums.

As she studied some of the photos, she noticed that in most of them, her great-grandmother was not smiling. In fact, she appeared angry. *If only these photos could talk. I bet they would have quite a story to tell.*

Then, Emily's eyes were drawn to a photo, which looked like it was done at an early professional photographer's studio. Katharine was sitting in a high-backed chair and her son was beside her. *What a beautiful young woman she was.* What made this particular photo stand out was that Katharine's smile seemed genuine.

Emily gently lifted out the photograph. She turned it over and read, "Michael Shoemaker, Photographer."

"Hey Mom, could this be the Michael from the note, "Michael moves in," and "Michael leaves?"

"Not sure, Em. I'm not familiar with who Michael was. I just know Grandmom took in boarders." Her mother continued talking. "This photo was taken when she was younger. I didn't know her then. She could be a mean old woman, who always used to get angry if I went near her dogs. And those dogs were snappy little things. I was happy not to go near them."

"Aunt Sally told me that your grandmother had a tubal pregnancy. That must have been a pretty dangerous thing back then." Since Emily's ectopic pregnancy many years ago, she had often thought of her great-grandmother and that particular connection they shared.

"I suppose it was."

"You know, I never did find out what 'BPO Midwife' meant. In all these years, it has really stuck with me and I've always wondered."

"Well, Em, perhaps you could talk to an older midwife or someone who might know something about turn-of-the-century midwifery. Hey, wait a minute. What about checking on the Internet for information?"

"Uh. . .all right, Mom. In all these years, it never really dawned on me to check there. I guess it was too obvious."

"I've been having a ball 'surfin the net', as they say. You can find out all kinds of stuff online."

"Yeah, I know." As Becky turned on the television, Emily walked into the den and sat down at her mom's computer. She connected to the website of her favorite search engine, then typed in the key words, "midwifery practices early 1900's." There were 152 hits.

Scanning the list, Emily saw that the tenth one was entitled, "Diary of a Turn-of-the-Century Midwife." She clicked on it, and immediately she was brought to the homepage of a feminist publisher, giving a synopsis of a midwife's journal.

Emily read it out loud. "Anne Gliddon was a turn-of-the-century midwife, who delivered babies, among other things, for middle-class women from 1900 to 1929. She worked from her home in South Philadelphia where she regularly delivered babies in their homes, as well as doing a procedure called menstrual extraction, or bringing a woman's period on in the early stages of pregnancy. Her daily journal shows a compassionate and caring woman who helped mothers in desperate situations eliminate unwanted pregnancies. These women would otherwise resort to self-induced abortions with wire coat hangers or hat pins, with many dying of hemorrhages."

"Compassionate and caring woman? I suppose she believed that she really was helping women, but I imagine the child in the womb might have had a different opinion," she said out loud.

Emily stopped reading and tried to empathize with women in the first part of the century or even now, whose boyfriends, lovers or husbands were abusive or simply indifferent to the woman carrying a child within. How horrible it must have been to find yourself in a situation which seemed hopeless. If only she could tell these women that abortion was not the answer, that although killing the unborn child seemed like a quick fix, it had far-reaching moral, physical and spiritual consequences for the mother, father and society as a whole.

"Eliminating unwanted pregnancies?" She wished that she could make women understand that when they resorted to such procedures, that they were actually 'eliminating' a part of themselves.

Now, for Emily, it seemed so simple. She tried not to judge these turn-of-the-century women, because she also understood there were abusive husbands and little, if any, help from society in the early part of the century. Now, there were many pro-life and religious organizations devoted to helping and supporting women in those circumstances.

"BPO," she said once more, searching for a connection to the website passage.

Emily recited a portion of the excerpt again, "...procedure called menstrual extraction, or bringing a woman's period on in the early stages of pregnancy." The words now seemed to jump off the computer screen. Emily's heart started beating more rapidly, her breathing stopped as she stared at the initial letters of these three words, "...bringing...period on."

"Oh my God," she said out loud.

Becky rushed into the room. "Oh my God what, Em?"

"I got it! It means 'bring period on.' Why else would she be going to the midwife?"

For a few seconds, her mom was silent. "You know, Em, I was hoping that you wouldn't find out about all that. In all these years that you've been studying those ledgers, I had no idea what those abbreviations stood for. I would never have imagined that she would actually write down what she did in a bookkeeping ledger. To be quite honest, I never really thought much about it."

"You mean you knew all along?"

"Well, I knew, but no one spoke about it back when I was a kid. Even though it wasn't talked about, from what I understand,

Grandmom didn't really hide it. These boarders that she would take on, they would often become her lovers too. I remember one incident where Grandpop chased one of her boarders with a gun."

"Really, mom? He chased one of her lovers with a gun?"

"Yeah. I didn't really understand it all that much, but I remember seeing Grandpop's eyes and they looked so angry. Anyway, I didn't find out for certain until I was much older, when Sal confirmed my suspicions. Besides, it's not something I'd want to pass on to the next generation. That kind of information needs to stay in the past, Em."

"Forget about it? Mom, how can I possibly forget about the fact that my own great-grandmother had many abortions?"

"Em, just leave it in the past."

Emily sighed as her mother turned around and walked out of the den.

Her heart beating rapidly, she stared at the monitor, the words "bringing on a woman's period," jumping out at her, shouting at her.

Her boarders would become her lovers? Emily wondered about the boarder Michael, whom Katharine had written about several times in her ledger. Could he have possibly been a paramour? And why would she have only mentioned him?

Another realization occurred to her. In the back of Emily's mind, it always seemed odd to her that Ruth looked nothing like her father and her skin was so pale, so white.

Could Ruth be the boarder, Michael's, daughter? Emily wanted to ask her mother about it, but Becky had seemed upset when she brought up her grandmother's abortions.

Now obsessed with an insatiable drive to know the truth, Emily's thoughts became consumed with discovering the complete story. Immediately, she recalled seeing a picture of Katharine many years ago which showed a tall man behind her. Emily rushed into the living room, pulled out the album and searched the contents. Page by page, she scanned the photographs until her eyes became fixed on the stoic-looking young Katharine. Emily could make out a tall man, but the photo was brown-tinged and somewhat out of focus so she couldn't distinguish any details in the man's face. She slipped the picture out of the album, then searched the photos for a shot of young Ruth. She easily found one, circa 1929 when Ruth was 20. Unfortunately, this photo was also a bit unfocused. Emily brought both pictures to the desk area in the den.

Carefully, she held the photographs side by side. The slightly blurry condition of both images reminded Emily of a conversation that she had had with Jason about impressionistic painters, how they tried to create an impression rather than paint something so detailed.

The 'impression' of the man, despite the unfocused state of the photograph, still revealed a characteristic set of shapes. Emily could tell that he had a strong jaw, high forehead and slight nose.

Holding the two photographs together, there actually was no mistaking the similarities, especially the shape of their heads and jaw line. Emily became convinced that this was Ruth's father. It seemed that the lack of detail reduced the distraction and, in fact, aided the comparison.

Still driven with a desire to confirm the truth, Emily walked out of the den and approached her mother in the kitchen.

"Mom, I know this is upsetting you, but I need to show you something."

"What, Em?"

"Is it possible that Ruth is not Grandpop's biological daughter?"

"Em, I told you to leave it in the past. How is dredging up any of this going to change it now?"

"It's not going to change anything, but after all these years, I need to know."

Becky hesitated, then sighed. "Nobody ever said anything, but it was a given. Grandpop was very dark and my father looked a lot like him, except as my grandmother used to say, 'a handsome version.' Aunt Ruth, well, she looks a bit like Grandmom, but. . . ."

Becky continued. "To my knowledge, Grandmom never admitted it, but we all kind of knew. I'm sure Aunt Ruth realized it as well. It didn't really take a genius to figure out that Ruth was the product of one of our grandmother's many liaisons. We just loved Grandpop so much and so did Ruth that I don't think it really mattered to her. She loved him as her father, despite the absence of genes."

"Do you think your grandfather knew?"

"I'm not sure. He may have realized it as well."

Emily handed the photographs to her mother. "Look at these photos."

"So this is Ruth and this is Grandmom. So what?"

"The gentleman standing behind your grandmother, look at his face."

Becky squinted as she looked back and forth between both photos. "This could be him, Em. There are definite similarities."

Emily stared blankly at her mother.

"Now, I never want to talk about this again, so please don't bring it up."

Emily walked into the den and sat down at the desk.

Her hands shaking, she finally disconnected from the Internet and sat quietly staring at her mother's computer screen. All those years, it was a mere point of interest, trying to find out what the notations meant. Now, it was a personal matter. She felt a deep sense of sadness and an emptiness at discovering the truth.

That night, as she lay in bed in her old room at her mother's house, she listened to the breathing of her five sleeping children and husband. She found herself overwhelmed with deep gratitude for her family.

Beneath the gratitude, there was a sense of despair about her great-grandmother. "Oh, God, is she in hell? How could an ancestor of mine possibly have done that? How could she have carried on affairs with those men right under the nose of her husband?"

Her eyes began to tear for her great-grandmother, an ancestor that she would never know, this woman who had already been dead for 40 years. Then, part of her felt anger at her great-grandmother who, so many years ago, misused God's precious gift of sexual expression and life.

She now wished that she had never heard the complete story of Katharine Clayman and now understood her mom's insistence with "leaving it in the past." It was much better when she was just a picture in her family tree album. Now, she was a lump in Emily's throat.

A year later, Emily sat quietly in the church pew. It was a challenge to find the time to pray before the Blessed Sacrament, while at the same time, dealing with the responsibility of raising and homeschooling five boys. However, she managed, often bringing her sons with her. As always, once she arrived, she didn't want to leave. It was difficult to describe, but when she was in Christ's Eucharistic Presence, her soul seemed to exude a contentment, a joy unlike anything else.

She had begun praying the Miracle Hour, a "rich grace-filled hour" as it is described in the booklet that guided one through this prayer. The 'hour' is a simple format that included praying in 12 five-minute segments devoted to things like praise, scripture, forgiveness. During the forgiveness section, there is a statement, "I forgive my ancestors for any negative actions that affect my life today and make it harder for me to live in the freedom of a child of God. I release them from bondage and make peace with them today, in Jesus' name."

She always remembered her great-grandmother, Katharine Clayman, when she said this prayer. Also in the Miracle Hour, there is a prayer of surrender that ends with, "loving Father, let the cleansing, healing waters of my baptism flow back through the generations to purify my family line of contamination. . . ." She thought about her great-grandmother and other ancestors and relatives who chose to live a life of sexual immorality: fornicating, contracepting, committing adultery, having abortions.

For an entire year, Emily had placed before God this uneasy feeling about her great-grandmother. Initially, she had been ashamed to be related to her. Through prayers like the Miracle Hour, she was able to begin praying for her in earnest, though she often wondered whether her prayers would do her great-grandmother any good. Her spiritual director, Father Dominic, had told her that no one knows the state of one's soul at the moment of death. He had given her hope that perhaps her great-grandmother had experienced a change of heart. Even at the moment of death, it is not too late for a conversion.

In her prayer before the Blessed Sacrament, she was also reminded of the Mother Teresa quote, "If you judge people, you have no time to love them." Once Emily stopped judging the kind of life Katharine had led, she was able to start loving her as a "human being of inestimable worth," as Pope John Paul II had said. Her great-grandmother, regardless of the life she lived and the choices she made, had been a human being of inestimable worth. When Emily focused on this, she was able to think of her great-grandmother as someone she could love unconditionally.

One particular Saturday afternoon, during a rare opportunity to be alone while praying before the Blessed Sacrament in her small parish church, when Emily came to the section of the Miracle Hour entitled "Wait for the Lord to Speak," she sat back and allowed her mind to clear.

A few minutes previous, she had prayed for Katharine, as she did every time she did the Miracle Hour. She also pictured her great-grandmother in the saving presence of Jesus. During this time, she often felt God telling her things. She never heard words as such, but she sensed that God was communicating with her.

In the silence of the small country church, in Jesus' Real Presence, she began to get a strong awareness that she and her great-grandmother were connected in more ways than she fully understood. From the depths of her soul, she could hear the words, "in reparation for my sins and the sins of others," the words of the prayer she recited first thing every morning.

She realized that her great-aunt, Ruth, and Aunt Sally had lost children before birth and neither had been able to give birth to children. In this way, it seemed that they were also affected by Katharine's choices.

However, no one else among Katharine's great-grandchildren had ever lost children through ectopic pregnancy. Most of the Clayman great-grandchildren went along with the morals of the time, with pre-marital sex a common occurrence, the majority using contraception or becoming sterilized. It's possible that some of the great-grandchildren had resorted to abortion. Emily's loss of six children was clearly unique in her extended family.

As she continued meditating and keeping her mind open to God's word, she began to perceive a stronger realization: that she and her great-grandmother were connected even more deeply and in some way, it involved Emily's losses and her ancestor's lifestyle.

Immediately, she felt a deep and inborn desire to help her great-grandmother in whatever way she could. It was not unlike the feeling one experiences when one sees a child drowning in the water. She wanted to reach out through the ocean of life and grab her great-grandmother's hand and pull her to the safety of Jesus' loving presence and God's infinite Mercy.

"God, how can I help my great-grandmother?" she whispered.

Emily bowed her head and continued to pray. She wanted so desperately to help this fellow human being to whom she felt a deep connection. Yet she felt helpless.

She lifted her head and was drawn to the stained glass window with the image of St. Joseph and the child Jesus.

Child-like purity, it seemed to call to her.

In an instant, she could hear a car pulling into the parking lot.

Saturday Mass is in half an hour.

Now, Emily felt a strong desire to participate in the most perfect prayer, Mass. She had told Jason that she might be away for a few hours, so she sat back and continued to mediate.

God, what you've given me is a beautiful gift, but I really need you to help me to understand all this better and to give me ways that I can help her.

Within several minutes, Mass began and Emily allowed herself to absorb the graces. She once heard the saying that Mass is a little bit of heaven and she certainly understood why this was so.

Consecration approached, the very moment that the bread and wine become the body and blood of Christ. Emily prepared for the solemn moment by bowing her head. She heard the words spoken by the priest, "This is my Body, which will be given up for you. Do this in memory of me," and the small bells rang in response.

The chiming of the bells now silent, Emily listened as her soul echoed the words, "in reparation for the sins of others."

A minute or so later, Emily heard the priest say, "This is the cup of my blood," and again from deep within her being, she sensed the words, now seeming loud over the sound of the bells, "in reparation for the sins of others."

It could only have been by a showering of abundant graces that Emily was able to grasp, in a small way, the knowledge of God's perfect plan for the salvation of all. His son died to redeem us. But we, in turn, have the opportunity to suffer in reparation for the sins of others. It is one of the special ways that we, as human beings, can image God.

She now felt within the deep recesses of her heart and her soul that indeed her losses were allowed by God to act, in part, as reparation for her great-grandmother's abortions, not unlike the actions of the young visionaries at Fatima who wore ropes around their waists to the point of drawing blood, in order to act in reparation for the souls in purgatory.

Walking up to communion, Emily pondered the words of the "Lord I am not worthy" prayer as she prepared to receive the Body, Blood, Soul and Divinity of her Savior.

"The Body of Christ," she heard the priest say to her. As she responded, "Amen," and opened her mouth, the host was placed on her tongue. At that very moment, again the words, "in reparation for the sins of others" resounded in her soul.

Now humbled, her whole body, her whole being, her whole life seemed changed. There, within her soul, was pure love, a minute taste of the perfect love that God has for us. There was also a deep faith, a sureness that God loves us unconditionally and without end. Finally, there was hope, a bottomless and never-ending desire to bring not only her great-grandmother, but every human ever created into God's loving presence.

Emily not only knew, but now experienced, that within the Mystical Body of Christ, we are all connected. Our actions and the way we think, good or bad, affect all those around us. It impacts the very unity of the human family.

She had often wondered why God had allowed those six children to be conceived when He knew that they wouldn't be born or live beyond a few hours. God is the one who opens and closes the womb and the only one who has the power to decide who will be born and who will not be born.

She thought of one of her favorite John Paul II quotes, "Human life is precious because it is the gift of a God whose love is infinite and when God gives life, it is forever." Her children, those now in heaven, were great blessings and eternal gifts from God.

The Mass now over, Emily returned home. Bursting with excitement to share with Jason her experience, she walked through the door to find Jake and Nate fighting over a computer game. Phillip was crying to be nursed. Tom and Andrew were wrestling on the floor. The dog was barking. "Binky, be quiet, girl," Emily called. And she realized how absolutely ridiculous that sounded. Why had they allowed the boys to name their dog after a character on a cartoon? Jason said, "I've got marking to do, Em. I have to go to the school." He kissed her, then walked through the door.

"Gimme it," screamed Andrew, as he and Tom continued wrestling on the floor.

"It's mine!" Tom screamed back at him.

"Nin-nin, Mamma," Phillip cried, putting his hands in the air in a motion for Emily to pick him up.

Gazing down at little Phillip, she thanked God for allowing her to go through the difficulties of being a mom and to experience those pregnancy losses. She was grateful for the knowledge of what her great-grandmother did, so that she could pray for her and suffer for her.

The noise and screaming still echoing in her ears, Emily was now able to deal with the turmoil without frustration and without anxiety, but with love for the "duty of the moment."

She scooped up her toddler and sat on the sofa. She lifted her shirt to allow her youngest child to nurse.

"Mom," Jake screamed. "Nate won't let me play Mario Kart."

"Yeah, I won't. He's being mean to me and I'm not letting him play my game."

She took a deep breath and relaxed. Filled with the grace from her experience at Mass, Emily felt blessed to have a wonderful, loving husband and these five rambunctious boys.

She thanked God for the Catholic Church, for keeping the truth alive and for allowing her to embrace it. Most importantly, she was grateful for the gift of her life and for the opportunity to spread His love to others and to help, even in a small way, stop her family's intergenerational sin and the effects of it which had prevailed for many years.

31

Hebrews 4-13

April, 1961

Katharine moaned when she realized what tonight's dinner would be. "I hate meatloaf. The food in this place stinks. No salt, no spices, no taste," she grumbled. *I wouldn't be surprised if the cook in this rest home once worked at a prison.* She grudgingly sat down at her place at the table. "It's damned hot in this place. And why does everything smell like urine?" She pushed around the food on her plate, barely touching any of it. She wasn't very hungry anyway. All day, she had had a nagging bloated feeling in her belly and strange shooting pains in her arms.

Katharine looked up from her plate and studied the other residents. Most were eagerly consuming the evening's dinner. After a few minutes, she stood up and walked across the hall toward the common room. She knew that the staff would be turning on the news at six o'clock and she wanted to get a good seat to watch.

Though there were two couches in the room, she sat down on the brown plaid couch facing the television set. The other sofa was a solid green one with its back to the one she had chosen.

No matter where I go, everything smells of urine. Reaching into her skirt pocket, she grabbed the tube of Ben Gay and rubbed it on her arms.

She enjoyed visiting the common living room when supper was being served. Very few people would be there and she so desperately craved time away from the other residents of the home. Its pale yellow walls and brown and beige furniture reminded her of a hospital.

"Hi, Grandmom," Katharine heard. She turned her head to see two of her granddaughters, Sally and Becky, walking toward her. Becky held her youngest child, Emily, in her arms.

"Why aren't you eating your supper or have you already finished?" Sally asked.

Not waiting for her to reply, Sally continued, "The traffic was so bad that it was stop and go the entire ride here. We would've been here an hour ago."

"Why are you both here? You didn't tell me you were coming, Sally."

"Yes, I did. I told you yesterday that I would be visiting on my way to pick up my husband from the train station."

Ignoring Sally, Katharine faced her other granddaughter. "How old's the baby now, Becky?"

"She's not quite two, but she's small. I had to bring her with us because Sally's going to drop me off at the children's shoe store nearby. Emily's so tiny that she needs special walking shoes."

Katharine looked up at her great-granddaughter and shrugged her shoulders.

"Here, Grandmom, feel how light she is," Becky said as she placed Emily in her great-grandmother's lap.

Katharine's eyes widened, then a frown replaced her usual stoic face, not as much a frown of disgust, but one of serious concern.

"Becky, babies are. . .well. . .messy," she said as she looked at Emily's small face. *I hope she doesn't need her diaper changed.*

A few seconds of awkward silence, then Emily's high-pitched baby voice spoke up. "Dess pwetty?"

At the sweetness of her words, Katharine cleared her voice, forced a smile and said, "Yes, dear, your dress is quite pretty with its pink polka dots. And look at your shoes, as shiny as can be."

Emily reached up and placed her small hand on the side of her great-grandmother's textured face and, with her tiny fingers, gently traced the deep lines that Katharine's facial wrinkles appeared to make.   This young child's small eyes captivated Katharine. She was not quite two, but she stared sternly at the lines. Then, as if a light switched on, she gazed adoringly at her great-grandmother, an expression which offered an unconditional love that Katharine had rarely noticed from a child or anyone else, for that matter.

She began to shift and move in her seat. "This child is certainly. . .well, animated."

Ignoring her grandmother's comment, Becky responded, "Isn't she light?"

"I suppose so." Emily became distracted by the noise of the console television and wiggled off Katharine's lap.

"Momma, TV," she said, as she ran over to the large television in front of them. "Watch Capan, Momma."

"No, honey. Captain Kangaroo isn't on right now. Besides, we can only stay a few minutes."

Emily's small eyes formed a frown. "No go, stay."   She stood by Katharine and patted her great-grandmother's knee.

The three adults exchanged a few moments of chatter, then Sally and Becky apologized to their grandmother for having to leave after such a short visit.

"Emily, let's go," Becky said, as she grabbed her hand and pulled. "Say goodbye to Great-Grandmom."

Emily beamed at Katharine, her tiny face glowing, and replied, "Bye, bye."

Sally spoke up. "Tootsie Roll, blow Grandmom a kiss like Aunt Sal is doing." As Emily watched her aunt, she put the palm of her miniature hand to her mouth and blew Katharine a kiss.

Sally leaned over to kiss her grandmother's leathery cheek, then she, Becky and little Emily began to walk away.

Katharine watched Becky and Sally turn around one more time to wave. Becky then leaned over and scooped her daughter up into her arms. Emily smiled at Katharine, then waved her hand.

What in the world is Sally calling that baby? Tootsie Roll? What an absurd name.

Katharine thought of her great-granddaughter and the expression of awe and wonder in her eyes and how her little hand had gently touched her face. She had seen this child only once before when she was a newborn nearly two years ago. Now, this mere toddler seemed to connect with her in a way Katharine could not comprehend. *That child is a lot like me.*

Katharine then watched as two women in their late thirties approached the green couch that faced away from the television, then sat down. Katharine sighed again, irritated that she might not be able to hear the news program. "I hope they're not going to jabber on about nothing," she mumbled to herself.

Ignoring Katharine, the women spoke openly. "I guess we'll wait here while mom is having her supper," one of the women said.

"I just couldn't believe it," the other one said, now in a hushed tone. "Jane came home last week and told us she was pregnant and that she and her boyfriend didn't know what to do. Well, I told her that I would take care of everything and arrange to get her an abortion. I mean, it wasn't their fault. The boy used a condom and she still got pregnant. Her dad was upset, but I told him teenagers will be teenagers. At least something can be done."

"Where did you take her?"

"To a doctor who works out of a clinic in Camden. It was expensive but well worth it. I hear it used to be much easier at the turn of the century than it is now."

"And Jane had no problems with the abortion?"

"Well, it's only been a few days and she does seem rather withdrawn and quiet and stays in her room a lot. I keep telling her that her dilemma was solved, but that doesn't seem to help."

"She just needs time. And what about the new pill? All you have to do is take a pill and you don't get pregnant. Seems like the perfect solution."

"Well, it does seem rather convenient, but my friend was on the pill and she said she was so sick with it, that she stopped taking it after a month."

"That's a small price to pay for convenience."

"As soon as Jane comes out of her room and starts acting normally again, I'll be putting her on the pill. That is, as soon as we can find a doctor who will prescribe it. It's still hard in some towns to get a prescription for someone who is unmarried."

Katharine listened, then shook her head. *Things sure have changed. A pill to prevent pregnancy. Lord knows, I sure could've used that. That young woman who decided to take matters into her own hands could've used it too.*

She reflected nostalgically about her life during the early part of the century. Immediately, her mind envisioned all the lovers with whom she had shared her bed. Michael's young, handsome face came to her mind. It was likely that he was now dead. How she missed him.

Too tired and in too much pain from her arthritis, it became difficult to remember what life was like for her back then. Small and pretty, it was usually a simple task to find someone to warm her bed. But what did all those encounters really accomplish for her anyway? It seemed like another lifetime ago.

She had to admit that she never really felt satisfied, not physically and certainly not emotionally. There was always this gnawing ache inside her being telling her that the way she lived her life had far-reaching consequences. She brushed the feeling aside. *What I did only affected me, no one else.*

Harry's place in their marriage was a prime example. She remembered thinking that he was not the nicest looking young man she had ever met, but he had obviously been quite taken with her. When he approached her at the harbor, he could barely talk to her with his stammering and stuttering. Day after day, Katharine would see him there. At that time, Katharine was desperate to get away from her father's abuse and she recognized that it would only get worse. She was told that she had been a mistake, that she had been the reason her father had to marry her mother. So when Harry nervously asked for her hand in marriage, she realized that he could be the key to escaping from her prison. It didn't really matter that she didn't love him. He provided the perfect solution.

Katharine admitted that she never had any intention of being faithful to her husband. After all, she gave him a pretty wife, one that he would not have been able to find elsewhere.

Strangely enough, she didn't care whether he remained faithful to her. *He wouldn't have had the guts to go elsewhere anyway.* However, she understood now that marrying Harry had two purposes in the end: to rescue her from her prison and to make her legitimate. When seeking out the midwife to bring on her period, there was never any question. Married women frequently have unexpected pregnancies.

So as part of her own plan, she recognized that it was important to stay married to him.

The nightly news came on but by this time, so many people had gathered in the common room that she could barely hear it. Somebody started to play piano. Shrugging her shoulders, Katharine looked up and, over the buzz of everyone's voices, she heard the elderly gentleman start singing "Nearer My God to Thee."

"Another holy roller," she mumbled under her breath. But she had to acknowledge that, even for an older man, he had a beautiful, soothing voice. She decided to listen. After all, she couldn't hear the news and there wasn't anything better to do.

> *Nearer, my God, to Thee, nearer to Thee*
> *E'en though it be a cross that raiseth me,*
> *Still all my song shall be,*
> *Nearer, my God, to Thee*
>
> *Nearer, my God, to Thee, Nearer to Thee*
> *There let the way appear, steps until heav'n*
> *All that Thou sendest me, in mercy given;*
>
> *Angels to beckon me nearer, my God to Thee*
> *Nearer, my God, to Thee, Nearer to Thee*
> *There in my Father's home, safe and at rest*

"Nearer my God to Thee? Where the hell was God when my father was giving me the strap every other day from the time I was just a little older than that baby, Emily? Where the hell were the angels?" Katharine mumbled under her breath. It was difficult for her to be thankful for anything.

"Excuse me, ma'am."

Katharine was surprised to see the elderly gentleman, the one who had been playing and singing the song, standing close and leaning down in an effort to talk to her. He had a thick head of white hair and surprisingly few wrinkles. She could tell that when he was much younger, he would have been strikingly handsome. "Yes, what would you like?"

"I couldn't help but notice that you seemed to be the only one listening to my song."

Katharine frowned. 'That's nonsense. There were other people listening. You have a beautiful voice."

"Thank you, ma'am. But I got this feeling that I was supposed to come over here and talk to you."

Katharine frowned again. "Now what could you possibly talk to me about?"

"Well, I feel like I need to tell you that God loves you."

"What?" Katharine could hardly believe her ears.

"God loves you. Perhaps you've never heard those words before."

Katharine hesitated. "Uh . . . I . . .well. . . ." she scowled.

The elderly gentleman continued, "That song I just sang, it's my favorite song. You know, my young wife was on the Titanic, in second class, and she was one of the survivors. She told me she heard the band playing that song while the ship was sinking. Ever since then, I've loved that song. It's brought me closer to God, I think, and to my dear Lillie, God rest her soul."

She stared at him intensely, then shook her head. "Look, I know you mean well, but I don't have time for this. I need to get back to my room." Katharine stood up and slowly started the journey back to her room. As she was exiting the large common room, she looked back and saw that the gentleman had positioned himself back at the piano and started playing a slow, melancholy tune.

She stepped out of the room and began walking down the long hall to her bedroom. She abhorred this place, with its lack of privacy, no pets, lousy food.

It seemed like the air was getting heavy and it was becoming harder for her to take a breath. *Damned hot in this place*, she silently complained. *Even this hallway smells like a men's urinal.* Slowly, painstakingly moving down the hall, she passed by one of the other occupant's rooms and stopped to catch her breath. Her eyes were drawn to a glare of light, the metal crucifix and wooden figure which hung on the wall over the bed. There, before her, was the image of Jesus hanging on the cross, blood on his head, face, side, feet and hands.

Katharine made her usual attempt to push away those fruitless thoughts in which one wonders if there really is a God. Suddenly, it felt like someone hit her in the chest with a sledgehammer. The pain knocked her to the floor. Her body stiffened, her arms and wrists full of tension, like she was a hard bronze figure from Rodin's "Gates of Hell." Lying on her right side, with her body partially blocking the hallway, her eyelids beginning to close, she strained to look down the hall and back towards the common room.

Her back felt the excruciating pain of her scars, the wounds which had remained open for many years. Her eyes caught sight again of the crucifix and of Jesus' bloodied form. Closing her eyes, she envisioned Jesus being scourged, his back taking on fresh gashes, wounds destined not to heal, and pain shot through her scars.

Help, she opened her mouth to say. She heard the faint sound of piano music, its soft melody becoming surreal background noise. She continued to keep her eyes closed, then opened them, letting out a small gasp.

The child stood calmly and peacefully before her.

"Em. . ." she tried to say her great-granddaughter's name. *What is she still doing here without Becky and Sally?*

Her great-granddaughter stood perfectly still and quietly gazed down at her. Katharine's eyes squinted as the toddler's form shone like a bright light and her eyes again radiated that pure, unconditional love.

"Where . . . are . . . the nurses, honey," she struggled to ask. *It isn't right that no one is coming.* As her heart questioned, she focused on the toddler's eyes and she became filled with the knowledge that though only the child stood next to her, there were many more watching on. Katharine couldn't see them, but she could hear their hushed murmurs, spirits without bodies, one in particular who had been with Katharine for her entire life, though she had been too unaware to sense his presence, too hardened to care.

Unconditional love. How many people had offered the same unconditional love that these spirits without bodies did? Her husband, her children, grandchildren, many of her customers, Michael, all came to her mind.

God loves you. Her mind and soul replayed the words spoken minutes ago by the man playing the piano. *God loves you.* Katharine now struggled to look up at the child. Her great-granddaughter's eyes displayed the complete and devoted gaze of an older baby recognizing her mother. *I'm not worthy of that look, child.* From behind her, she could hear the piercing screams of several infants. As Katharine lay motionless, the cries soon became distant but ever-present. *God loves you.* Her heart and her soul became filled with these words, the knowledge that she was loved without conditions, without restrictions, fully and without end.

"Allow your heart and your soul to take on the child-like purity of one such as this," she heard a voice say. Katharine might have identified it as the piano man except that she could still hear his melancholy chords from the common room. She reached up, tried to grab onto the little girl's pink polka-dotted dress, still bright with a white glow. *If I can just touch her dress.* She raised her left arm and made an attempt, but her arm and hand were too stiff, the pain preventing her from the task.

With every ounce of strength remaining within her, Katharine lifted her arm and finally felt the softness of the material and immediately it became the nurse's white uniform.

"Katharine, Katharine, can you hear me?"

She nodded.

"Are you in any pain, dear?"

"I. . .my chest. . .can't. . . ."

"You need your heart medication."

Katharine was gasping now. *Where is the child?*

Her eyes were heavy, but she managed to open them for a second and whisper "Emily."

"Who's Emily, dear?"

Katharine struggled, but mustered what little strength remained to use her finger to point out where the child had been. "Why, there's no one there, Katharine."

She tried desperately to take a breath in, but there was no air left. All at once, it seemed like she was high above the floor, looking down at the scene, the nurse patting her lifeless face. *The nurse need not fuss about me any longer.* Her physical pain, now completely absent, was replaced by an agony of a different sort, hungering, thirsting. . .seeking comfort and light.

Epilogue
Prov. 10:28

August 2004

Emily watched as her husband arranged the music sheets on the stand, then tuned his guitar. She sat in the front pew of the small church, then leaned over to quiet her youngest son. Though she was now considered middle-aged, Emily remained young-looking, her shoulder length hair just beginning to show streaks of gray.

Jason moved closer to the microphone and he began singing the pre-entrance song:

Amazing Grace how sweet the sound
That saved sinners like me
I was lost but now am found
Was blind but now I see

As she listened to the song, the words took on deep meaning for her. When she reflected on her life of so many years ago, she realized that she had been truly lost and blind. Then she thought of her great-grandmother and prayed that somehow before she died, grace had found her.

As the hymn echoed throughout the small church, Emily's heart filled with joy. She fell more in love with her husband every Sunday when they attended Mass as a family. Though they had engaged in some fairly intense arguments over the years, both had always been committed to their sacrament.

Although Jason played guitar and sang on the altar, and she remained in the front pew with their five sons, she always felt such a deep attachment to him while they were celebrating the

Eucharist. She felt connected, by way of the Mystical Body of Christ, to deceased members of her family as well, like her six children in heaven, her father, Aunt Sally and to her great-grandmother, Katharine Clayman. Since her discovery a few years ago, it was not uncommon for her to think about Katharine at Mass and about how deeply she and her great-grandmother were connected.

Distracted by her youngest child's crying, she picked up little Phillip, who was now half her size, offered some consoling words, then continued listening to her husband. She suddenly felt a deep gratitude for God's presence in their marriage. How could she and Jason have gotten through all those difficult times without God's grace? How could they ever have been truly one, physically and spiritually, except for Jason's refusal to allow them to use any form of artificial contraception? How could they have found true happiness without following all of God's laws, not just the ones that were comfortable or 'easy'?

Mass, for Emily and Jason, was spiritual fuel not only for their own souls individually, but for their souls together and that of their growing sons. Though it was a challenge getting her five boys ready every Sunday and dealing with them alone in the front pew, she realized that it was a necessary sacrifice to be able to have her husband lead the congregation in song.

At home and towards the end of the day, Emily wandered outside to begin the evening clean up at their small, but cozy, home in the country. A neighbor's large cornfield was their back yard and a smaller lawn and naturally occurring bedrock lined the front portion of their three-acre property. Surrounding their humble 'estate' on either side was a thick, lush forest.

It had been a glorious summer's day, a stay-outside kind of day, and Emily savored the sweet fresh air of the early evening. She leaned over and began to gather up the lawn toys, badminton rackets, balls and baseball gloves. Then she watched her husband and their five sons, now ages 5 to 17, running around playing, laughing and enjoying a impromptu soccer game. Emily stood still, transfixed by the bright colors in the sky. The sun was just starting to set and the sky was turning brilliant shades of orange and pink. She stared at the colors that only God could produce and wondered, *How could anyone not believe in God?* Then she thought of her great-grandmother. When she first learned about Katharine and the choices she had made, she felt a deep sadness for her. Lacking the gift of faith and any way to form her conscience properly, Katharine's life was one of pessimism disguised as hope. It was an existence sometimes hidden in darkness and filled with the misuse of God's gift of sexuality and the destruction of God's beautiful gift of fertility and new life within her. It was a life which cried out that she, and not God, was in control.

She remembered Pope John Paul II's quote, "every human being is a being of inestimable worth." Despite her misguided and difficult life, Katharine remained a being of inestimable worth and Emily had come to love her great-grandmother, unconditionally, and to hope that her eternal soul had been saved.

The intensity of the colors in the sky increased as the pinks became more deep pinkish-red and the oranges became more deeply orange-red. How could it become even more beautiful and awe-inspiring? *That is so like God.* Just when we think, in our own humanness, that we have seen the most beautiful and breathtaking thing imaginable, He allows us to experience even more deeply of His beauty, His goodness and His love.

Emily's thoughts turned to the tiny unborn child growing inside of her and her heart leapt with joy. At 45, she had settled into the acceptance that she and Jason would not be conceiving any more children. She also realized that after experiencing the loss of six babies, perhaps this child would not be born. She remembered John Paul II's wisdom when he said, "Human life is precious because it is the gift of a God whose love is infinite; and when God gives life, it is forever." Whether this child is born or is not born, she understood clearly that it was a tremendous blessing to be experiencing the wonder and miracle of pregnancy again, especially in these first few weeks.

Tear-filled with gratitude toward God, she glanced over to see that Jason was smiling at her.

"How can I thank God for such a great gift?"she said out loud to her husband, knowing that he would understand what she meant.

"Em, you already have, by your willingness to be open to another child. Now, you can continue to thank Him by trying to be positive even when you start getting migraines and nausea."

Jason sometimes understood her better than she understood herself. He knew that, far from being stoic, Emily readily complained whenever she had the slightest discomfort.

She realized how different her life had become since meeting Jason, then becoming faithful to living out the teachings of the Catholic Church. Life was a much bigger, much happier journey since she began trusting in God's will. What better way for God to bring her closer to Him than to allow her to fall in love with Jason? *If Jason and I love each other so much, how much more perfectly must God love us?*

Emily again watched her growing boys running and playing on the front lawn. The soccer game now over, Andrew, their small nine-year-old, was doing cartwheels. "Mommy, Mommy, do a cartwheel," he yelled. For a moment, her mind drifted to the time 25 years ago when she had met Jason for the first time.

"Emily, do a cartwheel," said Rose.

"Oh, okay," she replied. Even at 45, her still small body easily maneuvered the cartwheel. As she was standing up afterwards, she laughed. "I'm going to feel that in the morning."

"Yeah, Mommy, do another, do another," her boys were coaxing her.

"No, no, one's enough." *Besides,* Emily thought of her tiny unborn child, *I don't want to make you dizzy, little one.*

The sky was now pale pink and orange and the colors were reflecting off her boys' running bodies. Their children truly were "the living testimony of full, mutual self-giving."

She walked over to her husband and stood beside him,

whispering, "Those children exist because we love each other."

Jason placed his arm around Emily's shoulder and whispered, "And because God loves us. Pretty awesome, eh?"

She nodded and suddenly, Emily was filled with hope, stronger than any she had known before. Encompassing everything that concerned her, she was filled with hope for her unborn child's safe delivery; hope for her sons' future as godly men of Christ, hope for her great-grandmother's eternal destiny. Hope had turned to peace.

Author's notes:

The St. Augustine quote at the beginning is from "The Enchiridion on Faith, Hope, and Love," translated by J.F. Shaw (Chicago Henry Regnery Co., 1961), page 9.

"The duty of the moment" is a quote from Catherine Doherty, foundress of Madonna House, Combermere, Ontario, Canada.

The genealogy books mentioned are fictional. Any resemblance to those in real life is purely coincidental.

The particulars of the Titanic disaster which the Katharine character is reading about in the newspaper are true. However, the character, Lillie, is fictional. Any resemblance to a real life character is purely coincidental.

As well, the quotes from the "feminist website" and the character "Annie Gliddon" are fictional. Any resemblance to a real life character or website is purely coincidental.

The Walk for Life event spoken about in the novel is fictional.

Prayer for Purity

(from Christopher West's book, Theology of the Body for Beginners) *Lord, help me to discern the movements of my heart. Help me to distinguish between the great riches of sexuality as you created it to be and the distortions of lust. I grant you permission, Lord, to slay my lusts. Take them. Crucify them so that I might come to experience the resurrection of sexual desire as you intend. Grant me a pure heart. Amen.*
(Used with permission)

The Use of NFP in Serious Need

In his encyclical, On Human Life, Pope Paul VI wrote: *In relation to physical, economic, psychological and social conditions, responsible parenthood is exercised either by the deliberate and generous decision to raise a numerous family, or by the decision, made for grave motives and with due respect for moral law, to avoid for the time being, or for even an indeterminate period, a new birth.*

Kimberly Hahn, in her book "Life-Giving Love," writes: *"Prayer is critical in the discernment process regarding the seriousness of our reasons to use NFP. Ever respectful of the freedom within the sacredness of the marriage bond, the Church does not dictate the specifics. She entrusts this power to us."* She further states: *"Here are three questions to aid discerning use of NFP:*

1)Do we have serious and grave reason for using NFP?

2) Have we prayerfully considered how temporary our use of NFP needs to be?

3) Are we in agreement about using NFP?

(Used with permission)

Unbaptized infants

With regard to children not yet baptized, the following is a quote from the Catechism of the Catholic Church, English/Canadian edition: Number 1261: *"As regards children who have died without Baptism, the Church can only entrust them to the mercy of God, as she does in her funeral rites for them. Indeed the great mercy of God who desires that all men should be saved and Jesus' tenderness toward children which caused him to say: 'Let the children come to me, do not hinder them,' allow us to hope that there is a way of salvation for children who have died without Baptism. All the more urgent is the Church's call not to prevent little children coming to Christ through the gift of Holy Baptism."*

Like the Emily character in the book, we have lost six babies through miscarriage and ectopic pregnancy. In only one instance were we able to baptize the child. It is my firm belief, even though most of my unborn children were not formally baptized, that, through "the great mercy of God," He recognized that it was our desire to have them baptized and they are all now in heaven in the presence of our Creator.

Pope John Paul II in his encyclical, the Gospel of Life, writes: *"I would now like to say a special word to women who have had an abortion. The church is aware of the many factors which may have influenced your decision, and she does not doubt that in many cases it was a painful and even shattering decision. The wound in your heart may not yet have healed. Certainly what happened was and remains terribly wrong. But do not give in to discouragement and do not lose hope. Try rather to understand what happened and to face it honestly. If you have not already done so, give yourselves over with humility and trust to repentance. The Father of mercies is ready to give you his forgiveness and his peace in the Sacrament of Reconciliation. You will come to understand that nothing is definitively lost and you will also be able to ask forgiveness from your child, who is now living in the Lord. With the friendly and expert help and advice of other people, and as result of your own painful experience, you can be among the most eloquent defenders of everyone's right to life. Through your commitment to life, whether by accepting the birth of other children or by welcoming and caring for those most in need of someone to be close to them, you will become promoters of a new way of looking at human life."*

Bibliography:
The following books were used while researching the events of this novel:
Titanic, An Illustrated History, Don Lynch and Ken Marschall, Hyperion/Madison Press Books, 6th ed.,Toronto, 1998
Margaret Sanger, A Biography of the Champion of Birth Control, Madeline Gray, Richard Marek Publishers, New York, 1979

Rodin Museum Handbook , John L. Tancock
Philadelphia Then and Now, Edward Arthur Mauger,
  Thunder Bay Press, San Diego, CA, 2002

Acknowledgments:

Miracle Hour by Linda Schubert
quotes used with permission

Life-Giving Love by Kimberly Hahn
used with permission

"If the Morning," words and music by **James Hrkach**
"Forever Amen" words and music by **James Hrkach**
used with permission

"The Good News of Natural Family Planning," brochure
quotes, used with permission from the Couple to Couple League,
PO Box 111184, Cincinnati, Ohio 45211

"She Moved Through the Fair," traditional
"Amazing Grace," traditional
"Nearer my God to Thee," Sarah F. Adams, lyrics

Recommended Reading/tapes
Church Documents:
Catechism of the Catholic Church
Pope John Paul II, The Role of the Christian Family in the
Modern World (Familiaris Consortio),
Pope John Paul II, The Gospel of Life, (Evangelium Vitae)
Pope Paul VI, On Human Life, (Humanae Vitae)
Pope Pius XI, On Christian Marriage, (Casti Connubii)

Books and tapes:
DeGrandis, Robert, S.S.J. *Intergenerational Healing,*
  Praising God Catholic Association of Texas, 1989.
DeMarco, Donald, *In My Mother's Womb, the Catholic*
  Church's Defense of Natural Life, Trinity Communications,
  Manassas, Virginia, 1987
Drogin, Elasah, *Margaret Sanger, the Father of Modern*

Society, Coarsegold, California: CUL Publications, 1979.

Evert, Jason, *Pure Love,* Catholic Answers, San Diego, 2003

Evert, Jason, *If You Really Loved Me, 100 Questions on Dating, Relationships and Sexual Purity,* Catholic Answers, San Diego, 2003

Hahn, Kimberly, *Life-Giving Love, Embracing God's Beautiful Design for Marriage,* Servant Publications, Ann Arbor, MI, 2001.

Hahn, Scott and Kimberly, *Life-Giving Love, tape set,* St. Joseph Communication

Hahn, Scott, conversion story tape

Hampsch, Rev. John, *Healing the Family Tree*

Kippley, John and Sheila, *The Art of Natural Family Planning,* 4th. Ed., The Couple to Couple League, Ohio 1996

Kippley, John, *Sex and the Marriage Covenant,* Ignatius Press 2005, revised

Kippley, Sheila, *Breastfeeding and Natural Child Spacing,* 2nd ed., The Couple to Couple League, Cincinnati, Ohio 1989

Kippley, Sheila, *Breastfeeding and Catholic Motherhood,* Sofia Press, 2005

Kowalska, St. Faustina, *Divine Mercy in My Soul*

Kurey, Mary-Louise, *Standing with Courage,* Our Sunday Visitor, Huntington, Indiana, 2002

La Leche League, *The Womanly Art of Breastfeeding,* New York, Plume, 1991.

Lewis, C.S., *Mere Christianity*

Page, Geoffrey, *In Garments All Red, the story of St. Maria Goretti*

Pelucchi, Giuliana, *A Woman's Life, Blessed Gianna Molla,* Pauline Books and Media, Boston, 2002

Pope John Paul II, *Love and Responsibility,* San Francisco, Ignatius, 1993.

Provan, Charles, *The Bible and Birth Control,* Monongahela, PA; Zimmer, 1989

Schubert, Linda, *Miracle Hour*

Smith, Dr. Janet, *Why Humanae Vitae was Right: A Reader,* San Francisco, Ignatius, 1993.

Smith, Dr. Janet, *Contraception: Why Not, tape*

Torode, Sam and Bethany, *Open Embrace*

Von Hildebrand, Dietrich, *Marriage: the Mystery of Fruitful Love,* Sofia Institute, Manchester, NH, 1984.

Von Hildebrand, Alice, *The Privilege of Being a Woman,*
Sofia Institute, Manchester, NH
West, Christopher, *The Theology of the Body for Beginners,*
Ascension Press, West Chester, PA, 2004

Organizations and Websites

Vatican website www.vatican.va

Birthright International 1-800-550-4900, www.birthright.org

Morning Light Ministry, c/o St. Mary Star of the Sea Church,
11 Peter Street South, Mississauga, Ontario L5H 2G1, (416) 969-0545;

The Couple to Couple League International,
P.O. Box 111184, Cincinnati, Ohio 45111-1184;
(513)471-2000; www.ccli.org.

Serena Canada,
151 Holland Avenue, Ottawa, Ontario K1Y0Y2
1-888-373-7362 www.serena.ca

WOOMB Canada, Billings Ovulation Method,
1506 Dansey Avenue, Coquitlam, BC V3K 3J1
www.woomb.ca

Miracles of the Heart Ministries
P.O. Box 4034
Santa Clara, CA 95056 www.linda-schubert.com

Pure Love Club
www.pureloveclub.org
Jason and Crystalina Evert

One More Soul,
1846 North Main, Dayton, Ohio 45405-3832;
(800) 307-SOUL, www.omsoul.com.

One More Soul Canada,
P.O. Box 2961, Nipawin, SK S0E 1E0, canada.omsoul.com

Courtship Now
www.courtshipnow.com

Society of Blessed Gianna Molla,
P.O. Box 59557, Philadelphia, PA, 19102-9557

Priests for Life
PO Box 141172
Staten Island, NY 10314
www.priestsforlife.org

Priests for Life Canada
PO Box 31
Pembroke, Ontario
K8A 6X1

Women Exploited by Abortion
P.O. Box 267
Schoolcrat, MI 49087

Catholic Answers
2020 Gillespie Way
El Cajon, CA 92020 USA
www.catholic.com

Madonna House Apostolate
RR 2
Combermere, Ontario
www.madonnahouse.com

Emily's Hope, novel by Ellen Gable, copyright 2005
Full Quiver Publishing, www.fullquiverpublishing.com
a division of Innate Productions

About the author

Ellen Gable is a wife and mother of five growing sons, ages 6 to 18. Though she was born in New Jersey, she has been married to James Hrkach for 23 years and has called Canada her home for that entire time.

She has had several articles published (under her married name) in CCL's Family Foundations as well as the Nazareth Journal and www.domestic-church.com website.

For the last 20 years, she and her husband have been actively involved in Catholic apologetics, teaching Natural Family Planning and participating in Marriage Preparation instruction.

For more information, please check out the website: www.fullquiverpublishing.com

Ellen would love to hear your feedback regarding *Emily's Hope*. Please write to her at feedback@fullquiverpublishing.com.

To purchase more copies of this book, please go to the Full Quiver website: www.fullquiverpublishing.com. or write to us at

Full Quiver Publishing,

PO Box 244,

Pakenham, Ontario K0A 2X0

Canada